THE FORGOTTEN GOD

THE REAWAKENING
BOOK 1

ANDREW RYLANDS

ANDREW  RYLANDS

"Know Thyself"

Inscription at the entrance of the Temple of Apollo, Delphi.

PRINCIPAL CHARACTERS

Olympians

Achelois (Lois) – domesticated cat living near the abandoned Botrys factory. Also, a goddess of the moon.

Apollo – Olympian god of light. Amnesiac and reclusive. Shuns his peers and is content to remain within the confines of the Sanctuary of Delphi, his original home and seat of power.

Ares – Olympian god of war. Leader of the Plaka gang.

Athena – Olympian goddess of wisdom and patron of Athens. Resides on the hillside above the ruins of the former Agora in the heart of the city where she leads a tightly knit group of female cats who press her laws across the city, despite the increasing resistance of other gangs and groups. Obsessed by the activities of human archaeologists.

Deimos – son of Ares.

Hecate – goddess of witchcraft. Lives in seclusion at the Monastery of St John. Shuns her peers.

Hera – Olympian goddess. Wife and consort of Zeus.

Hermes – Olympian messenger god, also patron of thieves and tricksters. Resides on the summit of Mount Lycabettus, Athens.

Phobos – son of Ares.

Zeus – head of the Olympian gods and by extension, all immortals within the Greek pantheon. Currently living in quiet retirement at Delphi.

Titans

Bia – Titaness. Sister of Kratos and Zelus. Leader of the Davaki Park gang.

Kratos – Titan. Once sat at the right hand of Zeus and administered punishment to his foes. Chained Prometheus to the rock. Now leader of the Botrys gang, renowned for their harsh treatment of rivals, and ambitious to rule all of Athens' feline population. Has a particular dislike of Athena.

Mnemosyne – goddess of memory. Mother of the Muses.

Zelus – Titan. Brother of Kratos and Bia. Leader of the rival Gizi gang but temporarily allied with Kratos.

Mortals

Daphne – originally a stray who became a member of Delphi's feline community. Companion of Apollo.

Erichthonius – son of Herse. Grew up within the extended family of the Plaka gang in the centre of Athens. Convivial and intelligent. Likes football.

Hector – police dog in modern Delphi.

Herse – former street cat who found sanctuary with the sisterhood of Athena.

Homer – a tortoise. *

Jason – companion of Apollo and Daphne.

Melanippus – a seer. Member of the Botrys gang.

Olympia – close companion and occasional consort to Apollo.

Pandrosus – acolyte of Hermes. Lives on Lycabettus Hill.

Penelope – Athena's primary assistant and secretary.
Pythia – a seer and priestess. Guardian of the Oracle of Delphi.
Rea – daughter of Kratos.
Second Lieutenant Samaras – a policeman.
Tabitha – a member of the Plaka gang.
Yannis – son of Kratos.

* The Olympian gods have close bonds with animal species sacred to their respective cults. Athena has a bond with owls, which became a symbol representing her wisdom. Creatures sacred to Apollo include dolphins and cicadas among others, but also crows, ravens and hawks. He was said to use crows and ravens as messengers. The animal most sacred to Hermes is the tortoise.

CHAPTER 1
THE DISTANT PAST

I t wasn't his first murder, and it wouldn't be his last, but it was, perhaps, his most flamboyant, and his biggest regret. He never could remember the name of the place, deep in its remote valley in the mountains. It was little more than a village, though every hamlet was a kingdom in those days. This one came complete with a rustic hall, packed this evening with the local townsfolk, their king, and his retinue. All had gathered to watch the arrogant musician beat the best Olympus could deliver.

It is never wise to summon a god without good reason, and this could certainly not be described as such. In fact, Marsyas might have been drunk at the time. No matter; he exuded confidence, certain he could live up to his claim. It was true; his musical ability was sublime.

The god stood at the side of the stage, his natural radiance veiled, and his form scaled to little more than that of a man. He was the ageless epitome of youthful masculine perfection.

As patron of the arts, this god was in his element. Yet he dressed for the occasion in simple attire: tunic and sandals with a cord tied at the waist; modest yet elegant. He was here for a reason and as befitted his role as educator, he had, of course, brought the necessary tools.

Marsyas stepped forth and bowed before his admirers. From the wings, his opponent observed every movement in minute detail. He noted the subtle scents lingering in the evening air, picked up the sounds of lowing cattle nearby and the melody of the crickets in the woods across the fields. He sensed the rustle in the undergrowth across town that attracted a falcon's beady eye, and heard the air move beneath the wings of an owl. But mostly he studied the puffed-up virtuoso, preening himself before his admirers, so confident of his impending victory, that to him the contest had already been won, and the laurel wreath awarded. Let this counterfeit Icarus enjoy this fleeting moment, before his exposure to the full glare of the sun.

Solemnly, the man waited for the adulation to subside and silence to fall, then put his lips to the mouthpiece of his wood-wind *aulos* and began. He played his piece with skill and verve. The audience gasped at his accomplishment, hypno-tised by every move as his fingers flew to cover and uncover the tone holes. There was no doubting his skill; but, as ever with mortals, it was his ego that sealed his fate. He couldn't resist a smug, almost condescending, sideways glance at his watching opponent.

Apollo returned a broad grin, but there was no warmth in his expression; all semblance of friendly rivalry had drained away. He had no intention of losing, and it was unwise in the extreme to take him for a fool; maybe that lingering look was when his challenger got his first inkling.

The musician finished his performance and bowed osten-tatiously; first to the king, then the rest of the audience, then to the Muses who sat in judgement of this little contest.

The crowd rose to their feet, clapping and shouting for all they were worth. He stood centre-stage, soaking up the applause. They were certain, as was he, that nothing could surpass such a display.

The judges gave cautious but considered support, applauding and nodding and carefully avoiding his eye. The praise was deserved. He was indeed highly skilled; a master of his instrument, of composition and performance. He had wrought every drop of emotion from his tune. None could doubt he was a consummate musician; a maestro, even.

While the imbecile continued to milk the rapturous applause of his fans, his rival stepped forwards and his presence filled the room. A hush fell. The air became thick and cloying, catching in their throats. Anticipation grew; something special was going to happen tonight. They held their breath while the Olympian looked sidelong at his challenger; his eyebrow arched.

For the first time, Apollo spoke.

"So, can you do this?"

With unhurried grace, he moved towards the stool that appeared centre-stage and, sitting, casually flipped up his lyre high towards the rafters. He caught the inverted instrument and, still holding it upside down, started to play. Slowly it started: a lilting piece of exquisite beauty, building up layer by layer. A tune of his own invention. At its heart was a melody of heart-breaking simplicity but intense emotional depth; crescendos waxing then waning, before ascending once more. Then he sang, his rich baritone filling the hall. The audience gasped. They had never heard this tune, but the refrain was so enticing and the rhythm so infectious they couldn't help but hum along and tap their feet. He had them in the palm of his hand. This was artistry, the like of which they'd never witnessed for a player of a stringed instrument.

Apollo finished and basked in the applause before turning to his challenger.

"Surely, for one who claims to be the greatest, equalling such a feat is well within your capabilities?"

His voice was mild and quiet, but the mockery within the simple statement clearly hit the musician hard. He blanched; a scintilla of doubt behind his eyes.

For a moment, a sliver of opportunity existed for the man to extract himself from the rapidly closing jaws of his fate. A bow and humble acknowledgement he had met his match would have sufficed. He could have given in with grace and followed up by making an appropriate sacrifice and obeisance, recognising the futility of his boast. But the musician's hubris knew no bounds, and the window of opportunity slammed shut. He was beside himself, infuriated by the injustice of it all. Blindly, he careered on down the path to his own destruction.

"Ridiculous buffoonery. A clown's trick. How can a serious, self-respecting artiste such as myself be taken seriously if I am expected to emulate such circus tricks? Any idiot knows the *aulos* cannot be played back to front. It is an insult to suggest it."

That was it. The Muses looked down, studying their clasped hands, giving their judgement the appearance of objectivity, then solemnly declared Apollo the winner.

His opponent howled in indignation. Had they ears of cloth? Did they know true artistry when they heard it? Could they differentiate between a supreme performer such as himself and a tavern drunk strumming a few bum notes on an old guitar?

The god let the musician blather on for a while, then fixed him with a stare.

"It's time for your runner-up prize. But just remember, this is on your head. It was you who summoned me to this contest with your boastful bragging. Do you think your little skills surpass mine? You think you can overstep a god?"

The musician knew his fate then. His protest stalled in his throat. He tried to back away. Setting his lyre aside, the god took out a fine paring knife from a fold in the waist of his tunic.

"No. Please!"

Terror widened the man's eyes. Once more, the god fixed him with a humourless grin. There was no mercy there. Vengeance was due; the lesson would proceed.

It was said the musician's screams could be heard across the breadth of the valley and as far as the next town. Apollo left his victim's skin hanging on the branch of a nearby tree, dripping onto the bare earth. He pinned the rest of him to a barn door with a spear wrenched from the grasp of a dumb-struck soldier. At least that ended it for him. Let it be a warning to them all.

The Muses had long since departed.

CHAPTER 2
THE ART OF FORGETTING

A pattern emerged. Matters pursued with the best intent often turned sour, though not always with such disastrous consequences. His temper was tested again and again, and often found wanting, but all the time his mood circled back to the competition with Marsyas until it became a millstone around his heart.

Had the "punishment" exceeded the crime? Unquestionably. As lessons go it was as sadistic as there has ever been, yet through the years of his radiant Olympian heyday it cast a long shadow. Murmurs of his brutality reached his ears. Mortals began to cower in his presence, or try to avoid him. Efforts to reach out and teach them were met with downcast eyes and closed minds. He was no longer welcomed as once he had been. Among his followers he sensed fear replacing hope within their hearts.

At first he tried to ignore it, but the issue persisted, driven by his own short fuse. The god of light was too oft consumed by inner darkness. The sight of Apollo atoning for his sins became a feature of his existence. He was drawn into the plot Hera hatched to overthrow Zeus, and forced to build Troy's walls as penance. He wooed Cassandra but she spurned him, and he cursed her. At least, that time, his victim survived. His best intentions seemed destined to always end in cruelty, his image forever tarnished.

Bit by bit these episodes ate into his immortal soul, gnawing at his conscience until, down the centuries, they shook him to the core. One final episode brought things to a head, and incurred his father's mighty wrath. His future was finely balanced on the scales. Fortune, and the pleading of Leto, his mother, saved him, and this time his penance gave time for deeper reflection and led to change.

But though his behaviour improved, the memories of the past continued to burrow into his psyche like a tumour in the brain; a pain that would not be subdued. As a last resort he sought counsel from the one deity who could help him, and so the path to forgetfulness was set, and the past finally buried. Or so he hoped.

With his attention turned inwards he missed much of the debate about their future, and paid little heed to the plans that were set in place. The debates at their conference barely registered in his consciousness, and he gave his consent automatically, his attention elsewhere. By the time the Transformation took place he was only too willing to accept his new, smaller shape and be shorn of much of his powers. To wander the earth in permanent disguise was a mixed blessing, but at least it rendered him incapable of such barbarities as before. The tic that had caused such anguish had finally been isolated and buried, deep in a dark corner of his labyrinthine mind, never to be disturbed.

He'd had to lose a lot of other memories along with it, good as well as bad, but the numbness that remained was part of the price. Amnesia was a wonderful thing.

Apollo retired to the hillside of his ancient domain, living simply with others of his new kind among the stones, the origin of which he now barely remembered. The days blended into one another while he let daily routine wash over him and ceased to care. Time didn't flow there like elsewhere. In their temporal bubble, out of sight, and out of mind, playing their little games and scheming their little schemes, the cats of Delphi forgot and were forgotten by everyone. Everyone that mattered. Out there, beyond those self-imposed boundaries, things happened. Events took place, attitudes changed, people hatched plans and projects were pursued. They dreamed.

On the hillside they strove to stay the same. Nothing changed. They were slaves to the slow-turning wheel of the seasons, nothing more; a pride of feral cats, keeping watch over the ancient dream of Delphi. Animals were born and animals died, but for the others among them nothing much happened. With one exception. A ghost from the past sent to haunt him, or test him; unfinished business from the time of legend. Blissfully unaware of a past life, just as he had forgotten the ancient barb in his heart, the shot that, once upon a time, had pierced his soul. Suddenly restless, it stirred once more. Someone didn't want him to rest easy.

The cats of the Sanctuary preferred to stay out of sight of the tourists as far as possible, leading simple lives that revolved around eating, snoozing, playing, mating and watching, and that was how Apollo liked it. He was safe. His horizons had narrowed. Life was uncomplicated. This day was the same as the one before, and no doubt would be the same as the one after. He didn't care: the pain had gone.

CHAPTER 3
THE PRESENT

Nobody lives forever, they say, yet the ginger cat was older than the rocks on which he sat. Or rather reclined, in the pose of a sphinx, paws crossed before him. Like the Egyptian version, he looked as if he could have been carved from the landscape; immobile and unchanging. Yet this small facsimile, on the shoulder of Mount Parnassos in the Greek mainland, was very much alive.

The rays of the setting sun illuminated a handsome creature, his fur streaked with darker stripes above the eyes; a tiger in miniature. Below his chin, his chest and belly were white, as were his paws. He lay beneath a cypress tree enjoying the late summer heat. Golden irises resembled the glow of sunset, but with the fiery orb high above, his pupils were narrowed to a slit, as if to further shield his thoughts. But, impenetrable as they might be, they were not immune to distraction, and there was no one more capable of distracting than Daphne.

A cheeky sidelong glance. The suggestive wriggle of hindquarters.

It drove all other thoughts aside as a kind of madness descended upon him. The sap might have aged beyond measure, but it could still rise. Apollo watched her with parted lips, his heartbeat pulsing faster as he drank in her enticing, fluffy charm.

Daphne was different. It was as if she were designed for playful flirtation and deep, deep love. No, he reflected, not love: affection.

Put all thought of treacherous love far aside. Bury it. There is no need to let such a troublesome concept ruin the day. Stay in the present.

Instead, he focused on her perky pointed ears; drank in her delicious amber, black and white colouring; adored her perfect paws – so well maintained – and not least that bouncy live-wire tail. She did more than captivate his thoughts; she held them prisoner. He wanted nothing more than to tumble in the grass with her in a shared moment of fleeting ecstasy.

It was days since he'd last seen her. Apollo had wondered if she'd been deliberately staying out of his way. He drank her in until she drenched his every waking thought. To his frustration, she liked to maintain a certain distance, usually fleeing whenever he made a direct approach, but these past few months she was always there, on the periphery of his consciousness; a perpetual temptation on the fringe of his circle of friends.

Today she was in a playful mood. "Come on, then," she teased. "Try and catch me."

Hither and thither they ran, leaping the stones, darting around them, dodging overhanging branches and tourists' legs until they hurtled out of Delphi's entrance gates and across the road below.

That was when he saw her. Olympia. Perched on the wall near where the chase had led him. Daphne's tail flashed out of sight, but Apollo slowed and stopped. He turned to face her, and for a second their eyes met.

She looked away.

That single movement spoke more than any words.

And then it stirred once more; an emotion deep within his soul and so familiar.

Guilt.

His mouth was dry. He could not speak. Even if he could think of something to say, Apollo knew she wouldn't want to hear it, anyway. She'd become immune.

Helpless, he turned away.

She has no call on me.

But Olympia's face remained etched on his memory, her glassy stare burning the retina of his mind's eye.

A shake of the head to jog it onto a new path. No good; she was still there. Apollo moved slowly from her field of vision with as much dignity as he could summon. His insides churned, far more than she deserved.

Why do I care?

It was a relief to be out of her sight.

Ahead, Daphne waited in a half crouch, forelegs splayed, those gorgeous dark eyes fixed on him in a different way: playful, searching, flirting. His mood lifted once more, as if the sun had emerged from behind a cloud, though the sky above remained the deepest comforting blue.

He darted forwards once more – feinting left, switching right – but she spun beyond his grip and with barely a whisker's width, danced aside and set off on a mazy run, in and out of the gnarled tree trunks of the olive grove as old as time. Apollo followed, eyes fixed on her bouncing tail, and time stood still.

For just one moment, nothing else moved except his thoughts. He stood above, outside, and observed the playful flight below. He spied the hill behind, and in that instant saw it all anew. The gilded pantile roofs, held aloft on tall columns, floating between the trees. Among them, monuments and treasuries, and the busy winding road between them. Above it all, the marble theatre, and behind a screen of trees, the stadium. And in the centre, like a keystone holding everything together, a magnificent temple stood proud on a platform levelled into the hillside. A portico adorned with animated coloured figures, the lintel emblazoned with deep carved slogans.

The building commanded everything around.

The vision faded, leaving him momentarily bereft. Nothing remained beyond a scattering of fallen blocks that littered the hillside; a column here, a decorated plinth there, uneven stones where once was levelled road. His thoughts were drenched in loneliness and loss, and for once he wondered at his age. Why did he linger here for so long; a permanent fixture amid the season's whir?

Suddenly his heart was pounding, gripped by a primeval fear; a dread so vast it threatened to engulf him. But he knew, standing on the edge of the void, that it could not crush him, no matter how much he willed it. He would endure, and that thought was itself torture.

It had become a familiar friend, this deep-lying ennui, wrapped about his soul like a strangling vine. Its roots bored deeper within until he became immune to the pain; the echo of what once he'd been. He could not defeat it. His only defence was to forget, while about him like sparks from a bonfire, a million lives flickered, vanished and were gone.

The memory disappeared completely, as if it had never been, and without another thought the chase continued. Hurdling obstacles, dodging trees; onwards they went until she finally allowed herself to be caught. They tumbled in the dust and, parting, each looked deep into the other's eyes, as if searching for some fleeting recognition. Apollo bent his head and nuzzled her neck, seeking comfort in the present; sanctuary in the touch of another. He closed his eyes and probed insistently with his nose, enjoying her warmth as she lay on her side beneath him.

"Not now," she whispered. He paused, unsure. Now was the perfect time to claim his prize. She read his mind and with head twisted round, caught his eye.

"It's not time. Not now. Soon."

He stepped back, confused. It was his right, to end this chase in the appropriate manner. Aroused, his ardour demanded it. But something in her eyes made him pause, and his fervour cooled. He stepped aside, embarrassed now, and stared out beneath the trees, wishing he was elsewhere.

"I'm sorry," she said, rolling over to crouch on all fours. "I'm not ready yet."

Stirring, he bobbed his head towards her. "You shouldn't lead me on so."

Daphne said nothing. She rose to her feet and without a further glance, calmly walked away. Apollo watched her depart. Sinuous and sleek; desire personified. A million thoughts hammered against the gates of his memory, unable to break through.

He meandered along the quiet paths back towards the café and the road. He saw Olympia some way away, heading between two parked cars. Keen to avoid a confrontation, he stopped to watch as she approached two humans. The female bent down, holding something out. Olympia hesitated, drew closer, sniffed. With a speed that startled him, and a precision that defied their usual clumsiness, the woman grabbed Olympia with her free hand and scooped her off the ground. Her companion, a large bulky-looking man, held out a bag he'd been carrying and Olympia disappeared into its depths. He opened the rear of the car and hurled in the bag, with little care for its contents.

Apollo set off at a trot. How could he rescue her?

Doors slammed, and the vehicle reversed into the road, then set off away from him, faster than he could run. He watched it go, and deep within himself a fuse ignited, sparked by the anger, the injustice, the casual abuse.

"What's the matter?"

He scented Daphne next to him.

"It's Olympia," he said. "She's been eaten by a car."

CHAPTER 4
SUMMIT MEETING

T he walk across the night-time cityscape was a long one for a cat, but the Titan paid no heed to distance or the concerns of mortals. He was more than strong enough; it was written into every fibre of his immortal being, even in this despised diminished state. Kratos, god of elemental strength, and a rarity: one of the few of that elder generation of gods prepared to side with Zeus and his family in the great war long ago. Since that day, he and his siblings had been proud and mighty defenders of the king of heaven and enforcers of his rule.

Until she had her way. She with her ridiculous plans and stupid games.

Sundered from his lord and former role, Kratos hated every passing day in this new life.

He was large and muscular for his new kind; his coat a mix of chocolate and russet, though far from sweet, and bearing a face that somehow failed to mask the permanent resentment within. Kratos trudged along near deserted streets beneath the yellow lights and brooded on his fate. His anger burned deep, but never deep enough to prevent his fragile mood from kindling into rage at the slightest spark. But tonight he needed to keep a cool head. He was meeting Athens' patron, and if he wasn't careful, she would manipulate his mood to trap him with his own words, and get her way. She was clever, Athena. Clever and slippery, like all her generation; and to that list of crimes, he would add arrogant. But this very trait, Kratos reasoned, was her weakness. He must be careful of her cunning words and keep his plans hidden. This meeting was her last chance, and provided he kept his head, he would win, even if he failed. He marched on.

Kratos found Athena high on the wooded hillside above the ancient Agora, at the clearing where, in times long gone, Athenians would debate and vote on the important issues of the day. At the edge of this clearing was the place they called the *Pnyx*; a simple rock step on which orators would stand and speak to the assembled multitude before them, and receive their cheers or jeers.

She waited for him atop that rock, as her owl had told him she would. Her body was one more dark shadow beneath the stars, delineated by the glow of the rising moon, which lent her an outline of silver. Only the subtle movement of her head made him think her anything other than a carven image in likeness of a cat.

Never keen on small talk, Kratos got straight to the point.

"It is a fine evening," he said, unable to bring himself to use any of her formal titles. "But despite your choice of venue, I am not here to debate."

Athena remained still, looking down at him from the rock.

Inwardly, Kratos seethed at her choice of meeting place. The height advantage she held from the summit was infuriating. To hide his irritation, he paced up and down. "I propose a new settlement. A reorganisation of our territories across this city. One that reflects our current status."

He awaited her response, but Athena showed no sign of even having heard him. Kratos forced himself to wait, the flicks of his tail betraying his impatience. Finally, she stirred.

"And why do you think I might change our boundaries? I believe they work well."

He'd expected that would be her response. Her whole self-satisfied demeanour made his fur bristle.

"They do not. That much should be clear." He circled around, as if to make a point. "All this space you have, and so few followers." Kratos looked her directly in the eye. "What has happened to those who worship you? Where are your temples now? What has happened to those statues erected to honour the goddess across this city of yours?" He paused. Let that sink in. "Whereas my cult is large and growing. We are already too numerous for the streets we occupy." He tried to adopt a conciliatory tone, but it didn't come easy to one so used to dispensing threats on a daily basis. "I had hoped to come to an agreement. But if not, we shall arrive in force."

"And what do you think that will achieve?"

The interruption, as he was poised to launch into a long threatening tirade, wrong-footed the Titan. "One way or another we will take what is my birthright." The threat sounded lame, even as it was uttered.

"*We?*" she queried. "*Birthright?*" The mockery in her voice made his whole body tremble with suppressed fury. Kratos fought to control his temper.

"My siblings and me. And yes, our birthright. A status that befits our seniority. We are the older gods. And now, once again, we are in ascendance. More followers, and as a result, a growing influence. Yet we are constantly told to stay on the fringes, in barren urban deserts, away from the rich pickings of the centre. You tell us to keep out of the way. But why?" A sly tone entered his voice. "Is there some other reason you want to keep us at bay? A long time ago you promised to change us back, but what has happened? Why has the great reversal not taken place? And where are your fellows? Scattered to the winds. Or has something else made them disappear? Have they already made the change, and in doing so, somehow vanished? What are you hiding?"

Athena froze. The faint silver light of the half-moon caught a glint in her eyes. "Do not question my integrity, Titan."

Kratos gave an elaborate yawn. She was rattled. He tasted the night air on his tongue. It was fresher than in the suburbs; the scent of car fumes less pervasive. "No longer will we remain hidden on the fringes. Declare Athens a pan-Hellenic sanctuary and open to all of our cults. We will return to our home, and the natural order will be restored." He watched for a reaction, any excuse for him to attack, but she remained silent. "And once we're here, given our numbers, we can assist you in the search for the solution to our plight."

"This is no Panhellenic sanctuary, nor will it be. And as to worshippers... You can claim such, of course, but in your case they follow through threat and censure, rather than love. Unless I am mistaken. What freedom do they have to choose?"

"Freedom? You talk grandly of free will and choice? What about the freedom to starve? The freedom of loneliness, devoid of all company? The freedom to die alone and isolated, hiding from the wild dogs or brutal humans?"

Athena stood, as if bored with the conversation. She walked along the rock. "My dear Kratos, I'm almost touched by the sympathy you show to them. Yours must be a caring, warm community. Praise to you must ring out every time they sacrifice a sewer rat to your glory."

Her scorn almost made him break. "You may mock, but there are dangers out there that perhaps you are not aware of. Disappearances. Mysterious forces that wrench cats from the streets; the unwary, those that walk alone. No one sees what happens. There are none to report. But we know they're gone. Taken. And we find no bodies."

Athena paused, listening.

"And not just in our part of town. It's happening elsewhere, at Davaki and Gizi, too. Even here, I'm certain of it. One cat here, one cat there. Every few days. Sometimes more frequently. There's safety in numbers, and I offer more than casual succour. I offer them protection. What's wrong with showing a little gratitude in return for safety?"

"Protection?" Her voice rang with incredulity. "I know how you operate, Kratos. Caring doesn't come into the equation. The only thing you and your siblings understand is power in the raw. Don't pretend otherwise."

The temptation to spring at her and finally test her strength in combat was overwhelming. Almost. At the last minute, he held back; furious, but still cautious. *Words are all she's got*, he reminded himself. Words and... Prestige? Some other ancient power he didn't yet understand? In frustration, he realised he was still bound by ancient oaths and treaties. Olympians and Titans; so similar yet so different. But the old bonds were fraying, and it was time for change. She'd forced change on everybody else. It was about time she tasted some of her own medicine.

The two of them glared at each other.

"Scoff as much as you like," said Kratos. "But my worshippers are many, and hardened. Life is easy in the rich, soft centre." He changed tack. "You are alone, apart from a few rag-tag followers. Wandering lost souls, as far as I can make out. How can you stop me? Oh, there's the rest of your family to call on, I suppose. How could I forget them? But, where are they? Is Ares still your guardian? The messenger is always here, of course, flitting from one gossip to the next, desperate to prove himself relevant. Then there's... who?" He couldn't resist gloating. "None of you have any cult worthy of the name. Have you forgotten what you are, or were? Where are the adherents to your mysteries? Gone? Or are they too much of a burden in these modern times?"

Athena seemed focused on his every move, but Kratos was high on emotion by now and far more eloquent than he could ever remember. Resentment powered him like the most powerful drug. "Can you not feel it? The wind of change is in the air." He lifted his snout towards the breeze. "Do you catch its scent on the night air? What is it, that smell?" Her eyes fixed on him with laser-like focus. "It's powerful, and getting stronger by the day. What is it? It's the stench of decay. Of old ways gone rotten. Of a dying regime. Your time is at an end. You, and your feckless family. You've done enough damage to all of our kind."

"I disagree," she said, her voice cold. "And as to your suggested relocation, the answer is no. It would place too great a strain on the resources of the city centre. Over-crowding would force the humans to act, possibly by taking drastic steps to reduce our numbers. It would not work."

Below the rock, Kratos advanced a few steps. "What gives you the right to deny us? Who gave you permission to reign over us all?" He was standing close beneath her now, staring directly up. "Once we served at Zeus' command and acted as his bodyguard. As your protectors."

"I need no protection."

"No?" He let the word hang in the air. "And what of your father? What has become of him? Is his fate the result of another Olympian family plot? Where is Hera? Where is crip-pled Hephaestus, or the effete drunkard? What about slutty Aphrodite and proud Artemis? What have you done to them?" He stepped closer and tilted his head, looking up at her. "Come clean, Athena. Are they dead? Have you killed them? Is that what this was about all along? A way to weed out the competition so you can rule alone?"

Athena glared down at him, but Kratos cared not. His anger was the equal of hers. He pressed his advantage,

digging ever deeper wounds, finally getting to the real grievance at the heart of it all.

"I mean, I wouldn't blame you if you wanted to remove
one or two of the more troublesome ones. So why don't you
come clean? Admit it. Our transformation has removed so
much of our core essence that we are weak. Exposed to
dangers that were once impossible. We might live on, indefi-
nitely, but are subject to an assortment of deadly risks. I'm
sure you could put your formidable imagination to work and
come up with some interesting ways to dispatch them." The
stare was implacable, his voice a low, threatening growl.
Above him, Athena tensed, as if about to leap on him. His
tone dropped to little more than a gravelly murmur. "I don't
trust you an inch."

He took another step forwards, daring her to attack. "You
wanted to hide, and somehow you persuaded us to follow
you. The dream, whatever it was, has long become tarnished,
yet you claim you have forgotten or misplaced the means to
reverse the change and end our plight." A long beat passed.
"Or is it just that you are keeping it to yourself?"

"Don't be ridiculous."

Kratos stepped back, made a show of slowly circling
around to admire the night-time view of the city, then faced
her once more. It was tempting to leap onto the rock and
confront her nose to nose.

The tension eased. The time was close, but not yet. He'd
like it to happen before an audience.

His next address sounded almost conversational.

"We're moving into the city centre, and you can't stop us.
Think of it as a hostile invasion, or a form of assistance. It's
your choice, but it would be easier for you if you adopt a
more positive attitude. We can help you look for whatever it
is you've lost."

"I think not."

"Oh? And how do you propose to stop us?" Her impotent

fury gave him a jolt of delight that left a tingling sensation in his stomach.

"Take care, lest you overstep the mark," she said, finally. "You and your enslaved followers are not the only power here. This city holds secrets yet."

He couldn't help but scoff. "Hollow rhetoric, preached from an empty pedestal in a long-disused forum. Power? Secrets? You see the moon's reflection in a puddle and inform the gullible you have pulled it down from the sky. You have no power anymore. Your only choice is when to step aside. We will make it for you."

With that parting shot, Kratos stalked back down the hill, his confidence bolstered. Athena was even weaker than he thought. Her time was surely at an end. As he marched north through silent streets, he reconsidered his plans. There would be no more skulking in the suburbs. Everything was coming together, and earlier this evening, his spies had given him even better news: Ares had disappeared.

CHAPTER 5
KIDNAP

Apollo stood in the middle of the road, watching the car disappear out of sight. His outrage grew, but also his sense of impotence. There must be something they could do. He needed to tell everyone; but where to start? Daphne was still standing next to him.

"I'll see you at the meeting place," he said. "Gather as many as you can."

With that he hurtled across the road, flew through a gap in the railings without pause and scrambled up the hillside in search of his father. Regardless of their recent coolness, Olympia was a friend. Far more than a friend, in fact; a confidante, a lover, and someone he'd spent a lot of time with, watching the world and the dumb tourists go by.

He shadowed the well-trodden Sacred Way, following his own route up the hillside. There must be a council meeting about this.

Zeus was snoozing in a shady spot overlooking the remains of the temple. Apollo skidded to a halt, creating a small cloud of dust. The older cat's nostrils contracted in annoyance, and he raised his head, eyeing his son with suspicion.

"What?"

"One of those metal beasts has eaten Olympia and headed off down the road. You've got to do something. Punish it. Whatever. This is an outrageous attack. We shouldn't tolerate it."

"*We?*"

Zeus stretched a foreleg languorously and studied a pebble just beyond his paw. He yawned, then glared at the new arrival. His display of studied, languid indifference infuriated Apollo. Already tense, he paced the small clearing, unable to resist goading his father as he did so.

"I realise is it a lovely late summer's day, perfect for sleeping. The heat reflecting from these stones to warm your bones, the hypnotic buzz of the crickets. Why, it must be almost impossible for our elders to stay awake, let alone offer assistance when one of our kind is abducted."

Zeus seemed to find amusement in his son's anguish.

"You realise they're not alive, you know? They're metal automatons. Machines." Satisfied with his pronouncement, he lowered his head onto his paws again and settled down to sleep. Apollo stared at him.

"She's a friend."

Zeus raised his head a fraction. "So rescue her." He stared at the ginger animal.

Apollo sat and stared back. Rescue her? How? "What am I supposed to do against humans and their cars?"

"Do you not know who you are?" asked Zeus, softly.

"What's that supposed to mean?"

Zeus gave a small, shuddering stretch. He looked away. "Cats go missing all the time. It happens. Accept it and move on. You've got other friends. Tell them to be more careful." He gave the ginger cat another sideways glance. "If you don't like my advice, then feel free to go and do something about it."

He lay his head down again and closed his eyes, satisfied

with his pronouncement. Apollo glared at the pool of dark, cinnamon-coloured fur curled up before him. He circumnavigated the small clearing, trying to organise his thoughts as they tumbled around his head.

"I thought you were the leader of our group. Why don't you show some of that leadership?" He waited for a reaction, but got none. "Anyway, she's a friend. I like her. I spend time with her..." His voice trailed off.

The older animal opened his eyes to a slit.

"If you care so much, perhaps you should chase after her. It shouldn't be beyond your capabilities."

Apollo stared back, wide-eyed. "What do you mean? What do you think I am?" He groped for a suitable comeback, but Zeus raised his head and gave him an appraising look.

"I must admit, you surprise me. This level of care for Olympia is unusual, is it not? After all, she's not your only girlfriend, is she? I see you a lot more in the company of that other one. The little one with the longer fur. Daphne. I thought she was your *special friend* these days? What am I missing?"

Apollo squirmed beneath his unflinching stare. Was he so transparent?

Zeus was partly right. Daphne was more than just a friend; but she wasn't yet a mate. Soon he should put that right. He broke the stare, rescued by a twitchy ear which gave him the opportunity for a lengthy scratch.

"I like her. That's all," he said, eventually. "I don't want to give up on my friends so easily."

A fly buzzed between them and Apollo fixed it with a glare. Zeus would be no help; not that he'd really expected any.

"I've called a council meeting," he said. It was his last throw of the dice.

CHAPTER 6
OBSERVATIONS

The large grey cat lay under the shade of a low, gnarled tree on a comfortable bed of pine needles. To her right she could see the tops of the white columns of the restored Stoa of Attalos above the trees; to her left stood the classical outline of the Temple of Hephaestus. Behind her was Areopagus Hill, a vantage point thronged by tourists, jousting with their selfie sticks for the best view of the Acropolis. From her hiding place, Athena could observe the comings and goings of both the tourists and the other animals that moved within the archaeological park of the modern Agora. It was a pale echo of its millennia-old heyday when, as the city's main open space, it served as meeting place and entertainment venue, its beating commercial heart and the primary location for worship and ceremony. If only the stones, unearthed over the last century or so with such painstaking care, could speak. What stories they would tell. If only she could fully remember. If only they could remind her.

It was a quiet morning with few people about. Most of her acolytes – the select group of female feline followers who shared this urban woodland with her – were out and about seeking news or in search of breakfast. She would meet with them later, to instruct them about the day's comings and goings. For now, she watched. And occasionally napped. Then watched once more. Things were coming to a head; she knew it in her heart and sensed it on the sluggish morning breeze. There was change afoot, but she could not yet tell how it would pan out. It seemed likely that the activities of the humans down on the edge of the Agora had something to do with it.

If there was a maggot of uncertainty gnawing at her hope, it was born of her conversation with the oaf, Kratos. She could have bitten off her tongue. Why had she said anything about the city holding secrets? It had been foolish; a stupid boast to bolster her precarious position. But it had been a sign of weakness, not strength. She closed her eyes and regathered her racing thoughts. Until last night she'd been confident no other knew of the dig, but her confrontation with Kratos had shaken her. The excavation was important and had significance for all immortals, but it was imperative that whatever was uncovered in this place was kept by her alone. She trusted no other. That anyone else might seize it was unthinkable.

Whatever it was.

Therein lay the problem; she could not remember what she had lost, or was hoping to retrieve.

Athena was impatient for the archaeologists' excavations to bear fruit. Following her conversation the previous night they were her last hope against the coming storm. But their work was painfully slow. Did they need to examine every pebble with such painstaking care?

In recent weeks her followers had delivered tidings of increasing unrest among various tribes across the city, and even of disquiet among other species resident in Athens. Until last night Athena had ignored it. With the support of countless generations of followers through the years, she had long kept the peace among the fractious denizens of

Athens, despite the constant bickering of her immortal relatives.

Her thoughts returned to Kratos; this time it felt different. Unconsciously, she shifted position as her thoughts raced. Keeping the peace this time would take a lot more effort, with her chief enforcer and ally missing. Athena's followers were few, and although capable of looking after themselves, they were no warriors. They could not hold back a determined invasion.

Once more, she scoffed at the idea. Who did he think he was? If he was so confident of success, he must have mastered a new skill: how to herd cats. She lowered her head and closed her eyes, reassured by her knowledge of the creatures she and her fellow immortals walked among.

Athena's thoughts returned to the activities of the human animals, and in particular this little group digging among the ancient stones. They were on the point of uncovering something important; she felt it in her bones. Something she'd lost. An object that had been taken from her.

She couldn't remember what it was, but she was certain she'd know it when she saw it, and that it would change everything. But how? So far such knowledge had eluded her, and her frustration grew.

She got her first inkling of the excavation decades ago, but it had taken them years to get the relevant permissions, then clear the ground and start digging, rediscovering their past one pebble at a time. Archaeology took forever, but her confidence was growing that her long wait was about to end. She could feel it in the tips of her whiskers. But when? And then what? What could she do with the discovery they were about to make?

She would worry about that when the time came. In the meantime, with events so delicately poised, it was infuriating that the Titan had become aware of her interest. She'd worked so hard to keep it secret.

A stretch relieved the tension in her spine. It was time to have another look, as she had done yesterday and the day before that. She walked across the park, skirting the ancient ruins to the gate where humans came and went. It was a warm day; there was no need to hurry. Athena attracted little attention as she strolled out through the gate and down onto pedestrianised Adrianou Street. On the far side of this narrow thoroughfare was a row of restaurants and cafés, and behind them another set of railings overlooking the archaeological dig site. She made for her favourite café and hung around for a while, glaring at selected members of the clientele until they caved in and shared their food. Few could resist the piercing gaze of those bright, emerald-green eyes; they gave the subtle hint of retribution should the subject fail to comply. It wasn't healthy food from the feline perspective, but Athena had developed quite a taste for baklava, and who was there to reprimand her?

Hunger pangs sated, she found a quiet spot beneath an unoccupied table and observed the activity in the sunken space below. The dig had removed several strata of the city's more recent history to uncover foundations and debris of a building from a much older era, and everything built over this space in between. It was like looking back in time, and it fascinated the grey cat. Her focus flicked from one person to another as she observed their actions. Their painstaking progress was too slow for her liking. How many years had she waited?

A part-excavated pit between the base of two columns absorbed most of her attention. The earth at the back was different in colour and texture; not stratified like elsewhere. More jumbled. It looked like the site of an old well. Many things were cast into wells in the old days. Could the artefact she sought be in there? At the back of her mind whirled the faint, fleeting echo of cries, flames, burning buildings and smoke against a dark sky. People running everywhere; shouting, screaming, some carrying spears and swords, others their belongings and babies. An image of panic and slaughter and chaos. It faded as quickly as it had arrived, leaving her puzzled. Was it a memory? An echo from the stones? Or something else?

Athena retraced her route back into the wooded hillside above the Agora and called her followers. It was time to share the burden. To a degree, at least.

"Ladies, we are on the cusp of important developments, of which I cannot speak as yet. However, change is on the way, which should benefit all of our kind across this great city. I feel it. But the period just before this revelation is the most dangerous. If I am correct, the humans are about to uncover a tool that, if it falls into the wrong paws, will spread division and dissent. We have to place a cordon around the site where they are digging. It must be made secure. No cat is to be allowed through. You are the instruments of my authority in this. My gatekeepers. I urge you to use whatever force is necessary to deter intruders."

The demure sisterhood studied her with gravitas, despite their misgivings. They left it to one of their most experienced members, Herse, to voice their concerns.

"There is trouble brewing across the city, Athena. Our spies are hearing rumours of attacks, war between the gangs, and more. Surely, we should go out and speak to them. Try to prevent violence between our kin. Not turning our backs or hiding away here in the safety of the city centre?"

The grey cat studied her. "This is more important. War among the clans comes and goes. They're always squabbling over territory. What I'm talking about will affect all of us for the rest of our lives. Trust me on this. That's all I will say."

She looked across the animals gathered before her. All averted their gaze, and none spoke up, even though most shared Herse's views. Satisfied she had dealt with any dissent, Athena issued instructions to the guards, and turned to her most trusted supporter and second-in-command.

"Penelope, we must keep watch day and night. You will organise the changing of guards at intervals." She turned back to the others. "No one is to breathe a word to anyone outside of our group. Is that clear?"

Several of them exchanged wary glances, but there were no other dissenting voices. With the meeting over, they returned to their watch posts, prepared to carry out the instructions of their leader to the letter.

Yannis and his informant crouched on the edge of a flat roof, looking over a low parapet. They peered down into the fenced-off excavation of the Stoa Poikile. It was slow going. Nothing seemed to change, day after day. He was bored with the stakeout after only ten minutes.

"Wait a minute. You'll see her," his contact informed him. "She's usually here around now."

He was right. After a few minutes a cat appeared behind the railings opposite, about fifty metres away. It was a large animal, its colour difficult to determine given the angle of the sun, but Yannis was sure it was Athena.

He studied her for a while. She wasn't as large as the boss, but she was larger than most cats he knew. A bit more supple, he guessed, but not as strong.

Yannis followed her gaze. She stared at one particular human labouring down below. The subject of her scrutiny scratched at the earth with a small trowel. In its other hand, it held a brush which it used periodically to clean dust or small particles away from whatever it was it was trying to extract from the ground.

He watched for a few minutes more, then looked up to his fellow observer opposite. Every movement below entranced her. Was this it? The object she sought? He had no way of knowing, but he'd better tell the boss, just in case. He and his companion crept back from the edge of the roof and out of sight. Yannis looked thoughtful; not a frequent occurrence.

"You'd better keep a close watch on her. Let me know as soon as anything happens. I want to know if she makes a move. Any move. Okay?"

"But I can't watch round the clock. I need to sleep."

Yannis looked at him in exasperation. "Get your friends to help. You must have some."

The other cat looked doubtful, but consented if only to hasten his visitor's departure. As Yannis sauntered away he reflected on the instructions he'd been given, and the gangster's presumption. In fact, he had very few friends; just a few acquaintances, and most of them he could barely tolerate. He could imagine the response if he asked them to keep watch on a dull patch of earth for hours at a time. He'd be a laughing stock.

But getting on the wrong side of Yannis and his colleagues wouldn't do much for his health, either. He sighed and hoped nothing much happened while he was asleep.

CHAPTER 7
PYTHIA

nfuriated by his conversation with Zeus, Apollo passed through the Sanctuary, rounding up as many of the elders as he could. But his spirits sank further. The more he thought about it, the less convinced he was that they could help. There had to be a way of finding Olympia and mounting a rescue; someone must have an idea.

He fantasised about what he would do to the humans if he caught them. But without knowing where they had taken her, he was powerless. Someone should be punished for treating his friend like that. Who did they think they were? In the past, he'd exacted violent, deadly revenge for a single disrespectful word or deed. He shuddered to a halt, shaking his head.

Of course not. What a crazy idea.

He was a cat.

Most of the elders were equally disgruntled at having their peace disturbed. Their attitude did little to lift Apollo's mood. He arrived at their meeting place in the clearing below the ruined temple to find at least twenty cats had already assembled. They sat there, chuntering among themselves. Hera was particularly grumpy.

"This had better be good," she muttered for the benefit of anyone nearby, and staring across at Leto as if it was her fault. Their feud had lasted more years than either could remember and wasn't about to end. Some younger cats, who were usually out exploring at this time of day, were also arriving to find out what all the fuss was about. Out of respect, they stayed on the fringe of the gathering.

Their leader emerged, standing on a low wall at the side of the clearing.

"We appear to have a problem," said Zeus. "There is a story that young Olympia is missing. Has anyone seen her recently?" He gave Apollo a sidelong glance. The ginger cat could not contain his impatience. Giving Zeus a venomous glare, he stepped into their midst.

"They kidnapped her!" he miaowed at the top of his voice; his fury clear. "I saw it. Two humans, showing her no respect."

Her, and by extension, *me*.

Who were these people to act so high-handedly?

"They bundled her into a bag and put her in their car and went away. Up that way." He pointed with his nose. "We need to mount a rescue."

There was an abrupt silence as the older cats averted their gaze. A murmur of conversation started.

"He sounds way too excitable, to my mind," said one old boy. "Has he got any sense of decorum?"

"Too late to do anything about it now," grumbled an elderly black-and-white tom. "She's gone, and that's that."

"She should have taken more care," muttered a female.

"What was she thinking?" agreed another. "Some of these youngsters are far too friendly."

Hera was outraged. She rounded on the cat who had made the remark. "Don't be ridiculous. How can it be her fault?"

Around the clearing, heated arguments were breaking out as some ascribed blame or suggested precautions. None offered useful advice.

"Stop it. Listen to me!" Apollo could not contain his exasperation. "This is a crime against us. One of our family. It might happen again, to anyone. We stick together. We always have. We must do something."

"What can we do? We're cats!" came a heated retort from the crowd.

Zeus imposed his authority.

"Silence!" That had an effect. After giving the assembled group a threatening stare, he turned to Apollo. "You have no right to make demands of this group. They are not your subjects. They are your companions, relatives and friends." Apollo held his tongue, but his resentment was mounting. "You have given us your account of what happened, but what do you suggest we do? We cannot chase after Olympia. She might be anywhere. We cannot move with a speed to match their metal chariots. There is nothing we can do."

Apollo stood his ground, glaring into the distance. One or two of the older cats got to their feet, glancing at one another as if relieved to be leaving. Some younger animals talked about assembling search parties with groups of them hitching lifts in other cars.

"Let us hear what Pythia says," Zeus said, turning to the old priestess who had arrived later than most, unnoticed by the majority.

Pythia rose stiffly to her feet and jumped onto a fallen stone at the edge of their clearing. From her perch, she looked down at the assembled group, and the angry animal in their midst, savouring the moment. She paused for effect, closed her eyes in concentration, and summoned the essence of Gaia. Raising her face towards the sky, she spoke in a high-pitched monotone.

"While old Zeus studies his navel, chaos is unleashed and storm clouds gather. Doom will arrive from the north. The fortune of Athens lies in ruins that only great intellect can release. But love, twice renounced, will be lost."

After a pause, she opened her eyes and swayed until she regained her balance. A fleeting look of disquiet crossed her face. The other cats stared at each other in amazement.

The old seer had outdone herself. No one had a clue what she meant.

There was an awkward silence. At least her pronouncement defused the tension as they all grappled to interpret her words. Zeus, however, looked outraged.

"It's sad, but she's really lost it," said Hera to her neighbour.

"Maybe," the other replied, "but you've got to admire her timing. It was like something out of the old stories."

Apollo stared at the elderly cat, bewildered. What did she mean? He stepped forwards to question her further, but she gave him a warning look, turned tail and disappeared.

While the others argued among themselves about what she meant, he slipped out of the ring unnoticed and pursued Pythia. Still sprightly, the elderly cat circled the remains of the temple and followed a narrow track beside the ancient theatre, keeping up a good pace. Above this, she zig-zagged onto higher ground, skirting the stadium and out on the open mountainside. Apollo followed at a distance. Finally, she stepped aside onto a patch of level ground beside some low-growing bushes and turned to await him. Apollo arrived and stood next to her, taking in the view. He hadn't been this high up the mountainside for years and had almost forgotten how far you could see. Mountain ridges receded into the distance in different shades of blue and grey. In a gap between them, the sea sparkled.

He waited, but Pythia was in no hurry to fill the silence and continued enjoying the view. Was this where she spent her days? A quiet retreat, remote and peaceful, out of sight and out of mind of the rest of the clan? One of the oldest cats in the group, Pythia had no offspring of her own. Apollo knew her to be a recluse, avoiding the others and keeping herself to herself. She must spend her time wandering around the upper ruins and into the nearby deep cleft in the mountain where the spring emerged, he realised, and looked about him at the quiet slopes. There were worse places to be. Some said that she had explored the caves up in the hills where few dared to venture. Giving her a sidelong glance, he wondered if that were true.

Among all the Delphi cats, she was the only one Apollo avoided. When in her company, she always seemed to scrutinise and judge him. Now, perhaps, she was the only one who might give him answers.

"What am I supposed to make of that?" he asked, finally breaking the silence.

"Do you know how many have asked me, or my predecessors, that question down the years?"

Something squirmed in Apollo's brain; it stirred in slumber, leaving a residue of discomfort behind his thoughts, like undead spirits rising from their graves. He scarcely dared breathe.

"I am only a mouthpiece," she declared. "I say what the spirit tells me. It is for others to decide what it means."

"Spirit?"

The old cat stared at him through narrowed eyes as if he'd failed some crucial test.

"What spirit?"

"The essence of the earth goddess. The mother of all things. You, above all, should know that."

Apollo looked about him as if searching for inspiration, but any answer remained hidden. "You have mistaken me for someone else, I fear."

Pythia's stare grew harder; she looked right through him.

"Do you have any idea what you are?"

Without waiting for an answer, Pythia rose stiffly to her feet, then turned, pushed past the lower branches of two bushes, and disappeared. Apollo fought a strange reluctance, but followed her and found himself at the entrance to a narrow opening in the mountainside, beneath a high cliff. There was no sign of the other cat. With a deep breath, he plunged into the dark.

Instant night swallowed him. After a few steps, he was blind, relying on his other senses. Faint air movement detected by his whiskers told him he was in a confined but open-ended space, most likely a passage. He advanced. It was broadly straight with only a few minor turns, and fortunately, the ground was even. His nostrils told him Pythia was a short distance ahead. She must have been here before; he could sense her scent on the walls to either side. If he concentrated, he could hear her faint padding steps.

Onward he went. How far into the mountain could this fissure lead? Progress was slow, but after a long while, a more distant echo of footprints told him he was entering a larger space.

He turned a corner and saw the faintest shaft of light, grey against the blackness. It was too dim to illuminate any walls, but within it he saw vapours rising from a crack in the cavern floor, curling and coiling. It was warmer here. The gases hissed as they escaped and there was a pungent, almost metallic odour in the air, with a hint of sulphur. Silhouetted in front of the twisting pillar of gas was the dark outline of Pythia.

Apollo approached cautiously. Without looking at him, she spoke.

"You see? The Oracle still lives. It's just harder to find."

He stared, turning the name over in his mind. It was a word both strangely familiar, yet stubbornly incomprehensible. He studied the moving gases in puzzlement. Was something alive in the smoke?

"This is useless." He turned to go.

"I brought you here so you could ask your question."

He hesitated, torn. His question? How would this seething column of smoke help? With a suspicious glare towards Pythia, Apollo stepped forwards and closed his eyes.

CHAPTER 8
THE ORACLE

One step and he left the world behind. Blackness. Nothing. No senses, no sight, sound, smell, or direction. No up, no down. Just floating. What was this place? How big was it? Did it extend just beyond his reach, or did it go on forever? There was no scale; nothing to measure. It was the absence of everything. A void. The opposite of existence.

Did Chronos know of this place, or was it beyond his ken? Was this all there was? All there would ever be? The well of creation, or its grave? What was his purpose here? So many questions; his mind probed for answers, but the dark held on to its secrets.

Apollo had no fear. Instead, on the fringes of his awareness, there was a vague familiarity; he had been here before.

Faintly at first but growing rapidly, colours and shapes appeared. They swirled around, forming and dissipating in constant motion, changing hue, altering their shape, increasing in solidity before evaporating into ribbons of gossamer, only to appear again somewhere else. At least they brought some sense of scale, and with it, a sensation of nausea. With an effort, he suppressed the urge to vomit.

Then came the sounds. Not so varied at first; creaks and moans like wind moving through a long-deserted building. They ebbed and flowed; solidifying, then fading like an invisible storm. Then laughter; not joyous, but mocking and belittling.

A shape formed within the mass of colour. A man, perfect and chiselled like the finest statue; his skin bronzed, his golden eyes piercing, his expression unreadable. But also familiar. He was huge, filling Apollo's vision. With certainty he knew this was what he had once been, before the transformation brought utter change. But what remained?

Light shimmered around the figure, casting shadows across him. He began to change, morphing into something horrific. The face hardened into fury; his chest, arms and hands shining red as if he had bathed in blood. It smeared the once handsome face, dribbling down the chin.

What kind of monster was this? Vivid and terrifying, the golden eyes pierced Apollo with the sharp precision of an arrow from an unseen bow.

The gigantic figure faded into mist, and the mocking laughter swelled once more before morphing into speech.

"What is it you want?"

A simple question, but it caught him out. He had no straightforward answer. What *did* he want? So many questions raced around his mind.

Who am I? Where am I, and why?

He struggled to turn thoughts into words.

"I want to find Olympia."

It was a manifesto, a statement of intent, but with it arose an overwhelming sense of shame.

Shame he had allowed them to take her; shame at his neglect and failure to protect; shame that his love had been so shallow.

The laughter resumed, but more knowing now and more measured. He sensed he was being weighed on the scales, his fate uncertain while he hung there in the blackness, inert. Once, outrage would have consumed him; now, there was nothing. He was a blank canvas awaiting the artist. The voice broke the silence once more. He spun around, weightless and uncoordinated, but could see no speaker.

God of light,
   Shrouded amid Delphi's dreams,
   His soul polluted beyond Castalia's power to cleanse,
   His legacy a thread now grasped by brutal hands.
   Yet, should that filament Atropos shears escape,
   The fate of all forgotten gods will it shape.

The mocking laughter returned, assailing him from all sides. It gradually faded to be replaced by a swirl of visions in his mind's eye. Images rushed past at increasing velocity as he sensed himself pinned, unable to move, like a specimen on a board.

There were some scenes he recognised, but most meant nothing to him. He saw magnificent temples and devout ceremony, mingled with savage violence and destruction. Visions of anger, riot and bitter despair interlaced with scenes of peaceful serenity. They were replaced by the sight of overgrown shrines, barely attended as congregations dwindled. Vines clambered across toppled columns, and fallen porticos lay cracked and ruined in the dust, overgrown and abandoned.

There was no time to absorb or comprehend what he'd witnessed before new images vied for attention, cascading into his mind. Most he could not categorise: a blue-grey cat on the quayside of a small but wrecked harbour; scenes of butchery and horror in a grimy nondescript room, the screams cut short by the fall of a blade; an ancient city sacked and burning, then standing once more, vast and proud.

One scene he knew well: Prometheus chained, his sweat trickling down the stone.

The focus switched to the humourless and merciless laughter of a muscle-bound gaoler as he tightened the bolts fixing the Titan to the rock.

Then someone he thought he knew: kittens – some ginger, some dark – playing amid old stones tenderly watched by their tortoiseshell mother. Surely Olympia? Before he could look deeper, other scenes of horror flashed towards him: an animal tortured, its eyes wide and terrified; a broad shallow river twisting through a mountainous wooded landscape under a blue sky; an old man in a cloak with a staff beneath a dark rocky roof; a boat crossing a black river and then... No. Could it be? No, no, no.

Not that. Not him.

A memory he thought he'd locked away.

Apollo fought his invisible bonds, twisting with renewed vigour. But no matter how hard he struggled, his sight zoomed towards a rustic barn in a small village in a lonely mountain valley.

With one last effort of will, he hurled himself backwards and into the world of rock and air, panting, stunned, sickened and drained. What had he become? He was supposed to help, not punish. Was there enough water or blood in all the world to purify him now?

He fell backwards. Blind, nauseous, numb. Somehow he found the passage and, ricocheting from wall to wall, staggered and stumbled towards the light and fell onto the grass, gasping for air.

One thing was clear: his doom was set. He had no choice but to rescue Olympia. She was pregnant, and the future of all his kind depended on her survival.

CHAPTER 9
ENTRAILS

At the edge of their territory, by the perimeter fence of the disused factory, the Botrys gang had a dirty rat surrounded. It was dead. In fact, it had been dead for a week, lying here under a dusty bush in the summer heat, and it stank. The cats gave it as wide a berth as possible, apart from one whose mission had brought them here: the seer, Melanippus. He had the unenviable job of reading its entrails, and they would lap up every word. A lot hinged on his interpretation; were the Fates with or against them in their proposed war? What would be their leader's reaction? If the portents were bad, it could be disastrous.

He glanced over his shoulder. Kratos was watching impassively. The seer swallowed, relieved to see that the gang leader was, as yet, showing no visible sign of impatience; no twitch of the ear, flick of the tail or movement of any kind. Melanippus couldn't help but be nervous in his presence. Kratos' inscrutability came laden with menace, and his glance was returned with an intensity usually reserved for small, doomed rodents.

He turned back to the rat. Kratos had called him here for a reading and there was none better at interpreting the messy craft of entrails than him. Reading the mind of his master, however, was far more challenging. Melanippus knew the score; the rat was a sign. Melanippus had a strong suspicion his immediate future health depended on a successful reading. Get it right and his status within the group would be enhanced. Produce a poor reading, and… His stomach turned over at the thought. He banished such negativity and tried to focus. This was his chance to shine. His moment in the spotlight.

But, here on the front line, well inside the olfactory event horizon, the aroma was far from therapeutic, and his stomach already in rebellion. He approached the corpse. One wrong move might cause him to vomit; an omen he could do without. He swallowed, trying to bite down on the bile already threatening his throat, aware of his heart pounding against his ribs and the prickle of sweat on his pelt. With eyes half closed, he raked his claws down the distended belly of the animal from nose to tail. Its flesh split easily, like over-ripe fruit, and the stench of putrefaction had a near physical impact. He had to get this over with, and quickly. The contents of his own stomach were lurching around, and he was in danger of losing the battle to keep them still.

Concentrate.

Scents tell their own story and sometimes hold important messages: who was last here, what they'd had for breakfast, how long ago, and so on. He could do it, he knew, but right now, facing sensory overload, he couldn't think straight. Don't faint, don't squirm. Just do it. Melanippus stared down at the body and its spilled innards in acute discomfort. He did not lack evidence; getting close to it was the problem. He closed his eyes.

"You've had long enough."

The encouragement he didn't want. His mind went blank. *What does all this mean? What to say…*

He opened his dry mouth without the faintest idea what would come out.

"Er..."

He sensed, rather than saw, the impatient twitch of a tail behind him. Eyes boring into the back of his head. Where was his Sight?

Don't desert me. Not now. Calm, calm. Try to stay calm.

"Well, it's very clear..."

"What's clear?"

"Er, this. This is the liver, and you can tell a lot from the liver, obviously." He chanced a glance at his leader, trying to buy time, but instantly regretted it. Kratos cocked his head to one side, waiting.

Oh, well. In for a penny...

"Such as the diet of the deceased, for example, and what the weather was like when they passed away, of course." He looked around, desperate for support. There was none. Melanippus looked down again and once more struggled to avoid being sick. "You see that?" he squeaked excitedly, noticing something for the first time. "That's a kidney, and it's... it's facing over there to that building which means...." He stopped, groping for words. Almost imperceptibly, Kratos adjusted his position. Melanippus saw the subtle movement and speeded up his analysis, his voice squeaking up a notch.

"So, it clearly means whatever danger is coming is going to come from over there." He nodded to the south, and the building he'd been referring to, and glanced up, hoping it was enough. The look on the leader's face showed he expected more.

Melanippus tried to swallow but had no saliva, so he stared down again in desperation at the unfortunate rodent. The Sight arrived at last.

"Look!" he cried excitedly, treading the ground with his front paws and almost hopping up and down on the spot. "His nose is pointing north, which must mean a vital portent

is going to arrive from that direction soon, and, and..." He
again paused but this time his eyes widened in shock as the
distended stomach of the rat twitched.

It was as if it contained a seething mass of snakes; something was in there. With a sickening swell, the lining burst
and three fat, juicy maggots emerged, wriggling to freedom.
Melanippus took an involuntary step backwards, both fascinated and horrified. His own stomach lurched alarmingly.

"And there you have it," he croaked, his throat constricted
as he tried to keep everything down. "Danger from the south
and three important portents from the north." He looked up
triumphantly. Kratos stared back. "Or, er, three messages of
importance," equivocated the seer. "Or something like that.
Three of them anyway." He realised he might have to identify
and interpret these portents, whatever they might be. So he'd
better gain a little wriggle room.

Melanippus looked down again. The maggots were now
enjoying plenty of wriggle room of their own.

He turned and vomited spectacularly. The other cats
politely averted their eyes. Most of them were grateful to
have an excuse to back off. They exchanged glances,
impressed by the analysis, but anxious to see the boss' reaction. Did he like it? Was the seer safe? What would be the
mood of the day?

Kratos looked thoughtful. He watched the retreating cats, gave
Melanippus one last suspicious glare, and languidly made his
way back to the centre of his lair. This abandoned factory had
been their home for years and had so far avoided demolition
and redevelopment. Its high walls still stood, but the roof over
the main hall had long since gone. Within this larger open space,
trees now grew, providing excellent cover and protection from
prying eyes; an important consideration regarding his enemy. It
had the added advantage of providing shady resting places on

hot days. The factory, and the fenced-off wasteland on which it stood, made an excellent base, and gave the gang their name. Crucially, it was free from humans; apart from the watchman in his little hut by the road, but he didn't bother them.

This fortunate circumstance provided the Botrys gang not just with their home and safe ground, but also plenty of space in which to relax between their thieving and intimidation exercises in the neighbourhood. It also provided excellent hunting opportunities, attracting mice and rats from the surrounding area to meet their doom.

But Kratos, lord of this domain, had long since outgrown this urban backwater. He wanted more. He yearned for his old life, but better this time around: free of the sanctimonious gods of Olympus and their constant preaching and meddling. The novelty of hiding in plain sight, as they'd sold it, had long since worn thin, and he seethed with resentment at the fate her cunning fruit had delivered him.

He longed to get even, to rediscover his old powers, but the fury bottled within was matched only by his fear, a memory of the punishment the Olympians had delivered to his kin, all those years ago. If he shared his brother Zelus' haste, war would have erupted between himself and Athena long ago. But alongside his slow-burning hate, Kratos was cautious and filled with self-doubt. That innate hesitancy merely reinforced his perpetual grudge.

Never slow to demonstrate his strength to the mortals he lived among, Kratos enjoyed his dominion over them, and through physical confrontation bore the scars of a hundred one-sided fights to prove it. He resembled nothing more than a fur-covered boulder, but when this rock started to roll, no one wanted to jive. Other animals – even his many sons and daughters, the semi-divine who formed the malevolent core of the gang – got out of his way. With a mere whisper, his foot soldiers would run to comply.

The organisation and discipline of the Botrys gang made them feared by their peers across the city. Besides Kratos' extended family, they comprised a motley crew of ruffians and outcasts from across the neighbourhood and beyond. Known for their viciousness, a trait their leader both encouraged and required, their territory covered a large swathe of northern Athens. Most other beasts in those parts lived in fear of a beating from them.

Despite that, their ranks were swelling. The number of abandoned cats and lack of birth control had created a feline population boom, and many had nowhere else to go. Being a member of this most feared institution offered a refuge of sorts.

Kratos called them his worshippers and ruled them with absolute authority. He had done so since before any of them could remember; since before they were born. The crumbling walls of the former distillery served as their temple as well as their home.

They bowed to the power of his will. His dominion over them was such that none could contemplate or remember a time when he was not their lord, or when life was different. They had grown up under his spell, and knew no other existence.

Divination was the last piece of the jigsaw in his quest for vengeance, and there was enough in the seer's rambling analysis to confirm Kratos' belief that the time was ripe to launch an attack. Danger lay to the south; that was where his enemy lived. The nonsense about "portents from the north" he could live with; there were no meaningful gangs up there. No one with any force to trouble him. No reading was ever perfect, after all.

He should set one of his followers to watch the sky for birds travelling in threesomes; but there was no need to go overboard. Everything else stacked up, and there were no further omens. Nothing could now stop him. The time for action was nigh.

There was one last component to slot into place, and that would happen soon.

Back in the centre of his domain, Kratos called Yannis over for an update on the dig. He had no idea about the source of Athena's obsession, the "secret" she deemed so important, but whatever she craved, he wanted; not for its own sake, but to humiliate her. It would be the final insult; a precious treasure stolen from under her nose and the clearest demonstration yet of her waning influence. He ordered his lieutenant to redouble the watch and went to his sleeping quarters.

CHAPTER 10
THE QUEST BEGINS

pollo lay on his side, exhausted and confused. Nothing on this day made any sense. His experience in the cave seemed like just another fevered dream, already fading from memory. One residual thought remained: he had to rescue Olympia.

Gradually his racing heart slowed, and the nausea receded as the dreadful stench of the cave finally left his nostrils. Beside him Pythia crouched, watching. Why did she stare so? His discomfort in her presence was stronger than ever; he couldn't wait to get away.

He rolled onto his stomach, then got to his feet and stepped away, down the hill as slowly as seemed polite, grateful to be away from her. He could sense the old cat's eyes boring into the back of his head as he retreated. At least she offered no further advice and for that, he was grateful.

It was still mid-afternoon, with the sun high in the sky; its presence gave added relief. Now that he was out of that dreadful dark cave, he never wanted to see it again. Instead, with a renewed sense of purpose, he lifted his head and descended to the road. He had little idea how to execute his search, but that was the place to find answers. As earlier, he followed his own path to avoid the tourists thronging the Sacred Way. At a small clearing in the pine trees near the entrance, Daphne and Jason were waiting.

"We heard all those things they said earlier, and we didn't want you to sneak off without us," Daphne said, by way of greeting.

"We're going to help," Jason added.

Apollo looked from one to the other, grateful for their support. At least someone in this place cared. He led them to a quiet place, and there, beneath the shade of the trees, they spoke.

"I have to leave. I need to rescue her," he told them.

"Olympia's one of us. We've got to do something," Jason replied.

Apollo paused, unsure what to say and surprised Jason knew her well enough to want to help. He looked into the other cat's face to assess his sincerity. It seemed genuine enough.

"She's my best friend," said Daphne. "Just tell us what we need to do."

Daphne's presence always lifted Apollo's spirits in a way no one else could. It seemed natural that she would want to help. He gave her an affectionate glance.

"That's the trouble. I don't know what to do. All I know is that she's in a big city. Probably Athens. And she's in danger."

"I've heard of Athens," said Daphne. "But they say it's a long way away. How do we get there? And what did Pythia mean about Zeus studying his navel?"

"She was talking about an old saying," said Apollo. "You know, it's always said that Delphi is the navel of the world."

"But why would Zeus be gazing at it? Nothing that she said made sense," said Jason, voicing the thoughts of all of them.

"Athens, Athens…" Apollo muttered to himself, turning

the word over in his mind. It was so familiar. He must have been there before. But when? It was as if his brain consisted of cotton wool and his memories hovered just out of reach. The modern world was as much a mystery as trying to recall the true location of the Minotaur's labyrinth.

"If Athens is a big place, how do we find Olympia when we get there?" asked Jason.

They were at a loss until Daphne brightened and sat up, her tail twitching as an idea formed. "We must ask the police," she said.

Apollo looked doubtful. "But how will Sergeant Papadopoulos help? He can't understand us."

"None of them are good at our language," Jason agreed. "They can barely manage 'feed me.'"

"Not Sergeant Papadopoulos, silly," Daphne cried. "I mean Hector, the police dog."

The other two exchanged a glance. Hector was a large, somewhat overweight German shepherd, always avoided, as far as possible, by the other animals in the village. He was bad-tempered, had a vicious bark and was rumoured to bite those who dared to talk back. He was hostile to the cats of the Sanctuary; he regarded them as little more than outlaws or brigands.

"He won't help us," said Jason. "He hates us."

"He'll listen to me," said Daphne. She sat up, her back rigid with determination.

Daphne's fearlessness was one of her qualities Apollo admired most. No dog was going to faze her, regardless of its reputation. With Daphne around even the impossible seemed possible.

He swallowed and forced his mind back to the task in hand. "Okay, let's give it a go. We have no other ideas."

They set off, slipping through a gap in the railings, speeding along the pavement towards the village. It was a sultry afternoon and few tourists walked in their direction, but the three cats hugged the wall and did their best to stay out of reach, darting past as quickly as possible. The kidnap of one of their friends had shaken their trust in humans.

A couple of minutes after they'd left, a black-and-white cat, Polly, arrived in the clearing and looked about, sniffing for clues. She was crestfallen. She'd hoped to join the quest, but she was too late. The others had left, and she knew not where. Slowly she made her way back up the hillside.

CHAPTER 11
THE BUS

The place modern humans call Delphi is a short walk from the ancient site, hidden around a bending road. It is familiar to all the cats of the Sanctuary. Most of them scavenge for food from customers in the cafés on the edge of the village. The police presence – you could hardly call it a station – is the front room of Sergeant Papadopoulos's house which doubled as his office and operational centre. The house is set a couple of metres back from the narrow pavement, behind a dusty and rusty set of iron railings that had once been painted olive green. The cats slowed as they approached, keeping an eye out for both Hector and the villagers, and in particular the smaller humans who could be fast and were usually determined to make friends with them.

They spotted Hector sleeping under a wooden bench beside the front door. Apollo stopped at the gate, struck by indecision, but Daphne brushed past him and boldly approached the large dog, her tail rising in polite greeting like a furry flagpole. Hector slumbered on, snuffling and snoring. Apollo held back as she mewed at the dog, pushing her face in close, and admired her bravery.

"Hello," she said. "We need help."

Hector stirred, then started and jerked upright, banging his head on the underside of the bench. He barked at the sharp pain and lunged forwards sluggishly.

Daphne jumped back, the fur on her back standing upright. But she held her ground. "We need your help," she said again, flicking a glance from side to side, checking her exit was clear if she needed to run.

Hector lumbered to his feet, but Apollo preferred to study her perky little ears, rather than pay attention to the unfolding conversation. How did she maintain such poise in front of the big dog many times her size? Mortals could still surprise, and this one melted his heart, his affection melding into something stronger.

Hector looked poised to launch into a long bad-tempered tirade, but it died in his throat when he saw Daphne had not yet fled. Apollo was as surprised as the police dog to see that instead of running, she took a step back, then slowly, deliberately sat down in front of him as if passing the time of day. Her display of feline coolness was impressive. He turned his attention to the dog, hoping it would understand the subtleties of her body language as Daphne deliberately paid attention to the walls and door of the police station, all the time watching him out of the corner of her eye. Her fur was still fluffed out and he sensed her nervousness, but her poise was remarkable.

"We have an emergency," she said. "One of us has been stolen."

"Kidnapped by humans," Apollo added, snapping into the present and approaching.

Hector turned to him, still angry at being disturbed. There was a long pause. Curiosity got the better of him. "What do you mean, 'stolen'?" He addressed Daphne, but Apollo cut across her.

"Two humans put her in a sack and took her away in a

large car. Just after she had given them a lovely tour of the Sanctuary."

"Maybe they took a shine to her. Wanted a companion animal?"

"No, they were very rough with her. They didn't look nice," Apollo said, edging closer. "And besides, we don't play well as *companion* animals. We value our freedom."

"And you know the prophecy," Jason said. He stepped forwards, reciting from memory. "The cats of Delphi have guarded the Sanctuary since time out of mind. If anything happens to us, if we ever leave, then the world will crumble."

"Load of nonsense," growled Hector. "But if a citizen of Delphi has been abducted, then that is a crime." He sat down again. "So, what do you want me to do about it?"

"We need to find out where they've taken her," Apollo said.

"They took her this morning," Daphne added.

Apollo pointed with his nose towards Arachova. "They went that way."

"She won't be there," said Hector. "I know Clytemnestra, the police dog at Arachova, and she says the visitor cars never stop there. They go on down into the plains towards Athens."

"That's what we thought," said Apollo. "That's where we must go. To Athens. To find her and bring her home." He looked around at the others.

"Athens is huge," Hector told him. "Even if you get there, you'll never find her."

Daphne turned to face him. "If there are cats in Athens, we will find her."

Hector gave her a look, but said nothing.

"Where's Athens?" asked Jason. They all looked at him. "I mean, I've heard of it 'n' all, but…"

"Follow me," said Hector, turning and plodding into the police station. The cats followed, hesitant and sniffing for hidden dangers. But curiosity overcame their natural suspicion of enclosed spaces.

They found a room filled by an enormous desk that faced the door. Against the walls were lots of cupboards and filing cabinets. The whole room smelled of vinyl seat covers and furniture polish, mingled with paper and dust. At another time, it could have kept them busy for hours.

Hector stopped in front of an enormous picture on the wall and looked up.

"Wow!" said Jason, craning his neck to see it. "That's huge. What is it?"

"This is a map," Hector told him. "Of Greece." He pointed his snout towards a large red plastic spot stuck in the centre. "We are there," he said, "and the large black blob where all the lines join up is Athens."

The cats surveyed the map, with its pleasant colours and zig-zag lines. But it meant nothing to them. Apollo jumped up on the desk to get a closer look. He glanced down at Hector.

"So, how do we get there? Is it far to walk?"

The police dog snorted.

"For a start, you can get down from there. That's police property. It's not for walking on." Apollo ignored him. Hector pretended not to notice, and after a moment, continued. "You need to get a bus. There's one every afternoon to Athens. It leaves from the café at the end of the village at four p.m."

"When is that?" they chorused.

"A bit later. Halfway to sunset."

A door opened at the back of the room and Sergeant Papadopoulos stepped through, having finished his lunch. He stopped in his tracks when he spotted the cats. Apollo was still on the desk. "Scram!" he shouted, waving his arms around and advancing. The cats darted outside and ran down the street.

Apollo, Jason and Daphne approached the café at the end of the village main street. They slowed down.

"I've seen these buses," said Apollo, "but I've never noticed where they stop."

"We'd better wait here until one comes," said Jason.

They looked for suitable spots, in the shade, out of the way of clumsy human feet. Underneath parked cars was good: hidden from casual observers, but allowing them to monitor what was happening. Other cats would spot them, but with any luck, leave them alone.

The afternoon dragged on. An occasional vehicle passed by. Some tourists paused at the café over the road for a cool drink and something to eat. They considered heading over the road in search of titbits, but several warning glares from the café owner's cats made them think twice. A mutual hostility existed between the cats of the village and those of the Sanctuary. Scavenging for food on their patch didn't go down well, even though almost all the Sanctuary cats had done it.

"I'm bored." Daphne had her head on her paws and her eyes closed.

"I'm hungry," said Jason. The café food scents spreading on the still air were enticing, despite being mixed with the aroma of oil and grease from the underside of the car.

"We're on a rescue mission," Apollo reminded them. "We need to stay focused."

Jason was about to argue, when they heard a bus coming down the main street. At the café, people collected their bags and gathered on the pavement. The bus appeared and stopped at the roadside near the cats' hiding place, with a loud hiss from its brakes. They prepared themselves. Apollo gave the others a warning look.

"Ready?"

Humans milled everywhere, most of them carrying huge bags and suitcases. There were two doors – one at the front and another halfway down – but a scrum of people crowded around both, jostling to climb onboard. The cats tensed, waiting beneath their car, watching intently.

"How are we going to get on?" asked Daphne.

"It's a nightmare," groaned Jason. "We'll be trampled to death."

The bus driver clambered down the front steps, parting the crowd and opening the luggage hatches along the sides of the bus. People surged forwards, handing him bags, which he flung into the dark hold. The crowd thinned as more people climbed onboard, and the number with cases went down.

Apollo spotted an opportunity.

"When he's looking the other way, we'll get past him and into the hold with the bags," he told the others. They circled towards the back of the bus and edged closer. None of the humans noticed them; they were focused on making sure the driver took their luggage, then scrambled to get a seat.

The driver fell into a heated conversation with one passenger, giving the cats their chance. They shot behind him and dived into the dark of the hold, out of reach.

"Hey!" called old Kostas back at the café. "You've got stowaways!"

But the driver ignored him; he was too busy arguing.

Apollo, Jason and Daphne scrambled out of sight behind and between suitcases and backpacks. There was plenty of space to hide, but as they were settling down, the hatch slammed shut and they found themselves in pitch-dark. Their night vision was no help; there was no light at all.

Jason spoke, with a slight but detectable tremor in his voice. "This was a bad idea. I don't like this." Daphne whimpered nearby. Apollo somehow found her in the dark and butted his head against hers, purring reassurance. Despite the noise and vibration of the engine, the other two could hear it, or sense it, and the powerful calming influence it exerted.

"We'll be fine," he said. "They have to open the door sometime."

The huge vehicle, with its swerving movements, vibrations and constant background engine thrum, seemed almost alive. They tried to settle down, but as the bus lurched around corners, luggage shifted around them, forcing them to adjust position. As the journey progressed and the road became less twisty, they relaxed a little.

With every passing mile, the fog that had shrouded Apollo's thinking seemed to thin, and he became more confident of his decision to leave. He couldn't remember the last time he had been away from Delphi, but in the dark hold beneath the bus, and in contrast to his companions, he experienced a strange exhilaration.

Afternoon passed into evening, but for the travellers it remained dark, airless and hot, and the journey seemed endless.

It was mid-evening before the bus arrived at its terminus. The engine cut out and its familiar rumble was replaced by the shuffling and stamping of feet above them as the passengers gathered their belongings. In the dark the cats tensed, waiting for the luggage compartments to open and the opportunity to escape.

The driver finally lifted the hatches, admitting a little extra light from the dim streetlights. He hauled out luggage while a throng of impatient passengers gathered.

"We run as fast as we can," Apollo whispered to his companions. "Wait for my signal, then we go. We'll meet by those trees over there, at the far side of the asphalt." He pointed them out with his nose, through the forest of human legs.

The driver worked his way closer, methodically removing their cover. As soon as there was space in front of him, Apollo made a bolt for it, streaking out of the hold, followed by his companions. The driver pulled back in shock, and several people jumped aside as the cats darted past, swerving around and between them, dodging suitcases and backpacks, and the occasional grabbing hand. One or two laughed or exclaimed to see such enterprising stowaways. Several wondered aloud whether they'd ripped their bags open, or worse. A couple expressed concern about their welfare in the big city.

Apollo, Jason and Daphne weren't listening. They were free and running, relieved to be out of the hot and claustrophobic bus and into the open air. Wherever that was.

CHAPTER 12
OLYMPIA

Olympia sat in misery, head bowed, in a wire-mesh cage; one of many in a yard at the back of the building. The other cages were mostly populated by cats, but some contained dogs, either expecting or with a new litter of puppies. The filth and the stench were offensive to her eyes and nose. The place was never cleaned. How long would they keep her here? What would happen after?

To provide a distraction, Olympia tried talking to the small cat in the neighbouring compartment. She was unresponsive at first, but as trust grew, she spilled out her story.

"It happened while I was out burgling. I was looking for socks. Anything small and made of fabric, really. The boss likes that kind of stuff. He likes to rub his nose into them, roll around on them and soak up the scent of all the sweaty humans who've worn them. To each his own, I guess." She caught Olympia's look and tried to explain. "The good thing is, in return for a bit of thievery I get a safe bed, a fair share of the hunting spoils and I'm a respected member of the gang. We look out for one another."

She paused, lost in thought. "Or at least we did until I got nabbed. I suppose I got too cocky. I'd found an empty flat on the ground floor with the window open just wide enough for me to squeeze in. I had the run of the place. I found a basket where they dump their laundry." She looked up, with a gleam in her eye. "It was like a goldmine. I had the pick of anything. Of course, a lot of it was too big to carry, but there was plenty of underwear too. 'Smalls', I've heard them called. 'Bigs', for someone my size, but whatever. I got a mouthful of knickers and headed back out. It was all going well until I went round the corner into Kalama Street. I was concentrating on not tripping up, so I forgot to pay proper attention. It was a kitten's mistake." She sounded philosophical. "She came out from behind a parked car, all friendly like. Made some cooing noises. I was suspicious right from the start and backed away. I didn't want to let go of my prize, but there was something about this human that felt wrong. She was trying too hard to be friendly."

Olympia looked up. This sounded all too familiar.

"I paused to think. That was my undoing. Thinking. I should have just dropped the pants and run. But I'd put a lot of effort into getting them that far and I wanted to please the boss. I wanted to get the praise. To feel special. I still wanted to take them with me. I could have shared his den for the night. I might even have been invited into the inner circle, with all the important ones." She looked at Olympia, seeking understanding.

Olympia knew the politics of feral cat communities very well, with their jealousies and petty rivalries, but she was grateful that there had been no one of such a thuggish nature in charge at Delphi. Theirs had been a far more benign society.

Her neighbour continued.

"That's what did for me. Too many useless thoughts. She had something behind her back. A net. She was quick with it for someone her size. Once it had landed on me, that was it. I struggled but just got tangled up worse and worse. It was no use. I snarled at her, let her have a piece of my mind, but she put me in some kind of bag and bundled me into one of those cars they all have. So I ended up here." She looked around, disdainful. "There must be cats in here from every gang in the city. Some civilians, too. Not that I want to talk to them." She turned to Olympia once more. "At least you're not like them, bleating about how unfair it all is. I don't trust them." She cast her eyes down, bitterness in her voice. "Thinking. It's overrated."

CHAPTER 13
ATHENA AND HERSE

Beneath the twisted olive trees on the hill above the Agora, Athena was deep in conversation with Herse. The dusty-coloured cat with her darker brown ears and tail, was making another attempt to get her mistress to take the latest threat from the gangs seriously.

"The unrest is growing. My contacts among the citizens are getting edgy. They see many more comings and goings within the criminal community, and lots of them are feeling intimidated."

"We mustn't refer to them as criminals," Athena corrected. "They're wild. They live off their wits. They aren't all criminally inclined."

"I haven't met one yet that isn't a qualified burglar."

"Yes, but that applies to almost all our kind. We call it 'opportunism' when it is performed by one of our own."

Herse tried again. "Things are getting out of hand. We've got reports of mass raids on market stalls, particularly fishmongers. Large-scale fights on waste ground and sometimes in respectable neighbourhood parks. There's intimidation, increased theft. Basically, anything shiny is a target. I'm also getting feedback that quite a few cats are disappearing. It's serious."

After a long yawn, the grey cat licked a paw and began the process of grooming. She continued to address Herse between licks. "This sort of thing happens now and then. It's cyclical. The gang leaders get big ideas, they throw their weight about a bit, have a few run-ins with their rivals. It all settles down after a while. We're in the middle of the worst phase at the moment. It'll change. It always does." She started washing her face.

Herse stood, as if to walk away, thought again and sat once more, closer and directly in Athena's eyeline this time, determined to make her point. In previous years they had been much more proactive. They had gone out and knocked sense into the wayward souls out there until they got the message. Sitting here on the hill behind a screen of sentries and doing nothing seemed like an evasion of duty.

Athena had a good go at her right ear, then paused. "You should relax more. Spend some time with that young boy of yours. What's his name? Erichthonius? Check up on him. See who he's hanging out with. Take some time to enjoy the Plaka. Have some fun."

Herse couldn't believe her ears. She was being told to take a break, relax, go away for a while, stop pestering. She'd never heard Athena like this before; it seemed unnatural. The thought of being effectively cast out made her shudder. This part of the city, beneath and among the trees adorning the ancient Agora, was her home. She belonged here. Away from the twisting, narrow streets of the Plaka in the Acropolis' shadow; the heart of old Athens. It was the neighbourhood she'd grown up in, where she'd learned to jostle and fight with every other scruffy kitty for attention and food. She didn't want to go back. She'd been little more than an adolescent when the older toms started paying her too much attention, and too small to fight them off.

Worn down and abused, she'd had a litter of kittens, few of whom had survived. As soon as she felt able, Herse escaped and left them to fend for themselves within the gang. It was a selfish act, but she had to do it to survive. Or so she justified it.

Herse hated thinking back to her earlier life, but now she was being instructed to go there and, recurrent nightmares permitting, relax. It wasn't her current idea of fun. At least she was older, wiser and stronger now; better equipped to fight off unwanted suitors or accept them on her terms. Although there was little room in her life for desire anymore. Under the guidance and protection of Athena, the sisterhood lived a chaste life, and the worldly bickering and petty jealousies of the cats of the Plaka held little appeal. Herse followed a higher calling these days: maintaining order throughout the entire city. It was a mission identified and pursued relentlessly by her mistress and leader, Athena, for as long as she could remember. Under their leader's guidance, the sisterhood kept the feline population in line.

Her old life seemed small and pointless by comparison. But, given her responsibilities and those of her chosen clan, the thought of leaving without being on official business seemed like desertion. Herse had become used to travelling the city, poking her nose into other animals' affairs in an official capacity on behalf of her leader. What would it feel like to be free? To have no cares or responsibilities? To shake off the woes of the world, even if only for a short time? She was so used to minding everyone else's business, she found it hard to imagine. A tingle of apprehension ran down her spine. There was only one benefit she could think of: catching up with her beloved son. Erichthonius was, as far as she was aware, the only survivor of her brood. She'd seen him around occasionally, prowling the streets of the Plaka, sniffing out the shops and bars and dodging the tourists. But she'd always kept her distance, though she always kept an ear attuned for news of him. She'd heard he was popular and bright; she had high hopes for him. He had his own life now, but it would be nice to see him again; to see if he remembered her.

Still, being instructed to take time out – to unwind and relax – was so unlike her leader it felt like a slap in the face. Athena's watch on the archaeological dig was the only thing consuming her attention these days. It had become an obsession and she would brook no distractions.

Herse ventured a direct question. "What is it you're hoping the humans find with all their digging?"

Athena stopped her grooming and looked out across the city. "I'm not sure. But I think it's going to be something important. If I were to hazard a guess, I'd say it is something stolen from me many, many years ago."

That made no sense to Herse. Yes, Athena was old; she might be ten, perhaps even older. But how could something stolen from her be hidden so far underground? She could only conclude that her mentor was getting a little soft in the head. She was sprightly for a ten-year-old, but her obsession with the dig might be a symptom of a larger problem. She shuddered. Perhaps it was a good time to take a break and test the temperature down in the real world, amid the hustle and bustle of other animals. At least it would get her away from this obsession with things long dead and buried.

Herse got up and stretched.

"You may be right. I'll take a day or two off and check in with my son." She sauntered off.

Athena resumed washing.

CHAPTER 14
A BRIEF ENCOUNTER

Herse chose a quiet route through the Plaka, rather than approach the headquarters of the Plaka gang directly. They were always suspicious when one of Athena's people came visiting, and she had no appetite for a confrontation. Instead, she hoped to find Erichthonius out and about somewhere, or at least get word of him, but these days she had no knowledge of his preferred haunts.

Marching down the centre of the street, too late she saw a sleek silver-white cat hovering in the shadows, apparently entranced by scents deposited by the wall. She hoped he hadn't seen her, and kept walking, eyes fixed ahead. It wasn't that he was hostile – far from it, he was polite and friendly to a fault. But that was the problem; he could disarm you with a casual question or a kind word far more effectively than a brutal thug. Athena's business was private, and Herse took her responsibilities seriously; they all did. She had schooled all her flock to be as distrustful of Hermes and his scheming as any villain.

There were no side streets or alleys to provide an escape, she had no choice but to hope he didn't notice her.

At first she thought she might be in luck; he seemed more

interested in investigating the scent marks left by recent visitors than engaging in conversation, but her heart sank as she saw him look up and take note of her approach. He headed diagonally across the street to intercept her.

"Hi, er, Herse, isn't it? What brings you down among the mere mortals of the Plaka?"

"Hermes, hello. How nice to see you." She kept it polite, but was unable to keep a note of irritation from her voice. "I'm taking a little break. Catching up with a few old friends and my son."

"Ah, yes. Erichthonius, if my memory serves me. A fine young animal, I seem to remember. And how are things up on the hill? Is Athena keeping you all busy?"

She hesitated. "Well, yes. We're stretched, to be honest. I feel guilty taking time off."

Hermes shared an interest in a passing scent, making a play of sniffing the air.

"Mmm?"

She watched him from the corner of her eye. "Oh, it's probably nothing. Just business as usual. But it's keeping us on our toes." He could tell she was making a little too much effort to appear unconcerned. "You know, the gangs are in a ferment, the sky's falling in, that sort of thing."

Hermes exuded an air of indifference. He ambled on down the street, as if expecting her to follow. Herse hesitated, torn. Now was her chance to escape, to turn and quickly walk away, but like so many before, she couldn't resist seeking his opinions.

"I hear many rumours about Kratos and his mob wanting to grow their territory, and the Gizi gang is getting so out of hand. The raid on the market last week was shocking. What do you think?"

Hermes considered her question, then answered with one of his own. "Well, the more important thing is what Athena thinks. She must be worried, surely?" Herse halted in her tracks, unsure what to say.

"Er, no. She's not too bothered. Says it will all blow over."

"That's most unlike her, is it not?" He waited, but Herse, remembering her training, remained silent. After a while he went on, answering his own question. "Ah, well. I expect she has her reasons." He gave her a sidelong glance. "I'm sure she'll be back to business as usual before long."

Again she held her tongue, but against his unnatural calm she felt hot, and flustered; desperate to fill the silence, and equally anxious not to say anything. He waited, looking else-where, apparently unconcerned, damn him, while her thoughts twisted about one another.

"I'm sure it will be clear once we've got this current obses-sion out of the way."

Hermes looked up and she knew instantly from his reac-tion she'd said too much. "Oh, she's got a special project, has she? How interesting. Now I understand why you can't say anything. Don't worry. Your secret will be safe with me." He nudged closer until they were almost touching. He was bold, certainly. Disarming. This intimacy, an invitation to share his confidence, was a gift too tantalising to resist. All she had to do was share a little secret. It was no big thing, surely? Certainly no betrayal; she was merely demonstrating her initiative, gathering intelligence: something Athena would surely encourage.

But while she wrestled with her conscience she failed to see him playing out the line, enticing her like a practised angler. At that point, Herse made her mistake. She looked into his eyes and was lost in unguessable distance. Beneath her feet, the street lurched as if it were floating, and her head spun. She experienced a fleeting sensation of panic, leaving her stomach small and knotted. But she couldn't break his stare. Those blue eyes bored right through her, splitting her thoughts into fragments. They were a colourful kaleidoscope, swirling and dancing in a kind of inner space. Behind them, through them, she sensed something incomprehensible and vast beyond her imagination; a hint of terrifying power that could crush her with just a thought, if it so wished.

Herse was defenceless, her thoughts plucked, unpeeled and weighed on the scales by some invisible judge. She had no secrets anymore; only the horrible sensation that she was no longer alone in her own head. Startled, she heard herself speaking, as if from a great distance. Trapped in this mental vice, it felt as if the conversation was taking place between two completely different beings in another place entirely. Her captive mind bore horrified, silent witness to the things her physical body was saying out loud; things she had wanted to keep to herself.

"Well, she said something odd earlier today. Made me wonder if she might be losing her marbles."

"It's not that Elgin chap again, is it?" Hermes gave a sympathetic chuckle, as if, out there, an inconsequential conversation was taking place between friends. Imprisoned in this inner space, it sounded a million miles away and false, and there was no humour.

"What? No. She said they were going to dig up something stolen from her years ago. That doesn't make any sense, does it?"

He let her go, broke the bond, and looked down the street. She staggered, and a wave of nausea passed over her. But at least she was back on solid ground; alone once more with her thoughts. Herse stared, wide-eyed, in relief at the flagstones under her feet, and tried to regain her balance.

"No. Very odd," he muttered, as if to himself. "She hasn't said what it is, then?"

Herse shook her head, feeling confused again, not daring to meet his eye; now desperate to escape.

"You'd better keep a close watch on her in case of any other signs. If there area any, let me know." Orders issued,

Hermes turned his attention to a nearby plant growing in a pot. "Well, it's been nice seeing you. Pass on my regards to your youngster."

The spell was broken, leaving Herse feeling flustered. What had she done? What confidence had she betrayed?

"You won't tell anyone, will you?" she pleaded. "I shouldn't have said anything. I don't want to get her into trouble."

Hermes turned his head and flashed his most reassuring look. "Of course not. It'll go no further." He paused as if a thought had just occurred to him. "But if you are worried about her behaviour, I think I know how to get her back to the straight and narrow. I know someone who can help. I'll get a message to you." He set off before she could respond. Never had the promise of help sounded so sinister, but her over-riding emotion was relief to see him go.

A short distance across town, Herse's colleague Rena watched the comings and goings at the corner of Thisiou and Astiggos Street. The morning had been long, and she was bored. How long did she have to do this for? The sun wasn't yet overhead, and it would be late before her shift ended. The street was at least traffic-free, but the number of pedestrians was increasing. She kept a wary eye out for members of her own species. Dogs could pass – they were accompanying humans as often as not – but cats could go no further. She had turned four away already this morning, but the arguments were tiresome, and she hoped there wouldn't be too many more.

Her spirits sank as she spotted three more heading towards her; gang members by the look of it. They might be tricky to turn aside. She glanced down the street to her right, but there was no sign of Trixie, her back-up. The newcomers marched straight up to her, and without breaking stride, they attacked. She screeched in pain and surprise, but they overpowered her, and dragged her into a nearby alley by the scruff of her neck.

"You can't do this," she said, before further blows rained down. Then one of them got her in a chokehold and darkness descended.

She came to in a filthy back alley, well away from the main thoroughfare, behind the bins and rubbish bags piled up at the back of a large store. The place stank, with debris in the gutter, and coloured liquids puddling in cracks on the ground.

Yannis leaned towards her.

"Tell us what we want, and we might let you go."

She looked around, terrified. But there was no escape. The three of them had her boxed into a corner. Her eyes darted around, seeking an escape route, a hiding place, anything. But there was none. She was trapped.

"I don't know anything," she pleaded.

Her captors exchanged knowing glances.

"'Course you do. You just need to get it off your chest," their leader insisted.

She tried reasoning. "What is it you want to know?"

"Your leader. Her Ladyship. What's she so interested in? What are you guarding?"

"I don't know. She doesn't tell us anything. You've got to believe me."

A swipe across her face, drawing blood, told her they didn't. It loosened her tongue. All thoughts of holding out against these thugs vanished. She just wanted to survive.

"She said it's an artefact, whatever one of those is. It has power. We must stop anyone getting near it. That's all she's told us. That's all we know." She was desperate now. Sobbing, pleading. "There, I've told you everything. Let me go."

They didn't.

CHAPTER 15
THE BOTRYS GANG

The terminus was next to a metro station north of the city centre. From the new arrivals' point of view it was a sea of asphalt with sharp, angular buildings and far too many people. The cats ran under and around buses until they found temporary cover beneath bushes on the verge at the far side. Apollo would have liked to go through, but a high chain-link fence blocked further progress. He halted to wait for the others to catch up.

"Made it," said Jason, still out of breath. "Now all we have to do is find Olympia."

Nervously, they peered out from their hiding place, and the enormity of the task sank in. Athens smelled different to home, and Apollo sensed it was bigger than anything he had imagined. He glimpsed a wide road on the other side of the fence, busy with traffic. Behind them lay an open space with several parked buses and a now diminishing throng of people, mostly heading into a large building behind. Yellow streetlights illuminated the ground, and the air was filled with an exotic assortment of scents, most of which he'd never experienced: different plants, diesel fumes, and in the distance, the enticing aroma of food cooking. The cocktail was as intoxicating as it was disconcerting.

"Where are we going to start?" said Jason. "This place looks enormous, and we don't know anyone."

"I'm not doing anything without a proper rest," said Daphne. "I felt sick inside that awful bus. It was so hot. We need to find a safe place for a few hours, then we can make plans."

There was no obvious safe place to sleep nearby. More busses were coming and going, their movement difficult to predict, and what if someone was still searching for the stowaways?

"Let's move, then," said Apollo, turning to survey the fence. Its design made it difficult to climb, so they walked along beside it until they found a small gap where the wires had been cut and bent aside. On the other side was a narrow, quiet road. They crossed and followed a short street, keen to get away from the bus station.

Within minutes they arrived at the side of a major thoroughfare; wide and with multiple lanes of traffic racing in both directions like two opposing rivers. It was bewildering. Overhead the sky was dark, but bright sodium lights illuminated the road surface, and headlights on the vehicles dazzled them as they looked about.

Then there was the noise, ebbing and flowing against a constant background rumble. Athens looked horrific.

"It's not all like this, is it?" wailed Daphne.

"Of course not," said Apollo, more in hope than certainty.

The traffic was far busier than anything they had experienced in Delphi. From their sanctuary on the pavement they watched in dismay as vehicles thundered past their noses. At the far side Daphne glimpsed a small black-and-white cat.

"He might show us where we can rest," she said. The others gave no sign they'd heard her.

"Right, let's get across," said Apollo, in a loud voice. He stepped into the road; eyes set on the opposite side.

"Wait!" shouted Jason. Apollo paused and looked at him, as a truck thundered by, so close he was almost knocked over by the wind it gave off as it passed. "Are you mad?" Jason yelled. "Wait for a gap."

Chastened, Apollo re-joined him on the kerb. The grey-and-white cat edged forwards, looking right and left. "Now!" he shouted, and ran for it.

Trusting his instinct, Apollo followed with Daphne close behind. On the opposite pavement they paused, panting with relief. There was no sign of the cat Daphne'd seen earlier.

They headed along smaller and quieter roads to find somewhere safe; but the city was too busy. Over railway tracks they went, then along narrow pavements between tall buildings and parked cars. They were weary, but driven by nervous energy and desperate to find a safe place to rest. They had no idea where they were. The buildings and roads seemed to go on forever, as Athens' true size dawned on them. Finding Olympia would take a lot more than guess-work or luck.

At last they arrived at a piece of waste ground, amid which they could see the outline of several old, abandoned buildings. They were difficult to make out in the dark, and for once there were no lights, but encouragingly they could see no sign of a human presence. A badly maintained and easily penetrated wire-mesh fence separated the waste ground from the road.

It was a great find; a deserted and secluded place where they could rest and take stock of the situation. With spirits rising they crossed the overgrown ground until they reached the high outer wall of a large building. A sniff and glance around. The walls were intact, although few of the high windows had any glass. Nearby, a tall chimney prodded into the dark sky. Most of the roof was missing, but that was no problem. The tops of trees poked above the brickwork to provide cover from prying eyes. It was by far the best-looking place to hide they had yet seen.

"It's not like the ruins back home," said Jason.

"It looks lovely," Daphne ventured. "I like the trees. I wonder what it looks like in daylight? Perhaps we could stay here while we try to find Olympia?"

The first item on Apollo's agenda was food. "There must be plenty of mice or voles here."

They passed through a doorway into an empty room, where debris from old broken furniture littered the floor. Beyond that, they found themselves in a large, dark, tree-filled space amid the high walls they'd admired earlier. It was dark beneath the trees, and the scent of vegetation strong. Little light from the distant streetlamps penetrated here, and the moon was obscured by the branches above.

They hesitated while their eyes adjusted.

The place looked as if it had been deserted for a long time. There was no trace of recent human activity, but there was…

Apollo sensed movement and looked to his right.

A dark shadow against the darker background. The outline of a large cat standing on a pile of rubble, a metre above them. Eyes glinted in the low light.

The creature edged closer, and as more light fell on its face, Apollo thought it the ugliest cat he'd ever seen. He could just make out a nasty-looking scar below its left eye, running down almost to its jaw. It bristled with hostility; every movement was tight and tense. They had unwittingly strayed into the heart of its territory.

"Well, well. What have we here?" it growled. "Who are you, and what do you think you're up to?"

Apollo ignored the burly giant and glanced around, noticing movement all about them. Cats appeared from almost every crevice and nook. They were heavily outnumbered.

"Just as well I didn't nip over there for a snooze," murmured Daphne.

Turning back to their inquisitor, Apollo maintained the confident demeanour of a tourist on a sightseeing jaunt. He exuded inquisitive, naive friendliness.

"Nice place you have here," he said. "Very spacious and secluded. No sign of humans. I like it." His companions said nothing, but stood still, watching the shadows.

"Like it, do you? Fancy moving in, eh?" sneered the big ugly brute, as he carefully descended from his perch and drew closer. It was obvious he was the leader of this sizeable group. His manner spoke of an easy familiarity with violence. "Well, this is a private place. For us. There are no vacancies. Not without express permission. And you haven't got any." He glanced around, eyeing his followers, putting on a show for them, Apollo didn't take his eyes from him. A brief silence fell as they eyed each other.

The hostile animal took another step closer. "We could always do with some fresh meat," he snarled, his voice low and threatening.

Apollo took another moment to glance around, which only provoked the big cat further. "Do you often eat cat?" he enquired.

"We'll eat whatever we like," came the reply, followed by the obligatory boast, "We are the Botrys gang, and this is our territory. No one comes in here without our leave, and no sneak-thief intruder gets out in one piece."

The dark cat's voice became lower and softer, which only made him sound more threatening. Apollo watched his every move, never moving a muscle. All around, members of the Botrys gang edged forwards towards the Delphi cats. They looked hungry for blood. Apollo sensed Jason and Daphne instinctively edging closer to him. He held his ground, and tried to reason.

"There's no need to take offence. Coming here was a

simple mistake. We're visitors. We mean you no harm. We're just looking for somewhere to sleep for a few hours. Perhaps you have a quiet corner? We'll be off before dawn."

Behind Apollo, his colleagues' eyes darted left and right, looking for escape routes. But he could see that his calm reassurance seemed to be having an impact; there were one or two blinks and murmurs of agreement among the observing gang members.

The large hostile cat in their midst took the opposite view, however. He bared his fangs and advanced until his snout was almost touching Apollo's. Still, Apollo maintained his position. He returned the other animal's stare, unflinchingly. The seconds seemed to stretch, as the others held their breath.

The dark cat spoke to the Delphi group. "Who do you think you are, marching in here unannounced? Your arrogance is a little displaced, is it not? You are far out of your depth." He stepped back once more, spittle dripping from his incisors. "What are you doing here? She's trained you well, I'll admit. Takes a fair amount of bottle to stand here telling me you want to make friends. I'll give you that." He stepped closer once more. "But it won't work. It's over. For all of you. Her, him and the thug she likes to keep at her side. This is our time now." He paused, as if deciding what to do, then turned his attention to Daphne placing his face close to hers. He closed his eyes and inhaled her scent. She winced and tried to turn aside. Jason bristled, but remained rooted to the spot. "Ah, such a sweet scent to accompany so innocent a creature." He lifted his head, nostrils flared, and continued in a voice as melodious as gravel being ground in syrup. "So complex. So many notes. Is that a hint of… cypress trees, mingled with… narcissus, and…" With eyes open, he glared at her. "Asphodel."

"Look…" Jason said.

The brute turned towards him. "Or what?"

"There is no need for such aggression," said Apollo. Far

from placating the monster, this seemed to rile him further. He swung back towards the ginger cat.

"I need no lecture on aggression." Once more, he moved close, studying Apollo. "I would say you can deliver a message back to her, but it's too late for that. I've been reasonable. I gave her a chance. If this is her response, then so be it. You're going nowhere."

Before Apollo could react, a pawful of razor-sharp claws flashed towards his face. The ginger cat jumped backwards, but not quite fast enough to prevent a nasty gash across the nose. As if released from a dream, the other gang members followed their boss' lead and attacked in a blur of teeth and claws, yowling and squealing. They were wiry and street-wise, hardened by years of fighting but, lulled by Apollo's soothing words, confusion momentarily dulled the edge of their attack.

The Delphi cats had far less experience of combat. Relying on instinct, they found themselves fighting for their lives.

The big cat pounced on Apollo, trying to grapple with him and drag him to the ground, but found himself evenly matched. Despite the unprovoked attack, Apollo still felt a reluctance to fight. He experienced a flush of dislocation while he wrestled with the big bully, as if his waking mind struggled to accept what was happening. *It shouldn't be like this.* He was shocked at the power of the other animal; despite his opponents size, Apollo had expected to be much the stronger. It was many a long age since he'd come across anyone with such strength. But the overwhelming emotion was disappointment that his message had failed to chime. Why did they not believe him?

It became more difficult to keep the gangster at bay, but he still had little appetite for the fight. His own bites lacked venom; his claws remained sheathed.

His enemy, in contrast, used every means available to bring him down, targeting his vulnerabilities with deadly intent. Apollo suffered genuine pain from the claw marks on his shoulder and back, and felt his skin pierced by the monster's sharp incisors; yet he struggled to shake off the torpor. He was still musing on why his peaceful request for help had carried so little weight.

The requirement for him and his companions to survive finally took over his thoughts.

He tried to shove his opponent backwards so he could escape; but it was like pushing a boulder uphill. As they tussled, his hind paws slipped on the loose ground and he fell sideways, with the brute on top of him. The dark cat reinforced his grip, and bit down hard on Apollo's neck, sensing victory.

Around them, gang members attacked Daphne and Jason, pouncing, biting, snarling and slashing. But in the tight space, they often got in each other's way. Fortune had placed a wall immediately behind the Delphi cats, so they could not be surrounded. Both of them desperately tried to stay on their feet and spar with their opponents at a distance. Falling beneath an attacker would be fatal. The screeches of a dozen fighting cats filled the still night air, and a light came on in the night watchman's hut.

Things looked hopeless, but the Delphi cats fought with a desperation that clearly surprised their attackers. Daphne was nimble and quick-witted enough to make her enemies look slow and clumsy as they tried to pin her down. With a balletic move, she leapt over their heads and bounced from a nearby tree to gain some space and distance.

Jason – larger, stronger, but more earthbound – preferred to use the trees for cover as he darted between them, dodging attacks. Quick as they were, the odds were stacked against them.

Torchlight swung in their direction, surprising all the combatants and bringing salvation. A human voice yelled at them to shut up. The night watchman resented having his peace being disturbed by yowling, fighting felines.

As the light fell on him, the dark cat loosened his grip to look over his shoulder. With his attention diverted, Apollo squirmed out from under him. At that instant a shower of gravel flung by the human landed in their midst, accompanied by further choice words. Cats scattered in different directions. Jason freed himself from the brute who had his leg in his mouth and scrambled towards a panting Apollo. Daphne, on hind paws, shadowboxing with her attacker, broke off and joined them.

Sticking close, they charged away from the fight zone between piles of rubble and the detritus of the abandoned factory until they saw a gap in the wall. Onward they ran across more waste ground towards another fence, looking neither left nor right. Bursting through one of the many gaps, they emerged into the open once more, but they dared not stop. Without looking behind, they charged across another road, heedless of the traffic, and reached a quieter pavement on the other side. They ran on, down a narrow street lined with tall buildings. At a junction, they turned into another similar street. There they paused, panting, looking back and listening for signs of pursuit. No one was following.

"That was… intense," muttered Jason.

"Scary," said Daphne. She spat out a mouthful of her enemy's dusty fur. Her entire body trembled with nervous energy.

Apollo said nothing; just caught his breath until his heart rate subsided. His wounds felt raw, the pain searing; but rather than lick them he stared into the distance, trying to remember when he had last received such a reception. Standards of hospitality had lapsed since he was last abroad, but he had no memory of being anywhere other than Delphi and the comforting slopes and groves of Parnassus. This amnesia was troubling. Why could he not remember? Who was he, really? The image in the strange dream in the cave came back to him. Was that real? It had made sense at the time, but now all he could remember were distant fragments.

His legs trembled in a violent shudder, as if the stress of the last few minutes was catching up with him. He closed his eyes and tried to empty his head of all thought.

He was old, he knew, but how old? What had happened to him? His body was shaking in some kind of response to shock. He tried walking slowly between his friends, seeking reassurance in contact, rebuilding his own confidence as much as theirs. Head rubs and butts helped, and finally he remembered how to purr. With a juddering breath, he regained a sense of normality.

"Come on," he said, "we can't wait here. They may come after us."

As the effects of adrenaline wore off, all were sore and weary. Stumbling slightly and walking gingerly, they headed along the street. All had suffered scratches and bites; some quite savage. Jason's leg oozed blood from a deep bite, and he was limping. Bite marks decorated Daphne's neck and ear, and she ached from nose to tail. Apollo's wounds were deep, but already they seemed to be healing. Jason gave him a quizzical look.

"You played it pretty cool back there."

"Did I?"

"Yes. You didn't shout back at him, tell him what you'd do to him, you know? I thought you'd threaten him a bit. Instead, you just tried talking to him."

"I hoped he'd listen to reason. Violence should not be the answer, despite what our friend might think. That's something that I…" He paused. He'd almost said *learned*, but had he? What experience accompanied that thought? There was no associated memory; the words came automatically. After the events of the last hour, did he still believe them?

He shook his head to quell such regressive thoughts.

The gang leader's resistance to the potency of his call to reason disturbed him, leading his thoughts to spiral back on themselves.

This search is futile. Why did I ever come? What is the point?

He reflected further, doubt building on doubt.

Why were they so hostile? Why so much hatred?

Perhaps the worst thing of all was his opponent's strength; he hadn't come up against such power for as long as he could remember. Would it be the case with everyone he met outside Delphi? The worry left him subdued.

Every so often they passed a gap between the buildings that lined the street. Some were filled with parking spaces for cars, others fenced off, concealing small gardens. They soon came across one such patch of vegetation screened by a low wall, surmounted by railings.

"In here," Apollo said, his spirits low, and feeling more tired than he could ever remember.

They squeezed between the railings and passed into a triangular space behind the buildings. There they stood, looking around. They were in a small garden filled with trees and large plants. In the centre was a plastic table and several chairs topped by a sunshade umbrella on a small piece of grass. Screened from the street, they felt safe and began to relax.

Too soon.

CHAPTER 16
ACHELOIS

"I gather you're new around here," drawled a low voice from the darkness above them. They looked up, fearful again. A white face peered down from the flat roof of a small shack that stood beside the tall building. The owner of the voice jumped elegantly down onto the grass beside them. "You don't look very threatening. I'm Achelois, by the way. Lois for short. Pleased to meet you."

"What do you mean, we're not threatening?" said Jason.

"It's obvious what was happening, my dears. I could hear your little scuffle a mile off. If it's any comfort, you're not the first upcountry victims of the Botrys gang."

"How do you know we're new around here?" Jason asked.

Lois looked him up and down.

"Well, you don't speak like an Athenian, for a start. And you don't seem to know much about this neighbourhood." She circled around him and noticed his leg wound. "The more civilised among us give the hoodlums from Botrys a wide berth. They are trouble, especially their leader, Kratos."

"Why are they so vicious?" asked Jason.

Lois turned towards him. "It stems from Kratos himself. He behaves like no cat, although he inhabits such a body. He is different. Aloof, proud, determined. You might say he is like a human."

"He's a bully, that much is clear," said Apollo. "But he has nothing to do with the reason we came here."

"We're from Delphi," said Daphne.

Apollo stepped forwards. "I'm Apollo. This is Daphne and Jason." He glanced towards his companions. "We're here to rescue a friend. We didn't want to start a fight. We're not here to claim territory."

Lois stood still and looked him in the eye, holding his gaze for a long time. Rather than retreat, she sat down to study them all.

"From Delphi, you say." She glanced once more at Apollo. "How interesting. There have been rumours of portents. Gang members are unable to keep secrets for long – well, some of the minor players, at least. Recently I've heard talk of divination; of signs. Kratos is getting restless."

"In that case we should get a warning out to everyone else," said Daphne.

"No." Apollo gave her a warning look. "We stay clear of Athens politics. We can't afford to be distracted."

"I wouldn't worry on that score," Lois told Daphne, "the local inhabitants are well aware of Kratos and his gang." She looked them over once more. "But your arrival…" She hesitated. "You've come a long way. This friend of yours must be awfully important."

"She's just one of us," said Daphne, stepping forwards. "The cats of the Sanctuary. We're a big tribe. A family. We stick together."

"Altruism. How quaint. A commodity in short supply around here."

"What do you mean?" Jason sounded suspicious. Lois gave him a cool look.

"I mean nothing other than she must be special to you." Once more she scanned their faces. "A lot of gossip reaches my ears. We need to take care, all of us. There are dangers beyond Kratos and his unsavoury followers. I hear of disappearances. It's strange, because it has never happened before." They stared at her in silence. "New stories reach me almost every day. It doesn't seem to be accidents. There are no bodies. They simply vanish."

"Where are they going?" Daphne asked, her eyes wide.

Lois glanced at her. "If I knew that I would investigate. The fact is, nobody knows." She stood. "Follow me." She led them along a path around the side of the apartment block to a larger enclosed space at the rear, bathed in silver moonlight.

"It's very bright," said Daphne, looking up. "I thought the night was cloudy." The moon was so radiant they could make out tall apartment buildings on all sides.

They came to a meagre patch of grass surrounded by a few trees and bushes.

"You will be safe here. But before you sleep, let me have a look at those wounds." She ordered Jason to lie down and inspected his leg. He didn't protest, but lay on his side. Lois took her time, examining the wound both visually and by nose and tongue. After some time she concluded her examination, gave one final delicate sniff to be sure, and applied treatment in the form of rhythmical licking.

Jason closed his eyes. Soon he was deeply asleep and snoring.

After Jason, Lois administered similar treatment to Daphne's various bites and finally approached Apollo. He looked at her through narrowed eyes.

"Who are you?" he asked. She ignored the question but moved to his side to look at the grooves Kratos had scratched into his shoulder and neck.

"Remarkable," she said.

He turned towards her, even as she tried to get a better view. "It's just a few scratches. I heal quickly." She paused and studied his face once more, before stepping back, her expression unreadable.

"Is it really you?" she said. He was bewildered. Before he could think of a reply, she continued, "Achelois, daughter of Asclepius at your service," then performed a deep bow, her nose almost touching the ground in homage.

He didn't know what to say. "I…"

Rising to her feet, the white cat turned to draw his attention to some bowls by a nearby wall. "There are humans here who leave water and food for me. This evening it is yours."

"What about you? Won't you be hungry?"

Lois glanced back, tail swaying in thought. "It's a beautiful night. I'll hunt for something. I haven't enjoyed the taste of a fresh mouse for a while. Get plenty of rest. We shall speak again at first light." She disappeared around the corner of the building.

Daphne and Apollo had their fill, leaving Jason to sleep. They left some food and water for him, and, feeling replenished, found a sheltered spot to their liking at the edge of the lawn. They curled up together in a jumble of fur, before falling into a deep sleep.

Apollo's dream was vivid.

The sun was scorching, and he sensed the danger with every fibre of his being. They were being hunted by a monster; his mother, sister and himself. Anxiously, he watched the seas from the summit of Mount Cynthus, day after day. But of the monster, there was no sign. He tired of waiting.

"We cannot stay here. We're like rabbits in a trap," he told his mother.

"We're safer here than out on the open sea," she replied.

His agitation grew. Finally, he could bear it no more and took matters into his own hands. He leapt into the sea, transforming into a dolphin, and swam swiftly towards his enemy's domain. Below the slopes of Parnassus, he emerged and strode through the olive groves to the rift in the earth where Gaia's breath emerged.

Seeing him approach, Python, the mightiest serpent ever to have lived, emerged to do battle. Apollo wounded it with many arrows until it turned and fled back into the cavernous shrine. There he pursued it until, at last, he put an arrow through its eye, then, with a sword, cut off its head. The body he sliced into many pieces and burned on a massive pyre; the column of smoke was a warning to heaven.

The shrine he would take as his own. His father's punishment was nothing. He had found his home.

In this way was his legend born.

Stirring from his troubled sleep, Apollo opened an eye. It was still dark. Above him, sitting on a roof, silhouetted against the moon, was the dark shape of a cat sitting upright, perfectly still and darkest black, as if carved from the night sky. He turned over and went back to sleep.

Dawn arrived, and they slept on. It took time for the full light of day to penetrate the space between the tall apartment blocks. The sun had been climbing into the sky for a couple of hours before they stirred.

A nearby buzzing insect made Apollo open his eyes. He yawned and stretched, and for a moment wondered where he was. The tattered remains of his dream drifted through his head, then vanished.

He remembered the events of the previous evening and stood up.

"Good morning," came a now familiar voice. Lois was curled on a cushion on a garden seat nearby; a favourite perch. "You've slept very late, but you were so deep in slumber I thought it best not to wake you."

In the bright light of day, Apollo studied her more closely.

She seemed different, somehow; not as large as he'd thought her last night.

"There is more food, if you'd like to eat," she said, calmly returning his stare.

Apollo turned towards the re-filled bowls, shocked that he had heard no human arrive and replenish them. How could he have slept through it? His hostess appeared to read his mind. "You looked exhausted after your exertions yesterday."

Apollo shook his head to banish the last remnants of sleep from his sluggish thoughts and sat down for a quick wash. By now, the others were also stirring and studying their surroundings. The space between the tall buildings was a snug communal garden, little more than a small patch of grass and bare earth, with some trees and shrubs for shade and cover. But it was a wonderful haven of peacefulness in this strange, unwelcoming city. Despite its spartan appearance, there were some beautiful scented flowers that Daphne found irresistible. But they couldn't stay here forever. While Jason and Daphne ate, Apollo approached their hostess.

"You have been so kind. Thank you," he said. "But we've tarried here far too long. We'd better be on our way."

"Do you know where you're going? Or where to find this friend of yours?"

Once again, Apollo was lost for words. Athens was huge, and he hadn't a clue where to look for Olympia. She gave him another look of appraisal.

"You need some sort of plan, if you are to have any hope of finding her."

Apollo gave Lois a suspicious look, which she ignored. "The point is," she continued with exaggerated patience, "you will have to be careful. If I know anything about Kratos, it is that he won't like the fact you have escaped his clutches. Particularly when he was engaged in fighting you. He is not used to losing."

Apollo turned his head dismissively. "What is one self-important thug among many?"

Lois' eyes opened wide in shock. "Don't you know what you are up against? Whether through choice or chance, you have stirred up a hornets' nest. He will not take this well. As we speak, he will have his agents out, prowling the streets, looking for you. To be caught unawares would not go well, I think. If you head out there just blundering around, hoping to get lucky, you will be easy prey." The look she gave him made Apollo uncomfortable. "You need some idea of where to go, and how to get there."

"I'm prepared to take my chances." He knew that Jason and Daphne were listening intently.

"You won't get far alone. And what of your companions?" Lois glanced at them over his head. "Will you lead them blindly into danger? These days, death can be swiftly dealt to anyone caught alone and friendless."

A sharp look. "What do you mean?"

Achelois adjusted her position slightly on her cushion. "I mean that Kratos' followers are vicious, and used to dealing out deadly punishment." She held his eye. "And in these days of shortened horizons and shrunken ambitions, no one is safe. Not even you."

Her voice softened. "Do not shun guidance, and help when it is offered. You will need it if you are to stand any chance of finding your friend."

CHAPTER 17
DEBRIEF

I n the blue-grey pre-dawn light, the Botrys gang assembled on a clear patch of ground within one of the deserted buildings. The mood was sombre; most wished themselves elsewhere, fearing the reaction of their leader. Two dozen or more cats sat on the cleared ground, or decorated the mounds of rubble and rusting machinery, most of them trying to keep a safe distance. They cast around nervous glances. Even the dawn chorus seemed muted.

In their midst, Kratos slowly paced back and forth, his tail slashing from side to side, as he tried to keep the lid on his temper. His eyes blazed in fury.

"Last night was a disgrace," he told them. They averted their eyes. Most sought out exit routes through the gaps in the walls, but none dared make a move while in his presence. They digested his words, sifting them for any crumbs of comfort, no matter how cold.

"It was a failure on all counts. You earned nothing but my disgust. Another performance like that and our reputation will evaporate, and with it, the fear that precedes us. We will appear weak." He paused his stalking and glared at the nearest animals. They shrank back from his stare, averting their eyes. Kratos approached the nearest cat, towering over him. "Where were the sentries?" he demanded. His target lowered his head until his nose was almost on the floor. The gang leader's eyes bored into the top of the hapless cat's head. Getting no answer, he turned to another animal, this one sitting on the rotting hulk of an ancient bottling machine. "Well?" he demanded. "Where were they? Asleep?" His victim turned aside, unwilling or unable to offer a reply.

An uncomfortable pause ensued, before Kratos finally turned away, addressing his next remarks to the general assembly.

"You allowed three total strangers into the heart of our headquarters without challenge. Three moronic yokels fresh from the farmyard at that. I can't get the stink of olive groves out of my nostrils." Another pause. Another furious glare around the assembly. "At the very least, we should have taught them a lesson they would never forget. Made an example of them. Made them respect us." He glowered at the group, then resumed stalking, back and forth. "As for their cocksure leader. The eloquent and evasive ginger. I should have ripped his throat out. What a pleasure it would have been to save us all from his pretentious preening and his feeble excuses. And I would have done, but for you lot letting him go." Kratos licked his lips as if imagining the taste of his enemy's blood while staring at those around him. None could bear the terrible weight of his glance. Several tried and failed to suppress shudders, trying to pretend it was nothing more than the chill of early morning. All were in fear of a stinging claw swipe. Several cringed as he drew close.

"We wouldn't have let them go, but for the big human with the light," ventured Vasilis. A cuff across the side of the face was enough to show that his intervention had been rash. Kratos stood before him, a low growl at the back of his throat. The smaller cat backed away a couple of steps, not daring to take his eyes off the leader. The fury burning behind Kratos' eyes rooted him to the spot.

Finally, the gang leader relented. He circled once more. "Let me remind you." He raised his head and spoke loud enough for those at the back to hear. "This is our headquarters. Our secure secret place. No outsiders are allowed, unless we bring them here. But what do you do? You let them scamper right through, bold as brass." One or two breathed once more, confident the worst was over. Kratos spun towards the nearest cat, pinning it with a stare. "But instead of making an example of Mr Superior and his friends, *you let them go.*" The target tried but failed to avert his gaze. It shrank back, eyes wide. "So who was guarding the northern perimeter last night?" He delivered the question in a lower voice; gravel laced with menace. "Who was it?" He edged closer.

"Demetrios," came the strangled reply.

Kratos looked around. "Where is he?"

At the edge of the gathering, a beige cat turned to leave.

"Stop him!" called Kratos. The group surrounded Demetrios, waiting for their leader to approach. In their midst, he lay, supine and terrified, eyes darting from one to another, in a futile search for an ally.

Kratos stared down at him. He was calm now, but no less assertive. "So, what was it? Were you sleeping, or had you deserted your post and gone to pay a visit to one of your local house cats?" Demetrios gave no answer. "I hope she was worth it," Kratos purred.

"I..." Demetrios spluttered. Kratos leaned closer, never taking his eyes off the other cat. "I didn't see them."

The gang leader sat back and surveyed the ring of faces surrounding the prisoner.

"I think that excuse is more feeble than any I've ever heard. Surely you can come up with something better." Beneath him, Demetrios swallowed but said nothing.

Kratos turned to the others. "Are we taking that at face value? Are we prepared to let him off the hook?" They returned blank, dead-eyed stares; no one could show dissent. The gang leader focused his attention on the opposite side of the circle, to a mean-faced tortoiseshell with a ragged ear. "Do what you must," he said, the instruction delivered within a purr.

Without further thought she lunged down, snarling and biting. Those beside her immediately followed her lead, ripping at the victim in their midst. His brief screams soon died in the still morning air and with his passing, Kratos' mood lightened, as it tended to, following every demonstration of his power. The gang had gone some way to redeeming themselves after the previous evening's mistakes. He slowly wandered back to the clear ground he'd occupied earlier where some of the tribe still waited.

"Never drop your guard again," he said, glancing from face to face. "If you do, you know what your punishment will be." A pause. "Let us assume his was an individual lapse, and he had not shared his duty with another." The silence was stifling. Fur stood on end, whiskers quivered, every muscle tensed. As if flight could save any of them.

Kratos absorbed their attention like a malevolent black star, sucking in every photon of light. All felt the power of that stare like a crushing physical weight upon their shoulders as it passed from one to another. They hesitated, desperate to leave, but incapable of movement.

Kratos delivered the next question softly.

"Where was the chase? How come you scattered and let the intruders off the hook?" More pointed looks at the assembly. Several licked their dry lips, quivering beneath the scrutiny.

"You should have captured and brought them to justice." Still speaking softly, Kratos approached the nearest cat until they were almost touching nose to nose. His voice dropped to a whisper. "My justice." He looked deep into her eyes and held her gaze for a long while. He resumed, louder now. "You're going soft. You seem to forget we rule this part of town."

Among the wider circle, the cats exchanged more furtive glances. This meeting was the worst they'd known.

Turning suddenly, Kratos approached one of the smaller females perched on a pile of fallen bricks nearby. She shrank back, cowering before him, her ears flat. But unexpectedly, he lightened the tone. "Magda, when was the last time you did any serious tracking? Delivered some rough justice to an escaped spy?" She mumbled an excuse, but Kratos wasn't listening; he'd turned away once more.

"You've gone soft," he yowled. "You all have. Last night those three mongrels insulted our name and our honour. They need to be taught a lesson before they go spreading tales of their daring across this city of ours. One last proper lesson. A fatal lesson." Once more, he looked at the ring of faces surrounding him. "It's time they remembered who we are. It's time we reminded them all. We are the Botrys gang. We rule around here, and soon we'll rule this city. We don't let a few mangy strays from the countryside come and go as they please."

There was an awkward pause, then Melanippus spoke up. He was perhaps the one animal in the entire group feeling good about himself. "At least it shows I was right!"

The others looked at one another, scrambling to remember his reading of the entrails the other day. Kratos stopped dead in his tracks, staring into the distance.

"Spies," he said as the penny dropped. "And from the north. The portents were correct. They weren't simple rustics. We've been infiltrated by Athena's spies!" His fury redoubled, the large brown-and-russet cat paced back and forth, his tail slashing even more wildly.

The incident had been more serious than he'd thought. It was no accident. The seer had foreseen it all.

He addressed them again, scarcely able to contain his anger. "I want them hunted down, and an example made. They're going to regret the day they marched in here. Especially the ginger one." He looked around, staring into their faces. "Got it? Go!"

In relief, the group scattered, desperate to be out of his presence. As they departed, Kratos called to two of his children; his most trusted subordinates.

"You two will lead the intelligence gathering. Yannis, I want you to lead a team to scout out Avalos Street up to the north. Rea, do the same to the south. Take the sharpest trackers, like Menelaos. It shouldn't be too difficult. Just follow the stink of goat dung on their paws." He thought for a moment. "Question the local citizens as well. Use as much force as you want, although I suspect they'll cave in soon enough. Someone knows where they are. And when we find out, I want you to track them down and arrange a nasty little surprise for them. And anyone that's been hiding them." He looked at them, pleased to see how eager they were. Among all of his family, they were closest to his own heart; true believers in his cause. He trusted them implicitly. "Question, then kill. Whatever it takes. No one walks in here and gets away with it."

Yannis hesitated. "Menelaos is missing." Kratos glared at his lieutenant. The other cat gulped, then continued, speaking fast. "Disappeared. Can't find him anywhere. I've sent out some guys to look for him. We've even quizzed the locals, but there's nothing. Can't even pick up a scent."

"It's like what happened to Martha last week," added Rea, trying to defuse the situation. "The Snatchers have been busy again."

Kratos turned his discomforting stare towards her. When he resumed speaking, his voice contained shards of cold fury.

"This is *her* doing. I know it. She's in league with them, whoever they are." His thoughts returned to the conversation before the Pnyx rock. She had hinted at other powers in Athens. The thought was disturbing. "She's trying to whittle down our numbers, one at a time," he told them, his thoughts still whirling. "Well, there'll be no more velvet. It's time to unsheathe our claws." He addressed Yannis once more. "Change of plan. I don't care who you take, but gather a group together and get down there. Keep a watch on Athena. Find out what she's up to. I want the place staked out. Squeeze the locals for all they're worth." He looked at Rea. "It's time for us to act. Get over to Gizi and talk to Zelus. Tell him what's happened. We need to coordinate our attack. Find out the earliest he can get his guys moving."

He called to a third member of his offspring. "Kostas, get a hunting party together and track those three down. I want them punished. Dead or alive, it's up to you. But if you let them live, you'd better have a good excuse." The other animal bowed his head and left.

Kratos looked at them. They were still under his spell and hanging on his every word.

"What are you waiting for?" he shouted. "Get moving!"

They scattered to carry out his orders while he retreated to his favourite place to bask in the warming morning sun and ponder his next steps.

You can't escape. The noose is tightening.

CHAPTER 18
INTO ATHENS

Achelois hopped down to the ground and sat. Like obedient school children, they gathered before her. "Before we set out, I need to know more about your friend," she said, "and what you hope to do."

After a moment's hesitation, Apollo recounted the story of Olympia's capture and their mission to rescue her. He left out much of the detail but concluded with their escape from the gang. "If it wasn't for the human with the bright light, I'm not sure what would have happened."

The events of the previous night still consumed his thoughts. Being friendly and open hadn't worked. Maybe modern day mortals were different, and not so easily influenced. Perhaps he'd been too naive. But there was something unsettling about the big bully of a gang leader.

Daphne focused on the practical matters. "Do you know where Olympia might be?"

Lois' eyes widened; a feline look of incredulity. "Have you any idea how big Athens is? It goes on for kilometre after kilometre. I wouldn't have the faintest idea where to look."

Daphne slumped, her eyes downcast.

Lois dipped her head, looking into her face. "But I do

know someone who might help. He knows a lot of what goes on in this city, and he might have heard of something." Three faces turned to her in hope. "It's quite a walk to where he lives," she warned, "and if the Botrys gang is out looking for you, there's no time to waste. You should set off immediately."

"Will you take us?" asked Jason.

"No. It's too far for me to go. But I can start you off on your journey and point you in the right direction." She looked at them. "There is no time to lose. We'd better set off."

She headed to the opposite corner of the garden, and led them through the narrow passage between two buildings. It ended at a tall gate; no barrier to four agile cats.

They dropped onto the pavement beyond. Lois glanced up and down the street, then trotted south, keeping close to the buildings. The Delphi cats followed.

The streets were quiet. Old Leda, dozing in the morning sun on a balcony, opened an inquisitive eye as they passed.

For Apollo, Daphne and Jason, the stifling heat of the city streets proved energy-sapping. Their guide led them further south, towards the centre, hugging walls and staying on the quiet side of the street. They used parked cars as screens against prying eyes and changed direction several times at deserted intersections. The Delphi cats soon lost all sense of direction as the city's true scale unfolded. The endless warren of roads seemed without end.

Before midday they came to a square, shocked by the intensity of the traffic. Nothing in their previous experience had matched this. Not only was it hot and noisy; from their perspective at tailpipe level, the dust and fumes were over-powering. It was no place to linger. Achelois drew to a halt.

"This is where I must leave you," she said, tail twitching as she shouted over the noise of the traffic. "But let me show you where you need to go." She led them to the corner of a wide street. Across a busy junction, it continued into the distance. "You must carry on down there," she told them. "Do you see that hill in the distance? That is Mount Lycabettus. More of our kind live on its summit, with their leader, Hermes. If anyone in the city can provide you with help to find your friend, it is them."

Apollo looked up at the name. Achelois caught his eye but misread his thoughts.

"They are not like the Botrys gang," she reassured him. "They are more welcoming towards strangers, and if anyone knows what goes on in Athens, it is Hermes. He gets news from all over the city and sometimes beyond; he is more likely than anyone to know what has happened to your friend. But it is too far for me to journey. I don't like to venture so far from my home."

Apollo, Jason and Daphne looked down the long street to the steep-sided hill at its end. It looked a long way away.

"Thank you for all your help," said Apollo.

She paused and looked at him, then bowed her head. "You have a famous name." He said nothing. "I know of only one who bears that name, and it was said he was mightier than all others save one." She looked away. Her voice dropped. "Yet he was supposed to save us. A force for good, so it was said. Someone to look to for hope and succour."

"I am not he."

She gave him a long, appraising look. "No, I can see that. But perhaps some of his qualities remain."

She stepped back, and looked at each in turn. "I wish you well on your journey." Then, business-like and concerned about their welfare, she offered one last piece of advice. "You must take great care crossing the roads. These metal chariots move very fast. Don't be frightened of the noise they make, but be sure to keep your wits about you. I've seen too many young friends die under their wheels. Once you have crossed the junction, keep going straight ahead and always towards the hill. That is where you should find news. If any of them question you, tell them I sent you. Go now. Don't tarry, but take care." With one last look, she turned and left them alone once more.

"It's still quite far away," said Apollo.

"And we've been on the road for ages already," groaned Jason.

Daphne miaowed in sympathy. "Well, we'd better get started."

They studied the road junction in front of them, but it was so confusing. Traffic seemed to come from all directions. Buses, trucks and cars hurtled by, stopping periodically for no reason the cats could deduce, before roaring into life and speeding off again. The pauses offered no respite; other vehicles from different directions immediately filled the gap. Adding to the confusion, some of them went straight ahead while others veered off right or left. From the cats' point of view, it was chaos, and getting to the other side in one piece would be a lottery.

"Remember what I told you," shouted Jason, pushing himself to the front, standing on the lip of the kerb. "Look for the gaps."

"Ooh, this is horrible," Daphne muttered.

After a while, there was a brief pause in the traffic flow.

"Now!" cried Jason, and shot into the middle of the road. The others, nerves on edge, followed as fast as they dared. They could do this; it wasn't too far. A screech of brakes startled them as a large truck, coming from a direction they hadn't expected, shuddered to a halt. Behind it, horns blared. "Fucking cats!" yelled the driver from his open window. But they were gone; startled and scattering as they crossed the last few busy lanes. Engines roared and vehicles moved once more.

With the distant kerb in sight, Daphne froze, as out of the corner of her eye she saw a large bus bearing down. Instinctively she flattened her body and closed her eyes. It passed

over her head. The instant it was gone she bolted across the
last stretch of tarmac at top speed, hurdled the kerb, and ran
for the first safe place she could find: a narrow gap between a
chained-up bicycle and a wall. Panting, and close to panic,
she closed her eyes and tried to calm down; she'd made it.
But where were the others?

Despite his slight limp, Jason was ahead of the others, and
kept running where Daphne halted. He cleared the last lane
of traffic – a taxi missing him by the length of a tail – and
hurtled down the street ahead, as if three-headed Cerberus
were after him. Fifty metres down the road, he slowed down
and ducked under a parked car to wait for the others.

Apollo took a different line to his comrades, darting across
a second road, then veering past some human pedestrians. He
ran between them, dodging around their legs as they crossed
the road, and ended up on the opposite side of the street to
Jason. It was the street they had been targeting, but he could
no longer see his friends. Where had they got to?

"Where are you?" His frustrated miaow, lost in the traffic's
noise, got no reply. For a while, he stood in the middle of the
pavement as humans came and went on either side. Some
had to swerve around him, swearing and giving him fierce
looks, but most ignored him as just another obstacle.

One human bent down to scoop Apollo up, which stirred
him into action. He needed to find somewhere to think; to get
his head straight and plan his next move. Darting through the
crowd, he spotted an open door. It seemed quiet inside so he
entered and found himself in a small shop with two aisles,
each lined with tall shelves reaching up as far as he could see,
all stocked with the items humans seemed to value in tins,
boxes, bottles or packets, all lined up in tightly packed rows.
There was a gap under the bottom shelf, which was just large
enough for him to squeeze into. He tucked himself away to
collect his thoughts.

A flash of memory caught him by surprise, as he recalled

an indestructible sense of invulnerability, and the chance to move anywhere instantly with nothing more than a thought; the ability to solidify or evaporate into the aether at will.

It vanished, leaving just the faintest imprint in his mind's eye. That was no longer him. He was trapped in a far smaller body; admittedly agile, but vulnerable, and prone to weariness and pain. There was no escaping the fact he was footsore and tired.

Should he go back and search for signs of his friends at the junction? No. It was pointless; there was no way they would hang around near the chaos. They must have moved on together, hopefully following the directions Lois had given them.

His thoughts lingered on Daphne. It might have been unfair to let her embark on this quest. He should never have endangered her so. Daydreams of lazy afternoons in her company, ranging the hillside in Delphi, distracted him. Memories of chasing each other, lying together in the shade, in tranquillity; far away from this frantic place. Was it unfair that he worried about her far more than Jason? He suppressed a pang of jealousy at the thought of the two of them being together. Logic dictated they must have passed him and gone on ahead. It was time to get moving and catch them up. Perhaps he would meet them at Mount Lycabettus. Had Hermes changed much? Would he recognise him? He couldn't remember the last time they'd met.

Apollo sensed movement from the back of the shop. Not sluggish, oafish human movement, but stealthy, supple, feline tracking kind of movement. Then he saw it: a large, well-fed grey-and-white cat.

"Who are you and what are you doing in my shop?" it demanded.

"I just popped in for a rest."

"Oh. *I'm only resting*," the other cat mocked. "Well, rest out on the street, you scrawny little mongrel. No one comes into Stavros's Convenience Store without my permission."

Apollo sighed. What was the problem with these Athenians? Why were they so hostile? Why were they oblivious to his powers of persuasion? He noticed two humans enter the shop and walk down the aisle in front of him. "Have they asked permission?" he enquired, his voice dripping with sarcasm.

Rather than wait for an answer, he left, ignoring the jeers that followed him out onto the street. Once there, he took stock. The trees that lined each sidewalk limited his view, but he had a strong sense of the direction he needed to travel. It was a long time since he'd last been abroad, and back then, the ground he was now standing on was a mixture of fields and woodland punctuated by the villas of the wealthy and the humble cottages of their farmworkers and servants. Concrete, asphalt and paving slabs were a poor upgrade.

He set off slowly. Apollo was familiar with cars, buses and the occasional truck at Delphi, but the profusion of vehicles was alarming and the noise overwhelming. How many people lived here? Who was their leader?

He kept close to the buildings, out of the way of the pedestrians who rushed past in both directions. He passed a low plate-glass window. A ginger cat walked along in the same direction as himself. He studied it, before realising it was his own reflection. He had spent many centuries in this body, yet this still caught him out.

He stopped and looked at his reflection again. The shadows above and the dark interior made the shop front a vivid mirror. He explored the face, the whiskers, the ears, and then, looking deeper into the dark well of the pupil, he caught the faintest glimpse of something else; the echo of what he once was. He peered more closely. But, no. It was gone, leaving the fading impression of something long lost, as if he'd been caught in a camera's flash and had to close his eyes tight. No amount of staring would bring it back.

He walked on.

A little further on, he came to a large paved area, like a small Agora, but without the market stalls, or hustlers or orators. Also, it was far away from where he thought the centre of the city should be. The road he'd been following took a large detour around the edge, before resuming its course on the far side. Apollo stopped in his tracks.

Ahead of him, in the centre of the space, jets of water rose from the ground, squirting high into the air before falling back. What strange magic was this? He approached with caution. The jets of water formed a circle, with all those on the perimeter pointing inwards, and those in the centre ascending vertically to a great height. He watched, entranced, as the height of the jets altered according to a pattern. It was fascinating. Perhaps it could be improved?

Keeping to the grass surround, he skirted the water, as the jets changed their pattern and formed a new intricate dance. Some intertwined about each other in an ascending spiral; others played different gravity-defying games, changing direction in mid-air. Globes of water burst from the ground in staccato rhythm before exploding and cascading down to soak passers-by. The central jet climbed to an impossible height, casting a veil of spray as far as the perimeter of the square. People stopped, aghast, and stared.

Apollo ignored them and walked past towards the tree-lined street leading towards Lycabettus.

Another distraction caught his eye: a portal to some underground cavern. Confused, he studied it. Could this be an entrance to the Underworld? It seemed too obvious; not well enough hidden, and humans were emerging from the depths: Hades would never have let them go. He drew closer and saw a set of moving stairs leading down into the depths, and next to them, another set rising. Curiosity piqued, he made a detour, descending to a brightly lit hall criss-crossed by many pedestrians. What it was, he couldn't tell, but it was clearly not the Underworld. He remembered his mission; he couldn't afford to be distracted. Further exploration would have to wait.

The second staircase took him back towards daylight like any other commuter, but smaller. It was, he reasoned, another thing to add to his growing catalogue of strange contraptions humans had developed while he slept.

Daphne cowered in the gap between the bicycle and the wall. The noise and sudden movement of the huge vehicles had been terrifying, and she felt lucky to have escaped in one piece. Her body was rigid with fear. She closed her eyes and tried to take a few deep breaths to calm down. After a few minutes, the terror eased, but her relief evaporated when she found she couldn't see the others anywhere.

What's happened to them, and where am I?

Her heart still raced; her breath came in ragged bursts. Confused, she stared straight ahead, her eyes focused on a tall lamppost by the side of the road.

She struggled to calm her feelings. Her mind was elsewhere. Traffic fumes washed over her, dust filled her nostrils. But in the unmoving air and barely audible, she heard the distant, echoing voices of the trees that lined the nearby streets.

Poor thing. She's lost.

So far from home.

What are you doing here?

Go back to where you came from. Go before it's too late.

An itch catapulted her into the present, and she lost the thread. While she scratched her neck, Daphne recognised her breathing had slowed, and her panic had subsided. She was calmer now, and able to think.

Where had they gone? Why hadn't they waited for her? Irritation replaced bewilderment. Looking around, she could see no sign of them at all, which she supposed meant they weren't injured. But with so many humans around, and the horrible noisy traffic just a few metres away, she didn't feel safe. Someone was bound to spot her. And then what?

What had Lois told them? They should cross the busy junction and then go down a street to a hill. Perhaps the others were already on their way. Maybe she could catch up with them.

They might have waited.

Which street? Daphne had a choice: the one to the left of her, or the other to the right. How could she tell which was correct? She couldn't miss something as big as a hill. She left her hiding place and walked around the corner to the street on her right, hoping to see her destination ahead. But she had no such luck. Instead, she found a street lined with trees on each side. Between them and the tall buildings that seemed to close in on her, she could barely see the sky. With a deep sigh, she set off, trying to stay out of reach of pedestrians and keeping an eye out for dogs.

Just a small amber, black and white cat minding its own business on this hot afternoon.

She brightened up a little. There must be a few friendly cats around here who kept humans for pets and who might give her directions if she got lost. Buoyed by such positive thoughts, she headed down the street.

Jason sat under the car, unnerved and trying to regain his composure. He was appreciating the scale of the challenge they had undertaken in trying to navigate this enormous city, let alone find Olympia. He would need to keep his wits about him; Athens was so alien to everything he knew. This area, nearer to the centre, was much busier than the neighbourhood they had passed through earlier. What now? He pondered the question for a while, but a new one replaced it: *Where have they gone?*

Looking up and down the street from his hideout, he couldn't see his companions anywhere. He'd better go back and look for them. A horrible thought struck him: what if they'd been hit by one of those big metal things?

He suddenly felt sick; but there was nothing else for it. He would have to go back and find out.

Steeling himself, he crawled out from under the car, and, keeping close to the kerb, he trotted back to the junction. At the corner, he paused, looking around. It was a relief not to detect any dead or injured cats, but neither could he see them anywhere.

Where had they gone? Lois had told them to find Hermes, and he lived on top of a mountain. He looked around the square and down the roads nearby, wishing he'd paid more attention to her directions. After the trauma of the road crossing, he'd lost his bearings, and the more he circled around, the worse it got.

Trees lined the road behind. But to his left was a long, straight avenue with, at its far end, a kind of flat-topped hill with steep sides and an old building on top. It reminded him of home.

That must be it.

Having a firm destination to aim for lifted his mood. But first, there was the matter of another road to cross. This time, Jason studied his surroundings. He noticed the humans waited for a while on the pavement until the metal chariots all stopped before they crossed. Pleased with this insight, and confident of safety in numbers, he crossed the road with them, dodging feet and dashing ahead once safe on the far side. More alert now, he made his way south.

. . .

Achelois walked home through the heat of the afternoon, along deserted residential streets. She ambled back, in no mood to hurry, taking her time to enjoy the occasional butterfly darting between flowers, or to consider the multitude of overlapping stories hidden within the more interesting scents she came across. Along the way, she worried about the three visitors from Delphi. They seemed so innocent of the big city. They understood nothing about the place or how it worked. Was sending them to Hermes the right thing to do? Maybe she should have –

She was so deep in thought as she turned a corner that she almost walked straight into Rea. The russet-coloured thug slashed her tail from side to side and uttered a low, threatening growl from the back of her throat. Lois felt the fur rising along her spine. She normally stayed well clear of Rea and her associates.

"So, what have you been up to?" the gangster sneered, unable to hide her contempt. "Been acting the tour guide for our little out-of-towners, have you? Leda told me you'd brought them down here."

"What does it matter to you?" It was unsurprising that Rea had extracted information from her elderly neighbour; she seemed even more hostile than usual. It would be difficult to get out of this encounter without a fight, and Lois wasn't as young or as fast as she used to be.

"Where have you taken the little toerags?" Rea demanded. "What did you do with them?"

Lois crept backwards as Rea inched forwards, trying to maintain the distance between them while looking for an escape route: a gateway, a car she could get under, a fence to jump over, anything. But there was no shelter in her immediate vicinity. She tried to play for time.

"Why are you so interested in them? They're well gone now and they won't be back. They're no threat to your gang."

"They're spies, and I think you know who for. They left

without paying their dues and we can't let that happen, can we? We're going to make them pay, just like anyone else who crosses us. So you'd better tell me where you sent them."

"Asleep, were you?" Lois taunted. "What happened to your lookouts? Kratos has really let things slip."

Rea snarled, saliva dripping from her jaw. "No one gets past our guards without special skills and training. We're going to teach them the last lesson they'll ever learn, and then we're going after their masters. Or mistress, more like. And we won't let collaborators like you off the hook."

Lois froze. What had the intruders done to get under their skin so much? She'd never seen gang members so on edge; even one as vicious as Rea. She saw a car coming down the road towards her and thought about darting in front of it to put some distance between them.

Rea noticed the flick of her eyes and attacked. Lois could only react, but she wasn't used to fighting, whereas the younger cat was a practised warrior. Lois was no pushover, but she was no match for Rea, and she suffered a beating; an onslaught of painful bites and deep scratches which bloodied and closed one of her eyes and notched an ear. She didn't have the strength or speed to get away, and there was nowhere to hide.

Rea stopped. She stood over her opponent, gloating, unable to resist a boast.

"Times are changing. The fat cats of the Plaka and the Agora have had their day. Soon we'll rule Athens, then you'll pay your dues. All of you!" she shouted to any animals within earshot, then stared down with contempt at the older cat struggling for breath at her feet. "But it looks like you won't survive long enough to tell them."

With an arrogance befitting her gangland reputation, Rea turned tail and strutted away.

Lois lay badly injured and struggling for breath. Her head

was swimming, and she couldn't see properly. She was in pain from head to tail, with blood oozing from her wounds.

At least it was over. She didn't have the strength to crawl to find shade or shelter; she just lay there, drifting in and out of consciousness. She had been aware of her enemy's rant but hadn't been listening; they were all the same, these petty megalomaniacs.

Along the deserted street, insects buzzed, and the distant traffic noise continued, but the immediate vicinity was quiet.

The cat lay still, and the pain subsided as her life drained away.

CHAPTER 19
DAVAKI PARK

I n Davaki Park, Bia and her followers sat together under the trees in the eastern corner, close to the fountain. The park was shut at this time of night, but despite the hour, the traffic on Thiseos Street never stopped. As long-term residents, they had become used to it; at least the closed gates gave them respite from human pedestrians for a few hours. Having tested and overcome the psychological defences of diners at several nearby restaurants, many of the cats had taken their fill and were sleepy. But not all. Several gang members remained on the prowl. One or two raided the dwellings of the more easily intimidated local citizens via open windows or – a luxury item around here – cat flaps. The still, warm night air which encouraged people to keep their windows ajar aided their efforts.

Bia herself was feeling relaxed and content. She had carved out a nice territory south of the Acropolis. It was a good district, with plenty of pickings for the gentlewoman cat-burglar and her followers. Bounded by a busy dual carriageway to the east and a warehouse-dominated business quarter to the west, there were few territorial disputes with other gangs. They occasionally had trouble from the stray dogs who roamed the business quarter, but when they became a problem, the city authorities wasted no time rounding them up. The cats of Davaki Park found it paid to keep a low profile and look as cute as possible.

On this night, Bia was struggling to sleep. She pondered the latest intelligence her followers had brought back from an expedition up to Filopappou Hill near the Acropolis. This wooded central area provided excellent hunting opportunities but was little inhabited by felines, with the odd exception or two. They told her of some excitement among the humans at the ongoing excavations in the nearby Agora. The human diggers seemed to have unearthed some interesting finds, including a stash of bright circular metal discs; similar to the things they often used to buy items in shops. Evidently, these examples were old. They were dull and soil-encrusted when dug up, but her spies reported they scrubbed up nicely, and looked quite charming – and collectable. Bia pondered where the humans hid them and if there were any more just waiting there to be dug up. She might have to engage in a little burglary or excavation of her own.

She had a little pit she had dug in a quiet corner of the park where she kept some of her valuables, and it might be nice to add to her collection. It would also enhance her prestige and influence within Athenian feline society.

But the most intriguing thing was what her spies had said about the other watchers. They had spotted an owl in a tree overlooking the dig site and thought they'd glimpsed another cat observing from the shadows further away. Also, they stayed on, watching long after the humans had packed up and gone away for the night, and most mysterious of all, the cat then went nosing around the dig site itself.

They couldn't tell who the observer was, but it was likely to be one of the Agora cats, and Bia knew what that meant. Should she take the opportunity for some serious one-upmanship? Mount a raid on the dig and take whatever was there?

It was an appealing idea.

She was in the middle of planning the logistics when a flash of silver-white to her right caught her attention. There, circling the marble fountain, picked out in the moonlight, was a large, white, sleekly muscled cat. She gave it her full attention. Where had he come from, damn him, and what did he want?

Hermes approached. Mr Superior always appeared when she least wanted. What would it be this time? Well, he'd just have to wait. She was in no mood to play along with his little games.

"What a pleasant evening," he offered, looking around. Then, as if to wind her up some more, he hopped lightly onto a nearby stone bench and settled down. Bia was doubly annoyed. Not only had he barged in uninvited, but now she had to look up at him like some young kitten receiving instruction from an elder.

She tried to ignore him. The silence grew, and with it, her frustration. Eventually, she cracked.

"To what do I owe the pleasure of your company?" She tried to sound as sarcastic as possible, but he'd never given a straight answer to a straight question in all the time she'd known him, so she suspected he wouldn't start now. Time to begin the verbal chess.

"Just passing by. Thought I'd see how you were doing."

A likely story. He always wanted something, and she knew she'd have to be on her guard not to let any information slip out; even more so with half the gang listening in. She didn't want to share her plans with the King of Gossip.

At least Hermes had the decency to descend from his ridiculous perch. He hunched down, curling his tail neatly around his side, and glanced at the cats nearby, most of whom had heard his greeting and were now just pretending to sleep while keeping a nearly closed eye on proceedings.

Bia's frustration grew. What was worse, she could tell he was relishing her discomfort.

"So, what news from up on the hill?" she said, at last. "Are those buffoons in the north keeping their noses clean?" She knew the answer without asking. "Still doing your bidding?"

Hermes leaned towards her. "I can't imagine what you're on about." He flashed her a sidelong glance. "Actually, I have some news that might just interest you. How you use it is entirely up to you, of course." He paused for effect, looking straight at her. Bia shifted position, aware he was trying to goad her into questioning him, and determined not to fall into his trap. She could wait for a long time, if that was the game he wanted to play. After a lengthy pause, he continued. "They're getting rather belligerent at the moment. In fact, I'd say things might be about to get a little out of control."

"She must be slipping," Bia ventured. "Or you're losing your touch."

Hermes looked into the distance.

"That's as may be. It's not for me to say. However, the situation appears to be getting a little dangerous. A war is brewing between the northern gangs and those in the Plaka, and then there is a rumour something interesting may soon be uncovered by our two-legged companions. It's just speculation, of course, but there is a suggestion it could be a powerful object last seen centuries ago, back in the mists of history. And I suspect you might know where that line of thought leads."

This was more interesting. Was this what was attracting the watcher?

Something from the distant past... Bia rarely thought about it, these days; it was too painful to remember what she once had. But she dredged through her memories. What had been lost that was so interesting to her rival? Did she really think they were about to rediscover the Luck of Athens? She'd heard the name, but she didn't know what it looked like. An object of reverence and power, they said, but what was it, and what use could it be, beyond some memento of times long gone? She tried to recall snippets of old legends. It was said to bestow its owner great fortune in battle, she seemed to remember. Perhaps even to render them unbeatable? With an artefact like that under her control, she would rule all Athens!

Bia's thoughts ran wild. Think of the power and influence. Think of all the retribution she could deliver.

The fur along her spine rose in her excitement. But apart from not knowing what it looked like, how would she use it? Assuming it was this thing. How could she tell? She looked directly at Hermes, suspicious.

"Why are you telling me this?" she said.

Serious now, he lowered his voice so no one could eavesdrop. "Let us assume it is this item known as the Luck of Athens. You don't need me to spell out what it would mean if those two goons from the other side of town got hold of it. If the rumours are only half true, life for the rest of us would be very miserable." He looked around, checking no one could overhear them, and continued in a more conspiratorial tone. "I'm looking for someone responsible to hold on to it. Someone who wouldn't let it go to their head. I've been keeping an eye on you, and the way you run this neighbourhood. It works. If a war is inevitable, then I think you might be a far better keeper than either Kratos or Zelus." He stopped, watching her closely. Bia wasn't taken in for a second.

"What's in it for you?"

Hermes leaned back. He looked hurt. "Why, I trust you to look after me. To make sure no harm comes my way. Of course, I like to look after those in the business of thievery, it's a skill which is not respected as much as it should be, and one appreciates an artist. I like to champion their abilities. On the other hand, in the case of certain animals I could mention, criminal behaviour has become intertwined with more violent strains of activity, and *that* I do not condone. Should this object be what it purports to be, then I shudder to think what would happen if it fell into the wrong paws."

He fell silent. Bia's suspicions remained.

"Why don't you take it for yourself?" she asked.

Hermes looked into the distance. He said nothing for a long while, then…

"I've mused on that, and it has some appeal, I don't deny." He turned his shining blue eyes on her, and she had to look away. "But as you know, I don't have a huge number of followers and I like to keep on the move. I suspect I wouldn't be able to hold on to it for long unless I watched it night and day. And of course, I wouldn't like the responsibility; I'm not after power for its own sake. My currency is gossip. News."

"And what about her?"

"You know what a fearsome reputation she has as a warrior, and to have it dramatically enhanced is the last thing I want. And if she were to enlist the help of her brutish oaf of a brother, goodness knows what havoc they would unleash. No one would be safe. Fortunately, no one seems to have seen him for some time, so maybe he's no longer on the scene."

Bia remained suspicious, but she couldn't think of anything to add. Her own opinions of them matched his. Perhaps, just perhaps, he was telling the truth.

She shuddered. It seemed impossible, but here he was, offering her dominion over the entire city and beyond. The dream was tantalisingly close and with it a chance to look down on her *betters* after all these years; the Olympians who loved to belittle her and her kind. It would be such a pleasure. She allowed herself to dream a little. If she could unlock the power of this legendary object, she might even bend dogs to her will, which would increase her authority immeasurably. The thought was intoxicating.

Hermes stood and arched his back in a long stretch. He glanced at her one last time.

"There is one problem. You must act soon. Tomorrow night at the latest, I suspect. The humans are making progress with their digging and you-know-who is likely to make her move soon. If you are going to act, I know someone who might help. One of her followers, in fact. Someone more than a little disillusioned."

"How do I find her?"

"Astiggos Street. Approach from the west. Get there an hour before dawn. Her name is Herse. I'll warn her to expect you. Right, I'll be off." He made to depart, then halted. "Anything else?"

"No," she replied, then hesitated. "It's probably nothing, but when I'm over to the west, I hear dogs yapping on about being imprisoned."

"What do you mean, 'imprisoned'?"

"It's quite faint, but that's what I think they're saying. Of course, dogs always exaggerate. They're all drama queens, and their accents are a bit funny. Maybe I didn't understand them right. You don't think the humans are rounding up strays? You don't think they'll start on us?"

Hermes appeared unconcerned. "Who knows? Anyway, fewer stray dogs around the place is hardly a problem, is it? I don't think they'd start on cats. Where would they keep us all?"

Bia studied the ground in front of her nose and regretted asking the question; she hated showing vulnerability. Hermes watched her for a second longer, then turned away and was gone.

CHAPTER 20
THE CHASE

Apollo turned his thoughts back to his mission and walked on. He crossed a square and continued along the tree-lined street, paying little attention to his immediate surroundings; the streets all looked the same to him. The hill ahead was all that mattered. He had to find Hermes. Gaining his help looked like Apollo's best – perhaps only – hope of finding Olympia in this enormous, bewildering city.

From the corner of his eye, he detected movement and glanced across. On the opposite sidewalk, another cat walked in time with him, in the same direction. It focused ahead and avoided eye contact. Was it also seeking Hermes, and what might it want from him? Did Hermes grant wishes?

He trudged on. He and his companion across the street appeared to be going against the flow of pedestrians. Most two-legged traffic headed past him, lured by the strange moving staircase in the square he'd left, and the subterranean world it led to. After several minutes of dodging them, Apollo glanced across the road once more to see what progress his fellow traveller was making, and noticed the other animal now had a companion, both of them keeping pace with him. Both seemed determined to avoid looking at him.

Interesting.

Apollo slowed down, sauntering along the pavement and meandering in pursuit of interesting scents. He sniffed at some litter by the kerb. When he looked up, he found his shadows were also dawdling, waiting for him to move.

He set off again with a more purposeful stride. They matched him. A junction with a minor side street came and went, and they continued on their parallel courses. Then Apollo sensed movement; a change in direction from one of them. Dispensing with subtlety, he looked across the street. One of his stalkers had accelerated and was marching across the road ahead of him, the other heading directly towards him. Apollo considered the options. Should he challenge them? Find out what they want?

He thought about turning back and looked over his shoulder, only to spot a third, scrawny-looking cat with dark, mottled fur, following him. It seemed to stare right through him, but the look on its face was none too friendly. He was being led into a trap. Why?

The next corner was approaching. He quickened his pace, then bolted as fast as he could down the side street.

"Stop the spy!" yelled the cat behind Apollo. The other two arrowed towards him just too late to pounce, but the chase was on. His pursuers weren't as coordinated as they should have been. Taking the initiative had bought Apollo a few metres' head start, but nothing more.

Luckily, down this street, there were fewer humans to impede him.

Unluckily, down this street, there were fewer humans to impede his pursuers.

Apollo sped on, not heeding his surroundings. He sought new turnings to shake them off and careered around corners as if pursued by the hounds of hell. But they knew this place too well, and he couldn't lose them. At least he stayed ahead, for now, at any rate.

Once again, the cats of Athens had become aggressive. But why? Was it related to last night's encounter? Could he stand up to all three of them? After his previous battle, he wasn't so sure, and he didn't feel like finding out. The most annoying thing was he couldn't outpace his pursuers, but to his relief, they didn't seem able to close the gap. It was going to be a test of endurance. How long could he keep going?

As the adrenaline surged through him, he shot across a multi-lane highway, vaulting the low fence in the central reservation, heedless of the traffic. He dodged buses and cars by a whisker's length and hoped his pursuers weren't so fortunate. But they were just as adept at avoiding those metal chariots of death as he was.

The longer the chase continued, the more anxiety clouded his mind. The relentless pursuit was most unusual. What was driving them? Was it fear? Was it anger? If so, what had he done to annoy them?

Up ahead, he saw trees to his left. A park, maybe. It might provide extra cover. At least the trees would give some shade from the punishing heat and get him away from cars and exhaust fumes.

He swerved to pass beneath the arching branches, and as he did so, he could hear his pursuers almost snatching at his tail. In the distance, a dog barked at the sight of the chase and headed straight for them, its human guardian trying but failing to call it to heel.

Apollo ran on; his breath never seemed to carry enough air to his aching lungs. His paws, his legs, his muscles... all were hurting. It was impossible to keep this pace up, and he had to slow down to something more sustainable. Would it be fast enough? Surely his pursuers must also be suffering. But from the pounding he could hear behind him, there was no sign of them slacking. Their persistence seemed almost supernatural, and a horrible thought entered his head: what if they could outrun him?

How much further could he go? His lungs ached for him to stop. Sheer willpower was all he now had to drive him on.

Then, something strange happened. The weariness eased, and he felt he could keep going as long as he wanted. His body felt stronger, lighter. Was this what they call *second wind*, or was it something else? The self-doubt which had stalked his thoughts fell away, but the pursuit continued as the chasers found new reserves of their own.

Apollo changed direction at random, trying to force mistakes. He swerved around trees, through and between the objects in a children's playground, over or under park benches; anything that might cause one of them to stumble. But he was out of luck; the park ended far too soon, and he found himself at a roundabout where four roads met.

To his good fortune, the traffic was quiet at this time of day. He darted across and up a road opposite. A flimsy metal archway stretched across, and enormous gates stood open at each side. He passed them without thinking, but something in the air changed. Something he couldn't put a claw on. There was no longer any sound of pursuit.

He dared to look behind and saw his pursuers had stopped on the far side of the gate, their bodies heaving as they panted for breath. Apollo turned to face them. They glared at him across the invisible divide with raw hostility. He couldn't understand why they'd stopped; like many things today, it made little sense.

"Don't think you'll escape us for long," one of them sneered, "and don't expect her to keep you out of our clutches."

"You can't hide there forever. We'll find you. We'll get you," snarled another.

The third just uttered a guttural growl, deep in its throat. Apollo glanced at the flimsy arch. It wasn't designed for defence; it was just a simple barrier for cars. Why were they afraid to pass underneath, given the risks they'd taken chasing him here?

"Who are you?" he shouted. In reply, they just jeered at him but said no more. After a minute, they turned and grudgingly departed.

Apollo stood there for a while, watching them go, and letting his heart rate return to normal. He had no idea where he was, and worse still, he couldn't see any sign of Mount Lycabettus.

He sat down, deflated, wondering who or what had stopped them. Someone far more frightening to them than he was.

A deep frustration replaced the exhilaration he'd felt at evading his pursuers. He was being blocked at every turn. So far he'd been attacked and wounded, lost his friends, then stalked and chased halfway across the city, and he was no further forward in his quest. Being the prey of some mindless thugs seemed like the ultimate insult. He'd been pinning everything on meeting Hermes and enlisting his help, but someone was trying to prevent it. Who?

Could it be his attacker from yesterday? It seemed unlikely; why would he bear such a grudge? He thought about retracing his steps, but he wasn't confident enough to take on all three of them and however many more there might be. How could he ever find Hermes now? There was no one in this alien city he trusted to ask for help, and his word no longer seemed to carry any weight with mortals. He was alone, for perhaps the first time. He had no answers; he couldn't see a way forward.

Uppermost in his mind was the feeling he'd let Olympia down. Time was dragging and his quest had stalled. Poor Olympia. He had no idea how to find her and was no further forward than when he'd arrived in Athens.

He couldn't just sit on the side of the road forever; he had to go somewhere. Weary, he stood and turned to scan his surroundings. Behind him, the road curved upwards and soon passed out of sight. It was in a cutting; wooded slopes rose on each side. To his immediate left, a short rocky bank climbed a few metres and then levelled off. It seemed as good a direction as any. At least he would have the advantage of height over any fresh pursuers; Apollo didn't entirely believe they had given up the chase.

He paused once more and looked over his shoulder, thinking of Daphne, and again wrapped in guilt. He hoped she was alright. Jason, too, of course. But Daphne... Losing her was more than just misplacing a companion; she was his inspiration. He wanted her by his side when they finally found their friend. Olympia might be his most recent ex, but Daphne was his future. Where could she be?

Weary and more dispirited than he could remember, he laboured up the steep slope onto the gentler gradient beyond, lost in thought, and paying little attention to his surroundings. "Spy," his pursuers had called him. He thought back to his encounter with the gang. The leader was quite a character. Impervious to reason, bitter and full of anger. What made him so? Just trying to have a conversation seemed to aggravate him. Was he the one who had sent the chasers? Why was he so paranoid, and who did he think they were spying for? What did he think they might find? He must have mistaken Apollo for someone else.

His concerns for his friends grew. If those thugs had tracked him so determinedly, then they too would be in danger.

Apollo halted and looked over his shoulder, tempted to go back and try to find them. He hovered one leg in mid-air, gripped by indecision.

"Few dare venture through my gate," purred a low female voice above him. He turned and saw a large black cat perched on the trunk of a fallen tree not far away. Apollo's hackles rose. Who was this, and what did she want from him? His patience with Athenians was wearing thin.

He studied her. The cat was black from nose to tail with no other visible colouring. Yellow eyes surveyed him coolly.

"I'm lost."

"That much is obvious," she said. "I don't get many casual visitors."

Apollo looked around with fresh interest. He was in a quiet patch of woodland within the midst of a huge bustling city. He could hear no vehicles; even the birds were muted in this glade. He sniffed the air and caught the scent of vegetation and earth rather than the exhaust fumes and pollution he'd become used to in Athens. The abrupt change was welcome, but startling. Ahead was a long slope, the top veiled by trees which stretched out to either side. Why were his pursuers so scared of this strange black cat? He looked anew at his surroundings with narrowed eyes, trying to spot anything unusual.

"What is this place?" he asked.

"It's just my domain," she said. "My little kingdom. Enter at your peril."

Apollo felt hot in his fur. She was mocking him. "And who are you?"

She gave him a long look, then jumped to the ground and sauntered up the hill between the trees. Apollo watched her go, hypnotised by the languid sway of her hindquarters as she sashayed away. She had a dangerous walk.

He weighed up his options. To return the way he'd come, with the likelihood of bumping into those three gangsters again, held no appeal. The only alternative was to venture on into the lair of this mysterious and slightly sinister creature who seemed to exert a strange power over this territory.

He followed.

CHAPTER 21
DAPHNE ALONE

Daphne continued down the street. Where could Apollo and Jason have got to? Her worry increased with every step. Surely nothing horrible could have happened to them. If that wasn't bad enough, she still wasn't totally convinced she was heading in the right direction. If only she could get an unobstructed view down the street past the trees. She had never been great with directions, but Athens was proving a difficult education. Her thoughts turned back to Olympia.

Her legs ached. She had been walking across this enormous city all day, or so it seemed, and she wanted a nap somewhere nice and quiet. Maybe a little something to nibble.

She skirted an old plastic bag and surveyed her drab surroundings. The street was a busy thoroughfare, lined with shops on both sides. Cars, buses, vans and trucks rushed down the central tarmac strip, but she learned to ignore them. Provided she didn't go towards them, they appeared happy to keep out of her way.

None of the shops looked like suitable places to rest up. She needed some houses or apartments, but to find somewhere like that would mean deviating from the route. If she left it, she would soon be lost.

As she plodded on, worry turned to dread, and hunger gnawed. She felt footsore and weary, and frustrated that she still couldn't get a proper sight of her destination. With every step away from the square where she had lost her companions, Daphne's self-doubt grew. If only she had paid more attention to the directions.

She arrived at a crossing. The street she had been following ended at a wider, busier road. On the opposite side, her street continued; narrower and free of vehicles. But how could she get there? The prospect of another dangerous crossing filled her with dread, and the noise and bustle of the road before her was terrifying.

Not wanting to repeat her previous experience, she waited for a gap in the traffic. And waited. And waited some more. Sometimes, the vehicles seemed to stop from one direction, but only slowed down from the other. Then, without warning, it all speeded up again.

Despair increasing, she paced up and down the sidewalk. Then she noticed some bright lights on posts that kept changing colour. Some sort of shrine? The humans gathered beside the posts and, after waiting – to pray, perhaps – risked crossing the street. In homage to their piety, the noisy traffic stopped and waited.

She approached a post, hesitant. Then, still keeping as much distance as possible, she waited until the humans crossed and ran for it, her heart hammering.

Once safely across, a little of Daphne's confidence crept back. She turned into the traffic-free street she had seen, feeling much better.

Her reward was the sight of several restaurants, their tables covering much of the street. Some had people sitting at them. This was more like it; she could handle begging for food. She'd done it occasionally at the café in Delphi. She knew the ropes: have a quick wash to look presentable; gaze towards the humans sweetly, perhaps cocking her head a little to make it look like she understood what they were saying; pretend to be friendly, even allowing the odd pat on the head; watch closely and pounce on anything dropped before any rivals could steal it away. If the item amounted to more than one mouthful, be prepared to fight to defend it.

Simple. Provided there wasn't too much competition. Daphne surveyed her surroundings. Not too bad. Her chief rivals seemed to be a mother and kitten combination. She would have to watch out for the older cat, but the youngster wouldn't be too much of a threat. Apart from the cuteness aspect, of course. But Daphne was young and good-looking; just a few months beyond being a kitten herself. She could do cute as well as anyone. It was the streetwise mother who would be a problem. Would she share her pitch?

Daphne settled down in a prominent position near a promising-looking table. She maintained a reasonable distance from her rivals and kept a weather-eye out in case anyone else was tempted to join them. At this hour of the day, she was in luck. The occasional titbit came her way, and she ate for the first time since early morning. She spent the next few hours on watch, moving among the tables as people came and went, seeking the best scavenging opportunities. Now and then a waiter would shoo her and her rivals away, but they would soon be back at post, waiting for the next opportunity, eyeing the diners, and assessing the odds of them sharing a mouthful or two: a nibble of Daphne's favourite souvlaki here, a piece of kebab there.

Her companions would surely have arrived with Hermes by now. It would be nice to be together again. She missed them; particularly Jason. But hunger wouldn't allow her to reflect for long. She concentrated on the diners once more.

In the heart of the city, surrounded by tall buildings, it was difficult to tell if shadows were lengthening, but eventually, afternoon turned into evening, and it was time to move on. Before leaving, she tried to thank the other adult cat for allowing her to share.

"Don't worry. I won't stay here. I was just hungry. You can have your restaurant back."

"You're new here, aren't you?" replied the other cat, looking at her in suspicion. "How do I know you won't be back? This has been our place for as long as I can remember. My mother used to bring me here when I was a kitten. I only let you stay because there was enough to go round, but I might not be so generous next time."

"Thank you," said Daphne. "I understand. But I'm from Delphi, and I'm trying to find my friend, Olympia. Perhaps you might have heard about her? Humans kidnapped her and brought her here in a big car."

The other cat was unimpressed. "Have you seen that road down there?" She glanced at the street Daphne had crossed. "How many cars go down there every day? How am I supposed to know if there are any cats in them?" She snorted. "If you ask me, your friend's history. They might be okay here..." She indicated to the diners. "But some of them hate our kind, and like nothing better than to do away with us, or sell us to others who might do the same or worse. Forget her, and get back to your *Delfi*, or whatever it's called."

Daphne suppressed a shudder of revulsion, but her anxiety for her friend returned. Where could Olympia be in this immense city, and how might she be able to find her? Would she have time before something dreadful happened? Her spirits sank.

She tried a different subject.

"Do you know a place where I can get a proper rest around here?"

Her companion stared into space for a while, thinking.

"I'm not showing you my nesting place, but if you're in luck, you might find somewhere along there." She indicated down the street in the direction Daphne was planning to go, anyway. "Past the end of this bit, there are some quiet back streets where the humans live, and some of them might have left a window open." She said no more, instead turning her attention to her kitten, which was chasing a piece of paper blown around by the breeze. Daphne waited a while, but the other cat continued to ignore her, so she left, raising her tail in brief, silent thanks.

The street was short and pedestrianised, and another road crossed it at the end. But this one was much less busy. Daphne crossed without bother and continued up the street opposite. Absorbed in her thoughts, she didn't notice it headed in a slightly different direction. It had been a little demeaning to beg for food – and she was glad someone left bowls for her and her extended family at the Sanctuary in Delphi – but it was also a relief to realise she could survive on the streets of this never-ending city.

Away from the street with the restaurants, it was far quieter. She had entered a part of town where humans lived. There were few shops. Instead, apartment blocks lined the street, most with their windows shuttered against the summer heat. But some of the upper floor apartments had balconies, and some of those windows were open. Even so, they were just out of reach, even for a young cat like her.

But her luck was about to change. The street ascended, and Daphne followed until she reached a corner where the ground floor of an apartment building was set partially into the hillside, and a first-floor balcony she could reach with ease.

Once there, she found an open window, and hesitated a while, listening for any sounds from within. But there were none.

Daphne balanced on the window ledge, then leapt down, landing on a small cabinet with a polished wood surface. She skated across it, sending an ornament spinning into space to smash with a tinkling sound on the floor and froze for a second, shocked at the noise. There was no new sound. Relieved, Daphne jumped to the floor, skirting the remains of the thing she had displaced, and nosed around. Unused to the dwellings of humans, she failed to appreciate that she was in a neat, but sparsely furnished living room with a small settee and a couple of armchairs. A table stood against a wall. The chairs looked inviting. One of them might do for a snooze when she'd finished exploring.

Through a doorway, Daphne found an even darker hallway with several adjoining doors. She pushed her way into a bedroom filled with the largest bed she had ever seen. She jumped onto it and her paws sank deep into the soft duvet.

This was as pleasurable as it was unexpected. Daphne congratulated herself on her bravery, and how it had served her well. She walked to the centre of the bed and curled up. It was glorious and comfortable. She was in heaven. Within seconds, she was asleep. Fast asleep.

It is normal for cats to sleep with one ear open, instantly awake at the slightest sound, but Daphne was so tired after her long trek across town that she fell into deep, carefree slumber. Anyone listening would have detected the rare but delicate sound of a cat snoring.

CHAPTER 22
JASON GETS LOST

For the first few blocks, Jason made excellent progress. There was still no sight of the others, and that left a nagging doubt. Perhaps he would get there first, wherever *there* actually was. He pondered this as he dodged pedestrians along the pavement. Surely he should head for the big temple thing on the top of the flat hill.

After an hour, with only a few minor pauses to pursue interesting aromatic distractions, he reached the end of the street, but came across one of the busiest junctions he had yet seen. The road before him was narrow but teeming with cars and humans. On the other side was a large, open paved area; a reward for surviving the immediate danger. Getting there required all his powers of concentration.

Once across, Jason arrived in a large irregular square with people moving in all directions. Momentarily, he lost his sense of direction, but then he looked up at the skyline and saw the rocky mass of the Acropolis before him. He marched towards it, drawn by the distant ruins.

But how he was going to get there? The cliff face looked sheer and impassable.

A more immediate concern was to avoid getting trodden

on or kicked by the humans milling around. The square was extremely busy in the late afternoon, as people emerged from work and tourists went in search of refreshment following a busy day's sightseeing. Though he didn't make the connection, Jason had similar motivations; all he wanted was somewhere to rest and lie low for a while and gather his thoughts. A pleasant drink of water would be a bonus.

He wandered around aimlessly for a few minutes, pondering his options, then noticed a patch of what looked like waste ground just beyond the square. A few humans were wandering across it for reasons best known to themselves, but it looked promising. It was fenced off by iron railings and far quieter than the main square; a good place to find a secluded corner for a nap and to de-stress after his long, dusty journey.

He watched some people come and go through a gate, but decided he could just as easily squeeze between the railings. Once inside, he became insulated from the buzz of modern day Athens, as if transported back to an earlier, quieter time. The effect was soothing, and Jason paid a little more attention to his immediate surroundings.

There were a lot of old stones, some intricately carved with designs he couldn't work out. A few pillars or sections of wall of varying height stood here and there, with bare earth or patches of grass between. One high wall had a row of extremely tall, old columns in front of it. Jason had to crane his neck to see the top. He spent a few moments observing all of this, taking it in and looking for a good place for a rest. A couple of cats sat in a sunny spot on the far side of the site, while a gaggle of kittens played on some grass, play fighting and chasing their tails.

He looked around some more and spotted a quiet corner where few people seemed to venture, with no animals visible, and headed towards it, hopping over some low ruined walls on the way. This was a lot more promising. There was a wall to the rear stretching up to present-day street level above, and some old ruins before it, surrounding a small patch of open ground now in shade as the shadows lengthened. He looked around briefly, then settled down and curled up to sleep.

Jason's thoughts wandered to his companions. Apollo could look after himself. But he worried about Daphne. She was the primary reason he was on this quest; the cause of the spur-of-the-moment decision that had taken his life in such a completely unexpected direction. He hoped she was alright. Perhaps she'd already found this Hermes character Lois had seemed to hold in such high regard.

With a bit of luck, he'd make it there tomorrow and be reunited with her.

At the back of his mind, a slightly ungracious thought arose: what if something happened to Apollo? Not terrible; not life-threatening or a serious injury, but something to hold him up, or keep him busy elsewhere for a while so he could have Daphne to himself? He shook his head to erase such unworthy and disloyal thoughts, and tried to sleep.

It was no use; just a few minutes had passed before he was rudely interrupted by two aggressive-looking cats.

"What do you think you're playing at?" asked one.

"You looking for trouble?" demanded the other.

Jason looked up wearily.

"I'm tired," he said. "I just want a rest."

"A likely story," said the first, circling to Jason's right. His companion moved slightly in the opposite direction, making it difficult for him to keep both of them in sight at the same time.

Maybe they would go away if he just ignored them.

He lowered his head onto his paws again. He was tired of having to be always on the alert in this city, and longed for the simpler life he had back in Delphi.

"One more time. What are you doing here?" demanded the first cat, more aggressively. Jason raised his head and turned towards the interrogator, determined to ask a few questions of his own.

"My business is my own and nothing to do with you. What are *you* doing here? And why are you disturbing me? Are you always this rude to your visitors?" He made no other sign of moving.

The other cats looked at each other.

"Who do you belong to?" the second one asked. "Botrys or the Gizi mob?"

"Perhaps he's one of the nutters from the south side," his companion ventured.

Jason said nothing.

"Who sent you?" the first cat tried again.

"No one. I'm my own animal," Jason replied, staring levelly at his questioner.

Could he take him on, if it came to it? Not if they had some colleagues in the area. Jason paid more attention to his wider surroundings, alert to any new arrivals.

"I reckon he's one of Kratos' losers," the second cat said to his companion, talking over Jason's head, and ignoring him.

"Nah," said his companion, "he looks too well fed to be one of that scrawny crew."

"Maybe he's been sent to spy on us," the other cat suggested. He was about to say more, but Jason pounced, catching him off guard. He raked his claws across his opponent's nose and delivered a sharp bite to his neck. The speed of his attack had forced the other cat onto his back; a position of vulnerability. The second cat advanced, as if to join in, but held back, waiting to see how the fight unfolded.

Jason stood over his opponent, snarling. His opponent looked up fearfully, all his aggression gone in an instant. With tiny movements, he backed away, his eyes fixed on his dominator.

Jason looked from his victim to the second cat, now poised to flee. He noticed the other cat carried a little more weight than most of the street cats he'd seen in the city to date. A little more of his anxiety dissipated.

"I reckon I'm faster than you," said Jason. "So, I think it's time for you to give me some answers. Who are you losers?" He glanced at the animal at his feet. "And why are you trying to intimidate me?"

There was a pause. The first cat spoke, never taking his eyes off Jason.

"We're in the Plaka gang. This place is one of our bases. We come here to rest up between missions and before scavenging raids. We're just trying to protect our turf. You can't be too careful. These days you never know who's spying on you, and sometimes folk just go missing, know what I mean?"

Jason didn't, but he pressed on. "Where are your colleagues?" He looked around; he couldn't detect any other cats in the area. The second cat recovered its voice.

"It's still early. They'll be here soon," he said. "Perhaps you'd like us to introduce you?" he added, turning submissive and compliant. The first cat said nothing, but gave a small twitch of his tail in agreement.

Jason thought fast. He didn't yet trust this pair, but if what they said was true, he'd get little or no peace in this neighbourhood without agreement of safe passage from the gang who owned this territory. Better they accept him than see him as a threat. Perhaps they could show him the best places to get food and drink.

"Alright. Let's wait."

They sat in silence. The two Plaka cats acted as if nothing had happened and Jason kept a wary eye on them. He didn't expect any trouble; he'd shown his dominance. But they might feel braver when some of their companions arrived.

While they waited, he pondered what they'd said. Wherever he went in this city, the local cats seemed jittery and on their guard against one another. Territorial bickering was a way of life for all cat societies, but the paranoia of the cats of

Athens was exhausting and far different from the life he'd known in peaceful Delphi. And what was that reference to cats disappearing? His thoughts, shrouded in guilt, wandered back to Olympia. It was a while since he'd thought about the quest, but his fixation on getting to the Acropolis, hoping to find some answers and meeting his companions again, had driven her from his mind. Lingering here was a distraction he couldn't afford. But he needed to eat and sleep, and with a bit of luck, the gang members might give him some information about what was up there.

Soon, another cat appeared, followed by another, and then a third. More arrived, heading into the heart of their den. In retrospect, Jason had been bold to stride in and treat it like home.

Still, he fronted up to the newcomers. Before he could speak, one of the initial two cats piped up.

"Hi, everybody. This is… er…"

"Jason," said Jason.

"Jason. He arrived this afternoon. Well, not very long ago, actually. He's just… visiting." He looked around at Jason for help.

Jason stood up and raised his tail in what he hoped was a confident but friendly manner. "Hi," he said. "I'm just passing by. Visiting your magnificent city." He stopped, unsure what to say. "Look, it's like this. I'm here with some friends and we're on a quest to find another friend who was stolen." He sat down. The recently arrived cats sat and lay nearby, staring at him.

"How many friends?" said one.

"What do you mean by 'stolen'?" said another.

"Where have you come from?" added a third.

Jason looked around at them. "There are three of us. Apollo, Daphne and me. We're from Delphi. We're looking for our other friend, Olympia. She was taken a few days ago." It seemed like an eternity. Was it really only yesterday? "We think they brought her here. We have to find her..." His voice trailed off.

"Well, she ain't around here. We'd 'ave seen 'er," said a gruff old male from the back of the assembly. "Any strangers round here, we see 'em off with a flea in their ear, or worse."

"It was humans. They put her in a big car," Jason told him, raising his voice. "She's no trouble to you. None of us are. I just want news. We were told there would be some answers up there." He turned his head, pointing his nose towards the Acropolis.

"No one lives up there," said another quieter voice to his left; a tabby female. She glanced at the cliffs and back towards Jason. "Someone fed you a line." She looked pleased with herself.

"We were told he lived on a hilltop," Jason replied, his temper rising. "Hermes. We were told he'd help us." The cats looked at one another and a murmur of conversation started up. Several of them laughed.

The tabby turned towards him again.

"Have you no sense of direction?" she said. "Hermes lives over there on Lycabettus." She nodded in the other direction. Jason followed her eyes to a much taller hill. "No one lives on the Acropolis. We visit from time to time, but no one actually lives there."

Jason's head bowed as if the weight of this news had pushed it down. All this way for nothing. How could he have got it so wrong? Amid his scrambled thoughts, he tried to save face.

"I must have been given the wrong information."

"So what happened to your mates, then?" said a cat from the other side of the clearing.

"I don't know. I thought they might be ahead of me, but if you've seen no one..."

Perhaps they had gone in the right direction, and he was the one who had got lost.

The tabby spoke up again. "You could stay with us for a while," she offered. Several of the other cats looked at her, but there were no dissenting voices. She turned to the assembly. "Why not? He's young and strong, and as long as we teach him the best hunting and scavenging spots, he won't be any trouble. We can always do with new recruits." There was a general murmur of agreement. She turned back to Jason. "I'm Tabitha. Let me show you where we sleep. In the morning, I'll show you what we get up to."

CHAPTER 23
SANCTUARY

The black cat led the way through the trees and up the slope to a neat complex of buildings at the top. Well-maintained steps led to a paved rectangular terrace with three buildings and a low wall along one side. Apollo climbed the steps cautiously, maintaining a careful watch. He paused and looked around in surprise.

Surely this was a human dwelling of some sort. How many of them lived here, and how safe was it? He couldn't see any sign of life, but he remained on alert. He had little experience of the buildings they lived in, but surely this wasn't a cat-friendly environment.

The other cat paused by a tree planted in the middle of the terrace, its base surrounded by a low wall. She sat down in the shade and turned to face him once more.

"This is what humans call a monastery." She caught the blank look on his face. "It's where some of their religious people live." As if reading his thoughts, she carried on "I know. What am I doing, living here among the followers of this new-fangled cult? Me, a practitioner of a far older religion. The true religion." She paused and looked around, then turned back to him. Her tone became convivial. "The fact is,

they're quite benevolent. For their species. They keep themselves to themselves, mostly. They leave offerings of food for
me. It's almost as if they worship my cult alongside their
own. What's not to like?"

Apollo broke off his stare lest it be thought rude. What
cult? Who was she? He couldn't place her. Still, he was
grateful for any place of sanctuary after the day he'd had. He
sat down and tried to think of something to say. She studied
him closely and his discomfort grew.

He was just about to remonstrate with her, when she
averted her gaze, got up and walked to the middle building.
This one was the smallest of the three: a simple single room
with an open archway facing the courtyard and an altar in the
middle.

On the threshold, Apollo paused for a moment, suspicious. He scrutinised the interior. Before him, the altar, on a
raised plinth, took up most of the floor space, before a
painting of a man nailed to a cross, writhing in agony; or was
it ecstasy? The painting had an ornate silver frame and hung
behind a large carved cross, also made of silver. Above,
dangled a coloured glass lantern containing a candle. There
were more candles on a shelf halfway up, and on a low step at
its base. To either side of the altar, alcoves retreated into
darkness.

The black cat disappeared inside. Curiosity got the better
of Apollo, and he followed.

She disappeared behind the altar where, in a small alcove,
he found two large bowls containing food and water. "Come
on," she said, "there's enough to share."

Apollo needed no second invitation to join her at her feast.

Afterwards, they sat once more in the courtyard, enjoying
the evening air. For a long time, neither spoke. The black cat
didn't seem inclined to start a conversation, while Apollo
wrestled with whether to admit his predicament. Since he had
arrived in Athens, he had mainly dealt with suspicion and

hostility. He sensed this cat was different, but he still wasn't sure he could trust her. Yet he had so many questions. Would she be able to give him any help? Somehow, he doubted it. She'd hinted that she didn't move from this area, so how could she know anything of the city beyond? He took it slowly.

"What is this place?"

"We're still in Athens," she told him. "Close to the centre, in case you were worried. The Acropolis is over there." She pointed with her nose. He vaguely remembered the name but couldn't visualise it. He didn't want to admit as much; it was yet another mystery to resolve.

"How come it's so quiet?"

"This is a rather special area. It's been a place of sanctuary and worship down the years. It has centuries of spells and incantations laid about its boundaries. Can't you feel them?" Her eyes lit up as she talked and looked up at the canopy of trees, through the branches, to the early evening stars.

It would explain the change Apollo had noticed when he'd passed under the gate on the road. He had to admit it felt different: tranquil and secluded, the air heavy with the scent of pine trees. It was a relief to be away from the frantic noise and congestion of the city streets.

But he couldn't afford to relax. He still had a mission to complete, no matter how impossible it seemed.

"I wish I knew what to do next," he said, scarcely aware that he had accidentally given voice to his thoughts. Slowly his head dropped towards his paws as weariness got the better of him, and he fell asleep.

He awoke with a jolt. It was dark. He couldn't tell how long he'd been sleeping, but as he stretched and moved, his muscles felt stiff from being in one position for too long. He looked around. There was no sign of his hostess.

Slowly, he stood up and explored the courtyard. The moon was high and full; bright enough to cast shadows from the tree and buildings. Apollo approached a building lit from the inside by yellow candlelight.

He sniffed around the doorway. There were scents he couldn't place; they seemed familiar yet unfamiliar, as if once known but long forgotten. He stepped over the threshold.

A dark shape loomed in the shadows. He startled, only to realise it was the large black cat. She stared at him with an unwavering, unnerving gaze. She seemed able to read his innermost thoughts. How long had she been here and what was her game? If she was so interested in him, why didn't she just talk to him? He stepped forwards, but before he could open his mouth, she beat him to it.

"You seem confused. Not just about me. About this place." She glanced at the altar and painted ceiling before training her stare back on Apollo. "It's time to find out what it is you are here for, and what you must do."

"What do you mean?"

"Step closer. Here." She nodded to her left. "I have some herbs gathered locally beneath the light of the moon. They will help free your thoughts so you can find answers to your questions. Look into the flame."

Without further ado, she delicately picked up a bunch of leaves in her mouth and dropped them on top of the nearest candle. She stepped back, muttering an incantation in a language Apollo had never heard. Her eyes focused on the burning herbs.

It was entrancing. He'd seen nothing like it before. Dimly remembered images floated in his mind. He moved a centimetre or two closer, then closer again, watching as the leaves smoked and crackled in the flame. A powerful fragrance filled the shrine, overpowering his senses. It was both delicious and intoxicating; arousing and soporific. As he watched the flame, it took over his entire field of vision. Then it seemed he was watching from a great distance down a long tube or tunnel. Then it went out.

He found himself in a dark, desolate, rocky plain that seemed to stretch on forever beneath a not-quite-black starless sky. No moon. There was just enough light to make out the landscape, but not enough to see any detail. There was no sign of a living thing in any direction. In the distance, he thought he could make out a ridge of low hills. There didn't seem to be any vegetation at all.

He looked down, surprised. A small pool of golden light illuminated the ground around his feet before being swallowed up in the enormity of the all-encompassing darkness. As his eyes adjusted, he could see that he was standing on a road of sorts. He followed it; there was nowhere else to go.

Apollo trudged on and on. Nothing in this featureless dusty desolation seemed to get any closer or further away. He had no concept of time here. He could have been walking for minutes or days. But strangely, it didn't seem to matter.

Eventually, as seemed inevitable, he arrived at the bank of a wide, slow-moving river. Its waters were the colour of pitch; the darkest black imaginable. He stopped. Even the pale glow emanating from him had no power to illuminate it. As he looked across, he could just make out the far bank. Could he swim? The thought horrified him, but how else could he get over there? He looked to his right and saw, not far away, a small rowing boat beside which stood a tall figure in a dark hooded cloak. The figure took no notice of him.

A voice came from his left: loud, deep, strong.

"I wouldn't even think about it, if I were you."

Apollo spun around and found himself confronted by a huge, vicious-looking three-headed dog. His mouth fell open in astonishment. The beast's three heads glared at him. Each mouth hung half open, filled with fearsome teeth the size of daggers. It was so close that its slobber splashed on the ground in front of Apollo's paws. He stood his ground and looked up at this creature of hell, and strangely his fear and uncertainty were gone.

"I'm looking for someone. She may be over there. I need to find her."

He looked towards the distant bank.

The three-headed dog edged closer. Two of the heads growled menacingly; the third addressed him directly.

"You can't. You're not meant to be here. Begone. Lest I change my mind and make you stay forever." It made a strange, strangled sound that Apollo interpreted as laughter. The monster took another step closer, almost grinning in anticipation as the last thought played across its triple brain.

Apollo looked back at those baleful eyes, and something snapped. Instead of feeling cowed and intimidated by this monstrous, threatening beast, pure anger flared – and with it his confidence returned. He would not put up with threats anymore; no matter who the bully might be.

He looked down at the creature before him, the way a lion might study a mouse. A small part of his mind stood aside, surprised at the transformation; he was now the largest lion ever seen, and the light that had been glowing from his small body, kindled by his rage, flared so brightly around him it seemed a star had landed on the banks of the black river. Now blindingly bright and clothed in full Olympian glory, he threw back his head, shook his magnificent mane and roared for the sheer joy and release, and the sound travelled far across the river and the dismal kingdom beyond, even to the halls of its pale king.

"Enough of threats," he growled in a voice so deep as to make the earth shake. *"Answer me."*

The three-headed dog took a couple of steps back. Two of his heads turned away, unable to bear the light. The third bowed, but despite the turn of events, did not yield.

"I am Cerberus. I am the guardian of this place," he said, his voice now almost apologetic. "I cannot let you pass. You must go, or else face the wrath of my master." One of his three mighty heads looked across the river into the distance.

Apollo was in no mood to back down, and the dog unable to. A fight seemed inevitable.

But then he heard voices from the far side of the river.

"You're too late."

"You should have come earlier."

"It was so horrible."

"Why didn't you help us?"

"Why did nobody come to rescue us?"

There were so many voices; accusing, wailing, pleading. Apollo stared across the river, flooded with horror and pity. Transparent, disembodied shapes drifted on the far shore, imploring and shaming.

"No one came to help us, and now it's too late."

A desperate thought struck him. He felt sick, but he had to ask.

"Olympia?" he shouted; a roar heard miles away.

He got no response.

Then, *"I knew her. She's not here. Not yet,"* cried a spirit; a small lone voice among the multitude. "But she will be soon, if you're not quick."

"Where? Where do I find her?" Apollo yelled, but there was no further reply; just the hushed moaning and chattering of the dead talking among themselves.

"Go. Now!" urged the three-headed dog, becoming visibly agitated. "Before we answer to my master."

Apollo turned towards it once more.

"You do not give me orders."

"Neither do you belong here. This is my domain, not yours."

They stared at each other. Apollo's anger abated, and his golden light no longer burned so fiercely. He gave the three-headed dog one last withering glare. Before departing, he turned once more towards the lost souls on the far bank. Whether it was guilt or pity, or sympathy for their plight, he had a desire to help them.

A beautiful music began, building slowly. It seemed to grow out of the air surrounding Apollo, and flow across the dark waters to the other shore; a symphony so moving, so beautiful, so heart-rending yet somehow comforting, and ultimately, in some small way, uplifting. It sprang from his thoughts, and he breathed life into it, then set it free to linger on that sad shore forever, to soothe the souls of the departed. Above all, in this dismal, forsaken place, he wanted to leave them a small gift: hope.

With one last dismissive glance at the enormous dog, he turned and padded away on paws the size of tree trunks.

The music played on, ebbing and flowing, never repeating. It seeped into the stones, delivering its timeless message on the miserable riverbank forever more.

In this way, he remembered he was a god.

CHAPTER 24
DEADLY FUN

To the other side of Olympia, they'd imprisoned a small, miserable and uncommunicative tabby. She'd already been there when the Delphi cat arrived. At first, Olympia ignored her fellow prisoner, but with few other distractions, she tried to break the ice. Her neighbour, introverted and shy, somehow blamed herself for the mess she'd landed in. It took a long time for Olympia to tease out her story; a tale of misery that was at once heart-breaking and familiar.

She'd never been evil; just a bit mischievous. She'd stolen a few things here and there. Nicked another cat's dinner now and then; nothing bad. No, she hadn't been friendly with humans, but she didn't hate them. She just wasn't sure about them; they were so big, so clumsy, and she found it hard to read them. It was her own fault, really. She probably just needed to try harder. Have another go at making a connection.

That was what started it. Trying to make a connection. The woman distracted her when she was minding her own business on the street, following some interesting scents on her way to one of her favourite places for hunting. She'd bent down, making out she wanted to be a friend in that stupid way humans do. Of course, she had distrusted her immediately, and let it show, holding back. If she'd been sensible she'd have run away, but the woman dangled a little toy; a piece of coloured string of some sort. Oh, if only she'd had more sense. But there was something about the way it moved. She couldn't resist chasing it, pawing at it. She'd never come across anything like it before.

In fact, she'd had little that could be regarded as fun in her short life. She just got on with things, eking out a living, getting stuff for the boss, staying out of his way as much as possible and keeping her nose clean. Sometimes it was a struggle to keep going. Not just getting on the wrong side of the boss, but dodging vicious dogs, outraged domesticated cats – every one of them a stuck-up, self-centred, bourgeois abomination – and those horrible vehicles on the streets. But at least she'd been free. At least she'd had somewhere to sleep, and companions to pass time with.

Some humans seemed okay, but others hated cats and threw things, or worse. So, there she was, entranced by a twirling, dancing piece of coloured string. Totally off her guard. Having a little fun. Then the net dropped on top of her, and her freedom was over.

Suddenly, the human didn't seem so friendly. She had an ugly expression on her face and she lashed out at her as she dangled there, unable to escape. This attempt to shut her up only made her screech louder, but a second, heavier blow stunned her, and cold fear did the rest of the job.

More days of terror followed, penned up in a little cage with hardly anything to eat. How she hated this place. Other cats came and went. She had no interest in them; conversation was stilted. She distrusted them almost as much as her captors; but at least she didn't fear them. There was something about the humans in this place that terrified her.

One day, they came to her neighbour's cage, opened it and

roughly picked her up. They put her in a bag, took her into a nearby room and ended her life with several blows from a heavy club. At least that's what it sounded like to Olympia; they didn't think to close the window properly. They didn't care what the other prisoners thought.

It wasn't quick. It took several blows, each met with a terrified scream, before they finally took her neighbour's small, ordinary life. No one would miss her; she had few friends and no one close. Olympia never even knew her name. A week later, her coat was part of another one.

CHAPTER 25
BLISSFULNESS

Daphne awoke to the sound of a scream as a light flared overhead. Alert in an instant, she crouched down, trying to identify the source of the sound.

An older female human stood in the doorway. Had she screamed in alarm, shock or delight? She stood there, blocking Daphne's only escape route.

The two of them stared at each other. Daphne tensed, ready to spring away, but it seemed the new arrival wanted to make friends. This was unexpected; she wasn't sure how to react. She wanted to make her escape, but how quick were the human's reactions? The older ones could be slow, but Daphne didn't want to take any chances. She hesitated.

The old woman moved towards her, making no sudden moves. Her face melded into one of those human expressions Daphne interpreted as happy. She appeared pleased to have a visit from a total stranger. Wary, and ready to flee at any moment, the cat allowed the woman to stroke her between the ears. The woman made a move to pick her up, but Daphne shrank back, and she stopped.

The two of them surveyed each other once more. Then the woman disappeared. Daphne waited where she was for a few minutes, straining her ears to assess if she had really gone, and whether it was safe to make her way back to the room with the window. She jumped down from the bed and approached the door to the hallway cautiously. The woman was nowhere in sight. Daphne darted into the living room, but skidded to a halt in dismay.

The window was closed. She was trapped.

A little later, the old woman reappeared in the doorway, making sounds at her. Daphne wasn't as used to understanding human speech as some of her kind, but it seemed like the woman was trying to be friendly. She held out a small bowl with food in it. Daphne's nostrils twitched. Fish, and decent quality. It was a promising development. She might as well have a bite to eat and then leave with a full stomach. Better than going hungry. She followed the woman into her kitchen, where she placed the bowl on the floor beside the wall. Daphne looked up again and tried to read her expression. She remained suspicious, but the fish smelled too good, and her resistance crumbled.

While she ate, her mind raced. How long would it be before she could get out of this place, and where had she got to? She was in Athens on a rescue mission; she hadn't come to meet the locals. Poor Olympia was waiting somewhere; perhaps in a place like this, or maybe worse. She suppressed a shudder at the thought.

While her nose was deep in the bowl, she heard a door shut. She lifted her head. The woman had left, and she had missed a chance to run past her when the door was open.

She waited a while longer, but the door remained closed, so she returned to the tuna and finished the bowl, then walked into the hallway and sat facing the door. When the opportunity arose, she was going to have to execute her move with precision.

She waited and waited, but there was no sign of the

elderly woman returning and the door remained stubbornly shut.

Daphne surveyed her surroundings once more, but she could find no evidence of another exit. In pure frustration, she scratched at the hall carpet and found it pleasantly satisfying. Being brought up in Delphi, she had never had the pleasure of carpet to scratch, and this was so much easier than bark; it was as if they'd made it for scratching. It was delightful to see her claws plough grooves into the material as she vented her frustration. But she couldn't scratch all day, and as time passed, her outrage at being imprisoned grew. She was a creature of the fresh air and wide open spaces; not some lap cat! How dare this human imprison her like this? It was outrageous.

After a while, she gathered her thoughts. There was a chair in the hallway, opposite the door, and sitting beneath it made her feel a little better. With a sigh, she settled down once more to wait.

An hour passed, and then another. Finally, there was a sound outside and the rattle of a key in the lock. The door opened. Daphne tensed, waiting for a clear gap through which she could run, but the woman quickly closed the door before there was enough room for Daphne to make her escape.

A successful exit would clearly require careful planning, and perfect timing. But at least she now knew what she would need to do, and how quickly she had to move. Her dread of being kicked or trampled was just another operational risk to factor in. She had to remain patient and vigilant, then make her move quicker next time.

The woman placed a shopping bag on the kitchen worktop. She took out a bowl and opened a tin of cat food. At least Daphne wouldn't be going hungry. She placed the bowl on the floor, making the encouraging noises some humans make when trying to communicate with cats. Daphne studied her with curiosity. There was no doubt the woman was trying to ingratiate her way into Daphne's affections, but why did she believe Daphne would reciprocate? Did she think she was a simpleton? Ready to roll over at the first sniff of fish?

Daphne remained dismissive and determined to keep her distance. She was in no mood for faux friendliness from someone she'd just met and who was trying to keep her prisoner. She stayed under the chair.

The woman opened another door and entered a small room Daphne had not yet explored. The sound of running water pricked her ears. It sounded like a stream plunging into a pool. Did all human residences have such streams flowing through them? How come she hadn't heard it before? Curiosity got the better of her and she made the mistake of venturing out to explore.

With a speed that belied her age and size, the human grabbed Daphne by the scruff of the neck and lifted her. She hovered over the water; then, to her horror, the woman thrust her into it, submerging her.

Immediate panic.

She's trying to drown me.

Scrabble and twist for all you're worth.

Bite, scratch, wriggle. Don't go down easily.

But the woman wouldn't let go.

Head above water again. Deep breath, relief.

But then, the woman smeared something on her fur and rubbed it in. Nasty-smelling, greasy liquid. Bubbles and foam lathered up, invading her mouth and nostrils.

It tasted disgusting.

Spit.

Daphne continued to wriggle and grapple for all she was worth, but her opponent's bony fingers kept a firm grip. She smothered Daphne in the liquid a few more times, massaged her into a frothy foam ball, dunked her into the water repeatedly, then finally released her. She then swaddled her in a thick towel and vigorously rubbed her down.

After what seemed like an eternity in hell, the woman placed Daphne back on the floor, where she stood bristling with fury, glaring up at her tormentor with venom in her eyes. Daphne was fluffier than she'd ever been, smelling faintly of pine, and spotless. She despised this human with a passion her enemy could never conceive; her thoughts ran wild with the things she would do to her if she had the chance. What was worse, the woman didn't seem to realise the depth of the indignity she had inflicted. Instead, she scuttled back to the kitchen. Daphne, relieved to escape from the watery torture chamber, scrambled into another room, scanning for hiding places.

The woman found her again and pursued her furious and pristine prisoner. She held out a peace offering: a small cloth bag, sewn up around the sides, and just a few centimetres across.

Daphne stared at her gift with suspicion, sensing a trick, but then detected an aroma she had never come across, and which stirred emotions she could barely contain. It played with her senses; she had to get more of this wondrous scent.

Her eyes widened, and her nostrils flared. Her reservation became a thing of the past, and she approached the woman with her nose in the air. She wanted the bag. Needed it. She wanted to wrap herself in it and cover every inch of her body with that wondrous aroma. If she could, she wanted to bathe in it. *She had to have it.*

The old woman teased Daphne, dangling the bag just out of reach. Daphne almost snarled as the woman waved it back and forth above her head. She lashed out with a paw, claws fully extended, but narrowly missed.

All semblance of civility vanished now; she crouched, ready to pounce. She was a wild and primeval beast, prepared to do anything to get hold of that precious little parcel.

The woman ceased her torment and threw the bag on the floor in the centre of the room. Daphne spun and pounced on it like a mad thing, grabbing it and clutching it to her chest. She cuddled it and rubbed it all over her face, burying her nose in the heavenly fragrance. The outside world ceased to exist as she rolled around on the carpet, wrestling with the bag. A new world had opened up; something she had never experienced.

Now she knew she could never live without it.

CHAPTER 26
BACK ON THE TRAIL

Apollo woke in the pale light of dawn to a crushing headache. He tried opening his eyes, but the daylight hurt. For a while he lay still, breathing hard, as if he'd been running. After a few minutes, he tried to get up and struggled to his feet. He got two paces towards the door and threw up. Another few steps and it happened again. He flopped down, exhausted and feeling awful. What had happened? His mind reeling, he could barely remember where he was. Had just one night passed, or many? And what about that dream? Was it a dream? It seemed so real, but it couldn't be. He gave up and closed his eyes.

This was no good. His head was swimming. He had to try again. A few more minutes passed, then he readied himself for another effort. This time was better, and he stood up, swaying and feeling lightheaded. His mouth was dry; he needed water. Unsteady, he wove a path back into the shrine, to the alcove with the bowls, and drank.

Too much, too soon; the waves of nausea returned. He sat down, waiting for the feeling to wear off. It was no good. He needed fresh air.

Apollo returned to the courtyard and found a shady place to flop down. Gradually, normality returned. *Never again.*

It was some time before he could sit up with a head clear enough to think about what to do next. As he did so, the black cat appeared on the wall a short distance away. She examined him with a faint air of amusement.

"Perhaps I should have warned you not to get too close. Those herbs and enchantments can be quite intense. You went deep into your trance."

Apollo looked up at the trees. The weather was overcast but humid; not the best day for a hangover. He glanced across at his hostess.

"Who *are* you?" he asked, fixing her with a stare, his eyes narrowing. She returned his stare for a long time, considering how much to reveal.

"I am Hecate," she said finally. "I practice witchcraft."

Apollo nodded, absorbing this. "*Hecate,*" he repeated. The name was familiar; it was ancient and signified power, he was certain. But he remembered nothing about witchcraft, nor could he recall meeting any practitioners. Apart from maybe old Pythia back home. But she was a seer, and that was different. "What did you do to me?"

"That is difficult for me to say." She continued to look at him. "Normally, those braver mortals who dare come here are trying to gain some insights into their true nature, or to perceive the future, however imperfectly. I merely show them the way. I have no influence over what they find. Their experiences vary, but since you've been asleep for so long, I'd say your journey last night was longer and deeper than most."

He considered this. His memory was still sketchy, but fragments of his dream remained. They made little sense to him; apart from one thing.

"They said she wasn't there." He said it as much to himself as to Hecate. He looked up, hope rising in his throat until it almost choked him. "The spirits of the dead. They said she wasn't there. But there wasn't much time."

Hecate settled into a more comfortable position. "It is up to you to interpret or find meaning in your visions. They are personal to you only. I cannot offer much help."

"I came to Athens to look for a friend who was kidnapped. She's called Olympia. She was taken from us by humans. We think they came from here." He looked around as if expecting to see them appear around a corner, then recognised how silly it must appear. "I don't know where, though…" His voice trailed off.

Hecate broke the silence. "Few citizens ever visit me. The gangs are too frightened, and most of the other inhabitants are put off by my reputation." She looked quite proud. "As a result, I am not the best person to visit for gossip." There was a hint of disdain in her voice. "However, my gifts allow me to tap into the…" She paused, searching for the word. "Into the wider ambience of the city. The psychological undercurrent. And what I have detected recently is a level of fear within the animal population far greater than before. Your friend is not the first I've heard of who has gone missing. Nor will she be the last."

Apollo felt vindicated, almost relieved. But he couldn't see how this helped him. "Who is doing it? Why? Where are they being taken?"

"That I can't answer. Humans, probably. But whether for sacrifice or some form of worship, I can't tell. If they were being offered to me, it would be a different story, of course. Although sacrifice of a creature from our species would be rather impudent, don't you think? Possibly sacrilegious." She looked into the distance. "No, times have changed. It is a long time since I was offered a blood sacrifice. Food is the preferred choice these days. Plus the occasional mouse." She gave him a mischievous glance.

The talk of sacrifice conjured other memories. He nodded,

absently. His mind raced. More fragments of his dream from the previous night were coming back to him; but they made no sense. The one thing he clung to was the thought that Olympia was still safe, at least for now.

He stood up. "I have to go. They said I didn't have much time."

"And where are you going?" she asked. Apollo halted, confused. Hecate watched him. "As I said, I live my own life. I am no fan of news and gossip, but there is probably one animal who can help you. If anyone knows where to find your friend, it is probably him."

Apollo anticipated her. "Hermes. I was on the way to find him when I got waylaid and chased all the way here." The thought left a bitter taste.

She gave him a cool, appraising look, which only reinforced his embarrassment. "Then you know where to find him." It was a statement rather than a question. He hesitated.

"I've rather lost my bearings. I'm not sure which direction to take."

Hecate stood and walked along the top of the low wall to the corner, waiting for him to follow.

"Head down here and back through the gate you passed yesterday," she told him in a business-like fashion. "You must retrace your path to the other side of the roundabout and the park beyond. When you reach its far end, you should see the hill in front of you."

"But what if they are waiting for me?"

She looked him up and down. "What are you afraid of? You, of all people? Has your light dimmed to the extent that mere shadows confound you? Have you allowed yourself to become afraid of the dark?" She brushed past him and looked down the hillside through the trees. "You can no more hide your true self as change the colour of the wind."

Apollo chastised himself. This city and its inhabitants were testing him in ways he hadn't experienced for centuries.

I am Apollo.

What do they expect of me?

"For what it's worth, I think ambush is unlikely," she continued, "but you never know. Even at the unlikeliest moment, you may meet someone who can help you. Trust your instinct and heed their advice."

Yet another riddle to unpick. It was time to leave, but he hesitated, uncertain how to thank this mysterious witch. She read him, and with an almost motherly nudge of her nose, ushered him on his way.

"No need to thank me," she said. "Just find your friend."

He gave her a grateful look, jumped down and set off through the trees below. When he looked back, she had already disappeared.

CHAPTER 27
JASON IN THE PLAKA

Jason woke up, surrounded by his newfound friends, in a secluded corner of the ancient ruins on the site of Hadrian's Library. He stretched as much as he dared without punching his neighbours and rolled over against the back of the cat next to him. She grunted in her sleep but showed no sign of waking. He raised his head to peer over the top of the sleeping animals and examine his surroundings. They lay on a rectangular patch of ground, enclosed in part by the low foundations of old walls. A short distance away, most of the youngsters were already awake and engaged in their morning activities: competing for milk, play fighting or chasing one another. They were relentless; it all looked like too much effort. Jason dropped his head and dozed off for a few minutes more.

But not for long. Cats stirred around him, getting ready for the new day. Some had been out and about for hours. What would the day have in store for him? He needed to get back to the job of finding Olympia, but he had no idea what to do next. Perhaps he could persuade one of these cats to help him in his quest; he just had to find the right time to ask.

In the meantime, he needed to get to know his companions better and find some food.

He meandered around the place. It had some similarities to home, particularly the ancient stones lying around, standing upright, balanced on top of one another. What did humans see in all this? Some of them would most likely arrive soon to look around. He had enough experience to understand that they liked to do that, even though they never tidied things up. The old stones here had a fence around them to keep them apart from the rest of the city. This was nice because it kept the humans at a distance overnight. But he couldn't understand why the old stones were so important to them. Perhaps they worshipped them? There was little point speculating.

At least it kept them from interfering for a few hours, and in his limited experience of humans, he knew they did like to interfere. They were unpredictable, and a little odd, and it was a good idea to keep them at a distance.

Jason sauntered around the compound, following some unusual scents. They would tell interesting stories, if he could be bothered to interpret them; but this morning his mind wandered.

The small tabby who had spoken up for him the previous evening approached. She hopped from paw to paw, as if nervous.

"Hi, I'm Tabitha," she purred softly. "Would you like me to show you around?"

"Yes, why not?" He gave her a quick reassuring glance, then looked away, lest he appear rude. "Where shall we go first? No, wait. Before we do anything, where's the food round here?"

Tabitha brightened. "Oh, that's easy. There're loads of opportunities."

They spent the rest of the morning exploring the winding back streets of the Plaka, visiting some of the best locations to find food. At this time of day, the restaurants were closed, but several cafés and bars were open, serving breakfast to their two-legged customers. There were few inclined to share, but things were more promising by their back doors, where yesterday's leftovers and unused items had been bagged up and left for collection. But a little detective work with the nose, followed by some surgical bag-slashing here or there when no one was looking, could unearth some tasty delights. Jason was ravenous, but he soon had his fill.

Replenished, they continued Tabitha's guided tour of the neighbourhood. She showed him the best positions for watching the restaurants, the quiet residential streets where well-intentioned people sometimes left food out, and the houses where members of the local citizenry lived with their adopted human servants.

"Take this one, for example," she said. They were walking along a short, narrow street a matter of metres from a busy thoroughfare, but could have been in a different city, it was so quiet. Tabitha was facing a red-hued wall where crumbling plasterwork exposed bare bricks. Much of it was covered with the colourful graffiti that featured throughout the city centre, but verdant vegetation was spilling over the top, as if trying to escape. Blue flowers cascaded down towards the street. "This is a lovely secluded place to hide and rest," she told him. "But just along here," she resumed walking, "is a place where they keep a house cat." She saw the look Jason gave her. "Of course we don't talk to them," she said. "But if they're out, you can usually sneak in via the cat door and have your fill without anybody noticing."

"How do you know when they're not in?" he asked.

"Oh, you soon get to know their habits. They're usually out at the same time of day."

"But they must object?"

"Yes, but what are they going to do about it?" The upturned tilt of her nose spoke of a no-nonsense approach,

The cats of the Plaka gang weren't short of options for dining out, but who could resist the temptation of an unguarded bowl of premium cat food?

"Of course, I'm telling you all this in confidence," she added. "It took me months to find this place, and I haven't shown it to anyone else. It's my secret." She gave him a level stare.

"Don't worry, I won't tell anyone," he said, experiencing sudden, unnecessary guilt. Her eyes lingered on him a little longer, as if checking the message had been received, before they set off once more.

Tabitha was good company, and Jason relaxed for the first time since he had arrived in Athens. They paused often to explore interesting nooks and crannies, sniff out some beautiful flowers and plants, and just chill for a while, human-watching. By afternoon Jason's head was a whirl with all his new knowledge, and he needed a nap. Once more, his little companion came up with the goods. Behind an ochre-coloured wall, in the corner of a tiny secluded garden, she showed him to a shady patch of grass overhung by a bush and just big enough for two.

It was evening before they emerged and headed back to the Library of Hadrian. Tabitha left him to re-join her friends, and for a while, Jason was at a loss.

He wasn't alone for long. A dusty-coloured adolescent male approached him. He looked about the same age as Jason and introduced himself as Erichthonius. He asked Jason if he liked football. The question baffled him; he had no idea what football was, but, intrigued, he accompanied Erichthonius to find out.

They headed back towards the main street, with its many bars and restaurants. It was now mid-evening; the sun hung low in the sky and lots of humans milled around, eating, drinking, walking, talking and socialising. The two cats had to plot their course through a forest of legs.

Erichthonius stopped outside a popular bar and jumped onto a low wall separating the pavement in front from a narrow passage to the side. There was a small cushion in place, as if they expected him. The brightly lit interior was busy, but the large windows had been pushed wide, allowing tables to spill out onto the street, where the humans stared up at a box perched on a shelf high on the wall. Before he arrived in Athens, Jason had never spent much time people watching, so ritual behaviour such as this was a novelty.

The front of the box had a screen with moving pictures. Was it a religious ceremony? If so, the congregation seemed quite raucous; shouting and drinking seemed to be an essential part of the ritual. Jason stared up at the box, trying to make sense of the ceremony.

The pictures showed an enormous field with a lot of humans running around in random patterns, wearing two types of coloured shirts. There was a small white dot in the middle, which zipped back and forth among the humans. Jason focused on it intently, his head following its movement. How come he had never seen magic like this before?

He settled down to watch more. By his side, Erichthonius had already happily settled in, his attention focused on the box. A waiter approached, and Jason stiffened, ready to flee. But his companion was unfazed. He welcomed the waiter's greeting and even allowed him to tousle his ears.

"You've brought a friend," said the man, who placed a small bowl of offcuts between them. Jason remained wary, unable to understand a word the man said. But the tone of his voice seemed friendly enough. "Don't fight over it," the man warned, and walked away. Jason hesitated, trying to read his intent. Humans were challenging to interpret; hostile one moment, welcoming the next. He needed to improve his reading of them. For now, he would have to rely on the instincts of his new friend.

Erichthonius was clearly a regular here.

"They're friendly, and the food's good," he said. "The humans are watching a game called football. Barcelona are the team in darker colours. They're fantastic. The other team is AEK from Athens," he added, the pride in his voice clear. He talked and talked, but after the busy day he'd already had, Jason struggled to absorb any more.

"How do you know all this?"

"Oh, I pick up a lot from the commentary," the other cat replied. "I learned to understand human." Jason was astonished. A cat who could make sense of all the chitter-chatter of humans? Body language was as far as most of his kind went.

As Jason glanced over at his companion, there was a loud cheer behind him. He tensed ready, once more, to flee, but his companion was completely relaxed. Several of the humans nearby looked extremely animated. He tried to interpret the mood. One or two gesticulated wildly.

"It's a goal," explained Erichthonius, leaning closer. "AEK have scored." Jason looked blank. "They've got the ball into the net." A baffled look meant more explanation was needed. "You see the net? It's called a goal. They have one at each end." Jason looked at the screen, uncertain what Erichthonius meant. "Doesn't anyone watch football where you come from?"

"No." If it was as noisy as this, he didn't think any Delphi cat would venture within earshot of such a game. "It looks a bit dangerous."

Erichthonius cast a glance around the bar. "Not really," he said. "Only if it's two Athens teams playing each other." He turned back to the screen, absorbed once more.

Jason reappraised his companion. This young, intelligent, city-living sophisticate made him feel out of his depth. He missed his home and his extended family; even snooty Hera.

Life was slower and a lot quieter back in Delphi. There was a tranquillity and routine. Embarking on this ludicrous adventure had been the most stupid spur-of-the-moment decision he'd ever made, and by lingering here instead of trying to find the others, he'd made it worse. Guilt consumed him. What might have happened to Olympia while he dallied with his new friends?

And then there was Daphne. He longed to find her more than anything; more even than returning to Delphi and his familiar old haunts. But he didn't know where to even start. The scale of the city was overwhelming.

The match had just about ended. The humans were finishing their drinks and leaving. "Let's go," said Jason.

Erichthonius followed with a sigh. "They came close," he said, "but Barcelona is just too good."

They made their way in silence back to their sleeping quarters for the night.

CHAPTER 28
LYCABETTUS

Apollo descended the hill and retraced his steps from the previous day, passing the gate and roundabout. He entered the wooded parkland beyond. Was it only yesterday those thugs had chased him across this park? It didn't seem possible. Nevertheless, his senses were on high alert, he half expected his enemies to reappear at any moment. He still wasn't certain he was heading the right way, but he stuck with Hecate's directions.

He thought about his friends and where they might be. Jason could look after himself, he was sure, but he hoped Daphne was alright. Apollo was protective of her; maybe a little possessive. He missed her cheerful optimism and hated the thought of Jason having her all to himself. Even though their acquaintance had been brief, he now regarded Jason as a friend, but Daphne was a bit… special. She tugged at his heartstrings like no one else.

He daydreamed about her as he plodded on through the trees. A sweet reunion somewhere quiet; nuzzling and purring; then finally asking that question. He put the thought to one side and paid more attention to his immediate surroundings.

Towards the far side of the park, the prospect of ambush arose once more, and he slowed down. He was sure his enemies would be on the lookout for him. Putting himself in their paws, where would be a good place to waylay him? After a while, he stopped, no longer sure which direction to take.

"I wish I could fly above these trees," he muttered to himself.

A large crow, perched on the branch of a nearby tree, cocked his head, looking at him. Apollo had no more regard for birds than any of his species, and since this one was too big to eat, he ignored it. The bird shuffled along the branch until it was closer to his eyeline. Apollo glared at it, but instead of flying off as he expected, it spoke to him.

"Morning, guv. Perhaps I could be of service?" It tilted its head to the other side.

"What?" said Apollo.

The bird went on. "Well, sir. I couldn't help overhearing you, if I may say so, and it seems like you've got a problem and you want to fly to sort it out?" It studied him. Apollo stayed silent, so it continued. "Well, it's like this. Perhaps I could do your flying for you, if you like. If you tell me what it is you're looking for."

Apollo narrowed his eyes, suspicious. "Why are you offering to help me?"

The crow paused before replying. He sounded a little offended.

"We always help the Golden One," he cawed. "It's in our blood. Always has been, since before anyone can remember." He shuffled back along the branch, huffily. "But perhaps you don't need us anymore."

Apollo looked at the crow in astonishment, but at the back of his mind, some vague notion clicked into place. Yes, this seemed natural. A piece of an ancient puzzle slotting into place; aspects of his rule. He faced the bird, more enthusiastic now.

"Wait. You can help me."

The crow turned back towards him and shifted position again. "You just have to ask."

"I'm looking for Hermes," Apollo told him. "But there may be some cats ahead that are trying to capture me. I need to get around them without attracting attention. Can you help? Do you know Hermes?"

"Ha! Everyone knows the messenger. Stay here, my lord. I'll have a look around. Back in a jiffy."

It took off.

Apollo considered what had just happened. He would never have believed he could have a companionable chat with a bird. But then a lot of strange things had happened since he arrived in this city.

The crow soon arrived back.

"There's a trio of your kind about half a kilometre ahead. They're hanging around by the road. Two on this side, one on the other. They're not moving far. They're just sitting around pretending they're not with each other. Perhaps you were right to worry."

Apollo took stock. "Can you tell me how to get around them?"

"Easy," said the crow. "Follow me." Immediately it took off and flew north-eastwards. Apollo hurried after it before it drifted out of sight. A moment later it reappeared, sounding apologetic. "Silly me. I forgot you can't fly. I'll go in shorter hops." It set off again.

And so they went, via a circuitous route towards Lyca-bettus Hill, arriving from the southeast. The crow was as good as its word and took care to direct Apollo via less-used thoroughfares. They travelled down quiet streets, across small parks, through hospital grounds and passed a large concert hall. The trickiest bit was crossing a large multi-lane highway. But Apollo was used to them now, and had the patience to wait until there was a gap in the traffic.

On the other side, the gradient increased. A few more turns and he came to a flight of steps leading onto the hillside, leaving the buildings behind. He paused. The crow was waiting for him just ahead.

Apollo thanked it. "I think I can make it from here."

"Until next time, then." The crow took off.

Apollo looked at the slope ahead of him. The hill provided an airy viewpoint. Most human visitors ascended via a funicular, but a footpath also climbed to the summit. The path zigzagged upward to his left, but Apollo had no desire to follow it. He preferred to arrive unannounced, and he suspected the path humans used would be watched. That would mean navigating the steep, rocky slopes above. It would be a long, hard climb, but with luck he might have a look at this Hermes fellow and get a sense of his character before approaching him. It would be nice to be on the front paw for once.

Lycabettus, a famous viewpoint, was also home to one of the more distinctive feline communities of Athens: the Hermaeans, as they liked to call themselves; or "that bunch of hillbilly weirdos" as some of their less kind feline neighbours described them. They were regarded in similar wary fashion to the inhabitants of the Agora, always poking their noses into other animals' business. But they were less assertive, so most of the cats of Athens just left them to it. After all, everyone has a hobby of some sort.

Apollo started his climb. The oppressive heat of late afternoon made it hard work, but he was relieved to be above the city streets and away from the noise and throb of engines, and the fumes and dust that followed them. But though he was ascending, there was little or no breeze to freshen the atmosphere.

He toiled on, taking as direct a route as he dared, despite the increasing gradient. Above him, the hilltop was well defended by rocky outcrops, but he noticed gaps between the cliffs which looked passable. With the sun sinking towards the western horizon, he finally approached the summit.

Apollo had given no thought to the possibility humans might like to visit the terrace at the hilltop to watch the sunset, but his instincts had proved correct; by taking the harder route, he had reached this point unseen by any of those thronging the terrace.

"Ah, there you are," said a calm voice above him. "Glad you made it."

Apollo halted, annoyed. He looked up, trying to find the source of the voice, and then saw, perched on the top of a pier of rock some three metres above him, the silhouette of a pair of ears surmounting two bright eyes. The voice spoke again.

"I believe you're looking for Hermes," it said. "Over here. We'd better talk." The ears disappeared.

Apollo continued up the narrow cleft to the top, trying to slow his breathing and collect his thoughts. He stepped out onto a small plateau of flattened, naked rock. Waiting for him a short distance away was a silver-white male cat of medium build, with ears and paws tinged with brown. But his most striking feature was his piercing, unblinking blue eyes.

To his left, Apollo was aware of several other cats, lounging or sitting a respectful distance away. He knew they would observe him discreetly, and judging from the number of ears facing him like an array of miniature radio telescopes, listening to everything he said.

Hot and breathless from his climb, Apollo tried not to let his irritation show. Was this the Hermes of legend or not? Admittedly, his knowledge of the character known as Hermes was limited. He seemed to remember he'd been a friend, but was that still the case? What sort of welcome could he expect after such a long time? Hopefully better than most he'd received to date.

Standing still, Apollo pondered his opening gambit.

"I heard you could help me," he said at last. Once again, embarrassment arose to swamp his thoughts. Asking for help was so difficult.

The other cat continued to survey him coolly. The longer this continued, the more Apollo's exasperation grew. He returned the stare; for cats of any variety, this was close to outright hostility. Long seconds passed, and neither moved a muscle. Without averting his gaze, Apollo noticed a faint silvery shimmer around the other cat. It made him look larger; more imposing.

"So, you call yourself Apollo?" The white cat's tone was not welcoming.

"How did you—"

"I pick up a lot of things. I knew an Apollo once, but I thought him long out of business, so to speak. Imagine my surprise, when someone of that name appears out of the blue and stirs up some of our local citizens. Stirring them into a bit of a frenzy, in fact. Creating discord where we could do with a bit of harmony." He cocked his head to one side and paused, to see how his visitor would react. Detecting no response, he went on. "So, the first question on my mind is why now and why here? What is your little game? Please enlighten me. I'm all ears." He glanced to the side, as if to indicate the city below. "Mostly, we've enjoyed stability among our fractious little communities for years, barring the occasional territorial skirmish, soon forgotten. But as soon as you arrive, they are up in arms." The blue eyes narrowed. "So, forgive me for asking, but what is the purpose of this?" He took a step closer, his voice nearer to a hiss. "If you are here to claim territory, why now, and why so few followers? If that is your game, there is space on the fringes of the city. It is foolhardy indeed to take on the most fearsome group of all." Another pause; further scrutiny. Apollo remained statue-still. "If territory is not your game, then what are you doing here? One who disappeared so long ago his name is but an echo in the distant hills. A whisper in the grass. A label without meaning. Long dead." Hermes' voice was barely audible.

Apollo said nothing. Behind his frustration, he was trying to work out how this superior-sounding creature knew his name, let alone what he had been doing in this forsaken city. Was this blue-eyed monster an ally of the big bully of a gang leader and his bunch of thugs? Was it a trap? He crouched, muscles tensed and ready to fight. Taking down the smug white cat would be a pleasure. His only regret was all the wasted effort in getting up to this miserable eyrie. He decided on one last appeal to reason before he pounced.

"My affairs are no concern of yours, and I will not explain myself to you. I merely came here seeking information." He took a step forwards, eyes blazing.

Hermes looked aside, affecting a faint air of amusement. "Come, dear fellow. Information? You've got to do better than that. It's a long, tiring climb to get here, and you expect me to believe it was just so you could ask a couple of questions? If it's fortune tellers you're after, I'd try elsewhere."

"If it was fortune telling I sought, I wouldn't need to come here. What need have I for the pronouncements of Oracles?" Another step. His voice was a barely audible growl now. He was nearly within striking distance. The white cat stood his ground, as if hardly noticing. He seemed to enjoy goading his visitor.

"If it's riches you're after, I regret to inform you that the streets are really not paved with gold. You'd be better off staying in the country. Live your simple life. Leave the big city to us." He glanced over his shoulder towards his companions, all of whom were now watching intently. "Life must be a lot more straightforward for the rustics, up on their hillsides up north, eh? Perhaps the mosquitos have sucked up their brains along with their blood?"

Apollo's anger boiled to the surface. He took another step forwards until he stood nose to nose with the white cat. Whether it was the light of the sun setting behind him or his air of outrage, he seemed to loom larger, and his golden eyes were kindled to fury, his voice a low growl at the back of his throat, his words steeped in disdain. "This is the least welcoming city I've ever visited, and I don't much care for it. You may enjoy your petty muckraking in this cesspit, but I'm close to the end of my tether, and right now, harmonious relations between its inhabitants are the least of my concerns. They seem to have forgotten even the most basic rules of hospitality. I will pursue my quest with or without you. If you are unwilling to help, just say so and stay out of my way. I won't ask twice."

To his satisfaction, Hermes backed away ever so slightly.

"I too, have memories. Imperfect they may be, but to my recollection, Hermes was once known to be close to my father, and an honest go-between among us. How much has changed?"

Nose to nose, the two cats glared at each other, before Hermes lowered his eyes and changed his tone. "Son of Zeus," he said with a minute bow of his head. "Welcome. Please accept an apology for my greeting and apparent lack of manners. But with strange events occurring in our city recently, I needed to be sure you were who you said you were." He looked up, a searching look on his face. "My followers and I will be delighted to assist you as we may."

Apollo's host suddenly became business-like and friendly. "First things first, you must be hungry and thirsty after your climb. We can do something about that, at least. Follow me." He turned and led the way across the small summit to the back of the café.

Ready to fight one instant and treated as an honoured

guest the next, Apollo stood watching him while the tension eased from his body. He exhaled, then with a suspicious glance around, followed his host. What had been the purpose of the whole charade? Hermes' moods appeared to change more quickly than the weather. A dim recollection came to mind: his host enjoyed nothing more than verbal jousting. That, and thievery. He would have to keep his wits about him. In the distance, a few of the assembled cats rose and strode towards them with languid grace. The others resumed their business.

It reminded Apollo of home. Here, as in Delphi, some well-intentioned human had placed several large feeding and drinking bowls out in a quiet space behind the restaurant. It was out of sight of the human visitors and secluded. As with the other places where cats lived wild, this was a supplement to their main diet; it didn't negate all begging at the tables on the terrace, but it was good to have as a back-up. Hermes was right, Apollo was starving and thirsty after his long, hot climb. Out of respect, the other cats gave him some space; no one tried to jostle or crowd him out as they might have done back home.

Eventually, he stepped back. Hermes had been observing him for a while from a short distance. Saying nothing, he turned around again and sauntered across the rugged hilltop, away from the buildings. He stopped on the top of a raised, flat-topped boulder and hunched down. Apollo joined him. As he was settling, he caught sight of the view. Laid out before and below him was an enormous city, its expanse far exceeding anything he'd ever seen. The scale was daunting. In every direction buildings and streets covered the flatter ground as far as he could see, even down to the distant ocean. They also climbed up the slopes of hills far away.

Apollo raised his nose and caught the faint scent of salt water on the air. Somewhere out there was Delos, a name whose significance hovered on the edge of his memory, tantalisingly out of reach. As the sun set, lights came on, illuminating the entire vista and lending a magical air to the scene below the darkening purple sky. Above their heads, appearing almost close enough to touch, the first stars twinkled. But there was no avoiding the jewel in the crown of this vista. His eye was drawn to the southwest, to the structure on the spectacular cliff, looking like a mighty stone ship sailing on a sea of earth, stone and concrete. Its sheer sides were bathed in light from below, and on its flat deck was the most magnificent colonnaded temple Apollo had ever seen. He stared at it, lost in thought. Hermes followed his gaze.

"The Acropolis," Hermes told him, "and the Parthenon. Stunning, isn't it? Even now."

"It's wonderful." The sight brought back emotions he'd thought long gone.

"Yes, it is quite something," Hermes continued, now playing the role of tour guide. "It's looking rather battered, these days, but... Well, you probably know..." He trailed off.

Apollo glanced across at him but said nothing more. They crouched for a while in silence.

"I never believed for an instant that you came here purely to stir up the locals," said Hermes. "So, please tell me. Why are you *really* here?" In the light of a gibbous moon rising overhead, the white cat's fur gave off a soft silver glow.

Apollo sighed and focused his thoughts.

"We came here to rescue our friend, kidnapped from our home a few days ago. We think humans brought her here. At least that's what the Oracle indicated." As he was speaking, he tried to work out how long had passed. This was the third evening since Olympia had been snatched. They had been in Athens for less than seventy-two hours. It seemed a lot longer.

"'We'?"

"My friends, Daphne and Jason, accompanied me."

Apollo looked down at the carpet of lights. "Until we got separated."

Where had they got to? He'd hoped they would have arrived here before him. Were they safe? Was Daphne alright?

Apollo told the story of Olympia's kidnap, Pythia's prophecy and their vow to find her. He recounted their confrontation with the Botrys gang. He skipped the detail of his own encounter with the Oracle, and his visit to Hecate and the chase that led him there. Hermes said nothing until Apollo had finished.

"I'm not sure why Achelois sent you to me rather than straight to the Agora," he mused. "Unless she thought I might have some... influence," he added softly to himself. There was another long pause. The air grew chillier. "When did you say she left you? It's taken you a while to get here."

"I'm new to the city. I got lost."

"Well," he said, standing up and stretching. "If you'll forgive me, I've got a few things to attend to, so I'll leave you in the capable paws of one of my companions who will look after you. See you in the morning." With that, he set off into the shadows and was gone.

A smaller, darker-coloured cat appeared. "I'm Pandrosus," she said. "Let me show you where we sleep." She led Apollo to a small hollow just below the summit rocks. There was a dip in the ground, protected by rocks on three sides, with a gap facing trees on the other. Several cats were curled up together, sleeping or trying to. They included mothers and kittens of varying sizes, snuggling for warmth, and older cats as well. The sight brought him a pang of homesickness. Far away, but under the same stars. A couple of animals moved aside to make room for him, and he settled down, content in their midst.

· · ·

Standing on the north-facing side of the hill, Hermes pondered his next move. He called several of his disciples to him, issuing instructions. Without speaking they bowed their heads in acknowledgement, and departed, swift and sure-footed in the night, moving unseen on their own secret paths across the city to seek contacts and gather news.

Hermes himself set off north. He wanted to check out a couple of things for himself before deciding his next moves.

CHAPTER 29
CAPTURED

The sweet and heavy aroma of whatever was in the bag faded. Daphne struggled to make sense of what had happened. She'd experienced nothing like this before. Amid the drowsy after-effects was a dim awareness of having behaved in a strange and undignified manner. Had she really snarled and swiped at the old human, with all claws bared? It was as if her normal self had been possessed for a time, or some wild inner spirit released. The thought was disturbing. For the first time in her life, she felt a little dirty; shredded and exposed. Had those swipes been her real self?

She shuddered a little, placed a paw over her eyes and tried to get back to sleep. But the thoughts kept on cascading through her brain, and there, just across the rug, was the little aromatic bag of herbaceous temptation that had started it all.

Daphne rolled over. Sleep was impossible; she had to have more.

She rose to her feet, gave a half-hearted stretch and fixed her stare on the bag. What was in it? Whatever it was, it was wonderful. It made her forget everything. It made her happy

No, that wasn't an adequate word: blissful maybe? Euphoric? It made the world go away, and that was so nice.

Stopping short, she circled to one side, gave it a tentative poke with her paw, then hooked it with an unfurled claw, grabbing with renewed passion, smothering her nostrils and breathing in the heady aroma once more. For the next half hour, she was lost.

The day wore on and the pattern repeated itself: a light sleep or snooze disturbed by feelings of guilt that she couldn't quite pin down, punctuated by a love-in with those marvellous herbs, rolling over and over and forgetting all pretence of dignity. As the day wore on, the scent lost some of its power, and a little mental clarity returned.

"Olympia! What have I done?" In an instant, remorse took hold, gnawing at her mind. How much time had she lost? How could she have allowed herself to be captured so easily? What a fool she'd been.

She berated herself for her weakness; but that took her no further forward. So she chastised herself, instead, for being unable to come up with an escape plan. Escape was vital in order to mount a rescue, but it would mean leaving the little heady-scented bag of loveliness behind.

She looked at it wistfully. Could she take it with her? A picture formed in her mind of walking through the city, with her precious bag in her mouth. But it would be futile. She would be a target for every no-good thug and ruffian in this part of town, and they wouldn't be able to believe their luck. It would tempt even the soft, stupid domesticated pets to have a go. It would be madness. There were no hiding places out there that would screen her prize from the super-sensed nostrils of envious fellow felines, and they would stop at nothing to steal it from her.

Daphne collected her thoughts once more and focused on the matter of breaking out of the apartment.

She reviewed her situation. The apartment had one main

door and a second leading out to the balcony, which appeared to be permanently shut. She had arrived through a window from that balcony, but it too was closed, as were all the windows apart from one in the bedroom, which was only open a crack and far too narrow to squeeze through. So far, she had only seen the human come and go through the main door. So that seemed the most likely way to escape.

She would keep it under close watch. Her inexperience with humans was a problem. When in groups, they seemed to act similarly, but by themselves, they appeared more erratic and unpredictable. She had no idea what her guard was thinking, or likely to do next. The only course of action she could think of was to keep her under observation and be ready to act fast at the first opportunity.

A chair in the hall provided excellent cover. She should start right now; make this her base and keep watch. But it was quiet at the moment. So… was there time for a little more fun with the little bag of what she'd come to call *Blissfulness* first? She gave it a covetous look, then pounced on it once more.

Several hours passed before Daphne got her opportunity. In the late afternoon, a buzzer sounded, making her jump. She looked around for the source of the noise but couldn't see anything moving. It sounded again, and this time she heard movement from the living room behind her. The elderly human laboriously clambered out of its armchair and approached the door. She opened it a crack and spoke to someone on the other side. Daphne tensed, ready to move, but the door wasn't wide enough open yet.

She was in luck. The old woman opened the door wider to receive a parcel from a delivery man. This was her chance.

She made a bolt for the gap, catching the old woman by surprise. The delivery man was first to spot her and moved a leg to block her path. But, as he was waiting for a signature, he was neither quick nor decisive.

With a cry of dismay, the householder reached down and

tried to grab Daphne as she darted past. But she was far too slow. Daphne swerved past the legs and out into the stairwell, scrabbling for grip on the tiled floor. She spun away from the hands reaching towards her and shot off down the stairs; reckless, but desperate to escape.

At the ground floor, she came across another door; this was unexpected and unwelcome. Daphne glanced over her shoulder. How long before they arrived?

Both humans thundered down the stairs towards her. Frantically, she looked for a hiding place, zig-zagging from corner to corner of the small vestibule, but to no avail. The door was the only way out.

For the second time in a few minutes, fortune favoured her. Another resident arrived. He turned his key in the lock and opened the door to enter, but was greeted by a desperate animal flashing past him at escape velocity, followed by an out-of-breath neighbour and courier.

In her desperation, Daphne misjudged her trajectory, and received a glancing blow from the new resident's leg which sent her sideways into the frame of the doorway. But she was through, down onto the street and into the daylight. Blinded by the bright sun, she turned up the street and ran as fast as she could. The shouts behind her faded, and she took refuge under a car to recover. The ribs on her right side were sore where she had hit the door frame, but nothing seemed to be broken.

Her breathing soon returned to normal; her emotions took a little longer to stabilise. Elation at having escaped; satisfaction at being back on her rescue mission; anguish at having to abandon her lovely, glorious bag of Blissfulness.

Daphne shook her head and scratched an ear, trying to dislodge negative thoughts. She focused on what to do next. She had lost her bearings while she'd been in the apartment, and was no longer sure of the way.

I was looking for a tall hill.

Hermes lives on a hilltop.

Beneath the vehicle, her view was limited. But she had hope.

The street she sat on sloped upwards, and she was near the top. Peering ahead, it seemed to end in a park. The summit of a hill, perhaps? Could this be the place? At least it would allow her to get a proper view of her surroundings and find her bearings.

She ventured out and prowled up to the park, hopping through a gap in the fence. Amid trees and vegetation again, she felt better. Above her, the ground rose to a rocky knoll. Her heart leapt in anticipation; was this the place where Hermes lived? She set off to explore but soon realised there was no feline community here. There was, however, a trail to follow through the trees. But when she reached the top, her heart sank. Daphne was in the middle of a small patch of vegetation surrounded by endless streets and houses in all directions. She could see several areas of raised ground on the horizon, but much closer than these, and towering above her, was a far larger, steeper hill which dominated the view.

Daphne sat down, deflated. How could she have missed it? Lycabettus, if that was indeed her destination, was not too far away, but looked difficult to climb. Getting up there would take exhausting, and every minute lost was precious.

She had little time to dwell on the matter. Two cats emerged from the foliage behind her and strode in her direction. Birds chattered a warning in the trees nearby, but before she had time to think, both creatures sprang upon her and knocked her to the ground. Teeth and claws flashed, as the three of them rolled and scrabbled in the dust.

Daphne was still tender from her earlier escape and hadn't been in the best shape to start with. She couldn't free herself from her assailants. One of them had her by the throat, and she struggled to breathe. The only upside was that he blocked some of his companion's blows.

Daphne punched with her hind legs for all she was worth. But her opponents were strong and streetwise, and she couldn't break free. She felt herself weakening, and she couldn't breathe at all now.

Her prospects looked bleak, but her enemies stopped their attack and let go. They didn't back away, but loomed above her. Daphne lay on her side, panting, while her enemies stared down.

"Better not kill her," one of them said.

"Not yet, at any rate," her companion agreed. "We'd better take her to the boss. For some proper questioning."

Daphne's heart sank. She should have stayed with her Blissfulness.

"On your feet!" they commanded.

Daphne struggled to get up. There was a deep gash on her right foreleg, blood seeping into her fur, and vicious bite marks peppered her neck. But she was still just about in one piece. Limping and in pain, she managed to hobble down the slope between her captors. There was no chance of escape.

They led her down the far side of the knoll, away from Lycabettus. In the distance, camouflaged behind low-growing shrubs, a grey-and-white cat stood up and watched the departing trio for a moment. He stretched, then ambled downhill in the opposite direction.

Their base was a disused warehouse. It was the largest enclosed space Daphne had ever seen. Tall shelving units in long rows – empty of goods – covered half the floor, and in the remaining space, several large wooden pallets littered the ground. An old fork-lift truck sat in one corner.

She'd never seen a place like this before. Amid the pallets was an open space where she sat, nervous and trembling. Surrounding her on the ground and atop the jumble of wood was a ring of the meanest-looking cats she had ever seen.

Head bowed, and in considerable pain from her various wounds, she closed her eyes and tried to pretend none of it was real. The walk from the park, in the company of her two tormentors, had been hard. Several times she stumbled and almost collapsed, only to receive a nasty nip from her captors. All the time they complained about her "playing up", appearing to relish their sadistic little game.

After a while she heard the faint pad of footsteps and looked up to see an enormous cat approaching with purpose from the opposite end of the warehouse, his eyes fixed on her. He was taller at the shoulder than any cat she'd seen, apart from the big brute they'd come across the other night. Not as muscular, perhaps, but intimidating. He appeared much better groomed as well, but his face had a mean pinched look, and his eyes were close together.

He halted just in front of her, gave her a dismissive look, then paced back and forth, as if trying to decide his approach.

Daphne closed her eyes. Her head throbbed, her multitude of cuts stung and she ached all over. She just wanted the ordeal to end. None of the surrounding cats displayed the slightest sympathy; in fact, quite the opposite.

The big cat walked up to his captive and cuffed her across the side of her head. Her eyes still on the floor, Daphne realised she should be grateful he'd kept his claws sheathed, but her already aching head rang with the blow. Had he dislocated her jaw?

The big cat raised his voice. "Who are you?"

"Daphne." Her small voice died in the large open space. He moved closer.

"Don't be shy. Speak up!"

"I'm called Daphne," she answered, raising her head, but not quite looking him in the eye. Instead, she glanced at the ring of leering faces.

"And who might you be working for, Daphne? If that is indeed your actual name." He strode back and forth in front of his captive like a caged tiger, unable to sit still. Daphne felt faint and swayed slightly but tried to keep her eyes on him.

She was also a little confused; what else would anyone call her?

"I don't work for anyone," she replied. "And, anyway. Who are you? Who do *you* work for?"

One of the surrounding cats spoke up. "You are addressing Zelus. Leader of the Gizi gang."

Zelus turned to glare at his follower, who retreated into the crowd. He focused back on Daphne. "Come now. No need to lie." The pinched face moved closer, and Daphne shrunk back as if she'd been struck. She tried to avoid his stare.

"I'm not lying," she stuttered. "I'm from Delphi. I live there." How could they not believe her? Why were these animals so cruel? What did they want her to say?

Zelus resumed his stalking back and forth. "Let me recount the facts," he said, looking at his audience, as if making a case before a jury. "You were found not an hour ago, deep in Gizi territory, staking out our land and no doubt hoping to glean information about our movements." He flashed her a glance. "Why would someone like you be in a place like that? I suggest you were planning to meet up with a contact, perhaps to find out more about us?" He looked her full in the face again, his voice now lower and more danger-ous. "You wouldn't be the first of your order to try."

There was a pause. Daphne looked round in confusion. What "order"? Why all this nonsense about spying?

"Now," continued Zelus, "we can be reasonable about this. We can do it the civilised way, where you tell me every-thing you know about your operation, or I can beat it out of you." He sounded perfectly calm; chillingly so. After a brief pause to let his threat percolate, he continued. "So, just to reit-erate. My operatives intercepted you before you could meet up with your usual contact in that neighbourhood." He gave Daphne's captors a meaningful stare. "They should have waited until you made contact, but..." He turned back to Daphne, brisk and business-like once more. "In the circumstances, I can understand their excitement. Now, here's what you have to do. Start talking. I want names, faces, fur colouring and distinguishing marks. Addresses, and full disclosure about who or what was your next target. And above all, how much does *she* know?" He loomed over her, huge and menacing.

Daphne's mind was racing. How could she be in this position? She was a straightforward animal. She'd been brought up to tell the truth, but the truth didn't interest this brute. He wanted conspiracies and lies. She groped around in her befuddled mind for a convincing story.

"I can't tell you. She… she'll kill me."

Zelus stepped back. "Who?" he demanded.

"Her Ladyship." Daphne played for time, thoughts whirling around her brain. "You know what she's like when she gets angry. She takes no prisoners." She warmed to her theme. "She sent me to find…" She groped for a name. "Alejandro. From the… from the…"

"From Strefi Hill Park!" Zelus thundered, finishing the sentence for her. "Keep going. What did you want him for?"

"He was supposed to help me find your base." She looked around. "We were going to stake it out. See where you went. That sort of thing…" Her voice trailed off.

The big cat said nothing. He narrowed his eyes and stared at her.

He wanted more.

In her scrambled brain, Daphne made connections. She must have unwittingly stumbled into their territory at just the wrong time. But who was this mysterious, powerful female they daren't name? A storyline formed in her head. She looked directly into her interrogator's face.

"She's obviously a little worried about you." Daphne stole a furtive glance around the assembled gang while Zelus absorbed this information. She pressed on. "Although I don't quite know why," she added, sounding dismissive.

She snapped her head around towards the gang leader again, just in time to receive another heavy blow. Daphne's vision blurred. She staggered but regained her balance. Zelus pushed his nose close to hers so she could taste his breath and feel it on her cheek.

"*Who?*" All semblance of coolness had dissipated. He was on edge, agitated, impatient. "Spit it out, damn you!"

"Hera," Daphne replied.

The gang leader's eyes widened, and he took a step back and sat down. Clearly, this was not the response he'd expected. The encircling cats, seeing his reaction, became a mite less smug about baiting their victim. Daphne, still in pain, dizzy and swaying, held her breath. Had she gone too far?

"Hera?" Zelus echoed. He looked stunned. Surely the Hera she knew couldn't have caused this reaction. Maybe he was thinking of someone else with the same name.

"But… she's not here," said Zelus. "She disappeared. Years ago. She doesn't exist anymore."

Daphne pressed home her advantage. Let him think what he liked. She would build a legend around the staid busy-body who liked nothing better than to poke her nose into everybody else's business.

"She does," she shouted, her voice small but clear in the big space. "I saw her just the other day. She's heard about you, and she's obviously worried enough to ask me to take a look. I don't know about any assassinations she's got planned, but she doesn't tell me everything, and it wouldn't surprise me if she's got some other agents on the case." She looked around the room. "They might be closer than you think. There might be someone here now, for all I know."

The surrounding gang members looked at one another and shuffled, uncomfortable at the thought. Their confidence was evaporating, and one or two looked distinctly nervous.

The atmosphere changed. Zelus regained his composure.

He addressed Daphne again, but more cautiously now, as if questioning an equal rather than intimidating a spy.

"This is Athena's city. What business does Hera have here?"

Daphne looked him in the eye. "Perhaps they're in league," she said. "Maybe they're working together, and if they are, you wouldn't want to get on the wrong side of her."

How had he heard about Hera? And why was he so scared of her? Was there another Hera in these parts? A really, really angry one?

"Don't think this is over," Zelus warned as he loomed over her. But the menace had left his voice. "Tomorrow you're coming with us as our prisoner. Try any funny business and we'll kill you on the spot. Got it? Assuming you survive, we will continue our little chat later, until I get to the bottom of your schemes." He turned to face her captors. "Guard her carefully and don't let her out of your sight."

CHAPTER 30
OUT AND ABOUT

Travelling by secret paths known only to himself, Hermes soon arrived at the Botrys factory. In one corner of the largest hall of the former winery, Kratos was in conversation with his most trusted subordinates, briefing them on recent discussions with his brother, Zelus. Hermes held back for a moment, listening, then strolled around the corner and into their midst.

"Who let you in?" Kratos rounded on him, annoyed and alarmed that yet another intruder had walked past his sentries without being spotted or challenged. This one, at least, had a history of turning up when least wanted.

"Is that how you welcome me? Patron of thieves and tricksters and the one who's looked after your back all these years? You should watch your tone."

Kratos tensed, but held his tongue.

Hermes lowered his voice and adopted a less confrontational manner. "I'm just passing by and thought I'd see how you were getting on. What's the news from Botrys?" He circled the assembled animals, and peered into the shadows beneath the trees, as if this were his first visit. As he strolled, he noted the gang members present. Beams of moonlight pierced the canopy of trees, segmenting the floor into pools of silver and shade. His circuit complete, the white cat sat down and washed his paws, as if it were the most natural thing in the world to do, here at the heart of the gang's headquarters.

Kratos scanned his followers, clearly annoyed to see them spellbound by the intruder's presence; they were watching as if hypnotised.

The fur on his back rose, and he shifted position slightly.

Hermes halted abruptly and stared directly at him. "Come on, Kratos. Spit it out. Keep quiet much longer and I might think you're trying to hide something."

The command in his voice drew gasps. Who could dare speak to the boss in such a manner?

"You should take care," said Kratos. "Your sense of humour might catch you out one day. You caught us by surprise, Hermes. We've become more wary of spies trying to infiltrate our base recently." He sounded uncharacteristically sulky.

"Spies?" said Hermes. "How exciting. But what do you have to hide?" He looked around once more, peering into the further corners of their den. Then his deep blue eyes returned to the gang leader.

Kratos stood and moved to a new position from where he could look down on his visitor.

"Three of them," piped Rea, unable to remain silent. "The little bleeders marched in here, bold as brass, a couple of nights ago."

Hermes turned to her in mock surprise. "What happened to them?" Another glance around. "Are they still here? You don't mean to tell me you let them go?" Now it was her turn to handle that stare. She squirmed in discomfort. He turned back to Kratos. "They must have been awfully big and strong." All those watching were transfixed, hardly daring to breathe. What would be their leader's response?

Kratos remained still, wildly thrashing his tail. "The interrogation was interrupted. If that human oaf of a night watchman hadn't come blundering in, they'd never have escaped."

"So, you never found what they were after then?" Hermes' voice was mild and disarming once more. He looked around at the assembly, but no one volunteered an answer. "Anyone?"

Rea spoke again. "Said they were looking for a pal."

"Just a cover story," said Kratos. "We know they must have been after something, coming out all this way. It is clear that they must have been sent by Her Ladyship. It's another sign of her meddling. Testing our defences and checking our strength. She's always hated us. Can't bear the thought of someone in this city having just as much clout as her. Maybe more."

Hermes tilted his head, scrutinising him. "Clout? What clout?"

"You must know how few worshippers she has. My cult is growing. The number who worship me are growing all the time, and we become more powerful by the month. What you see here is but a fraction of our strength."

"Worshippers?"

Kratos cast an eye at his followers. "Yes, worshippers. They bow to me. Everything they do is at my behest." He glanced in Hermes' direction. "I guess you are not so well supported. You seem to have forgotten about the old ways."

Hermes pondered. "No, I've never placed much importance on numbers. I'm only interested in those who might cleave to me of their own free will. Who seek me out for their own reasons. I never coerce anyone."

Kratos simmered. "Esoteric nonsense. You should try living in the real world for a change. Here, in return for their service, they receive support, companionship, a combined purpose."

"What purpose?" The intrusion was sharp.

"They do as I tell them."

"Is free will a thing of the past?"

"You can have as much free will as you like, but will it fill your belly?"

The two of them exchanged tense looks; any pretence of cordiality was long gone.

Hermes broke the silence. "And what have you done about them, these 'spies'?"

"They've become the most wanted animals in Athens. They'll be found and dealt with soon enough. You can count on it."

The piercing blue eyes were at their most intense. "So how come the ginger one came to visit me this evening?"

Kratos blinked, clearly caught out by the news. He recovered quickly. "She must rate him highly. Or she's desperately short of alternative sleuths. Perhaps she thinks you're going to join us?" It sounded lame. What threat could Hermes be to Athena? The thought of them battling each other was laughable.

"You'd be better off keeping me out of it," Hermes said. "I've got problems enough without having to worry about Athena."

"What did you do with him, then?"

"I have done nothing yet," Hermes hissed. "My people are guarding him while I try to find out what his little game is, and if he is who he claims to be."

Kratos scoffed. "Who does he claim to be? He's clearly one of Athena's agents. What other explanation is there?"

Hermes gave him a sidelong glance. "I'm not yet certain he isn't her spy. From what you've told me, that looks the more likely option. But his story doesn't fit the assumption. Not completely. If he is her poodle, then what is she trying to achieve by sending him to me?" He paused. When he continued, he sounded more reflective. "The alternative is that if she isn't his master, then what is his game, and how has he tied you to me? I'm not convinced he would have plans of his own. He doesn't look bright enough. But he must be in league with someone." Hermes looked around at the assembled animals. He changed tack. "What about the other two? You must have been able to nab one of them?"

"They were a slippery little bunch," Rea admitted.

Hermes persisted. "Well, where are they? What has become of them?"

"Do you think they work for one of the other gangs?" Yannis asked. "They didn't look it. Too weedy by half. Too young, too pretty, not streetwise. They didn't look like fighters."

"Nah, they work for Her Ladyship, I'm certain of it," snarled Rea, unable to keep the venom from her voice. "They'll be heading back there. No doubt about it."

Hermes watched their debate with amusement.

"Enough!" Kratos gave his children a warning look. "We will track them down, and deal with them."

Hermes persisted. "Let's assume they were working for her. What could they have found out?"

"Might have noticed we're below strength," Yannis chipped in. Kratos glared at him.

"What do you mean by 'below strength'?" asked Hermes.

"Snatchers," Rea spat. She also received a warning look from her father. From the corner of his eye he could see Hermes was studying every interaction.

"Snatchers?"

Kratos looked at him, then the other two. "Some of our number have disappeared."

"Might they have just deserted you?" Hermes asked.

"No."

"And you think Athena's behind it, somehow?"

Kratos looked aside. "Consider the alternatives? Who else would it be? We have good relations with the other gangs in the district. They're too scared to try and funny business," he growled. "No, it's her alright. She is deliberately weakening us. Trying to get into their heads." He looked at the cats nearby. Finally he returned Hermes' stare. "She's deliberately trying to spread terror. We can't just wait and be picked off, one by one. We have to act. Even you can see that."

"I know she doesn't like you, but isn't it a bit of a stretch to suggest she is systematically wiping you out? We both know Athena. It's not her style."

"Yes, I'm saying she took them. She's always hated us. She'd like nothing better than to get rid of us. Erase us, just as she has the others. Ever since that futile transformation she persuaded us to undergo, things have gone wrong. Almost everyone has disappeared. They're probably dead. Except her. She hangs around like a bad smell. What is she planning? What's her big idea? Enough is enough." He paced, tail thrashing. "She thinks we're a pest. A menace to her friends in high places. The humans. I've heard she's always sucking up to them. That's the word on the street. She tells them we carry diseases, make the place look untidy, breed too fast. She wants us eradicated. Pest control, they call it. The disappearances are just the start."

"So, you believe she's in league with humans to destroy you? And what evidence do you have?"

"She's up to something. Everyone knows it. What is it she's so secretive about down there in the centre? Her followers are preventing anyone getting too close."

"What do you intend to do about it?" said Hermes.

Kratos said nothing.

"Do your siblings feel the same way?"

Still, Kratos refused to be drawn.

"We march on the Plaka!" Rea announced, unable to hide the pride in her voice. "We've got the numbers."

"Is Zelus going to help?"

"We don't need him or his gang," Kratos replied.

"What about Bia?"

"Says she's not interested."

"Are you sure she can't help?" Hermes persisted.

"She's a turncoat. A splitter. Just in it for herself. The only good thing is that she hates the Agora crowd as much as we do."

Hermes sat still, absorbing this news. "Still, I hear she talks to your brother now and then." He looked away, keeping Kratos in his peripheral vision.

"Told you that, did he? He wouldn't go behind my back. Wouldn't dare."

"It sounds to me like you chat quite a lot."

Kratos clamped his jaw shut, fuming.

The white cat continued. "So, you've made your frustration clear. When are you planning this raid?"

Kratos didn't answer.

"And Ares is going to sit back and let you do all this?"

"He's not around anymore," said Yannis. "Gone AWOL. Disappeared. Lost the plot. Done a runner. Departed the neighbourhood." Having run out of insults, he pawed the ground in delight. "He must have realised he's past it now. And with that slob gone, they've no more big hitters. They're sitting ducks."

Kratos glared at him, and he shut up.

"It'll all be ours," said Rea.

"You're not expecting any resistance from the Agora?"

Rea continued. "She might try, but there are so few of them, and they're all better at talking than fighting. She gets the humans to do her work for her, and they won't want to get their hands dirty chasing us all around the tourist hotspots down in the centre. As long as we do the business nice and quick, and keep a low profile, they'll be happy enough." She glanced at the boss, caught his body language and clamped her mouth shut.

"What about Ares' sons?"

There was a pause while the gang members looked from one to another.

"Sons?" said Kratos. "What sons? I don't care how many kittens he's spawned. They'll all be feeble without their old man. They won't be a match for street fighters like us. There'll be no escape."

"Good luck in organising your troop," said Hermes, mildly. "You sound confident that all of your people will behave exactly as you want."

"They have no choice," Kratos growled. "As I said, free will has not afflicted us in these parts. They know what's good for them. They do what I tell them."

"It sounds like you've got it all covered then," said Hermes. He got to his feet again.

"What are you going to do with him?" asked Kratos as an afterthought.

"Ah, yes. Our ginger friend." Hermes sounded unconcerned. "I'm not the violent type. I might send him off on a wild goose chase or something. Or maybe I can arrange for him to fall into your clutches sometime. If you come across him wandering into your path somewhere in the centre of town, think of it as a little gift."

He ambled through a gap in the walls, turned a corner and disappeared out of sight. Above, out of the corner of his eye, he sensed motion. He looked up and spotted the dark shape of an owl rising against the moonlit sky.

Hermes' next port of call was a disused warehouse in the district of Gizi. Zelus and his leadership team sat in a circle discussing the findings from the prisoner's interrogation. They had bundled her to the back of the warehouse, behind the forklift, with guards keeping a constant watch.

Hermes strode in, purposeful and business-like.

It was time to go fishing; he dangled a speculative hook.

"I gather you're going to support the Botrys gang's little excursion," he announced by way of greeting, walking towards them and inspecting his surroundings, as if visiting for the first time.

"Ah," said Zelus. "You'll have been chatting with my dear esteemed brother. What's he been telling you? He's always had an issue with confidentiality."

"As long as he doesn't spill the beans to the authorities," squeaked Nestor. "He's desperate for our help." Zelus shot him a look and he shut up.

Hermes ignored the Gizi gang boss and his garrulous little subordinate, but continued strolling for a while. He inspected the tall shelving units and sniffed the air, then approached them and stopped.

"He says he doesn't need you," he said, addressing Zelus as if the others weren't there. "Thinks his mob can manage by themselves, deal with Athena and all, and then, if you turn up, play you off against Bia and her south-siders. I think he's persuaded her to mount a flanking operation via Hadrian's Arch. I'd say he's even divided the centre up between them. She can keep most of the Plaka while he takes Monastiraki and the Agora, and whatever's found up there."

Zelus sat immobile, his tail twitching. "And how come you know all of this?"

Hermes looked around once more, taking his time before replying. "I get around a bit. I like to keep an ear to the ground, see what's going on. I don't like it when things become unbalanced. That could be dangerous. I'm sure you agree? This current plan seems a little unfair, if you've already got some sort of arrangement in place." He shot Zelus a direct look. "Of course, it's none of my business, and perhaps you're perfectly happy here. You have a nice territory, after all. Best quarter of the city. Apart from the centre, of course." He tilted his head, his look turning sly. "You never know. Maybe I can help with your strategic planning, offer advice. We can do some brainstorming together. You can bounce some ideas off me. That sort of thing?"

Zelus stared at him.

"Kratos has always been a troubled soul," Hermes continued in confidential tones. "I often think he seems a little…" He paused, considering his choice of words. "Unhinged. He's got a real flea in his fur about Her Ladyship, of course. Well…" He gave the assembled gang members a conspiratorial look. "We all have. She's never been the easiest to get on with, has she? But this time it's different. I detect a genuine animosity. More than any other time I've spoken to him. He's really out to get her, and he thinks she's got something of value he can use."

"Like what?" Zelus bent his head forwards, focusing on Hermes' left ear.

Hermes sat upright, pleased to have such an attentive audience. "I don't know yet, but whatever it is, Kratos wants it badly. Badly enough to first ask for your help and then try to double-cross you, or at least use you as a distraction while he goes searching himself." He stopped a while for effect and then continued in convivial tones. "Between you and me, I'm surprised he hasn't mentioned it by now. I mean, it seems so important to him, and you are family. Of course, maybe it's just too precious to share. He must want to keep it for himself. Whatever it is." He raised a forepaw and started cleaning between the toes.

"The scumbag never mentioned Bia." Zelus' voice trembled with suppressed anger. "If he thinks we're going to do all the dirty work against those fat wasters in the Plaka, while he gets all the treats up in the Agora…" He left the sentence unfinished, his volume rising in unison with his feelings. "He'll get nowhere without us. We will not let him collect his treasure and keep all the best pickings."

Hermes paused his manicure. "Quite," he said, and settled down, folding his front paws together. He surveyed the group. There were around a dozen cats present, but at this hour, many more would be out on errands and missions, causing mischief, hunting rodents or hapless birds, stealing trinkets and intimidating house cats. All to add to the legend and influence of Zelus, who regarded himself, and not his brother, as the leading gangster in north Athens.

"You need to take care and watch out. That's all I'm saying. You know what families can be like. Sibling rivalry and so on. But blood is thicker than water, and all that..." Hermes paused, lowering his voice so that only the two of them could hear. "If you have to act alone, have you sufficient strength to pull it off?"

"Of course we have." Zelus sounded calmer once more; back in control, confident. "What he has in brawn, he lacks in finesse, and he's far too cautious. He can't plan, and he cannot see the bigger picture. He might like to think he can act alone, but in reality, he needs us." He looked around proudly. "I've got plenty of muscle, and the meanest, sharpest claws in all the city. Think strategically, then act quickly and decisively. That's our approach. He's forever coming up with excuses to delay. He's all bluster. When it comes down to it, he won't do anything without us."

"We've lost a couple recently though," his second-in-command Demitrius ventured.

Hermes turned towards him. "Really?" His eyes widened in surprise.

"Oh, yes." Zelus cut across his deputy, his tail slashing out a warning. Demitrius and Hermes duly picked it up. "Just a couple. Nothing major."

"Five, according to my count," Denna piped up.

Zelus rounded on her. "I said nothing we can't handle."

"Five? Dear me," Hermes said. "That seems rather careless."

"Like I said, it won't affect us. We can take the Plaka

ourselves, without Kratos' dubious help." He tried to sound calm but couldn't help fidgeting under Hermes' scrutiny.

"What's the problem, then? Is it a lack of foresight holding you back, or is it because you don't have the balls?"

The other cats looked stunned; no one ever spoke to their leader like that.

Instantly, Zelus stood over Hermes, his eyes blazing. The white cat didn't move a muscle, maintaining his relaxed pose. "You tell me you're keen to get going and act decisively, but from where I'm sitting, you don't look to be taking the initiative at all. In fact, I'd say it looks like Kratos is calling the shots and you're just waiting for his instructions, like some tame little pet." He stared up at Zelus, unnerving the other animal, who turned full circle, trying to maintain his temper.

"You've got a nerve coming in here and saying that." He struggled to keep his voice level. "We have a plan. Jointly agreed. A pact between equal partners. He won't get anywhere without us. But I can act alone if I have to. I don't need him."

The white cat stood, taking the other cat by surprise. Zelus flinched a little. Hermes looked him full in the face, inching closer until their noses almost touched. His stare was hard as flint.

"It's nothing to me whether you pad along in his shadow, or take the lead. But, a little advice. Your ally's planning is more advanced than you think, and you'd better get wise to his agenda, or you'll just end up as his doormat. Someone to do the dirty work while he picks up the prizes. If he needs you at all, it's just to watch his back." He made to go, then turned back. "Oh, and better keep an eye out for interested third parties. There's more going on in this city than you know. It might be a good idea to look after any extra bargaining chips you've got. You never know when they might come in useful." His eyes flicked to the forklift truck in the corner of the warehouse.

Zelus stood transfixed and glowering. "What have they found at the Agora?" he asked in a quiet voice. Hermes backed up a pace.

"Well, isn't that the exciting thing? Nobody knows. Take the initiative and perhaps you'll be the first to find out."

CHAPTER 31
A NIGHT-TIME RAID

Bia hated being bounced into any sort of action, but she recognised this opportunity wouldn't last. A cloudy night was just what she wanted; nice and dark, no annoying patches of moonlight illuminating the place. She padded along quiet streets, using her intimate knowledge of central Athens to skirt the urban woodland and reach her destination without attracting the watchers' attention. She hugged the walls, and sought the darkest pools of night, one shadow among many.

Her route passed along quiet residential streets, avoiding major thoroughfares as much as possible. She was alone. This was a mission she trusted to no one else. If this thing fell into the wrong paws… She shivered at the thought. No, this was something she wanted for herself. To retrieve this sacred object from right under the nose of Her Snootiness would only add to her satisfaction.

If half the rumours Hermes had told her were true, it would be transformational. Once she mastered it, she would become the most powerful animal in the entire city.

The all-powerful Bia, Queen of Athens. They would all

have to bow down to her; she could order them to do whatever she liked.

She allowed herself to dream; wouldn't it be fun to get
Kratos to look after the little ones while she and the other
mums had a nice relaxing time away from all the mewling?
How about forcing Hermes to run a few errands on her behalf?
Maybe bring her some appealing trinkets. She could coerce
Athena to bring catnip toys to her. Yes, how marvellous to see
her crouching submissively and taking orders, watching but
unable to join in. *Delicious*. Her tail tingled with excitement.

As she turned a corner into Astiggos Street, Bia snapped
back into the present. She halted behind a chained-up stack of
restaurant tables and peered down the street.

Movement. A cat-shaped silhouette stepped out from a
doorway and stared back in her direction. Bia hesitated, then
moved forwards a couple of paces. The other cat raised, then
lowered her tail in recognition. Having to rely on support
from an enemy was annoying, but then again, her accomplice's betrayal was delicious. Athena would be beside
herself.

Bia sniffed around but could detect no signs of a trap. She
padded forwards once more, slowing as she approached her
contact. In the dark, she could sense the other animal's scent
rather than make out her features. The other cat bowed her
head in recognition and moved off, leading her along the
silent street.

They skirted a shuttered restaurant, where Herse stopped.
To their right was a metal fence at least two metres high. It
presented a difficult obstacle for a human, but with gaps
between and below the panels, it might as well not have been
there at all for a cat. Bia paused beside her companion.

Herse broke the silence. "This is where they are digging,"
she whispered. "The area Athena seems most interested in is
over there by that bank of earth." She pointed with her nose.

"Just in front of it is the place where they have been most busy. That's what she focuses on. The object must be just under the surface there. A good poke around should let you get it out, I'm sure."

"Do we know what it is?" Bia asked. Hermes had shared no information on its appearance.

Herse hesitated. "I'm not really sure, except Athena says she will recognise it when she sees it. It must look impressive. Or pretty. Beyond that, she hasn't said."

Bia thought for a while. Hermes had said it was an object of power, but was vague about the details. All these hints seemed to show something unusual. She had never paid much attention to the stuff humans dug up at these sites. Most of it seemed to be little pieces of pottery that they got excited about and put in museums, but she could never understand the attraction. Athena didn't seem too bothered about such stuff, either, so the thing she was looking for had to be something different. It was time to take a closer look. She moved forwards.

"Wait! One more thing," Herse whispered. Bia looked over her shoulder. "Be very careful down there. Athena has other followers around here on guard. They're looking outwards, rather than in, but if you make any noise, they are going to hear you and investigate. Be as quiet as you can."

It was a useful reminder. The gang leader turned back to the challenge and took a moment to plot a route through the ruins towards the area Herse had shown. It looked to be partially obscured from the railings on the street opposite, but in plain sight from her perspective. Hopefully, Herse's colleagues wouldn't be traipsing along this street tonight.

Bia squeezed under the fence and dropped to the lower ground level, which the archaeologists' work had uncovered. There were a few shallow pits, and between them the raised foundations of walls and the occasional column. Bia skirted around them as stealthily as possible, trying not to attract undue attention with sudden movements, should any passing animal take a look. Not that there should be any, if Herse was telling the truth.

She arrived at the spot her collaborator had indicated and took some time to sniff it out. Even in the low light, the most recently turned earth was clear to see. But she could detect no clues where anything precious might be buried. She walked back and forth, thinking.

What was that?

She sensed a slight vibration. The tips of her whiskers trembled, picking it up like radar. But the signal was so faint. Bia shook her head vigorously, to clear her thoughts, and stayed as still as possible. Yes, it was something; right on the limit of her detecting ability. A sensation she'd never previously experienced. It told her something different lay here, right under her paws.

She bowed her head towards the ground and felt it again, then she moved a metre away and detected... nothing. Her excitement mounted. This had to be the mystery object. She moved back to where the strange sensation was strongest and dug with her front paws, scrabbling urgently at the dirt, forgetting Herse's instruction to be quiet.

Her scratching attracted the attention of an owl perched in a tree overlooking the site. He swivelled his head, watched her for a moment, then returned to mouse-spotting.

After several frantic minutes, something glinted just in front of her nose. She stepped back to inspect it. It was still dark, but she had uncovered something promising. An embedded circular object, encrusted in earth. She scrabbled at the surrounding soil and extracted a muddy blob, placing it on the ground next to the hole she'd dug. Then she licked it, removing as much loose material as she could. It fell away easily.

Stepping back a short distance, Bia studied the item, tilting her head to see if a different angle would deliver new insight.

Something shiny glinted beneath the dirt at the side. Was it gold? Bia loved gold. Anything golden and shiny, in fact, as long as it was metallic. She could tell from its weight this was metal, not plastic.

She cleared more dirt away with her rasping tongue. The object repaid her effort, reflecting what little light was available, and from the way it shone Bia was sure it was gold.

If truth be told, it was a little small to be so special and so powerful, but it was ancient, judging from the funny pictures carved onto the surface. It appeared to be something important and rare; the treasure she had been searching for. It had to be.

She ran through the salient points in her mind. She'd found it in the place shown, and those strange vibrations had pinpointed its precise location in the ground. It was just below the surface, like Hermes and Herse had told her it would be, and where Athena was expecting it to be. True, it looked a little small for something so powerful, but size meant nothing of itself. She would work out how to use it once safely back at her base, where she had time.

It also had the advantage of being portable. She picked it up in her mouth, tasting earth mixed with metal, and looked around. No sign of watchers.

Bia plotted her way back to her entry point into the compound and jumped back to the base of the fence. On the other side, she found Herse. The Agora cat gave her a questioning look.

Bia dropped her precious object and cleared her throat. She looked up. "Found it," she said. "Now I'm going to disappear from your life, and most likely never see you again. You'd better not breathe a word."

"You don't need to worry on that score," Herse replied. She inspected the other cat's prize. "I'm hardly inclined to go bragging about this."

CHAPTER 32
NO FURTHER FORWARD

Once again Apollo had a restless night, disturbed by a dream so realistic he felt he was reliving it. This time he found himself among the olive groves on the slopes above the Corinthian Gulf, amid a chase that was nearing its end. He sensed the girl was near exhaustion, her energy spent. She would have to stop, make her stand. She was feisty, this one; no easy conquest. Not like the others who just melted in his arms. It was part of her appeal. He saw her slow and stop and turn to face him. He saw, with the strange clarity of dreamsight, the defiance in her eyes, her determination not to be a victim.

Evening was approaching, the shadows deepening beneath the trees, and he was elated. Would victory have ever tasted so sweet? She was above all others, the special one; the woman who would complete him. He had to have her. It was providence; a gift so sweet. None could equal her; not even Aphrodite herself. Inside his fantasy, his emotions felt vivid and real. His passion was unrestrained; he could almost taste her exquisite lips. Soon he would lose himself in the softness of her kiss and the sweetness of her breath. He would feel her lithe body, with its firm young breasts, press against his.

And there she was, in the middle of a small clearing; facing him, standing straight and breathing hard. Her hands were on her hips, she had a fierce look in her eye, and her chin raised in just the manner he found so enticing.

He stopped. Finally, she would be his; they would become one.

"You'll never have me. I defy you. I won't be just another of your conquests. I hate you!"

He paused, admiring her spirit, lusting for her even more. Everything about her was perfect and so different; beautiful and independent of mind, confident in manner. Her defiance just deepened his ardour, if it were possible.

His passion was unbounded; he would build her a palace, set her on a throne of jade encrusted with diamonds and precious stones. He would give her servants to wait upon her every need, and take a delight in pleasuring her in all the ways known to the divine, their union founded in bliss. Like a huntsman approaching a cornered animal, Apollo moved a step closer and held out his hand.

"Come on. We can take it slowly if you like. Just talk for a while." The honeyed words fell smoothly from his lips, and the corners of his mouth turned upward to a smile. It was an approach he'd used countless times before, but never with so much resting on it.

"Never!" It was a scream of resistance; a declaration of war. Behind it, she uttered a silent prayer to the god of the river, and was answered.

She closed her eyes. He stepped closer, reached out to take her wrist and grasped… a laurel branch.

"No!"

His anguished shout echoed in his mind, around the glade and beyond. He grimaced, staring wildly around him as if trying to spot an accomplice hiding in the shadows. Someone he could vent his rage upon; someone he could split asunder like matchwood.

But there was no one.

He turned back. The beautiful tree trembled before him. He glared at it, beside himself with frustration.

"Daughter of Peneus, at the last, all trees die and return to the earth," he snarled as if it could hear. "You can't hide in there and expect to escape me forever." He looked up at the sky, his arms flung wide, shouting in a mighty voice for all to hear, whether they were far across the gulf or high in the mountains. "This isn't over."

In this way, desire conquered reason.

He woke in the early light of a grey dawn, an hour before sunrise; still tired. Troubled thoughts scudded through his head like storm clouds before a gale. There was no chance of further sleep. Instead, he got up, picking his way past the sleeping cats around him, pausing at the edge of the clearing to stretch, then sniff the air. At this hour, before the city below awoke and resumed its daily business, the scent of the trees was strong.

First things first; he needed to scratch something. He decided upon a convenient tree trunk and let rip, with his ears tilted back. It was good to get some frustration out of his system. As he stopped he heard, nearby, the sound of scuffling feet. On a patch of dusty, pine-needle-covered ground, some of the little ones were playing and fighting. He watched them clumsily chase and tumble over one another, happy and carefree.

None of the adults were awake, so he settled down close by and immediately became part of the game; a climbing frame of sorts. Unafraid, they clambered over his flanks and along his back, trying to dislodge each other, while he twisted his head to check they were okay. One of them repeatedly tried to pounce and pin down his tail. It felt like home. No, he realised, it felt like home should have been, if he wasn't always so wrapped up in his own ever-circling thoughts. For half an hour he gave himself up to the antics of the kittens until relief arrived in the form of Pandrosus, the female who had led him to their sleeping place the previous evening.

With one last look, he left them to it, and set off to explore the hilltop, weaving a path between trees and rocks until he ended up near the spot where he and Hermes had chatted the previous evening.

As he surveyed the concrete jungle below, the enormity of the challenge struck Apollo afresh. The city seemed to go on forever. He couldn't count the number of buildings, so how could he find the one which held Olympia? And where was Daphne? And Jason?

He looked around again, needing to talk to his newfound friend, the crow, and saw it perched nearby. Apollo inclined his head slightly. The bird recognised the sign and set down in front of him.

"What can I do for you today, guv'nor?" it asked.

"I've got something else you might help me with. I'm looking for a friend." He paused. "More than one, actually." Indecision overwhelmed him; who should he look for first? An intense yearning for Daphne swamped all other thoughts. Surely it made sense to find her first, before they redoubled their efforts to rescue Olympia. While he hesitated, the bird remained still, eyeing him intently.

The words of the Oracle came back to him; finding Olympia was more important. He described her to the crow and told it what had happened. "I think she's somewhere down there, but I don't know where, and there may not be much time." It was embarrassing to have so little information to share. How was this bird going to be of any use with just the feeble notion that she was *somewhere down there*, in the enormous urban sprawl below? The crow listened. Briefing over, he made ready to depart.

"It'll be a challenge and no mistake, but I'll put the word

out and we'll see what turns up. There's quite a lot of us about." He spread his wings.

"How will you find me?" Apollo asked.

The bird looked over his shoulder as he took off.

"Don't worry. I'll spot you."

Apollo watched him go, still feeling torn. Had he made the right decision? Maybe he would find Olympia, but his worries for Daphne intensified. He couldn't bear to lose both of them. It was still just one bird within a huge urban sprawl. What chance did it have?

In the east, the sky was turning pink as the sun drew closer. Sunrise always lifted his mood. It was time to find something to eat and put his anxiety aside, at least for a while.

As he set off across the rocky plateau, Hermes approached.

"What did you find out?"

"Quite a bit," said the white cat, "as a matter of fact."

"So?" Apollo waited.

"All in good time, old chap. Shall we see if there's any food left in those bowls? I'm starving." He set off to the place where they had fed the previous evening. Apollo trailed after him, impatient for news.

They ate in silence for a few minutes, then Hermes led the way to a different perch with another spectacular view. As they walked, he nodded to another couple of cats to join them.

"I've asked Angelia and Pharis to join us," he told Apollo. "They've spent the night gathering such information as they can to help your search, as have I."

They sat. At first, no one spoke. Apollo's frustration mounted.

Hermes scanned the scene below, as if unsure how to start. Eventually, he broke the silence. "Perhaps I'd better give you a synopsis. I visited a few old haunts last night and found out more than I expected. Things are happening at a pace." He gave Apollo a sideways glance. "You've certainly set a few hares running, so to speak."

"Did you find out anything that would help me find Olympia?"

"Maybe, and maybe not. There is a lot of agitation among the gangs, and war seems inevitable. But while they are all busy with their preparations, several of their members have defected, or gone missing." He looked at the ginger cat. "Don't get your hopes up. Disappearances happen all the time. The leaders say it's not unusual. Just normal staff turnover. Bit inconvenient for them, but that's life. What is unusual is that, given it happens all the time, both of the gangs mentioned it." He turned to his two lieutenants. "Did either of you pick up anything?"

Angelia spoke first. "I went east. I spoke to Hecate at her hilltop retreat."

Apollo glanced at his companions. He didn't feel like having to explain his visit there; he hoped Hecate felt the same way.

"The old witch?" Hermes scoffed. "Remind me, where's she hanging out these days?"

"The Monastery of St John."

"She's changed. Has she converted?" He looked across to share the joke with Apollo, but the ginger cat gave no response.

Angelia continued. "It's a quiet spot. The priests are kind. They give her food. Nobody else seems to know that she's there."

"You're telling me. She's certainly slipped out of mind. Well, I suppose I ought to pay a visit sometime. Before she puts a spell on somebody."

Apollo's agitation was growing, and this irrelevant small talk was getting them nowhere. "Can't we just get on with it?

Did she have anything useful to say that might help us find Olympia?"

Angelia gathered her thoughts once more, staring into the middle distance. "She did her usual thing. 'The old ways are dying. No one has any respect for the elders anymore.'"

"She's heard nothing on the grapevine?" Hermes asked. "I suppose she's out of the loop, these days. Stuck out there. And she was never the life and soul of the party."

"There was one thing. She said that a great evil was afoot, and it threatened everybody, and some humans had begun to farm dogs."

Apollo and Hermes stared at her. Dog farming? What could she mean?

Something clicked in Hermes' memory. "Ah, yes. It might explain what Bia was on about." He gave a quick, selective summary of his earlier conversation. "They're keeping her awake barking all night." He grinned. "Anything else? No? Nothing to do with us, then. Seems like a bit of a dead end." He turned to Pharis. "What did you find?"

Pharis spoke more slowly. "I went south and talked to the gangs in Ymittos and Agios Dimitrios. They reported one or two cats going missing, but they assumed they had just been run over, or were victims of assault. They tended to be the younger ones." He looked around at the others. "No road sense, of course."

Apollo shuddered at the recollection of his own introduction to Athens' busy streets. It was a steep and unforgiving learning curve. "So, you've learned nothing," he said. "We have no idea who is taking these animals, or where they're being held. We're no further forward. This is useless."

Hermes gave him a look. "Well, I learned that there's a price on your head. You and your pals. Kratos has put the word out, and he's got animals looking for you, and they mean you harm."

"I don't care about them."

"You shouldn't dismiss them. They're dangerous, and there are more of them than you might think. You should stay here until it all blows over."

"No."

"What did you do to upset them so much? They want blood. They're sure you're spying for Athena, out to do them harm."

Apollo snorted in derision, but the white cat continued on his theme.

"They're certain you went there to test out their defences. To get an idea of their strength, and gather information that would give Athena a chance to prepare a welcome. If that was your mission, you've stirred up a hornet's nest, and maybe forced them into action sooner than they would like. That's not good for any of us."

Apollo looked away, seething at the implication.

Hermes persisted. "Well? What exactly were you up to? Have you passed on whatever you discovered? I think you owe us an explanation."

Apollo was, by now, beside himself with frustration. The point of visiting Hermes had been to get information about Olympia's whereabouts. It had been a waste of time; he would do better by himself. He stood up, glared at his host, then pointed his nose towards the Acropolis and set off.

Hermes caught up with him.

"What are you doing?" he asked.

Apollo stopped and turned to face him.

"Coming here was a mistake. I don't know why anyone advised it. You're no help at all. I'm not just going to sit on my arse all day and count flies. I'm going to go over there to start looking." He nodded in the vague direction of the Parthenon and set off once more. Below him, the track wound down the hill.

Hermes caught up with him again.

"Why did you come here? So you can report back on what

I'm up to? I think not." His usual demeanour of smug superiority had vanished.

"Don't worry. You're doing nothing worth reporting on." Apollo continued walking.

Hermes tried a different tack. "It's dangerous down there. You're top of their hit list, and more to the point, you don't know where you're going."

"For one thing, they don't frighten me. Second, yes I do. Over there."

"Oh, so you *are* working for her?"

"I don't know what you're talking about."

"You can stop playing the innocent. Just admit it. You're in league with Athena. You might as well spill the beans. What's her special project all about? It's got the entire city seething. If she's not careful, her precious *Pax Athena* is going to come crashing down around her ears."

Apollo stopped in his tracks and stared at the white cat, a glint of fury illuminating his golden eyes. Despite his anger, he kept his voice calm, knowing his words would resonate more. "I seem to remember I used to like you. But for an immortal, you're so full of shit. Stop playing games for once, and just get out of my way. We came here to rescue a friend, nothing more."

"Ah, yes. Ever the altruist. You and your little friend Daphne. That name rings a bell. Peneus' daughter, if I recall. The one who gave you the run around. I thought you'd got her out of your system?"

Apollo's eyes narrowed. "What are you talking about?"

"Come on. You must remember. It was quite a story, back in the day. Eros was—"

"I don't have a clue what you're on about."

"No? Too bad. Because if you dared to climb down off that high plinth, you might like to know she's—"

"She's just a friend from Delphi, and she knows Olympia. She volunteered to help."

"Sounds like she's quite attached to you, then. Something must have changed."

Apollo had no answer. Hermes' probing left him confused. On the fringe of memory, he felt he should know something. But what?

Hermes continued. "So, if Daphne's just a friend, what does that make Olympia?"

The ginger cat looked at him, bewildered. "We were close," he breathed.

"Close? As in, *let's have a family*?"

Apollo gave a snort and looked the other way.

Hermes looked pleased with himself. "Ah, I see it now. You came to rescue your wife and brought your girlfriend along for the ride. Only now, they're both lost and you don't know where to turn. Do you follow your duty or your dick?" He pushed his face closer towards the ginger cat until they were almost touching. "I knew the old Apollo was in there somewhere."

He looked insufferably smug, and Apollo started to hate him. But then the white cat continued his musing, as if talking to himself.

"But where does that leave the other one? Jason."

"I don't really know him. He came along for the adventure."

Hermes gave him a long look, followed by a tiny, pitying shake of the head. "You don't make a very good shepherd, do you? You'd only been in Athens for five minutes and you lost your flock." Hermes' voice hardened. "But that's only the half of it. You show up after all this time, acting the innocent, but then throw a grenade into an already volatile situation. Do you seriously expect me to believe it's all because you want to save a mortal? What's so special about this one? How is she different from all the others? What's she got on you?"

Apollo didn't answer; he just set off down the hill.

Hermes shouted after him. "There's far more at stake right

now than the fate of your little friend. And if you think Athena is going to give you any help, you're beyond naive. When did she ever help you? She won't be remotely interested. You'll get a better hearing from the human police. I was trying to help you, but if you don't want to know, then you can go to hell." He turned around and retreated up the slope.

Hermes' acolytes stayed well away from him when he returned. They hadn't seen him in a mood this foul for a long time. When he'd calmed down a little, he sought Angelia and Pharis, and indicated north.

"Head down there and get me an update on our ginger friend's pals," he ordered. "I'm pretty sure Zelus is holding one of them, and if that insufferable ginger fool had allowed me, I would have told him. Keep tabs on her and try to find the other. Let's see what they've got to say. And keep an ear out for any news of this so-called friend of theirs, if she exists. I want to know who she is and what makes her so special. What or who was she spying on? Did she survive? We're going to find out what's happened to her before he can and wipe the smug expression off his face."

CHAPTER 33
APOLLO ALONE

pollo continued his descent of Lycabettus Hill without a clear idea where to go, let alone a plan. He was furious with Hermes. Why did the white cat have such trouble believing his story? Why did he think he knew Daphne? Surely he was holding some information back. But what?

His thoughts circled round as he marched down the slope, looking far more purposeful than he felt. He needed to control his frustration and think clearly. He had to find Athena. She alone seemed capable of helping him locate Olympia; he just hoped she would be more helpful. A phrase from Hermes echoed in his head.

'When did she ever help you?'

As the street levelled out, he found himself by the side of the busiest road he'd yet seen, with three lanes of traffic in each direction. His attention snapped back to the present; he'd be no use to Olympia if a bus flattened him.

A few minutes of concentration allowed him to spot a gap in the traffic, and he darted across. At the other side, he lost his bearings. He wanted to avoid the busy thoroughfares, if possible, but as a result, his route took him south, across the landscaped grounds of some museums and the ancient site of Aristotle's Lyceum. He hopped over fences and boundary markers, but at least his chosen route was unimpeded by the city's pedestrians and vehicles.

Continuing on his bearing, making sure he always headed towards the Acropolis whenever he could see it looming behind buildings or trees, he found himself in the National Gardens, an extensive park filled with exotic plants and trees. He marvelled at the enormous palm trees and sniffed around the edges of the central pond. It was all quite a distraction. At one point, he thought he saw a tortoise, but it was no big deal; there were a few at Delphi. He could have stayed in this restful corner of the city all day, but duty nagged him back to his task. Despite the attractions of the park, he made excellent progress and emerged at the side of another busy road; the worst yet.

As he surveyed the acres of tarmac in front of him, Apollo's attention was taken by a tram; it was the first he'd seen, gliding down the centre of the road, between all the cars, trucks and buses. Another form of transport to avoid. He froze, keeping a wary eye until it was past. How many more strange vehicles did the modern world of humans have, waiting to catch him out? At least this one seemed to stick to the grooves in the tarmac, which was a relief.

Fortune was on his side. He'd emerged close to a major pedestrian crossing and, taking his cue from the humans when they ventured across, he followed in their midst. His confidence was increasing, but the big city was still strange. From this far pavement, he could see Mount Lycabettus in the distance to his right, but ahead was a warren of narrow streets and tall buildings, and he no longer had sight of the cliffs of the Acropolis to guide him. He would have to rely on instinct.

Apollo launched himself into the maze of buildings. He had no idea how to navigate through to the Agora where the mysterious Athena was said to live, but he hoped some cats in this part of town could direct him. They couldn't all be as rude as the members of his species he'd met so far on this trip.

The further he penetrated into the urban jungle, the more disoriented he became, until he was no longer sure he was heading in the right direction. The streets were narrow and winding, and he soon lost his bearings.

A tour guide, pursued by a gaggle of elderly humans, approached, holding an umbrella aloft despite the warm weather. Apollo couldn't resist following out of professional curiosity. This was an opportunity to learn from a leading practitioner; a bona fide expert. He became embroiled in a sea of legs as the group passed him, then, freeing himself, followed them for a while. The group trooped down the street to a large ceremonial archway where they blocked the street while the guide delivered a lecture on its history and significance. How lucky Apollo was to work in Delphi. Imagine trying to shepherd a gaggle of humans this big in the city, with all of its distractions. How many would she lose before the end?

They set off again, Apollo tagging along, his quest momentarily pushed to the back of his mind. They ventured down more streets, dodging the local people. But he still had no clear sense of the direction they were going. With luck, the group might head towards the Agora and his immediate target.

After a while, the buildings on the right side of the road thinned out, and to his relief, he caught another sight of the Acropolis towering above, much closer now. It was to his right, which meant he was passing to the south of it instead of the north as he'd intended, but now he had a clearer idea where he was heading.

The group paused while the guide delivered another talk, this time about the remains of a large amphitheatre on the hillside before them. It was described as the Theatre of Diony-sus, and the guide had a lot to say about it.

Apollo's attention wandered. Why had they named a theatre after that waster? He sniffed at some nearby plants while reflecting on the strange motivations of the human species. The tour had become a little boring, and he considered leaving, but the group set off again, so once more he followed.

After a short while, they paused in front of a low modern building with enormous glass windows and several statues inside. It seemed they were heading inside.

Like the museum at home, but with bigger windows.

He continued on his way down the narrow road, occasionally glancing up at the temple on the skyline and the monuments below. This was better. It reminded him of Delphi. His mood lifted as the sun warmed his back; he had a renewed sense of purpose. The direction was more or less clear and the surroundings were vaguely familiar. It was a relief to leave the concrete and steel world of men, even if just for a little while.

On a whim, he took a detour along the hillside in preference to the road, wandering past inscribed stones, gnarled trees and low bushes. At one point, he passed a sleeping adder, hidden in a secluded suntrap. Further along, he spotted another tortoise chewing on a ground-hugging plant. He savoured the scented vegetation of this more open land-scape; another lovely contrast to the city streets.

The sound of flapping wings attracted his attention as the crow landed on a nearby rock. It cawed at him.

"Greetings, my lord."

Apollo stopped, somewhat taken aback, but not displeased by the salutation. "What have you found?"

The crow, pleased with itself, performed a little dance on top of the rock. It tilted its head to one side and addressed him again. "We've found something you might be interested in. After I left you, I talked to my fellows at our daily murder. They agreed to keep an eye out and get back to me if they saw anything. I got a response quicker than I expected." He shuffled his feet once more, turning to the other side. Apollo waited.

"Well, a short while ago, one guy came up to me. He said there's been talk of a lot of dogs making a racket over in Tavros, so he went to check it out."

"I'm not interested in dogs," Apollo said. He turned away, disappointed.

"No, no. Wait," the crow urged. "That's not what I came to tell you. My mate did a couple of flypasts to get a proper look. He says there're a lot of animals down there in a big yard at the back of a building. It's not just dogs. They've got cats as well. But there are very high fences around it. They can't get out."

Apollo's eyes narrowed as he studied the bird. Was it telling the truth? Would they have taken Olympia somewhere like this? It sounded as plausible as anything else he could think of.

"Could be worth checking out," finished the crow, pleased with itself.

Apollo thought for a moment. What should he do? His intention had been to find Athena and try to persuade her to lend him the resources to search for Olympia. But if this was indeed where she was being held, then there was no time to waste. He had to rescue her. But how? There was no back-up now he'd lost Jason and Daphne, and he had no faith in Hermes.

So there was no alternative but to find this place himself and check out the crow's story. He wondered how much he could press him and his friends for further help.

"You have done well," he said. "You have my thanks, but now I need you to do more. I want you to show me where this place is. I have to get there as fast as possible. How do I find it? How far is it?"

The crow flapped his wings in delight. "It's not far to fly, but it's quite a long walk. I'll guide you, though." He set off in a flutter of wings and alighted on a tree a hundred metres further on. Apollo gritted his teeth and followed him at a brisk trot. He had renewed hope for the first time in days, but alongside it came a surge of concern. Would he get there in time?

They made rapid progress across the city; the crow made short flights ahead, and the cat followed as quickly as he could. They left the precinct of the Acropolis, surmounted Filopappou Hill, and descended towards the Tavros district, back into the world of modern men.

CHAPTER 34
THE GANGS ADVANCE

The Gizi gang assembled in the centre of the warehouse as the first glimmer of light touched the eastern horizon. One of Daphne's captors cuffed her awake. She struggled to her feet, her wounds and limbs aching. Her heart sank. Today was going to be difficult. She hoped they wouldn't march her too fast, or too far, or be too rough. How much more punishment could she take?

Across the dirty concrete floor, she watched Zelus stalking among his troops, cajoling and encouraging. He had a spring in his step, as if he'd gained some renewed purpose. Would she have to face any more questioning?

As if reading her thoughts, he turned and walked in her direction.

"No funny business. You're staying with us today, and we'll have another cosy chat this evening. We might have quite a lot to catch up on." His eyes narrowed. "Cause trouble and we'll just execute you on the spot. Got that?"

Daphne avoided his eyes and stared at the floor, mute. She wasn't ready for another bout of mental sparring, or worse. Zelus observed her for a moment, then turned away to attend to his troops.

They moved shortly after, streaming through the pre-rush hour streets in columns, silent and swift, each led by a senior lieutenant. In the grey dawn, there were few vehicles about, and they could cross major roads with ease. Daphne found it hard to keep up. A fitful sleep had left her feeling marginally better, but the beating she had endured only a few hours earlier had left her in poor shape. She ached all over, and her wounds hadn't healed. Her guards – the same pair who had attacked her so brutally the previous evening – hadn't allowed her anything to eat and were merciless in urging her on.

Zelus might have shown genuine fear at the mention of Hera last night, but having recovered his composure, he didn't seem too bothered if Daphne died on this route march. She limped and struggled on, panting for breath and in constant pain. Every few minutes, a jab in her flank from the snout of a guard urged her forwards, faster than she felt she could manage. Somehow, she kept up, breath rasping in her throat, heart pounding.

She should have never set out on this adventure. She could have just stayed in calm and peaceful Delphi, playing among the ruins and the trees, enjoying good company, chasing flying insects and small rodents. Having fun. Instead, she was in a dungeon of concrete and asphalt, enduring endless torture.

They crossed Stadiou Street and zig-zagged through narrower streets and alleys until they reached Athinaidos Street. Here, Zelus called a halt. He waited until all the columns caught up, then gave them one last set of instructions.

"Just remember why we're here. We are going to take over this neighbourhood. Look around. This is our new manor. But first, we've got to turf out the slobs who live here. Put the place under new management. Think of it as a hostile takeover. This place looks good. The pickings are rich, the food better. Just a minor dispute to resolve, and it's ours. Are you with me?" He looked at his assembled troops. They miaowed, nodded and tail-signed their agreement, impatient to get started, fired up to be taking part in something that would become legendary: the day the Gizi gang took over the Plaka. They would talk about it for years. They would be famous and feared throughout the city. This was their day.

They advanced more slowly now, keeping a careful watch for any local inhabitants who might sound the alarm as they drew closer to the square and the target of their attack. Shop-keepers were opening their shutters and setting up for the day; cafés put tables out, and the motorised carts and small vans of delivery men puttered along the narrow streets. The cats streamed past, silent, intent on their destination, obliv-ious to the looks they were attracting from the few surprised humans.

As they reached the edge of the square, Zelus signalled them to slow down again, but one was not paying attention. She advanced into the open.

"You," he shouted. "Zinovia, come back."

She ignored him, or lost in the excitement of the moment, did not hear. She had spotted a local cat sauntering across the middle of the square, all thought of instructions gone. She sprinted forwards on the attack, and within a few seconds, the rest of them followed.

Zelus tried, but it was impossible to call them back; their blood was up, they were on their way. The battle of Monasti-raki had started, whether he liked it or not. He chased after his troops, leading from the rear like many a general over the centuries, now able to only respond to events, rather than shape them.

Daphne had no desire to take part in any fighting, and certainly not on the side of these bullies. She just wanted to keep out of it; but her minders were straining at the leash to get involved. Maybe she would get the chance to give them the slip. So far, though, they kept a close eye on her, and she was too weak and battered to outrun them. She would have to wait. Her guards pushed her forwards as fast as they could, nipping her if she slowed down.

A short distance across town, another troop of cats headed south along Aristofanous Street, arrowing in towards Monastiraki Square from a different direction. Kratos led the way. To the west, on Agias Theklas, was Rea and her column, while Yannis and the rest tracked down Athinas Street. They were making rapid progress, each vying to be the first there, to get ahead of their ally. Kratos regretted inviting Zelus to this little shindig. He had no desire to share this prize; it had all been his idea. But could he win this war on his own? He would have kept the entire operation in-house if the omens hadn't been right, and those verminous little spies had not appeared. If he could get his paws on that bunch again, he'd make them squeak.

As his column turned into Thermidos Street, he slowed the pace. He didn't want to arrive too far ahead of his lieutenants; there were limits to even his ability to restrain a group of agitated, wound-up cats. Nor did he want to risk losing the element of surprise and attacking with less than his full force. An elementary mistake like that would give the defenders time to get themselves organised.

Not that it'll do them any good.

At the junction with Ermou Street, he paused, checking for Rea's group. In only a few minutes, they appeared to his right. In silence, Kratos led his cats across the street and under the cover of the modern building opposite. Rea's group joined them. There, they halted to wait for Yannis's unit.

As they waited, the leader struggled to contain his agitation. Though he would never admit it, tension was gnawing at him. He mulled over Hermes' visit once more, particularly his mention of the sons of Ares. Kratos would never have dared this venture if Ares himself was still around; his reputation still hung over the city like choking smog. He hated to admit it, but Hermes had spooked him. How many sons did Ares have, and were they still with the gang? On that point, his intelligence was lacking. If any of Ares' sons were here, how much of their father's prowess had they inherited? Kratos took pride in the brutal martial abilities of his own offspring. If there were several of his enemy's brood still around, that might even up the odds. But if they were still young, they could be eliminated with ease.

At the back of his mind was a vague recollection that they were to be feared. But surely nowhere near as much as their old man. Kratos was sure they'd never be a match for his own offspring. He glanced at them among the throng, herding the troops and keeping them in order, reminding them of their duties. Strong family ties were the spine of his outfit; they provided strength and discipline. He cast his mind to his enemies. Unless Ares had left capable deputies in charge, they were sitting ducks, but he should take care. Eliminating any potential future threat from offspring would be wise. History was littered with legends of orphaned youths seeking revenge.

While the big cat was deep in reflection, many within the group were struggling to keep still. Returning to the present, he became concerned that one of them might inadvertently wander out into the square, giving the game away. Discipline was wavering as the fear of what lay ahead displaced fear of himself.

Given the chance, most of this lot would flee.

Put to the sternest of tests, was his authority wavering? Had he reached the limit of how far he could push them? Kratos put such negative thoughts to the back of his mind: there was grim and bloody work to do. He would worry about the limits of his power once he had won.

He grunted orders to those nearest, and they reluctantly stepped back. All were nervous; they just wanted to get on with it. Several of them used the enforced wait to disappear under parked cars and relieve themselves in preparation. Kratos gave them a sour look. He had little sympathy for signs of weakness. They had to keep it together for a little while longer.

There came a strangled cry of annoyance from behind. One of his spotters was peering around the corner of the building into the square. He turned to Kratos.

"Over there," he urged. "It's Zelus' crew, I'm sure."

Kratos followed his gaze and saw numerous cats streaming out into the square from the far side. What was going on? All thought of waiting for Yannis and his troops was forgotten. The Gizi gang had already started; they wanted the Plaka for themselves. He turned to the animals surrounding him, most of whom were now creeping forwards to watch events across the square.

"Those swine are trying to grab all the glory for themselves. Well, we will not let them. Follow me. Attack!"

Kratos charged into the thick of the action. There would be a reckoning for this. His supposed ally had better have a good excuse for jumping the gun.

The others needed no further encouragement. Rea was first to respond, overtaking her boss, eager for action, as ever. Her troops were just a hair's breadth behind, spreading across the square. Glory for Botrys was at stake, if nothing else.

CHAPTER 35
THE BATTLE OF MONASTIRAKI SQUARE

Old Nikos meandered across the square on one of his regular morning routes. He often left the rest of the group before sunrise to enjoy this quiet hour alone, exploring the nearby streets. It proved to be a good move tactically, as it made him a familiar face for local café owners and shopkeepers when they were setting up for the day, and they often flung a few treats in his direction. He never let on to the rest of them; it was his secret.

This morning had been unremarkable. It was not a day for hurrying. He had said hello to one or two of his friends from his regular round and was considering where to head next when a sudden movement brought his head up. A group of cats, streaking across the pavement of Monastiraki Square in his direction. He looked over his shoulder to see what might have attracted them, but a rapid reappraisal of their trajectory left only one conclusion: they were heading for him.

He turned and bolted towards home but saw another group moving diagonally to cut off his escape. Nikos veered right in a desperate move to shake them off, hoping a long detour down the side streets might evade them; but his pursuers were gaining. He was older than them and had lost some of his speed and stamina, but he hoped he had enough in him to reach cover, even if it meant entering a shop.

His plans came to nought. With a flying leap reminiscent of a lioness bringing down a wildebeest in the Serengeti, Rea caught his flank, raking her claws down his haunches and bowling him over. He tried to use his momentum to regain his feet, but the other pursuers were on him, and he was buried beneath a seething mass of enemies.

He didn't suffer long.

So began the Battle of Monastiraki Square.

The Plaka cats were caught by surprise. Most were just waking up, stretching, sniffing the air, washing and planning their day. In a matter of moments, they were fighting for their lives. One or two were picked off in the main square itself, but most of the fighting took place within the fenced-off area of the Library of Hadrian, which the Plaka cats used as their home, or in the neighbouring Roman Forum. The Botrys and Gizi gangs raced to outdo each other to get into the action first, and dozens of cats streamed through or under the metal railings surrounding the site. They scented blood and an easy victory.

Kratos and Zelus had wound their troops up to fever pitch, and there was a wild but purposeful fury about them. The cats of the Plaka were pitched into a fight for survival against a bewildering array of aggressive foes who outnumbered them at least two to one.

Jason was as startled as everyone else, but at least he hadn't moved far from the collective sleeping area, and he was with some younger adults. His first thought was to flee; he had no argument with anyone and saw no reason to get caught up in someone else's fight. But his options were limited.

Behind and to the left was a wall; too high to jump. The attackers streamed in from the right and ahead, and there would be no simple way out. His decision was made by a bulky black-and-white cat charging towards him. The only option was to stand his ground and fight. Events moved too rapidly for him to feel nervous. As the adrenaline surged, his only thought was survival.

Savage duels arose around him. If he'd had time to think, he might have wondered at this unusual behaviour. Their species didn't go in for pitched battles. A brief skirmish to establish territory, over in seconds, was all. This assault was clearly organised, and the invaders were unnaturally persistent and aggressive. But the luxury of reflection was for later. In the short term, he just reacted to events as they unfolded around him.

Out of the corner of his eye, he recognised Erichthonius engaging with an amber-and-black attacker; but before he could help, an enormous cat leapt at him. The two animals grappled with each other, rolling in the dirt. Jason bit hard into his enemy's neck and sank a good number of punches to his opponent's stomach with his hind paws before he shifted position. The other cat's weight and power threatened to overcome him, but the fluidity of their movement allowed Jason to break free as they rolled over, and he put half a metre between them.

He crouched, facing his opponent, paws splayed and ready to pounce. His blood was up now. He wanted retribution for this unprovoked attack; the black-and-white animal would pay. Feeling invulnerable, almost giddy in the heat of battle, he zoned out everything but his opponent.

His enemy hesitated.

Seizing the opportunity, Jason launched himself; his fury giving him the edge. With a more forceful leap, his enemy's hind paws slipped on the gravel, giving Jason momentum. He pushed the bigger cat backwards, putting it on the defensive, then dumped it on its back. Now on top, he delivered multiple blows with his hind paws and raked his claws across his opponent's shoulders, drawing blood, oblivious to the blows he was taking in return. In the heat of battle, he couldn't feel them; the pain would come later. But for now, he had tunnel vision and he could hear little. This duel was all that mattered.

Once again, he broke contact and moved back just far enough to deliver several savage scratches to the other cat's face, closing one eye. With his sight limited, and unable to detect where Jason's next attacks were coming from, the larger cat howled in anguish and fled, with its tail between its legs. Jason snarled after it, but had no time to bask in victory. Another attacker emerged, while all around him the battle was going badly for his companions.

Kratos scented victory. He'd never doubted he would win. The soft, easy living of the Plaka cats made them pussies compared to his hardened street fighters. Part of him was surprised they'd put up any fight at all; he'd half expected them to slink off without raising a paw. But victory wasn't yet complete. He had one more job to do. He had to eliminate any threat, no matter how remote, from any future offspring of the seed of Ares: successors to the former leadership.

Systematically, he tracked down younger male cats in a methodical killing spree. They were no match for his power and size. His victory would be decisive, and would sow fear among the defeated ever after; it would be so absolute that none of them could rise again. He meant to snuff out the threat completely, but how many sons were there?

Standing over the body of his latest victim, he spotted the youngsters in their little creche in the corner, mewing pathetically. They were confused and afraid, not knowing where to turn amid the turmoil and noise. Most of their guardians had fled or were fighting for their lives.

Kratos savoured the moment that would seal his victory once and for all. He descended on them like a raging tempest, lashing out left and right. All were defenceless against him. Some tried to resist, but bewildered and far too small and feeble, they had no chance. One after another in rapid succession, their brief lives were ended with little more than a pitiful squeak or mew. A few of the older ones tried to form a group to break free, but Kratos' own offspring, fastidious and vicious in their filial duty, herded them back towards their fate.

The youngsters' parents and minders were dead or scattered; all except one.

A mother, reacting instinctively to the mayhem, grabbed her kitten by the scruff of the neck, somehow dodged pursuit and leapt higher than she thought possible to escape over the retaining wall and through railings. She set off into the maze of narrow streets, never looking back. Kratos caught her out of the corner of his eye and barked an order, but no one was close enough to intercept.

He returned to his bloody murder spree. The fugitive would be tracked down in time, but first things first.

In the immediate vicinity, he repelled the few remaining adults who tried to come to the rescue of the little ones, destroying any remaining resistance. The Infanticide of Hadrian's Library, as it came to be known among their kind, was renowned in their later folklore as the worst of all deeds on the darkest of days.

Jason was some way across the battlefield and unaware of what was happening further afield; he was just fighting for survival. Weariness had replaced the adrenaline surge, but a dogged determination to save his newfound friends was growing, bolstered by the savage treatment they were getting all around him.

He launched himself against another opponent to assist Tabitha and was pleased to see her break free and retreat, limping, to relative safety while he kept her attacker busy long enough for her to escape, then looked around for other animals needing help.

By now he was panting, his heart hammering, and fatigue

taking its toll. But somehow he felt more alive than ever, and in his element. For the first time in his life, he had a purpose: to help these creatures. To rally them and help them fight back against these oppressors. His wounds smarted, but the light of battle was in his eyes, and seeing his bravery, some of them were responding. He scanned the square to see who was most in need of help and stiffened as he saw someone he recognised. This duel would be a pleasure.

Daphne held back as much as she could when the attack started. In part, this was because she could no longer run fast, but she also wanted to stay clear of the fighting, no matter what they tried to do to her. Her captors taunted her and cuffed her to ease their frustration at not being able to grab any glory for themselves. They wanted to be in the vanguard, seeking glory, not guarding the prisoner at the rear; but they dared not leave her. They took out their frustration by regularly cuffing, biting and clawing at her. Rough and vicious, they pushed her towards the heaviest fighting so they could get a better view.

Favours from Zelus depended on being seen to take risks, obey his orders and polish his ego. Holding back would earn them no credit. There was no glory in guarding a prisoner. Could they pick off some of those fleeing in this direction and win approval that way? As they got closer, they paid less and less attention to their captive.

The closer she got to the battle, the more dismayed Daphne became. She couldn't bear to watch, but neither could she look away. The squeals of the dead and dying pierced the morning air, but there was nothing she could do. Worse, the wrong side was winning. She knew nothing of the Plaka cats, but she was sure they couldn't be as bad as Zelus or Kratos' gangs, and they didn't deserve this evil abuse. As if to rub it in, her captors were relishing the success of their comrades.

She lost the little hope she'd had of escaping; where would she go in this strange place if all her surroundings were under their vicious control? She had no family here; no one other than Jason and Apollo, who she'd lost days ago. Daphne hated Athens with a passion. Where were the other two?

Her eyes swept across the battlefield one more time, but she could scarcely take in the carnage. Time and again, Zelus' gang defeated their opponents. The lucky ones fled; far too many didn't, their bodies slumped in the dirt. She assumed Kratos' crew were doing the same.

Then, in the distance, she caught sight of someone with familiar grey-and-white colouring. Jason! Her heart leapt. But hope was matched by an intense fear for his safety. What was he doing here? What if he got injured or killed?

She could no longer keep still; it was as if she'd sat on an ant's nest. She had to get close to him somehow.

She glanced at her captors, who were absorbed with the scene playing out before them. Could she, dare she, sneak away? Tentatively, she tried to shuffle backwards out of their peripheral vision. It worked; they didn't move. She became bolder, moving with more purpose. Paying full attention to them, she sidled away in slow and measured steps. Progress was painfully slow, but before long she'd put ten metres between them.

"Where do you think you're sneaking off to?" came a sneering voice behind her. She looked around. It was Yannis. His column had just arrived after their long detour across town and most of them were streaking past, eager to join the fray. But their leader had spotted an opportunity to curry a little favour with his father by delivering back to him the pretty little spy from the other night. No doubt he would have fun extracting her story.

The big cat growled down at her with gleeful malice. "Well, you can think again."

He was about to leap at her when there was a shout from

Daphne's guards, who had belatedly noticed her disappearance. They ran to her.

"Oi! This one's ours!" one of them shouted.

"We're guarding her," added his companion. "Zelus has plans for her."

"Not doing a very good job of looking after her then, are you?" Yannis sneered. "Anyway, she raided us first, and Kratos is keen to get a word."

There was a stand-off as the allies glared at one another. Daphne looked from side to side, caught in the middle.

A grey-and-white missile flashed across her peripheral vision and hit Yannis side on. Focused on Daphne's guards, he'd not seen Jason coming, and he had no time to react. It proved his undoing. Bloodied though Jason was, he seemed possessed with maniacal energy.

His momentum sent the two of them tumbling over and over, across the polished marble flagstones. Yannis, winded and caught by surprise, was always on the defensive, unsure where the next blows were coming from. He might have been the bigger animal, but size counted for nothing against such intense rage.

Daphne's captors were agape. They didn't want to get involved, but their little prisoner was edging forwards to help her friend. Seeing her moving released them from a spell; she was in danger of escaping.

They sprang forwards, but with hope rekindled in her heart, fuelled by the cruelty she had suffered at their paws, Daphne drew on reserves she didn't realise she had. She was a Delphi cat; not a pushover. She was no pussycat. She could fight like anyone if she had to, just as her friend was doing for her.

Daphne whirled round to face her tormentors, the light of battle kindled in her eyes. She bared her fangs and snarled at them, all thought for her own safety gone.

They stopped in their tracks as Daphne prepared to spring. She just had to decide which one to go for first.

Behind her, Jason held Yannis's throat in a death grasp, strangling him. One of Daphne's guards noticed and fled. In that instant, Daphne attacked the other one, releasing a pent-up flood of rage. She was smaller and less experienced, but the fight had gone out of her enemy. The cat scrabbled to break free, and once she did so, she ran as fast as she could. Daphne spat out a mouthful of fur and made to follow when a familiar voice cried out behind her.

"Oh, Daffers. I'm so pleased to see you."

She stopped, paused, and returned to her normal self. She was hurting all over, but relieved to be free, and seeing Jason again washed the pain away. She turned to face him. Slowly they walked towards each other, sniffing, watching, then tentatively, tenderly, each proffered a delicate nose-kiss, and with more confidence, a long head rub. For a moment they were lost in their greetings, but in the distance, the battle was ending, and they needed to leave before the victors hunted down any remaining stragglers.

Jason raised his head, looked her in the eyes. "Just as well I was here. That's the second time I've saved you."

She tilted her head. "Second?"

"The first was when I was in the right place at the right time to get mixed up in this crazy adventure back in Delphi. How mad was that?"

She took a step back and looked him up and down. He seemed changed, somehow. More confident. A little arrogant? He moved closer and nuzzled her once more, and she forgot her concerns; she wanted him, needed him, and soon. A low growl-yowl escaped her lips, and she nipped his neck with gentle urgency, then rolled over in front of him. It was a come-on more blatant than any she'd ever given, and not like her at all.

Jason raised his head and surveyed the fighting behind them.

"Not here," he said. "Come on. We'd better go. Let's find somewhere safe."

"But where?"

He looked around. The Botrys and Gizi gangs, who were already eyeing each other in suspicion, had control of the Plaka gang's headquarters; but the exit from the square in the opposite direction looked clear.

"Down here," he said. "Quick. Before they spot us."

They hobbled across the square, past the front of the metro station and down Ifestou Street, heading away from the fighting. Instinctively, they hugged the walls, seeking cover from the display stands, rails of clothing and shelves the shopkeepers were still in the process of putting out. The less visible they were, the better they felt. They were heading towards the site of the archaeological dig.

Close to the end of the road, at the corner of a side street, a well-groomed light-brown cat stepped out from behind a rack of sunglasses.

"This area is closed to visitors," she informed them, sounding both haughty and officious. "You must go back."

Jason's hackles rose. "You will not tell me where I can and can't go," he said, in no mood to back down.

Daphne glanced at him, admiring his newfound confidence. She noticed a slight doubt in the other animal's expression. "Those terrible gangs have attacked us for no reason," she said. "They've been doing dreadful things to our friends back there. You can't make us go back. They'd kill us."

She didn't have enough energy to go back, even if forced to. She was exhausted. She needed rest, and she needed Jason. The brown cat looked them up and down, then past them down the street. Anyone with ears and cat-like senses could hear the commotion right across town. It was obviously a major incident. She adopted a different approach.

"Athena has banned all cats from the area behind me," she said.

Jason, his chin raised, was in no mood to argue. "Try stopping us." He tried to walk around the other animal, but she stepped in front of him.

"Why are you being so difficult?" asked Daphne.

The brown cat looked at her, then came to a decision.

"You can head down here," she said, looking to a side street. "At the bottom, ask for Nina and have her direct you to the Agora. Say Thalia sent you. The Agora is safe and quiet. There's plenty of space. You should be able to find some respite."

They thanked her and followed her directions. At the end of the street, they found Nina, who was less agitated than her companion.

"Ah, more survivors," she said, studying their cuts and grazes. "Nothing too serious, I hope?"

"We'll be fine with some rest," Daphne assured her.

"Good, good. Yes, of course," the other cat replied, distracted and flustered by the morning's events. "Well, you're nearly there. Just to the left is the entrance to the Agora sanctuary. Just go under the turnstiles. Don't mind the humans. They take no notice. Once you're in, you'll see plenty of spots to curl up and get your head down. You should be fine. There are already quite a few of your comrades in there. If you're wanting food later on, the restaurants further down the street usually provide pretty good pickings."

They followed her directions and were relieved to see trees, cover, shade and lots of spots to hide and recover away from prying eyes. The place had a sense of serenity, despite the tourists wandering about. It was quiet, and insects buzzed in the early-morning heat.

As they meandered across the open ground, they spotted

a few other refugees who had already arrived. Jason halted to watch them.

There were so few.

He caught up with Daphne and led her to a sheltered hollow beneath an ancient tree, where her shyness evaporated. She wanted him, rolling over invitingly to demonstrate. Playfully, he nosed and butted her with his forehead. They tumbled together in intimacy, nipping and scratching each other like two small tigers. Daphne rolled onto her belly, and Jason stood astride her, pinching her neck in his teeth. She felt his hot breath in her ear as his head bent close, and instinctively pawed the ground with her hind legs, her eyes half closed in ecstasy.

The second time was gentler and slower, the release more satisfying. Afterwards, he pushed his head into hers, and they lay side by side, wrapped in each other, lost in the moment, enjoying the comfort of bodily contact. The rest of the world faded away to insignificance. They could deal with it later.

Kratos surveyed the scene of carnage with grim satisfaction. There were bodies everywhere; he'd leave it to the humans to clear them away. They did that sort of thing. Over by the far wall, a few captives were being subjected to the tender mercies of Rea. They'd survive as long as they did what they were told.

Victory had been decisive, although more of the enemy had escaped than he'd have liked. But they wouldn't evade him for long. Best of all, he'd eliminated any future threat of revenge from the spawn of Ares, their former leader. Victory felt good. It was just a shame he'd had to share it with Zelus.

He had achieved phase one of his grand plan: the Plaka, the biggest honeypot in the city, was his. But he wasn't satisfied yet.

There was still plenty to do.

· · ·

Atop Lycabettus, Hermes lay on his side, failing to sleep, staring into space. Despite the distance, his sharpened senses picked up the faint wails and screams from the battle below. He winced. Such brutality was most unnecessary. So many lives needlessly cut short, including the little ones. So many souls to escort. He sighed, pondering whether he could have done more to prevent the carnage. Why had Athena not acted to stop them? The responsibility for this mess lay at her door. This trinket she wanted couldn't be that important, could it? How high a price was she prepared to pay?

In the normal course of events, he enjoyed nothing more than to mess with her plans, and he liked to think he'd been successful on this occasion as well. But this intervention appeared to have caused a lot more collateral damage than he'd expected; it seemed like a throwback to the old days. Was this a one-off or was there something else going on? Something he hadn't picked up yet? Had he inadvertently made things far, far worse?

He put the thought aside with a shudder and concentrated instead on his ginger visitor. He called himself Apollo, but he was nothing like the super-confident, somewhat arrogant lothario he used to call a friend. This individual was far more contemplative and reserved; maybe even a touch shy. Nor did his story stack up; there was a missing twenty-four hours between his departure from Kratos' headquarters and his arrival at Lycabettus. Also, he had arrived from the wrong direction.

So where had he been? That story about a missing friend didn't add up. Cats went missing all the time; Hermes' conversations with the gangs had proved it. So what was he doing? Was he really in league with Athena? And if so, why? They were never usually allied; in any case, he felt sure he would have already heard about it. And if *he* was here, what about the others?

With reluctance he had to acknowledge the fact that his

visitor, despite the gaps in the timeline, may have been telling the truth. But chasing after an ordinary mortal, rather than just leaving them to their fate, was more than unusual. It would be unprecedented. It was time to get a better handle on exactly what was happening down there, and find out how his old friend wove into the wider tapestry of events.

He stood up, and he set off down the hill, in Apollo's paw prints.

CHAPTER 36
THE CAGE

Olympia looked up through the wire mesh. The sky was grey, and heavy with clouds. It was as good a day to die as any, she supposed, her fragile hope long gone. Who wants to go when it's nice and sunny? That would just make it worse. She could have been lounging in the shade of a tree, having a leisurely sleep, or keeping a friend company, not preparing to meet her maker.

She had been lucky.

Her neighbour had been taken; but it could easily have been her.

They had come for another at mid-morning, opening his cage and marching right in. Humans are so slow and clumsy, and this one had looked no different. But when he had the black-and-white cat penned into the far corner, he reached down surprisingly fast. Of course, his victim had nowhere to go. He'd put up a bit of a fight, though. Good for him. They'd taken him out of the yard, still struggling, spitting and hissing for all he was worth. She could still hear him in whatever room they'd taken him to, because they'd left a window open a crack.

Olympia heard his agonising screams for some time. Maybe it was just a botched job.

She shivered. It made her go cold, but she couldn't help it: the thought that she'd find out herself one day. When it was her turn, she hoped it would be quick; that poor soul had taken too long to die. She'd never discovered his name, and she was glad. Knowing him would have only made it worse.

She looked around the dreary compound. The fear in all the pens was tangible. When one or more of them was taken away, it had a sobering effect on them all. How could it not? All they did was pace about in their little cells and await their fate, praying it wouldn't be too bad. The noisy demise of their colleague took away even that last small hope. Nearby, some were curled up, eyes downcast, trying to sleep. But it wasn't easy with fear hanging over you, smothering you in layers of icy dread. And passing their time asleep just made the end come faster.

Olympia's attitude towards humans changed from tolerance and curiosity to dislike and even hatred. Some of her kind sucked up to them and tried to befriend the brutes. Why, she'd never know. They were savages. Monsters. All they did was dish out pain and misery. Cats should have stayed well clear. But like idiots, many insisted on living in their midst, scavenging off the detritus surrounding them and their wasteful lives. It just put them in constant danger.

They were cunning. She'd give them that. But also vicious beyond even the most savage predator. She might play with her prey, but usually she made sure it was over quickly. This endless hell was unremitting mental torture of the worst kind.

She thought about the dogs. How ironic. *Man's best friend*, they'd always claimed. Not this lot in here, judging by the state of them. They got more food than the cats, but not much. She supposed they were only there to deliver their puppies: scrawny little souls that were taken away far too soon, still yapping for their mothers while they were carted off. Sold into slavery, she guessed. They'd be alive, at least. But what sort of life would they have, with such a bitter and paranoid beginning? Didn't these humans know anything about animals? Most likely they just didn't care.

A night passed, and the following morning they brought in a new arrival to occupy her former neighbour's cage. Olympia watched him. He looked bewildered and terrified, like everyone else. Nothing she could think of saying would make it any easier for him. They all just counted the hours until it was their turn.

CHAPTER 37
THE BEAUTY OF AN ARC

Athena stalked back and forth in front of the dusty-coloured cat, who crouched submissively before her. Athena's whiskers quivered with righteous anger.

"You did what?" she howled.

Herse was almost inaudible. "I'm sorry, my lady," she whimpered, cringing. She stared at the ground in front of her nose, her whiskers drooped.

"You let her inside the cordon, allowed her access to the excavations and told her where to find the object I've been seeking for weeks? No, months. You betrayed me. Not just me, but all those who rely on us to impose law and order across the entire city. How could you?"

Herse said no more. It was pointless. She'd admitted her guilt; anything she said now would only make things worse. But Athena wasn't finished. She wanted all the facts. All the miserable details. She wanted to know exactly what Bia had found, the thing she'd been waiting for herself. She demanded the other cat recount the entire sorry story.

Hesitantly and between sobs, Herse told her everything. As she spoke, Athena stood stock still, as if carved in stone, her emerald eyes boring into the animal before her. Herse never lifted her gaze from the ground in front of her paws. She didn't dare meet her stare.

The story unfolded. The actions of the gangs worried her, and she felt worse that nothing was being done. She had shared her concerns with Hermes. He'd told her Bia might help, so she'd ventured across town to Davaki Park to hatch the plan to steal the object. Herse had hoped that would be the end of the matter, and things would get back to normal. Even as she recounted her tale, she recognised how stupid it sounded. Since Athena had been so obsessed with this thing, of course she wouldn't just let it drop once someone had removed it. And since she was so bothered about it, of course it must have been important. Very important. She'd ruined everything.

Herse finished. Athena's merciless stare never wavered from the wretched animal. There was a long, tense silence.

"I can't believe you colluded with her: Bia of all creatures. A gang leader…" Athena fell silent. Herse remained pinned beneath her gaze. "You can't even comprehend how long I have been waiting for this moment. And you have ruined it."

Her words stung. Pierced her to the core, Herse didn't know where to look. How could she repair the damage? While her thoughts roamed, Athena carried on.

"It was not a mere trinket. It was far more than that. Something…" The grey cat ran out words. Herse dared glance up, but took no solace, her mentor still glared at her. "It's not just the item itself," Athena continued, "I trusted you. You have betrayed me. Deceived me; and not only me, but our whole group." She gathered herself. The heat went out of her voice, replaced by a dreadful coldness. "I have no more use for you. I dismiss you from my service. *Begone*. Get out of my sight."

Herse staggered to her feet; her anguish uncontainable. Her mind was in turmoil; she didn't know what to do, where to go. The words stung as if she'd been whipped. She stared blankly around but could barely see her surroundings. Her sisters turned their faces away, unable or unwilling to acknowledge her; she found no comfort there.

The world had rejected her.

Stumbling, she left the clearing, her head hanging low, and set off for she knew not where. She wandered aimlessly up the hillside through the wood, with no idea where to go. How could she have misunderstood?

Her throat felt constricted; breaths came hard, and still the thoughts circled around and back on themselves endlessly.

I just wanted to help.

I didn't mean to hurt anyone.

I just wanted to make things better.

How could it all go so wrong?

Her meandering path led to the foot of the Propylea, the entrance to the rock of the Acropolis. She stumbled up the stairs, dodging between the human visitors. At the summit, she wove a path across the rocky plateau to the wall at its northern edge and raised her head to look out. From here, with the breeze ruffling her fur, she had an eagle's view over the city. Her city. It looked spectacular. Herse thought of all the people and animals below, and all the cats she had lived alongside; their foibles and their strengths, the squabbles and the camaraderie. She thought of her kittens, all grown up now, and making their way in the world, including her beautiful Erichthonius.

With a heart almost bursting with pride, she wished them well.

She paused.

It's for the best, she thought, and jumped.

CHAPTER 38
ON TORTOISES

Tracking Apollo was easy at first. Hermes had watched him set off and assumed he intended to pay a visit to Athena; although given her security cordon, he would find it easier said than done. Vasilissis Sofias Avenue was busy as ever, but once across, Hermes considered the options. Which route would Apollo have taken? Following the busy thoroughfare would have seemed the most logical route, but a few hundred metres further, it veered off to the north, away from the Acropolis. Would Apollo have spotted that? If he'd headed straight for the Acropolis, he would have, instead, left it and navigated through the grounds and gardens of several public buildings before crossing the National Gardens themselves.

Hermes moved along the pavement, sniffing at the railings, and eventually came across a post which the other cat had rubbed against in passing. The gardens route it was, then. He set off again with renewed purpose.

Crossing the Lyceum of Aristotle, now little more than a patch of scrubby grass and exposed foundations, he came to the National Gardens; a major area of landscaped parkland in central Athens. Following Apollo's trail through here might be challenging, as there were several routes he might have taken.

Hermes considered Apollo's destination. The Acropolis lay between him and Athena's abode. Would he pass to the north or south side? The northern route meant travelling the crowded, twisting streets of the Plaka, but the southern route, past the museum and the Odeon of Herodes Atticus was more straightforward. There would be many pedestrians at this time of day, but it was harder to get lost. He opted for the marginally less busy southern route.

There was no sign of Apollo's scent lingering on the street furniture, nor could he detect it on any vegetation. Perhaps Homer would know? He tried to recall the last time they'd spoken. It must have been decades ago; but tortoises live for… well, a long time. Maybe he was still around?

As Hermes passed the entrance to the Acropolis Museum, a sixth sense told him it might prove profitable to wander up past the remains of the Theatre of Dionysus and along the narrower paths under the cliffs, known only to animals. Sure enough, after a few minutes, he came across an elderly tortoise sunning itself next to a low rocky outcrop.

"Hi," he said. "Long time no see and all that. How's it going?" The tortoise showed little sign of having heard him, and Hermes didn't wait for it to respond. "Let me get to the point," he said, a touch louder. "I'm looking for someone. Ginger, with some white markings on the belly. Might have come through here earlier today? Have you seen anyone who might fit the bill?" He peered down at the other animal expectantly.

Homer extended his head a little further from his shell and looked up at him. "What sort of greeting is that?" he chided. "Where's the, 'Hello, Homer, old friend? How have you been keeping? What have you been up to since our last little chat?'" His beady eyes focused on the cat. "Instead, it's all crash, bang, wallop. Tell me this, tell me that. Then I'm off." He looked away.

Hermes sighed. He'd half expected something like this; tortoises could be notoriously touchy. *Typical. Just when you're in a hurry, your affinity animal gets a strop on.* Why did he have to get the sodding tortoise in the first place? Why not a squirrel or bird of some type? Something useful. An eagle! That would shake things up a bit. But, no. He was stuck with this recalcitrant twit. He paused and started again.

"Sorry, old friend," he said, in a more convivial tone of voice. "Got a bit carried away. Spur-of-the-moment thing. In a bit of a hurry. You know what it's like." The old tortoise snorted again. "Anyway. How are you? I should pop over here more often so we can catch up properly. It's quite nice here." He looked around. "How d'you like that? We could sit under a nice bush like that one over there and have a good long chat, eh?" He paused, looking for a sign the tortoise's mood was softening.

"I'll believe it when I see it," said Homer.

Hermes tried again. "Anyway. Sorry we got off on the wrong paw, but it's like this. I'm trying to find one of my colleagues. He's been staying with me, but he doesn't know his way around town, and I think he may have got lost. I don't want him coming to any harm. You know what some folks around here can be like. As I said, he's mainly ginger with a few white markings. I think he might have come through here earlier. But tracking anyone along here is impossible with all those humans trampling over anything that holds a scent. Do you think you might have seen him?"

"That's better," acknowledged the tortoise. "You should have started off like that. Been a bit more humble. Helps you make friends and influence animals." He stopped, satisfied he had made his point.

Hermes waited, his tail twitching involuntarily in his frustration. He wondered why he put up with this insolence from someone who was supposed to be a supplicant. He briefly fantasised about zapping the thing with a borrowed thunderbolt and suppressed a sigh.

"So?" he said, somehow maintaining his most polite expression.

"I'll have to think," answered the tortoise, retracting his head most of the way into his shell.

Hermes was, by now, inwardly seething. He looked around impatiently, half tempted to leave, but to do so would only give Homer the satisfaction of seeing him off. It simply wouldn't do to let one's affinity animal, no matter how annoying, get the upper hand. Who knew where such disobedience might end? He brought his attention to bear once more on his tormentor. He was tempted to poke a stick into his shell and give him a jolt. The tortoise spoke again.

"Well, I might have seen such a creature," Homer ventured.

Hermes' eyes widened in exasperation.

"Yes, I think I have. Someone matching the description came through here about an hour ago. Thought he was a tourist at first, and maybe a bit lost as he seemed to be taking the scenic route. He passed right by me. Didn't say hello."

Hermes' hunch had paid off.

"Great," he said. Now for the hard part. "You wouldn't have any idea where he was going, would you?"

"Well, yes. As a matter of fact… A crow came down and landed just in front of him, over there." He pointed with his nose. "Had a bit of a chat, they did. I thought that was unusual. Few cats would pass the time of day with birds. Let alone crows. That's when I thought there was something odd about it…" He broke off, thinking. Hermes waited, suddenly taking great interest in a pebble just in front of his paws. After a moment, the tortoise continued. "I don't like eavesdropping, you understand. But they were talking so loud it was impossible not to hear. The crow was all excited. Full of himself, he was. Did a little jig. Went on about some search for dogs and cats. Said he'd found a place. Old ginger liked that, he did. Got very excited."

Hermes was all ears but affected an air of nonchalance. This wasn't what he had expected. "Hmm. Sounds strange. Whereabouts?"

"Where was it now? Let me think..." He bobbed his head slightly, looking into the distance. "Oh, yes. They're in Tavros. That was it."

"Tavros?" Hermes computed the travel times, distances, routes.

"Yeah, they set off straight away. Ginger got the bird to guide him. Went off at quite a lick. Like they were in a hurry. 'What's that all about?' I thought. Still, why should I care? Nobody ever tells me nothing. I just potter about here, minding my business. I mean, even you can't be bothered to say hello more than once every couple of decades."

"Yes, jolly good," said Hermes. "You take care." Condescension laced his icy politeness. "I'll be on my way and let you get back to doing whatever it is you do all day." He waved his paw in the general direction of a flowering shrub. "'*The end of labour is to gain leisure*', as someone once said." He turned to go.

"Yeah, 'cept he never really said it," grumbled Homer. Hermes turned back, eyes narrowed.

"What?"

"What you said. Bollocks that is," said the tortoise, with exaggerated patience. "Although you're not the only one to get it wrong. What he actually said was '*business is for the sake of leisure*', along with all sorts of other claptrap. Anyway, he was overrated."

"What?" Hermes repeated, louder this time. Homer caught the cat's stare.

"Aristotle," he replied. "Overrated. All that wandering around pontificating. Load of old cobblers, if you ask me. Peripatetic? Peri-pathetic, more like. Now, Nietzsche, he was a proper philosopher. '*God is dead.*' That's profound, that is." He looked up at Hermes. "Present company excepted, of course. Anyway. Never liked Aristotle. A miserable sod if you ask me, and I met him."

Hermes felt wrong-pawed. He looked at the tortoise in astonishment.

"You can't have," he blurted. "He lived over two thousand years ago. You're not that old."

"Might be," grumped Homer. "I've got good genes, me. It's in the DNA, you see. Tip-top, it is. Quality. Runs in the family." He paused. "Actually, it might have been Grandpa who knew Aristotle. Had some stories to tell, did Grandpa. Always had time for a chat, no matter what." He looked accusingly at the white cat. Hermes was almost speechless. He pulled himself together.

"Aristotle had some other sayings as well that you might care to remember, including '*wit is educated insolence*'. It's a fine dividing line between banter and insubordination. Don't let your scholarship get you into trouble." He stared at the tortoise, pointedly.

"'*Character is that which reveals moral purpose*'," retorted Homer, unable to let things rest. Hermes took a step forwards, looming over the tortoise. Homer retreated into his shell. The cat crouched down until he could look inside.

"'*The aim of the wise is not to secure pleasure, but to avoid pain*'," he breathed, almost purring, a subtle hint of menace hanging in the air.

· · ·

In a quiet corner of his new headquarters at the Library of Hadrian, Kratos gathered several of his sons and daughters; the hardcore of his gang. The delay he'd agreed with Zelus allowed him to step up his watch on Athena's dig while his brother's attention was elsewhere.

Now it was time to up the ante.

CHAPTER 39
SUMMONED

Hermes headed in the direction of Tavros, prepared to conduct a street-by-street search if need be. Bia's reference to dogs howling came to mind. He'd dismissed it at first, but now it seemed the Delphi cat's story did stack up, and he really didn't want Apollo to have bragging rights over this one. At the back of his mind, an uneasy feeling was brewing: that his casual dismissal had been too hasty. Was this what guilt felt like?

Never say sorry. Never go back.

That was the mantra of his kind.

What continued to surprise him was the ginger cat taking such an interest in a mere mortal. Now that was quite a story. He was certain there was more to it than met the eye. Perhaps there was something in the water up in the mountains.

He spotted the owl from some distance, perched on a branch overhanging the path, and groaned inwardly. What does she want now? He approached the tree and sat down, fixing the bird with a hard stare and flicking his tail in frustration; a sign he expected the bird to read and understand. He was pleased to note its growing discomfort.

"You're wanted," said the owl. "My Lady requests an audience with you, sir. As soon as is convenient, if you will."

"Requests, or demands?" enquired Hermes, determined not to let the owl off the hook.

The bird shook itself and rotated her head from right to left.

"Requests," she said finally. "But firmly. Very firmly." She hooted. Hermes cocked his head slightly, enjoying the owl's discomfort. It was a shame she was just out of reach. It might be fun to ruffle her feathers a bit.

"I can do next Tuesday," he replied.

The owl became more flustered than ever. "It's urgent," she shrieked, and vomited a pellet of last night's undigested supper onto the path.

"Urgent, eh?" he said, sniffing and studying the deposit with forensic intent. "So, really more of a demand than a request?" He fixed his stare back on the frazzled owl.

"Yes, it is!" she squeaked. She flapped her wings.

Reluctantly, Hermes concluded his sport.

"Tell her I'll be there directly," he said, and stepping delicately around the pellet, walked on down the path.

CHAPTER 40
TALKS ABOUT TALKS

He found her on the summit of Pnyx Hill, surveying the city. She was aware of his arrival without having to turn around.

"Good of you to come," said Athena, still looking at the view. Hermes stepped up beside her, following her gaze, saying nothing. He remained wary of getting on the wrong side of Athena when she was in a grim mood, and this was not a time to be probing for point-scoring opportunities.

The silence between them stretched. In the distance, he could hear the city: traffic, the occasional siren, metro trains emerging from tunnels. They coalesced into an unabated backdrop; the soundtrack of urban life. Nearby he picked out birdsong, the buzz of insects and the chatter of tourists. Always tourists. They love to come and gawp at the remnants of their past.

Pnyx Hill provided a fine view of the Acropolis, the Propylea – the ceremonial stairway to the summit plateau – and the incomparable Parthenon. Athena followed his stare.

"Time was when my statue towered above that thing," she said. Hermes murmured agreement. He could remember it. A wave of irritation took over his thoughts.

"That was when you cared about this city," he said, looking her in the eye. He expected resistance, a sharp, stinging response, but it didn't come.

Instead, she looked away and sighed. "Yes, I may have let things slip." This was quite an admission. The closest thing to an apology he'd ever heard from her. What was going on? Athena led the way to a more sheltered spot beneath the low-spreading branches of a pine tree and settled down. She waited until he joined her.

"I've been distracted," she conceded. "I've rather let things go." She looked at him. "But you haven't exactly been helpful." There was little accusation in her voice; Hermes' nature was all too familiar. The city was her responsibility. She might step away for a while – a century or two, perhaps – but it was ultimately her domain.

They sat in silence for a while.

"So, what's to be done?" the white cat enquired.

"Well, we have to stop the gangs wreaking havoc," she said. "My authority... our authority is being undermined, perhaps terminally. They are waking up and flexing their muscles, so to speak, and they're not finished yet."

"What do you mean?"

"I think they're venting old grievances. They seem more purposeful than ever before. I think they want to usurp me. Not just me. All of us."

"How do you know?"

The look she gave suggested he should have known better than to ask. Of course, her silent winged spies got everywhere.

Hermes recalled his recent conversations with the gang leaders. He liked to think he had their pulse, but had they been keeping things back from him? Were there signals he'd missed? He'd known for some time they had developed a dim awareness of their past, but they'd never made an issue of it. Not to him, at any rate. They seemed ignorant, or uncaring, focusing instead on their little daily power-games and territorial disputes. He might have to re-evaluate.

"And you're sure about this?"

"Not yet. But I am worried." She sighed. "I'm afraid I housed a turncoat. A double agent. Because of her treachery, something important has been taken."

The white cat waited. The story of Athena's strange behaviour was about to unfold. What would be the consequences of his own role in recent events?

Athena glanced at him, then began. "A very long time ago, I lost something. Something precious. Not just to me, but to the whole city. It was a small statuette of me. A replica of the larger one that once stood yonder." She glanced over to the Acropolis. "It was lost during a sack of the city. You know, they used to occur often in the latter days of Roman rule. I wasn't here. I'd taken a sabbatical. Otherwise, I may have been able to prevent it." She was lost in thought for a while. "Anyway. It got lost. And it's been a problem ever since."

"This is your long lost artefact? The one you supposedly couldn't call to mind? Losing an old treasure is a shame, yes, but hardly a disaster. If they dig it up, they'll just bung it in a museum to collect dust."

She gave him a sly look. "I wasn't likely to tell my followers what it was. They're loyal to a fault, but they still gossip." Her stare became more pointed. "Anyway, the point is that it's more than just a statue. I imbued it with a power. The ability to communicate, mind-to-mind, across the boundaries between species, and across distance."

"You mean mind manipulation? How come I knew nothing about this?"

"No one did. I kept it to myself." She looked a little smug. "It's tuned to my thoughts specifically, but there's a risk that anyone who has some power might reconfigure it and use it for their own ends." She looked pointedly at him. There was no need to say more. In the long silence, Hermes tried to unravel the implications of what he'd heard. She'd been right to keep it under wraps. If he'd known about this earlier, he would have taken it for himself. Any of them would.

"So, anyone can use it? But what could they do with it?"

"Not just anyone. You need sufficient mental strength or power. In the right hands, a skilled user can project their thoughts into the mind of a target, control their emotions, plant ideas, get them to take actions they might not otherwise have considered." She caught his sceptical look. "It worked with Odysseus. And many more besides. A powerful mind can control many at once. Like a large gang, or a small army."

Hermes experienced another novel emotion: shock. This was a most unusual day. At the back of his mind, he replayed his conversations with Herse and Bia.

"And what's worse," Athena continued, "I think Bia has got it."

This was not good. This sounded much worse than a little territorial squabble over control of the Plaka. Hermes might have just handed their enemies the power to unseat them all, with unforeseen consequences; none of them good. It might be difficult to hide his role from the others if the full cast were to be assembled, and an inquiry started. He scarcely dared ask his next question.

"Do you think she knows how to use it?"

Athena gave him another sharp look. For once he was on the receiving end of those implacable emerald eyes and he didn't like it.

"I'm not sure. I'm going to pay her a visit to find out, but at least we should be prepared."

"I guess you'd like me to find that big fat slob of a brother of ours?"

"If you'd be so kind. But don't call him a slob. He has so many hidden talents, you know."

CHAPTER 41
PARK LIFE

I t had been a while since Athena had ventured down into Kallithea, but to her satisfaction, many of the shops and restaurants were still as she remembered. She had regained her composure following the regrettable dismissal of her treacherous servant. She experienced no guilt at her treatment of the unfortunate wretch; standards had to be maintained and the stupid cat had been acting far beyond the normal scope of her responsibilities. Athena just hoped the damage wasn't as great as she feared. Who could tell what manner of mischief Bia and her thuggish brothers might unleash?

She pondered the scenarios as she walked. What if Bia used the artefact to turn humans against her, or her followers; perhaps against stray cats across the city? What if she allied with her brothers to take over the Agora and force her into exile? Where might it end? She might need to consider putting out a request for reinforcements; but she couldn't bear the humiliation. It would be the last resort option, and she no longer knew where they all lived, or how many had retired or fallen into senility. And the thought of the endless barracking, the snide remarks and suppressed laughter were more than she could bear. It might last for centuries. And that was if they won.

It would all be behind her back, of course; no one would dare say anything to her face. Hera would be worst. Then they'd be wanting to interfere; they were already angry enough with her.

Athena valued her independence. She didn't want the rest of them meddling; not here in Athens, at any rate. She shook her head violently, as if trying to banish the thought, and walked on.

Hopefully, things wouldn't be so bad; it would be something she could contain. It took time to master the use of these objects. If the wielder didn't have the experience or the mental capacity, it could take days or weeks. Of course, Bia had more than enough mental capacity if she used it. She was a Titan; a goddess even older than herself, although saddled with the limited imagination typical of her generation.

Once, it wouldn't have mattered, of course. Athena could have haughtily dismissed any challenge with a swipe of her thoughts. Now, in this diminished state, the extra leverage the artefact gave was a game changer. Athena's one hope resided in her not understanding how to release its full powers. Bia would need to learn how to bend it to her will, how to project her thoughts, how to focus them into the mind of the recipient. She'd need to experiment, find a willing victim to test it on. It would take time to master the techniques. That would present a window of opportunity, but Athena would have to be quick.

She turned off Thiseos Street at the corner of Davaki Park and headed down Mantzagriotaki Street. Approaching the park she saw several of Bia's followers resting in the shade of nearby trees and shrubs. Few of them would be active at this time of day, and Athena guessed Bia wouldn't want to leave her treasure to the care of someone else, so she too would remain close by. She crossed the road and entered via a pedestrian gate and immediately spotted her target sniffing at some flowers near the fountain, as if without a care in the world. She headed for the gang leader, who stiffened as she sensed her approach.

Athena didn't dwell on ceremony. "Let's talk," she said briskly and headed straight to a secluded patch of grass nearby, waiting for Bia to join her. The other cat sauntered after, visibly irritated by the way her visitor had taken the initiative. Athena scarcely waited for her to sit down. "I've dismissed the traitor," she said.

Bia pretended to ignore her, staring into the middle distance. "None of my business. If that's what you came to tell me, this should be a short meeting."

Athena studied an unsuspecting beetle scurrying across the ground between them. "I just thought I'd let you know, just in case you wanted to recruit her permanently." She let it hang.

"How you manage your people is entirely your own affair. It really is nothing to do with me."

"Whereas stealing from the Stoa Poikile dig clearly is."

Bia gave her a sharp look.

"It's fair game. Exploring, discovering, unearthing, stealing. They're all legitimate activities. Any cat in Athens would agree. There's no law against it."

Athena's jaw clenched. The other cat was correct, of course. All felines acted on their wit to turn situations to their advantage, whether through stealth or cunning, or by manipulating others. The only crime was that the dig theft had taken place under her nose, at a place she'd been watching for months. Somewhere she'd set a guard around.

"Yes, you conducted a very skilled operation," she said. "So, enlighten me. What do you intend to do with your prize?"

Bia squealed in delight. "Aha, so this is what's bugging

you? You're so precious about your blessed antiquities. Well, this one's mine, and a nice little object it is, too. Finders keepers, and all that. I can see why you're annoyed. It's special, isn't it? Beautiful. I could feel the hum of power as I dug it out." She paused, enjoying Athena's discomfort, and continued her mockery. "Tell me. What would you like me to do? Put it on display in a glass box in the museum? Well, you can think again. It's staying with me."

Athena studied the trees for a while and watched some human children chasing each other around the fountain. Her mind raced. Did Bia even realise the significance of what she'd stolen?

"There are worse things you could do," she said.

The gang leader gave her a contemptuous look. "Do you take me for a fool? It's part of my treasure, my hoard. Perhaps the key piece. Something that I can use. Just the fact I've got it, and how I came by it. Swiping it from under your nose. That enhances my legend, my fame. I wouldn't be surprised if the storytellers are already composing the tale at their evening gatherings across the city. My reputation and the fame of my gang, is growing. Yours is in decline. How many followers have you got? You're a loser, and from what I hear, you won't have a home for much longer." She stared at the grey cat. "Do you think for a moment that I'm going to give it all up just so the humans can put a rare and beautiful gold coin on display in their precious house of relics? Think again." Bia stretched, flaring her claws.

Athena didn't move. A long, tense pause ensued before she got to her feet. "This city's history is important to me, but given your attitude, you can keep it. I thought it would be pointless reasoning with you. So I'll say farewell. I wouldn't want to delay your victory parade." She looked around, then stiffly walked away, not waiting for a reply.

Athena left the park, jumping through a gap in the railings. She crossed the road and turned back into crowded Thiseos Street. Bia could enjoy her petty victory.

As she walked, she allowed a slight spring to enter her step.

CHAPTER 42
PRISON

The street was dusty but deserted. A few untidily parked cars filled the gaps between the stunted, scruffy trees down one side. None moved along it. What sort of place was this? Just a few minutes ago, Apollo was passing along crowded, busy streets lined with shops, offices, apartment blocks and people. A couple of turns off the main road and he was in a netherworld of shutters, graffiti-covered windowless walls, high fences and deserted, dusty streets. This was a district of warehouses and industrial yards, most of which seemed abandoned.

He plodded along, as dusk turned to night, questioning the crow's intelligence. Why had it brought him to this wasteland? Did it understand who he was looking for?

He turned a corner and then another, as he traced a zig-zag path across the deserted quarter. Another hour passed and the roads and buildings all looked the same; he yearned for some sign of life.

Then he heard it. Faint at first, but growing louder as he homed in.

The barking of restless, unhappy dogs.

As he drew closer, he also detected the distressed yowls of

cats. His stomach felt small. Who could ignore the calls of so many distressed animals? Even the most cloth-eared two-legged passer-by should detect the pain and fear in their voices. He was fast developing a scorn for the stupidity of humankind and mounting anger towards those who held these animals captive. He should—no. Free the captives. Forget about the humans. He couldn't afford any distraction.

Apollo drew closer, anger building with each step. He needed to keep a clear head to plan a rescue. The crow perched on a branch of a misshapen apology for a tree just ahead of him.

The compound containing the imprisoned animals lay on the opposite side of the road. Apollo couldn't see in; a high wall topped with another metre of sturdy wire-mesh fence surrounded it, and he could see no foothold that would allow him to climb up.

At one end was an adjacent building with an even higher wall. The other end of the wall ended in a right angle and continued down a narrow passageway ending in another building. Apollo followed it and entered a small forecourt between the building and another road.

He was at the front of the compound where the dogs wailed. The only entrance was a sturdy locked door. Grimy windows to either side were reinforced with metal bars. The owner clearly took security seriously.

He retraced his steps along the side to the back of the site, studying the wall and fence, but could see no holes or weaknesses. At each corner, security cameras peered down on the road outside.

He sat squarely in front of one, not comprehending its function, and gazed at it. An inscrutable black lens peered back. Apollo turned to face the wall, wishing he could see what lay behind. But it was just too high. He would have to rely on the bird. He glanced at it, but it anticipated his question.

"This is where they are. What now?"

"I need to know if my friend Olympia is in there," he said. "Can you circle overhead and tell me who is inside? Tell me what it's like?"

The crow gave him a long look. "It's dark, in case you hadn't noticed. I won't be able to see much." He took off and spent a few minutes flying back and forth above the compound. He perched on the edge of the adjacent building's roof, peering into the gloom. Then he returned to the impatient cat.

"Dunno," he said. "Looks like there are lots of dogs and cats down there, in pens."

"How many?"

"More than five."

"How many more than five?"

"Don't know. I can only count to five."

Apollo sat down, exasperated. If only he could get up there, he could make a proper assessment. As it was, he was relying on a counting crow with limited mathematical abilities.

"Can you go up there and shout for Olympia?" he asked.

"No," replied the bird. "I can't talk to cats."

Apollo scrutinised him with a look that, to a casual observer, gave the impression he would happily eat him.

The crow was not a casual observer and immediately recognised the significance of the focused stare. "It's not my fault," he countered.

"You can talk to *me* perfectly well," the cat told him, fighting to maintain a steady voice.

"You're different. Believe me. Before I met you, I'd no sooner have dreamed I could talk to a cat than drive a car."

Apollo bit back a comment. There was no time to dwell on the shortcomings of affinity animals. He needed to find his friend. He broke his stare and turned towards the high wall. "Olympia!" he yelled at the top of his voice.

There was a momentary silence from the animals inside the compound.

"Who is it, and what do you want?" came a deep-voiced reply from a large-sounding dog.

"I'm looking for my friend Olympia. Is she in there?" Apollo bellowed.

The cacophony simmered down to murmured discussions. He strained his ears to make out the detail. There seemed to be a big debate among the dogs, perhaps because they had the louder voices. They spoke over each other, but he could make out a few comments.

"What's going on?"

"Who does he want?"

"What's it to do with us?"

"Who cares? Just tell him to get us out."

"Shh. He just might be able to help us."

Eventually, the dog who had first responded shouted back.

"Maybe. But what's so important about her? We all want to get out of this prison. We've been stuck here for ages, having puppies that get taken away before they're old enough. We're all desperate to get out. You've got to help us."

Apollo paced up and down, casting exasperated glances at the high wall. "What about the cats? I can hear cats in there with you. She's one of them. I want to talk to her."

"Who cares about the cats? Just get us out. We want to go home."

Apollo stopped pacing and stared hard at the wall as if willing it to collapse in a cloud of dust and rubble. He struggled to keep the frustration from his voice. "Look, I'll try to help you all, I promise, but first I need to speak to the cats."

There was further muffled discussion among the dogs, and in the background, some high-pitched feline voices could be heard.

"What's going on? Shut up for a minute and let us talk to him."

The debate went on for a short while, but then the din subsided, and he heard a cat.

"Who are you, and can you help us?"

This was progress. At least he was now speaking to one of his own species.

"I'm Apollo from Delphi," he shouted. "I will try to help you, but first I need to know if there's someone called Olympia in there. I'm looking for her." Nerves knotted his stomach. So much of his hope was resting on getting a response. He could only wait as more discussions took place behind the wall.

After a while, a faint but familiar voice replied.

"Well, you took your time, sweetie."

"Olympia! I'm so pleased to hear you. I've come to rescue you."

"And how are you going to do that, darling? Have you brought the army with you?"

Her natural sarcasm shone through the adversity; although she sounded strained.

"No..." he faltered. "It's... just me. But don't worry. I'll think of something. I'll get you out."

There was a longer pause while they digested his words. In the background, other impatient voices clamoured for news of the outside world. Some of them seemed to expect an immediate breakout. The last thing Apollo wanted to do was give the captives false hope. It was now clear that rescuing them would take some planning.

Eventually, Olympia replied, her voice cracking.

"You'd better be quick. I don't know how long I've got. They take some of us away every day, and I think... I think..."

She couldn't bring herself to say it.

She started again. "It's awful in here. It's..." She paused, collecting herself. "There's hardly any space. Some in here are their own worst enemy. They stop eating or lash out. They take them away soonest. I don't know what happens to them, but I don't think it's good. They keep the dogs for breeding. When they get too old, they disappear as well, and they take the puppies before they're weaned. Everyone's desperate. There isn't much time. I can't..." She trailed off.

Apollo had never heard her like this before. Olympia always had a quirky outlook, a snarky comment or a lofty look.

"You have to be quick..." Echoes from his dream.

He shivered.

"Don't worry. I'll get you out."

The words sounded hollow; he had no idea how he was going to do it.

CHAPTER 43
THE RAID

Athena waited until well after midnight before making her move. By this time there were no humans around; restaurants and bars had closed and even late-night revellers had retired to bed and the streets were quiet. Clinging to the shadows and moving with the grace and stealth that came naturally to her kind, she approached the site of the archaeological dig. She was less bothered about spies by now; even so, she didn't want to attract undue attention.

The distractions of recent days meant she could not keep as close a watch as she would have liked; but she was confident no other intruders had made surreptitious visits, and couldn't wait any longer. Once news of Bia's raid got out, other opportunists might try to see what goodies they could unearth.

She slipped through the fence and descended to the dig site, then made her way to the spot she expected to find treasure; the place indicated by Herse at her interrogation. It underlined what she had taken from her own observations.

But something was wrong. Athena stopped in her tracks, dismayed. Even by the dim light from nearby streetlamps, she could see the evidence of rough, hasty digging. Someone had scrabbled at the dirt, careless of the disturbance, and had extracted something from exactly the spot she'd been focused on all these weeks.

Athena glanced around. How had they known where to dig? Bia was convinced she had uncovered an item of power. So what had given her the impression?

She bent closer to the freshly dug earth, sniffed it warily, then buried her nose further into the hole. Just on the edge of her senses, she detected the faintest vestige of energy, like static electricity. It tickled the tips of her whiskers, giving the tiniest echo that something powerful had once been present.

Stepping back, Athena studied the area more carefully, checking for any evidence that might show who the raiders were; although she had strong suspicions. There were signs of entry on the far side of the compound: fur snagged on the edge of a rough gap in the chain-link fence; disturbed dirt where the invader had jumped down. Looking at the landing place more closely, she saw a couple of faint paw prints in the dust. The gap in the fence was the part of the compound closest to Monastiraki Square. So, what had happened to her guards? She couldn't blame Bia this time; this raid looked like the work of one of her brothers.

Rooted to the spot, her mind in turmoil, she whirled through the different scenarios, then she slowly made her way back to the Agora. After all the waiting across all the years, and despite her careful precautions, someone had stolen her prize. It was almost impossible to take in; the enormity of her loss was bad enough, but having it stolen from under her nose was far worse, and she dared not think about the consequences.

Anxiety replaced the numb feeling, then a howling rage.

She could not let this go; the fate of her kind depended on it.

CHAPTER 44
APOLLO IN THE AGORA

I t was clear to Apollo he could do nothing by himself. Staring at this high-walled compound would not help those inside, either. He turned to the crow, still sitting in the tree beside him.

"I need to find help," he said. "Can you keep watch?"

"Certainly, squire. In fact, I should be able to do better than that. There's a lot of us willing to help. I can rustle up some lads and lasses, and keep this place under proper surveillance, round the clock."

Apollo thought for a minute. "'Us'?"

"Other crows, ravens, jackdaws. All my relatives. There's a lot of us about, you know."

It might work; intense scrutiny from the air. Enough of a racket to attract the attention of even the most dim-witted human. If it were noisy enough, they might even investigate. The more he thought about it, the more he liked the idea.

"Round up as many of your kind as you can and keep this place under observation. It doesn't matter about the noise. In fact, make as much as you can. If anything happens, anything even remotely interesting, come and find me as quickly as possible."

"And what about you, guv?"

"I'm going to get help," Apollo told him.

"Okay. I'll get my mates."

He flew off.

Apollo turned and retraced his path, as fast as his tired body would allow. As he left the deserted quarter and reached the places where humans lived, the eastern sky lightened. His mind wandered, recalling recent events, his concern for Daphne never far from the surface. But now he'd found Olympia he was even more aware of the importance of speed. He remembered the strange dream and its ending, and he imagined music, as if an orchestra were playing inside his head. It energised him, lifting his mood. As he walked, his tail swayed with the beat. A distant part of his mind wondered why he'd never done this before; it was a welcome distraction from the weariness in his paws as they trod the dusty roads and pavements.

The sun rose before him, and he stared unflinching into its glare; not far to go now. He crossed railway lines, and trotted over the normally traffic-choked major roads, still quiet at this hour. Skirting the National Observatory, he left the streets and entered a wooded area, homing in on the Temple of Hephaestus. It seemed somehow familiar. He got his bearings. They said Athena lived in or around the Agora. This must be the place; much changed as it was. What had happened to the bustling inhabitants of yesteryear, with their relentless debate and discourse?

Through the trees, he spied the Acropolis and its monuments. Below it was the long roof of the Stoa of Attalos. Paying more attention to his immediate surroundings, he noticed movement beneath the trees: cats, lots of them. There must be some sort of community here. He moved closer and was confronted by a superior-looking amber-and-black female.

"Who are you that dares to come among us?" she challenged, looking him in the eye.

Apollo halted. He hadn't expected he would need to argue his way past guards.

"I've come to see Athena," he said, unable to keep the irritation out of his voice.

"Does she know you? Do you have an appointment?" came the smooth reply. Her tail stayed firmly and impolitely down. She looked at him with ill-concealed disdain, and if he'd been minded to sympathise, he might have seen her point. It was some time since he'd last had a proper wash, and he was dusty, travel-weary and a little dishevelled. But he didn't feel like turning on the charm.

He returned an appraising look of his own before answering, pleased to note she found his scrutiny a little disconcerting.

"She knows me."

He detected a momentary flicker behind the eyes, and her manner softened a degree.

"I need a name." She remained the epitome of bureaucratic obstinacy.

"Tell her Phoebus Pythius Acesius is here." His eyes narrowed. That should challenge her powers of recall. If she passed the test, he had plenty of others to throw her way.

"Hmm." She looked him up and down, her doubt clear. "Okay, follow me."

She wove a path between trees, over and around fallen stones, exposed ancient tree roots and modern pavements, gradually ascending the hill known as Pnyx.

Halfway up, in a small clearing, on an ancient fallen altarpiece, a magnificent grey animal reclined. She turned her piercing green eyes to study the intruder and addressed his escort.

"And what have we here, Penelope?"

"This is Fee, er, Pithy…"

Apollo stepped past her, glaring at the grey cat.

"It's me. It may have been a while, but you can cut the attitude. I'm here to tell you about some serious wrongdoing in this city of yours. But if you're not interested, just tell me and I'll be on my way."

To his left, Penelope was clearly aghast at his lack of decorum. But he ignored her. She tried to get a word in.

"He says he knows you. So I thought I'd better bring him up here. Just in case."

"I seem to recall him taking better care of his appearance," the grey cat replied.

Apollo gave Penelope a scornful glance and focused all of his attention on her superior. As he looked into Athena's emerald eyes, he sensed the faintest ghost of a memory: of thrones and a mountain and long white robes, and feasting and music and laughter. But also argument, rivalry, point-scoring, bickering and conflict. It vanished as quickly as it had arrived.

"I understood you had some authority in this city," he said icily, glancing at his surroundings. "But if this is the best you can do for a palace, perhaps I've been misinformed."

The grey cat interrupted him. "I have enough on my plate right now, and I have little need of further distraction. If you want my help, you'd better have a good story. Though if you are who I believe you to be, I'm surprised you can't deal with it yourself."

The barb stung all the more because of the truth it contained. Apollo needed to rediscover how to manipulate humans. It used to be so easy in the past, when he could just seduce them or intimidate them, according to his mood, or occasionally even appeal to reason. With a conscious effort of will, he swallowed his pride.

"Requesting help is the last thing I want to do, but I have no alternative." He recounted the salient points of his story, keeping it as brief as possible. He glossed over the detail of his encounter with the Botrys gang and the chase, but he left out all mention of Hecate. He detected surprise on the grey cat's face at certain points. She was not as informed as she might claim.

"So," continued Apollo, "I have located my companion and discovered there are lots of animals imprisoned with her. I've set a watch, but I need support to get everyone out. I have…" He hesitated, unwilling to admit it. "I have unfortunately lost the ability to converse with humans." He looked down, as if ashamed of this weakness, then met her eyes again. "Time is running out, and we need the humans to intervene. We need back-up."

Athena rose to a sitting position and gracefully curled her tail around her paws. She looked surprised to find herself on the receiving end of a call to reason; his case was irrefutable. "An extraordinary tale," she declared, and looked across the treetops towards the city. "And what do you think I can do about it?" Her voice was distant; she sounded almost bored.

With an effort of will, Apollo silenced the turmoil in his head. When he next spoke, his voice carried such a calm authority and assurance that Athena had no choice but to pay him full attention.

"All over Athens and beyond, cats have been snatched and held captive. Some are dying. Others are being sent to goodness knows where. Dogs and their puppies are also being mistreated, and in addition, there is an undercurrent of fear throughout the animal population; even you might detect it, if you cared to listen. Also, the inhabitants of the outer regions are in a ferment of frustration and their leaders are spoiling for a fight. You always prided yourself on your duty of care for this city, but with the current degree of turmoil, is that still the case? Can you maintain any pretence of control, or is your time at an end?"

Athena glared at him as if caught in a trap.

How would she respond to his challenge? Athena could

be prickly, but she'd usually been even-tempered and receptive to reasoned argument; she could even be friendly. Perhaps something was bugging her?

After a pause, her tone became a little more accommodating. "Wait in this vicinity while I investigate further and organise our response. I suggest you get some rest." She turned tail and left with no further word.

CHAPTER 45
AFTERMATH

Kratos walked around it, peering at it from several angles. But it was no good; he couldn't make it do anything.

"What's it for?" he growled. He was in a secluded corner of the Library of Hadrian, as far away from the prying eyes of Zelus' gang as possible. The snatch squad – the four of his children who had mounted the raid – stood by at a respectful distance. They watched his every move as he inspected his prize. He turned to the nearest.

"Are you sure this is it?"

"Yes, sir. We've been watching her for days now. We dug it up at the exact spot she's been studying, and there was nothing else like it around."

Kratos turned back to the object and continued his inspection. It was disappointingly small for something of importance: a statuette of a goddess holding a spear, just a few centimetres tall. It didn't look special. What was he missing? It was an image of his archenemy; of that, he was sure. What other goddess would pose in such outlandish gear? But why did she value it so? Was it just vanity?

Across the site, on the far side, he saw Zelus. He was

approaching, purposefully; what did he want? Before he arrived, Kratos stepped in front of his prize. That was one subject he had no desire to discuss.

Zelus wasted no time getting to the point. "We need to talk."

"So, talk."

"We need to agree our next steps. I expect Athena will seek some sort of retribution, so we need to be prepared for the eventuality."

"Let her try. She hasn't got the numbers, and the remnants of this mob won't be up for round two." He studied the pitiful group of captives in the far corner. They were few, most of them injured, which had prevented their escape. How many would survive the tender mercies of their handlers, given their fragile state?

Kratos turned back to the other cat. "But you're right. We need to decide how to press our advantage and finally get rid of her." He paused, appraising his ally, then addressed the issue closest to both their hearts. "And we need to divide the spoils. I started this war, so it's appropriate that I get the lion's share of the territory. My guys will take the Plaka itself, and everything on this side of the square. You can have everything on the other side." He watched for his rival's reaction; Zelus did not disappoint him.

"Not so fast. Your undisciplined rabble would never have managed this without us. You couldn't even get here on time, and half of your unruly mob only turned up when it was all over. We will have the Plaka. You can take Syntagma Square and the streets down there. That's more than enough for you to handle."

Kratos had half expected this response, but he and his forces could easily see the Gizi gang off if he chose. That might be sooner rather than later, unless Zelus backed down. The two of them squared up to each other.

"The prisoner's escaped."

Both leaders spun to face a nervous-looking cat who had just arrived. It was the male half of the guard team Zelus had assigned to look after Daphne. His colleague hung slightly further back, stepping from paw to paw, looking even more nervous than her companion.

Zelus vented his fury on the hapless animal. "How did you let that happen, you useless fool?" He took a step forwards. "You'd better have a good explanation for this."

"Yes, you being *crack troops*, and all," Kratos added, glancing sidelong at his rival.

The Gizi gang boss stared with laser-like intensity at his unfortunate underling, who looked like he might melt.

"We didn't stand a chance," he stammered. "He came from nowhere."

"Who did?" Zelus demanded.

"Never seen him before. It was this grey-and-white guy. A real warrior. Deadly. He took out Yannis in seconds." He shuddered at the memory.

"Then the little assassin showed her true colours," the other cat added. "She turned into a real viper. Savage."

"She looks like she's a bit of a ninja," the first cat agreed.

Zelus was shaking with anger. "But you just let her walk away?"

"What's that about Yannis?" said Kratos.

Quivering with nerves, the guard addressed him. "He wanted to take our prisoner away with him, but we said she belonged to Zelus. Then the grey-and-white guy just appeared. Took him by the throat. Killed him."

"Then the two of them turned on us," his companion added. "We only just escaped."

"You don't look as if you put up much of a fight." Zelus advanced on the pair; they both edged backwards. Behind them, Kratos' offspring drew closer, cutting off their escape.

"Wait a minute…" Kratos' mind raced. "Grey-and-white, you say? And what was your prisoner like?"

"Amber, black-and-white. Longer fur. Looked too well groomed to be a gang member, if you ask me," offered the female.

"But no sign of a ginger?" They shook their heads. "Sounds like two of the spics that infiltrated our headquarters the other night." He turned to Zelus, a fresh note of urgency in his voice. "That's two of them. We need to find the ginger one and track them all down. He's the ringleader, and I've got a bone to pick with him. Once I've taken him apart, limb from limb. He can't be far away." He turned back to the guards. "Where did they go?"

"They set off down Ifestou Street. But you know where that leads…"

The guard let it hang.

"Just as I expected. They work for *her*. They must be special forces or something. We'd better root them out before they come back with their friends." He continued, more eager now. "It's time to take the Agora and all the scum who lurk there. We have to get rid of Athena and her rag-tag gaggle of followers, once and for all."

"How soon can you be ready?" Zelus looked as if he wanted to attack straight away.

Kratos glanced at him, his instinctive caution returning. "We need to plan for this. We don't know what powers she's got hidden in the woods, or what friends she can call on. And the troops are still recovering. We need to give them a bit of time to rest and prepare, and everyone's scattered around the neighbourhood."

Zelus gave him a long, calculating look. "How long do you need?"

Kratos scowled. Why was his brother so desperate to rush in? Was he so naive as to never plan? No one had ever really tested Athena's power. She might have resources they weren't aware of. Otherwise, how could she have effectively ruled over this city for so long? He didn't like to admit it, but those three spies or assassins or whatever they were had spooked him. Melanippus' divination had highlighted them, and they might still have a role to play. What if they were part of a much larger secret army?

"Tomorrow, we gather our forces," said Kratos. "We do a little reconnaissance and make the call."

CHAPTER 46
POOLSIDE CHAT

I n the leafy northern suburb of Kifisia, the houses were large and swimming pools de rigueur. Beside one of the more spectacular examples was a wide patio set with comfortable sun loungers and umbrellas. Bright sunlight sparkled on the still water, casting playful reflections on the whitewashed walls of the rear of the house. A glass-roofed extension enclosed an alfresco dining area and barbecue, behind which was a dark, cool interior.

The garden was deserted apart from a large russet-coloured cat which was curled up on one of the sun loungers, in the shade. He was, Hermes reflected, quite the biggest brute of a cat he'd ever seen, and judging from his recent regime, he was getting even bigger. Probably a lot of Maine Coon in there, mixed with *souvlaki* and *kleftiko*. It was undeniable that the beast was overweight despite his enormous frame.

"Morning," he said, gently hopping onto the adjacent sun lounger.

The big cat didn't move a muscle, but from somewhere within the depths of the mound of fur, a disgruntled-sounding voice emerged. "Don't you ever knock?"

"Bit tricky with hedges," Hermes shot back. "Anyway, you know me. I always like the element of surprise."

The large cat grunted and continued snoozing. Hermes made himself comfortable and examined his surroundings. He was in no hurry.

"Nice place you've got here," he ventured after a while.

Wearily, Ares raised his head to get a proper view of his guest. "It's not too bad," he agreed, keeping his tone neutral.

"Yes. A comfortable pad." Hermes studied the reflections playing on the surface of the pool. "I didn't know you could swim."

"Of course it's comfortable. It's my palace," growled Ares, in a voice deeper than the sea. "I'm not going to live in a shed, am I? Or scratch a living on the top of a windswept hill." He looked across at the other cat. "I've never understood why you don't get a proper place of your own. Why don't you put your paws up occasionally? Enjoy a bit of luxury? Get some servants of the human variety to run around after you. You might like it."

Before they fell into a discussion on local real estate values, Hermes changed tack. "Don't enjoy swimming. Too much chlorine is bad for your fur. I'm surprised you do it." He looked his neighbour up and down. "Thought you might sink, given that thatch."

A rumbling sound rose from somewhere deep inside the big cat's body. Either a growl or a laugh. "Who needs to swim? This is a great place to hang out. The food's fantastic. Lots of tuna and seafood. And I get spa treatments and grooming into the bargain. Had my claws done the other day."

"Enough of tittle-tattle," said Hermes. His tone became sharper. "You're missed. You're shirking your responsibilities. Since you disappeared to your little hideaway, the situation has changed. There is near anarchy down in town. Your gang is scattered to the winds, and a lot of it is your fault. If you'd been there, they would never have been brave enough to attack."

Naturally, Hermes ignored his own role in stirring the pot.

This was all news to Ares; he was clearly out of the loop.

"What do you mean? My 'fault'? I'm not responsible for every cat in this city. I'm just taking a break. It's perfectly reasonable."

Hermes looked around the garden. "Unfortunately, your timing wasn't great. Kratos and Zelus have taken advantage of your absence. They mounted a raid on the Plaka and have taken over."

"What's happened to my boys and girls?" demanded the big cat, suddenly concerned.

Hermes caught his eye. "Decimated, unfortunately. It was carnage. Quite a few killed, several badly injured. Some escaped, but not the kittens." Ares went still, waiting for more. "Kratos seemed to target them, so I've heard, wiping out a whole generation, like he's making room for his own foul brood."

Hermes broke eye contact and silence fell between the two cats.

Ares filled it.

"Disgusting beast," he spat. He stared into the distance. "I'm going to enjoy giving him his comeuppance." He thought for a while. "Why didn't Athena do something?"

Hermes paused, unsure what to say. "She's been acting strangely of late. Watching the archaeologists near the Agora. From what I've been able to find, she's waiting for a statue or artefact to be dug up. Apparently, it's important to her. It's become something of an obsession, but I have to say it just means she's taken her eye off the ball elsewhere. She's just ignored other events and didn't even raise a paw to intervene. It's most unlike her. In the end, Bia seems to have nabbed it from under her nose." He stopped, reluctant to share what he now knew of its significance and capabilities, let alone his own role in its disappearance.

Ares grunted. He stared into space for a while, thinking.

"Statue, you say. Little one, was it?" Hermes nodded. "Where have they been looking?"

"The dig near the old Agora. They're sifting among the remains of what I believe was the Stoa Poikile."

Ares reflected some more. "Oh, well. Bound to turn up sometime." He sounded dismissive. Hermes gave him a quizzical stare; Ares stared back. "I think I dropped it there. A while ago." He ruminated further. "I think it was the Vandals, or maybe the Herulians. I dunno. Long time ago. Anyway, whoever it was, they sacked Athens, and I joined in, have a bit of fun. Well, why not? They'd stopped worshipping us, they'd gone soft. Temples were being allowed to go to ruin. Offerings had ceased. Things were slipping. They deserved a kick up the backside, so when the opportunity arose for a bit of mayhem, I couldn't resist. I found it, if memory serves me right, in a side alcove in the Parthenon. I knew it was precious to her, but she wasn't around, so I stole it. But it was just a trinket. After a while I decided I didn't want to be found red-handed, so to speak, so I dropped it in a well in one of the stoas down by the Agora." He finished and gave his companion a defiant look. "Didn't know she'd go all dewy-eyed about it, did I?"

Hermes considered the story. It explained a lot. Mostly, it explained that even Ares was nervous of a wrathful Athena in her full glory. "And that was your idea of a bit of 'fun'? You and your famous sense of humour. You should do some stand-up. You'd have 'em rolling in the aisles."

"Minus their heads, if they're going to laugh," came the reply.

Hermes looked to the heavens; time to change the subject. "Well, then. Time to get moving, eh?"

"I need something more to go on," growled Ares. "What's

the situation on the ground? Who has control of what? Where are they basing themselves, and what is their strength? Above all, what is Her Ladyship going to do? Or is she still planning to sit this one out? And what about our oh-so-superior Titaness, Bia? Is she going to join the fun, or is she content to leave it to her brothers?"

Hermes sighed. "Zelus and Kratos and their forces have control of the Plaka. They've got at least sixty, maybe more. They've taken over the site of the Library of Hadrian. Your old HQ." He glanced at the other cat. "As for Athena. Who knows? At least she does now seem a bit more bothered about things, so she will probably want to join in. Regarding Bia, I don't have a clue. If I were a betting animal I'd say yes, she'd join in." He paused. "There. That enough to be going on with? Oh, and one more thing. Apollo's in town and he's searching for a missing friend. He doesn't seem his usual self. Not bothered with local events at all. He's acting strange." He looked up. "Okay. I think that about covers it."

"Apollo? Haven't seen him in centuries. What's dragged his prissy little ass here? Missing person investigation? Give me a break. Probably just wants to deliver a lecture or two, hook up with as many of the girls as he can get his paws on, and act all smug and superior to the rest of us."

"Bit harsh," Hermes countered. He got up. "Anyway, time is of the essence. Let's get going."

"Hang on, hang on," Ares grumbled. "I'm not going anywhere without some victuals onboard first." He looked expectantly at the rear of the house. As if on cue, a woman appeared, carrying an enormous bowl of food. She looked across at them.

"Mr Tubs. It's lunchtime. Here you go." She carefully placed the bowl down and went back inside.

Hermes stared at the food. "Mr—"

Ares snorted. "One word," he warned, his voice rolling like thunder in the distant hills. "Just one word, and I'll rip your tail off and ram it down your throat. Got it?" Without waiting for a reply, he jumped down and waddled towards the food. Hermes watched him for a long moment, then sauntered behind.

"Thinking about preparations, it might be useful to bring your boys along."

Ares grunted his assent. He stopped and glanced around at the shrubbery at the far end of the garden. "Phobos, Deimos. You're needed," he shouted. "We've got a job to do down in town, so you'd better get your backsides into gear." He turned his attention back to his meal.

The bushes parted and two sleek young cats appeared; almost mirror images of each other. One was black with white markings, including a patch over one eye. His companion was mainly white, with black markings and an eye patch. They sauntered over, tails raised in greeting.

As they approached, Hermes glanced towards their father. "Are you sure they're yours?"

CHAPTER 47
THE SLEEPERS

A pollo woke up, still aching from his previous exertions, but sweating and troubled by the vestiges of his nightmare. He felt weary, but the thought of further sleep brought only fear. He stumbled to his feet. He had to find out how the plans here and now were progressing; anything rather than dwell on those unwelcome fragments of memory.

He turned his thoughts to the time; how long did Olympia have? Then there was the question of his travelling companions; where were they? Restless and impatient, he set off in search of answers.

The size of the Agora and its wooded hinterland surprised him; nothing looked familiar. Where in all this district did Athena live? He continued his perambulations, hoping to find her. Her followers kept their distance, regarding him with suspicion, but avoiding eye contact. He spotted small groups of other cats here and there among the trees, all beaten down and dejected. Curious, Apollo spoke to some of them to find out what was going on and how this place was run. Instead, he found he was talking to refugees from the Plaka gang, exiled in their own city.

Over several stilted conversations he pieced together the story of the battle at Monastiraki Square, and the unprovoked attack of Kratos and Zelus, and their merciless brutality, most clear in the massacre of the innocents. Most turned away or ignored him, unwilling to answer, still gripped by the horror of their experience. He should reach out to them; offer comfort in some small measure, but he couldn't. Reticence stayed his tongue as unwelcome thoughts hovered on the edge of his consciousness. *What right have I to speak soothing words of peace, after all I've done?* From those blank, unseeing looks he turned away, unwilling or unable to break the barrier of misery that surrounded them, uncomfortable in their presence.

Some were more animated, eager to share what they had seen, able to respond to his brisk questioning. Some spoke of heroic defenders overwhelmed by the sheer number of attackers, and others who held off the attackers and so bought time for their comrades to escape. He heard their anger and sorrow; they had suffered so much, others stayed silent unable to confront the horror. But amid the recollections, he heard mention of a brave grey-and-white stranger who rallied to their cause and even took down one of the most savage attackers.

Could it be Jason?

"I'm looking for someone," he said as hope surged within. "Female. Black, white and amber. Longer fur. Have you seen anyone like that?" The desire to find her, be with her, blossomed in his heart until it was a tangible, physical ache. At last, he found someone who thought they'd seen her, with a grey-and-white companion, hiding under the trees with the others. Apollo searched with renewed urgency.

He found them curled up together in a cosy bower, linked by experiences he had not shared. Their adventures had brought them closer and woven a kind of magic around them. Apollo looked down at the sleepers, their bodies entwined, their breathing synchronised. At peace. In love. Safe within the little nest they had made beneath the cypress tree. Daphne, nestled within the curve of his body. Jason's paw across her shoulder. Safe.

The moment stretched and twisted while unwanted recollections tumbled around and tormented his waking mind until it seemed his head would burst. Daphne and Jason looked as if they were meant for each other, and always had been. Them. Not him. He was an outsider. The eternal outsider to their love story.

He listened to their gentle purrs that, far from soothing, pierced his heart with savage blows. Jealousy, mingled with desire, consumed every corner of his soul. Inside him, something broke.

Beneath him, Daphne yawned and scratched an itchy ear, then opened her eyes and recoiled in shock. She struggled to disentangle herself from the still sleeping Jason and get to her feet. Behind her, coming to, he stretched and rolled over. Apollo loomed closer, driven by torment ages in the making. With deliberation, he looked from her to Jason then back. Jason saw him and started.

"Apollo, how wonderful to see you. Boy have we got a lot to catch up on, but what's the news? Where have you been?" He faltered.

"How dare you," Apollo said, a growl at the back of his throat. "She's not yours, she's mine."

"Now wait a minute." Jason scrambled to his feet, shaking off sleep, confusion written on his face. Without warning, Apollo delivered a stinging blow to the side of Jason's head with a force that bowled him over. Before Jason could get back to his feet the ginger cat was standing over him threateningly, but Daphne was just as quick.

"Apollo, no!" she screamed, her face thrust in front of him.

"Stay out of it. I'll deal with you later." Looking past her, he addressed Jason once more, "Get away from here while you still can."

Daphne was having none of it. "No. You go, you big bully. Get lost." She was furious. Fearless, she moved closer until their whiskers touched. She was quivering with indignation. "What's happened to you, this isn't you? You used to be our friend."

Apollo stared deep into her eyes and realised he had lost. Lost a contest he'd been destined never to win. The world faded away as he trod ancient paths of memory. He looked from her to Jason and back, then suddenly, without another word, spun on his tail and left.

"What was that about?" Jason watched Apollo's retreating form.

"I don't know. He frightened me." Her voice was distant.

Jason stood at Daphne's shoulder. They both watched until Apollo had disappeared from sight. He nuzzled her neck and gave her ear a reassuring lick.

"I think he needs a lot of time to himself," he added. "That wasn't the Apollo we know."

CHAPTER 48
THE AWAKENING

Kratos returned to his prize and looked for a suitable spot to lie down. This new headquarters wasn't yet a home, in his preferred sense. He'd had to leave his comfortable bed of stolen socks and underwear behind, and despite instructions to the troops, they had yet to amass any kind of haul to pad out his new surroundings with creature comforts. It would come; but for now, his quarters looked decidedly spartan.

Curled up against a wall, head on his paws, he peered at his acquisition. But his thoughts dwelt on recent news. Yannis had been a reliable lieutenant; obedient and ruthless, faithful to a fault. Kratos would miss him. His death was another crime to add to the growing charge list against the three spies. When he got hold of them, punishment would be delicious. What was it the guard had said? The smaller one had been their captive? He should have explored that more. What had Zelus wrung out of her? It should have been him asking the questions; he'd have made her squeak alright. It had been dark the night of their raid, but he still had a vague recollection of her. He pictured her in his mind's eye: patchwork colouring, diminutive but confident despite being outnumbered and surrounded, agile. A formidable little assassin indeed.

He stared at the statue.

Just what were you after?

Kratos experienced a strange, brief sensation of falling, as if he'd broken through some invisible barrier and dropped into a deep, deep hole, dissipating into space. His perspective changed, as his mind's eye took control of his waking thoughts.

He was looking out from under a tree somewhere. In front of his paws was loose soil...

Except they weren't his paws; they were white. What was happening?

A voice sounded in his head. It wasn't his own. *"What's this?"*

"Who are you?"

"What do you mean?"

Kratos concentrated hard. He didn't know what was happening, but he was talking to someone as if he was in *their* head. They seemed bewildered. From somewhere among his brooding web of thoughts, he gathered an idea of who this might be. If he was right, this was an encounter he would relish.

"You're one of her spies, aren't you? I know all about you," he lied, pressing his advantage. In his imagination, he loomed over the small, hapless animal, as if made to a different scale, intimidating it with his sheer size. It seemed to have some effect.

"My head hurts. Stop it!"

"All in due course, little one. Once you've told me all about yourself and what you've been up to." A sense of exhilaration filled the spaces behind his foremost thoughts, which suddenly sounded small and far away, as if spoken aloud in an enormous open space. Kratos shut his mind to such distractions and concentrated on his target.

"I can't think. My head's splitting!"

The other cat groaned, clearly in real discomfort, if not pain. Kratos relished the fact. He wanted to torture it and make it suffer. But he didn't want to break it. Not yet, anyway; he needed information.

He pulled back a little.

"I'll stop it hurting, but only when you've told me everything you know."

There was a brief pause while his target took a breath. He could sense it panting, as if it had been running. While it recovered, Kratos revelled in his discovery and the joy it brought him. He couldn't remember the last time he'd been able to exercise this kind of mental power over a subject, if at all. The strange sensation of unfolding the true scale of his mind was disconcerting, but marvellous; the possibilities were endless.

He had the disorienting sensation of his thoughts expanding into an infinite space that opened before him. Ideas flooded in, visions floated within reach, memories long suppressed came forth, jostling for attention. He perceived himself anew; understanding – or was it relearning? – his place in the universe. He felt he was floating above the world. Looking down, he saw the human multitudes and billions of other creatures crawling, running, flying and scurrying across its surface, tiny and fragile.

A world in ferment.

With a thrill, he sensed how easy it would be to manipulate them all, and eagerly grasped for the levers that would empower him. How could he have lived for so long in ignorance? How long had the Olympians plotted against him and his kind? Sneered at them; kept them down, servile and ignorant. He and his siblings were Zeus' allies; his adopted ones. The children of Styx, herself the honoured guardian of oaths. How could they treat him like this? The treachery of Zeus' spawn enraged him. What sacred oaths had they broken?

From his lofty position, he looked across the city and far beyond, saw the brief flashes of their immortal souls lit up at a distance, like tiny beacons lurking in their respective boltholes.

You have no hiding places anymore.

I will find you all. Find and destroy you.

Suspicions long held bubbled up in his consciousness anew; that burning sense of injustice he'd carried without knowing why. But it was no lie, and he knew precisely why he'd carried the grudge. From this distance, without focus, he couldn't tell who was who. It could wait. He would take his time and plot a strategy. When retribution arrived, he would relish it.

Kratos' thoughts continued to unfold and spread. This wonderful object gave him a glimpse of his true unshielded power. It was valuable beyond measure; a way to turn the tables and reclaim his true strength. No more would he or his kind pay dues to the squeaking, mewing gods of Olympus. It was time for a New Age. A Titan Age. To put an end to their tyranny. He would be subordinate no more.

His thoughts extended across the city and its human population for the first time. He wanted them as followers, obedient servants, slaves to do his will. Just like his gang, but on a far larger scale and with enormous power. An army that would bend to his will, driven and cowed. He would teach them to obey or face oblivion.

A fit of anger allowed him to test his new powers. On the fringes of his consciousness, he encountered strange energies he'd not come across before: electricity, and the engines it drove, and the things it powered. Other systems; networks; intricate and interconnected, but with so many weak points.

Kratos flexed mental muscles long unused, and tested his power. Across the city, there were power surges and grid outages. Blocks and neighbourhoods lost electricity. Traffic lights flicked off, causing collisions, mayhem and death. On opposite sides of the city, two gas explosions turned houses to rubble and triggered panic. Water mains ruptured, flooding streets. Kratos observed the destruction and the panicky human response with satisfaction, and turned his mind to more mundane and familiar items: stone and metal. Railway lines twisted like spaghetti, derailing trains, smashing them into tunnel walls or adjacent buildings. Further chaos. The cables of the Lycabettus Funicular snapped, leaving passengers at the mercy of the failsafe mechanism.

Death, destruction, mayhem. A small foretaste of what was to come once he learned to use this power. They would fear him and obey. For the time being he withdrew, satisfied with his experiment, while across Athens, sirens were wailing as the emergency services tried to restore order.

Kratos' thoughts turned inwards. How long had they imprisoned him in this small body with all of its limitations, and why? He had a dim recollection of a pact; a plot to limit the power of his kind, delivered as a strange fruit for all to eat.

It had been a trick. A crime. He had to undo it and eject the poison from his system. But how? This object was useful, but could it help him discover the antidote to that dread apple, and regain his correct form? Did the tree still exist?

There was so much to consider; but all in good time. First, he had to establish his power over those whining Olympians, and pompous Athena in particular. He pondered what to do with the spy, who wriggled and squirmed under the influence of his thought. He observed her as if she were a specimen under a microscope, recognising a simple spirit of streams and woodland groves. A nymph; the lowest of the immortal low. Almost powerless. A servant to his mighty kindred. A minion but possessing just enough mental capacity to put up some feeble resistance to his efforts to control her mind.

Once more, he gave her his full attention.

"Tell me everything you know. Tell me all about your mistress."

"I'm not a spy," she pleaded. "I've already told you everything. Please, just let me go."

Kratos flexed his newfound mental muscles again and heard the squeal at the receiving end. "That's a little reminder of what I can do. Now, let's pretend you haven't told me anything. Start from the beginning. When did she recruit you?"

"She didn't. No one did. I just wanted to help Apollo."

Kratos stopped, wrong-footed. He probed further into his target's mind but met unexpected dead ends; there was still a lot to learn about this device and how to use it, particularly the fine tuning necessary to probe and unpick individual thoughts.

"Better come and tell me all about it, then," he told her, wrapping velvet around his mental cosh. He threatened her in his most condescending voice. "Come and see your old friend, Kratos. We'll have a cosy little chat and you can tell me all about this boyfriend of yours."

He detected some feeble resistance, so he twisted and pushed his thoughts further in an effort to control her muscles, and if possible, move her limbs. The connection was haphazard at first; his target jerked like a marionette, and he felt her fighting him. But she was puny, and as he worked at it, his control improved, and her movements became smoother. She was powerless to stop him. Looking out of her eyes, he saw an unfamiliar view through trees of open ground sloping down to a gateway and pavement beyond. That must be the way towards his headquarters. His victim's head bobbed up and down, making his vision shake, as he forced her forwards in a robotic walk. It would take time before he mastered a smoother form of mind control; but for the moment this would do, despite the rough edges.

. . .

Jason returned to the little nest under the cypress tree that he and Daphne had made their own, just in time to see her leaving. He stopped in his tracks and watched her unusual staccato movement. She made no reply when he shouted; didn't even move her head.

He bounded over and stood in her line of vision, shouting her name. Looking through her eyes, Kratos noted the interloper with relish. This was the other accomplice; the grey-and-white one who'd killed Yannis. He'd deal with him in due course. First, he wanted to move his prey somewhere safe so he could get to the bottom of all this; even if it meant stripping her down to her muscle fibres.

Jason ran in circles around Daphne, trying but failing to understand what she was doing. Daphne just ignored him and kept moving in the strange, jerky walk, right past him. He raced around and stood in front of her, but she just barged him aside, still saying nothing, her eyes glazed and fixed straight ahead, her path unswerving. Jason watched her for a moment, then jumped at her, side on, knocking her down. Hating himself, he delivered a sharp bite to her neck.

"Ow!" she said, and went limp. The sharp jolt of pain sent a shockwave through her nervous system into her brain and broke the connection. Kratos sensed it and opened his eyes, losing his focus and his viewpoint. He tried to re-establish the connection, but back in this smaller container, his thoughts fell away, and he found it difficult to concentrate, distracted as he was by the remnants of what he'd just experienced. He fumbled, became too hasty and grew frustrated.

He glared at the statuette and attempted to relax, but sensed movement in his peripheral vision. One of his lieutenants had arrived to deliver a report on the afternoon's scavenging activities. Kratos listened to him with only half an ear. His mind was elsewhere, still trying to understand the revelation he'd just experienced.

After his subordinate had left, he studied the statuette in a new light and marvelled at it. Before him was a device of astonishing subtlety and power. Not only had it enabled him to make the mental connection with the spy, but it had given him a glimpse of his true self and allowed him to wield power of a kind he could barely remember. He'd been able to manipulate material and systems across the city, and do it with ease. It had revealed his true nature and hidden power; but with that knowledge arose an even greater bitterness towards the creature that had imprisoned him in this tiny, constrained body, with her evil tricks and spells. What had they done to him, Athena and her co-conspirators? Why had he agreed? It must have been against his will; the result of trickery and deceit. The devious behaviour for which the inhabitants of Olympus were famous. Trapped in this body for so long, no wonder it had melted his mind and eroded his memories.

For the moment, he had to put aside his burning resentment and find out how to regain his true form permanently, putting an end to the injustice. Questions piled upon questions. He'd always resented Athena, but now he had reason anew to despise her and all her kind. She had been keeping him, all of them, cooped up like this for centuries. It was time to forge a new future, one free of all Olympians. A future with himself and his peers in charge and humanity slave to their will.

Where were they now? Mighty Atlas, bold Crius, powerful Oceanus, bright Helios and all the rest. Individuals he'd all but forgotten. The older gods. Now he had a new mission: set them free and then make war on their feeble successors, scattering them to the winds, or worse.

There remained unfinished business with the spy, but she was just the start.

A stepping stone on the path to glory.

CHAPTER 49
ORDINARY ANIMALS HAVE NO CHANCE

"What if he tries again?"

"I don't know." Daphne was frightened, but Jason was no help. The episode had shaken them both. They sat beneath their favourite tree, trying to understand what had just happened. Daphne had been snoozing in the middle of the day, then suddenly she had the most awful crushing headache, as her head was filled with someone else's thoughts. Not just anyone, but the brute who'd attacked them the other night at the disused factory. Then, worst of all, he tried to make her walk.

He nearly succeeded.

She stared, unseeing, into the distance, scared and helpless.

"What was it like?" asked Jason yet again.

"I can't describe it. He was just in my head, asking me questions. Then he tried to make me go to him." She shuddered.

Jason came to a decision. "I'm going to see if I can find help. There must be someone around here who knows what's going on." He bounded off up the hillside. Daphne didn't move. She didn't see how anyone could help, but she had no other ideas. She tried to compose herself; her heart was still racing.

After a while, he returned with Thalia, the cat they'd met when they fled from the battle.

She studied Daphne, both curious and concerned. "I've never heard of anything like it. I don't know what to suggest." Daphne and Jason stared at each other helplessly. Thalia looked at them. "Maybe my lady would know what to do?" Immediately, she turned tail and left without further explanation. Jason set off after her.

Alone, Daphne racked her brains. Why would Kratos have such an interest in her? He must have talked to Zelus, she supposed. One interrogation had been bad enough; she couldn't face another. They were both obsessed with spying, which seemed odd. Then she remembered how frightened Zelus had appeared when she mentioned Hera. And Kratos seemed a little spooked to hear Apollo's name. Why? How come he'd heard of Apollo? Had he ever been to Delphi? Someone would have mentioned it, surely?

Questions crowded her mind, but who could give her the answers, and where had Jason and Thalia got to?

She got up and set off into the woods. Anything was better than sitting here waiting to be summoned by that evil monster.

She wandered the hillside in search of them, but they remained elusive. She was on the point of giving up when she heard voices. It sounded like Jason, but who was he talking to?

"What do you mean, possessed?"

"It's like there was someone in her head. At least that's what she told me, and I believe her."

"That's impossible. You need to tell her to calm down. It must have been a bad dream or something."

"I saw her. It was no dream. She was walking, but she

didn't seem to be in control of her legs. She couldn't hear me. I was there."

"Enough. I've told you, it's impossible. It sounds as if you're both getting a little hysterical. I'll come and see her in due course. But first you need to tell her to calm down. Relax. She's been through a lot recently with the battle, and her imprisonment. She's probably just suffering the after-effects of all the trauma."

Crouching down, Daphne edged as close as she could. She could see Jason, but a low bush hid the animal he was talking to. Abruptly, he turned and left. Daphne didn't move a muscle. After a moment, another cat appeared: Athena's assistant, Penelope.

"I suppose you heard that?"

"Most of it, my lady. But I'm not sure I understand any of it."

There was a long pause. Daphne had a desperate urge to scratch an itch behind her ear, but she dared not move.

"It's worse than I feared," Athena said eventually. She sounded tired. "It appears our enemy has somehow found out what it can do. Some of it, anyway. You've heard the sirens across the city? The human population thinks it's under attack. But his real target is probably me."

Daphne held her breath. She peered through the branches at Penelope. The other cat was agape.

"So, the story you told me is true?"

"You didn't believe me?" Athena sounded indignant.

"No, it's just… I…" Penelope struggled and failed to correct her faux pas. "It just seemed incredible."

"Well, it's true." There was a hint of satisfaction in the grey cat's voice. "However, it is now imperative that we retrieve the object before he uses it to cause even more harm. If he's learned to use it properly, it may be too late. I need to speak to Hermes again. Can you send an owl? Better see if you can find Apollo, as well."

Penelope hesitated.

"What now?"

"Well… what can you do if he uses it against you?" There was a tremor in her voice.

"Very little. Only the powerful can truly defend themselves against a direct attack, and only then, with difficulty. I'm afraid ordinary animals have no chance." She must have seen the shocked look on her assistant's face, as she softened her voice. "Don't worry. If he's going to use it against you, he needs to know your name or at least have a good mental image of you first. The statuette is an amplifier and focus. It strengthens thought waves and also projects them powerfully into the mind of the recipient. But when used against an individual, it needs a known target to aim for, otherwise it's useless."

Penelope left on her errand. Shortly after, Athena followed.

Daphne was dumbstruck. She tried to absorb what she'd heard. Not only had Kratos had a look at her the other night, she'd told Zelus her name. That had been a mistake. She turned the other details over in her mind.

"Only the powerful can truly defend themselves… Ordinary animals have no chance."

Daphne had never thought of herself as special, but she was not prepared to be dismissed as "ordinary". At least she now had an idea what had happened. How could she defend herself against another attack?

Fear knotted her stomach. She supposed her only defence was what she'd always done when someone tried to persuade her to act against her better judgement: be stubborn as hell.

CHAPTER 50
A TIMELY THEFT

Kratos finished speaking with the last of his officers. Evening drew near, and he was impatient to have another go with his new toy. He didn't want to let it out of his sight, so he issued orders for his subordinates to come to him, rather than visiting them on his rounds as usual. He had to find a good hiding place for his new treasure, but for now, fear of retribution for any who went near it would have to suffice. As his last lieutenant left, he issued instructions not to be disturbed, and settled down in front of the artefact. He was building a list of targets and projects, but first it was imperative he concluded the unfinished business with the spy. Kratos closed his eyes and conjured her image in his mind, then projected an instruction.

Daphne was still on the hillside when the new attack came. She jerked and struggled in an attempt to block the invasion, but he was too powerful, and his thoughts overwhelmed her.

"I don't believe we'd finished our discussion." A simple command followed the unwelcome greeting. "Walk."

Kratos could sense his subject fighting back, making tiny

adjustments to soften the impact of his will. But he was too powerful, and it was an insignificant act of rebellion.

Kratos concentrated on moving her in the direction he wanted. It proved easier than last time; he was growing familiar with the control mechanisms. He settled back to enjoy the view as she trudged out of the Agora and along Adrianou Street. She would soon be with him.

Atop the walls of the Acropolis, Apollo strolled aimlessly between the weathered blocks that littered the ground. Lost in inward dreams, he'd arrived here without conscious thought, troubled by his recent encounter. His rescue mission had stalled, and what should have been a joyous reunion with his friends had most likely destroyed all semblance of trust between them. At least his explosive rage had stopped short of total disaster this time.

He paused and raised his eyes to the tall columns looming nearby. *What am I here for? Why did I come?* The stones ventured no opinion, but their silent presence drew him closer. Hopping onto the marble platform on which they stood, and passing between them he came to the inner sanctum; once a sacred place, now open to the elements, and filled by a large crane and the tools and equipment of modern workmen. Such mundane items were an intrusion. He turned to leave, but a vision from the corner of his eye made him pause, and as he looked closer he found himself in the centre of the temple as it once was. Beside him was a huge twelve-metre-high statue of the goddess herself, helmed and holding a shield and spear. Her golden floor-length gown glinted in the flickering light of oil lamps. A figure of ancient mystery and reverence, she seemed alive. The distant head turned towards him.

"So you came at last. I sensed your reluctance from the start. Here, take it, eat." Setting aside her spear, she proffered a bright red fruit. It looked enticing, delicious, even. But as his vision was drawn from it, back towards Athena's face, he spied Demeter in the shadows at her side. Her face spoke a different message. She cast a nervous glance at her companion.

"It is not forever. Remember that. There will be another dawn in due course, when we return in glory." As an attempt to reassure, her voice lacked conviction, the cat thought. Athena cut her off.

"Wait. Let us not yet speak of what might be. We all agreed on this course many years ago, and our path is set.

"As is our return…"

"Indeed, but for the present such thoughts are a distraction." Athena turned back towards him, still holding out her hand, her condescending smile like a mask. "Here," she said, bending down towards him. But as she leaned forward her smile was replaced by an expression of concern. "I know you've been struggling recently. You are bearing a heavy emotional burden. This will help you set it aside for a while." He glanced at the fruit in her hand. "It will help you sleep through the ages until it is time to return."

He moved forwards, sniffed the item and took a bite. Even as he crunched down he caught Demeter's expression of concern. What was wrong? Then the pain hit, and he blacked out: a novel experience for a god.

The vision faded and a ginger cat stood among the ruins of the Parthenon once more, alone amid the columns of weathered stone. He shook his head and stumbled, his stomach queasy, gripped by the urge to vomit. He closed his eyes, and the sensation passed.

Relieved, but suspicious, Apollo retraced his steps, no longer sure what he had seen, then headed directly to the boundary wall, driven by a sudden need to feel a breeze on his face. From its flat surface he looked out across the city. His eyes moved from the distant sea to the maze of streets below and he marvelled at the speed and endeavour of humanity in the years he'd been asleep. Before him were countless buildings and within and between them, thousands of people went about their business, criss-crossing the squares and pavements, en route to he knew not where. He envied them. They had a purpose, whereas he felt lost and out of place. Even his rescue mission was mired in politics and hanging by a thread.

As he scanned the scene below, watching the interplay of vehicles and humans, something caught his eye. A small figure he recognised, glimpsed briefly in a gap between tall buildings. Daphne. She was stiffly walking, as if dragged against her will by some invisible rope. She disappeared from sight. With staccato movements Apollo scanned the area, trying to see what might have attracted her, his vision sharp despite the distance.

His eyes were drawn towards the ancient ruins of the Library of Hadrian and he froze. In a moment of clarity, alternate futures danced before him, tantalisingly close; so close they almost mingled; almost gave him a chance. But his vision failed, lost in a fog. Could he do it? Could he save her? Could he save both of them? He had to try. The mocking voice echoed in his head once more, like an actor in an empty theatre: *His soul polluted beyond Castalia's power.* With jaw clenched tight, he knew that whatever the outcome, he would, at least, purify his soul. In blood.

Apollo turned and flew, faster than the wind, towards the Propylea. Arrow-straight, he sprinted across the uneven, rock-strewn plateau, his belly skimming the stones as he vaulted them. At the gap where the grand ceremonial staircase once stood, he didn't slow, but bypassed the steps built for tourists, oblivious to their startled looks, and leapt down in huge bounds from boulder to ledge to slab, each precise landing inch-perfect and true. He streaked through the tourist entrance and into the woodland beyond, arcing his trajectory downward towards the Agora.

Jason, wary and alert, saw the golden cat hurtle past him. He watched him go, then followed slowly behind.

Under her enemy's control, Daphne could do little but try to smooth her passage. Her body was no longer her own; the sensation was most odd. She attempted to work with the flow of Kratos' instructions rather than against them, smoothing the effect rather than stopping him. As a result, her movements were slightly less stilted than before, but it was only a matter of degree. It did nothing to prevent her feeling like a prisoner in her own head.

Soon she saw the entrance to Kratos' new headquarters. The human gatekeeper paid her little attention as her staccato movement took her past him. She went deeper into the lion's den. Gang members looked up when they saw her approach. A small crowd soon gathered around her, following her progress as she headed for their leader.

Finally, she arrived. The source of her problems lounged on a scrubby patch of dry grass, next to a little item made of stone. She glanced at it from the corner of her eye but couldn't make it out properly. Why was it here? Why was *she* here?

She could guess, but didn't like any of the answers she came up with.

After a while, Kratos' mental grip relaxed slightly, allowing Daphne a little free movement. She took in her surroundings as best she could, but then had to snap back to attention as he issued a new command.

"Sit." Inside, she bristled at this new humiliation. This was how you spoke to a dog! Futile anger flickered briefly in the small space of her thoughts she still controlled. Kratos stood up and skirted the object to inspect her more closely. Around them, a crowd gathered.

"We could continue this interview in our private little thought

bubble, thanks to my new toy. Do you like it, by the way? Pretty, I think you'd agree." He glanced at the strange object. *"But perhaps my devoted followers deserve to hear what you have to say."*

Suddenly it stopped, and Daphne staggered slightly as if a huge weight had been lifted from her shoulders. She took a deep breath but remained silent. Kratos looked at the crowd assembling around them.

"Let's pick up where we left off the other night, before we were so rudely interrupted."

She glanced at the thing he was so proud of; a little stat-uette. How odd. She'd seen nothing like it, even in Delphi. But then she'd never been into the museum; that was for humans. They were keen to keep cats out.

"I think we can guess what your mission was. But before we hear your confession, tell me about your companions the other night." Suddenly, he was in her head again. *"Yes, spit it out. All of it. Or else."*

"Or else what?" she said out loud. There was an audible ripple through the crowd.

"You have courage, I'll grant you that." Kratos' paws threw up plumes of dust as he paced. What did he want to hear? Was there any point playing for time?

A thought germinated at the back of her mind, so ludi-crous she couldn't take it seriously, but just maybe…

"Come on." There was an urgency now. He didn't like to be kept waiting.

"One is called Jason." She paused. He glared at her. "The other is Apollo." The stare he gave her felt almost physical in its intensity. She had to look away.

"More."

"There weren't any more."

She readied herself for a blow. Again, she heard him inside her head.

"No funny games or I will prolong your agony as long as possi-ble, believe me."

She concentrated on the ground in front of her and swallowed.

"We're from Delphi. That's all. We're looking for a friend."

"I'm not interested in your cover story. Tell me about this colleague of yours. The ginger one."

"Apollo? He's just someone I know. There's nothing else to say. We're friends."

"And how long have you been friends with him, daughter of Peneus?" He caught the confusion in her eyes. "Yes, I've done you the honour of thinking about you. I know more about you than you think. There's no point lying to me anymore. At what point did you put aside your hate? Or is there more to your story? Another twist that you want to share? Someone else in the mix?"

Daphne faltered. A fleeting image passed into her thoughts, of a chase, or a hunt. Maybe. No. Desperate flight. A frantic escape, just in time. From a man, beautiful and golden. It vanished, leaving her confused.

A shout went up from the edge of the crowd. Kratos looked up, impatient at the interruption. What he saw seemed to enrage him. He stepped back, then with a screech of anger, departed. Daphne watched as her tormentors turned and followed.

Straight through the entrance to the Library of Hadrian, Apollo ran. Inside were a few gang members, the majority had gathered at the far side of the site, where Kratos held court – could he buy her some time? Time to maybe try and escape? – but even so, his reckless attack seemed suicidal. Kratos was holding court over on the northern side of the site, behind the ancient wall, and that was his target. Apollo caught the gang members by surprise, descending on them like a lion onto docile antelope. Cries for help went up, and in the distance, some of their colleagues at the back of the crowd turned to see what the fuss was about. A few, led by one of their boldest, sprang into action, closing the ground fast as they sought to rebuff this surprise attack. Apollo saw them coming. He singled out the leader and leapt at him, taking him in mid-air. A sickening rip followed a strangle-grip to the throat as his claws opened his enemy's body from his neck to his belly in a spray of red. The gangster fell dying while the ginger cat moved to his next target, nostrils flared, a ferocious light kindled in his eyes.

As the noise grew, more of Kratos' mob heard the fight and the cacophony reached those surrounding Kratos and the spy. Their attention diverted, they hesitated, looking this way and that as if unable to act without some sign from their leader. How would he react to this lunatic attacker? As confusion grew, those in Apollo's immediate vicinity had little choice other than to fight or die. More of them turned to repulse the attacker, others to flee.

Despite Apollo's initial success, the odds were turning against him. He stood over the body of his latest victim and looked up to see many more cats charging towards him. Unfortunately, the animal he wanted most was not among them; he still lingered at the rear.

The numbers confronting him were overwhelming; there was a limit to what he could achieve alone. It was time to retreat. Past the startled gatekeeper he ran, back onto the street, then turned to the right and fled towards the square. A large contingent of Kratos and Zelus' combined troops pursued him. He passed the entrance to the metro station and turned onto Ermou Street, dodging human traffic and staying well clear of vehicles. In his fury, traffic lights fused and a fire hydrant burst from its mooring, sending a jet of water climbing into the sky. Cars screeched to a halt at the gridlocked junction. Apollo didn't care; he ran on, slowing now as the pursuit dwindled, then stopped.

He looked back. He'd wanted the bully dead, but he had

failed in that objective. Hopefully he had, at least, bought Daphne a little time, but now his legacy called. There would be no waiting for others to act. He'd abased himself to ask for help, but it was not forthcoming, and he wouldn't ask again. He was on his own, and the freedom was invigorating.

Jason followed Apollo as quickly as he dared, but paused short of the entrance to Hadrian's Library. He watched, astonished at his friend's bravery – or stupidity – and paid little heed to the pedestrians dodging around him. There was nothing he could do. It was a relief to see Apollo escape unscathed, but disappointing that he left in another direction. Despite their last encounter, Jason wanted to talk to him to ask about Daphne's strange behaviour. It would have to wait. Instead, he retraced his steps to the Agora, trying to find anyone who might have seen her.

In the growing noise and confusion, they all forgot Daphne. Amid the distraction and without pausing for thought, she picked up the statuette in her mouth and ran in the opposite direction. She thought she'd seen an entrance there to the world outside; it was the only chance she had. She'd not gone more than half a dozen paces when a cry went up behind her. Someone had been paying attention.

The gang was split. Many continued towards Apollo to join the fray and see off this impudent intruder. But Kratos heard the alert and turned, remembering his captive. He flew after her, eating up the ground. Dozens of gang members followed his lead.

Daphne had only a few metres' advantage. She darted towards the nearby gate and hurled herself at the gap between the railings. It was just wide enough for a small animal like her to fit through, but it wouldn't be easy for anyone larger. There was an instant logjam behind, as her pursuers fell over each other in their eagerness to follow. Kratos, large as he was, struggled to squeeze between the railings, costing him valuable time. Daphne sped on as fast as she could, not daring to look back, but extending her advantage. She ran straight ahead down a short street, then came to the corner of a plaza with several restaurant tables beneath large sunshades. She ran among them, hoping the obstacle course would further delay her pursuers. Dodging between waiters and around seated customers and their bags slowed her down more than she liked.

Once through the gate, the pursuers gained on her. They sped in and out of legs – of both the human and table variety – and homed in on their prey.

Daphne sensed them gaining. At the edge of her vision, she glimpsed her tormentor; he had almost caught up. In desperation, she darted right once more and headed for the entrance to the nearest restaurant. Her pursuers hadn't expected the move, but instantly changed course, concentrating on their target. Kratos and two other gang members ran into the legs of a waiter carrying a large tray of food at shoulder height, knocking him off balance. As he struggled to stay upright, other cats got under his feet, and he fell sideways onto the nearest diner. The tray and its content clattered into the middle of a table, smashing plates and glasses, spilling drinks and splattering food over those nearby.

The cats streamed past, oblivious to the outrage, still focused on their pursuit. Other waiters and angry customers kicked out at them, sending some flying, adding to the mayhem. Someone slammed the restaurant door shut, blocking many of Daphne's chasers. But Daphne, Kratos and half a dozen of her fastest pursuers were already inside. She bolted through a doorway at the end of the bar, a whisker ahead of the gang leader.

The kitchen was small, hot and crowded. Pots and pans

filled with bubbling liquids and frying meat covered all available burners. Chefs and assistants moved between stations with rapid precision, preparing ingredients, filling or emptying pans, ovens and larders, assembling meals onto plates, all amid the paraphernalia of a busy lunchtime service. Daphne hurtled into the midst of this ordered activity, adding a huge dollop of chaos to the mix. She twisted and turned, dodging chefs and waiters alike, looking for an escape route, while they tried to block her progress or kick her into submission.

At first, there seemed no way out, and she was close to panic. Hard on her tail, Kratos tried to anticipate her moves and pounce. Mentally, she braced herself for the impact, but then she spotted the back door open as a staff member came in from the yard beyond. The hydraulic hinge closed, and the door swung shut, but she squeezed through as it slammed behind her.

She took a blow to her side as a result, the impact spinning her over and partially winding her, sending the statuette flying into the gutter. She'd landed in a quiet back alley. Painfully, Daphne hobbled over to the object and picked it up again. It was slimy with both her saliva and whatever it had just fallen in.

She walked on, limping a little as she caught her breath. The alley was short, and Daphne soon arrived at a narrow, busy thoroughfare. She turned left, in a direction she hoped would take her away from the gang's headquarters, avoiding shoppers and keeping an eye out for cats.

Chaos ruled in the kitchen. In his pursuit, Kratos had to veer around annoying humans while his target seemed to slip straight past them. The delay prevented him from following her through the back door. He charged into it, but it was just too heavy, even for his size and bulk. He made a tour of the kitchen, looking for another way out; a window, anything. He was oblivious to the furious gesticulations of chefs and other staff as they waved dangerous-looking knives and cleavers in his direction. Someone opened the front doors once more, allowing his companions an escape route; but that was no good. Kratos looked around for an open window.

While he paused, a cook gave him a hefty kick, sending him sideways into a storage rack. Pans and dishes clattered around him, but Kratos ignored them. He fixed his eyes on his assailant and ran straight at him, leaping upward power-fully. Using the jutting handle of a pan as a springboard, he launched himself at the man's face; a mass of teeth and claws. The force of his leap dislodged the pan, tipping its boiling contents into the cook's crotch just as the furious animal reached his face. In shock and sudden pain, the man dropped everything and fell backwards, screaming in agony from both the cat and the liquid scalding his groin and legs, scrabbling to get the frenzied animal off him. His momentum pitched him into the door, forcing it open as he fell backwards into the alley beyond. Kratos hurdled him and charged after his prey.

Moving more slowly now, Daphne took a right then left turn, hoping trackers wouldn't be able to follow her scent amid the tourists and shops. She was weary and sore, and the artefact made her jaw ache. But if it was as powerful as she'd heard, she had to keep it out of her pursuer's paws.

She emerged onto another, much quieter street. But she'd lost her bearings amid the labyrinth of narrow, twisting passages. At the end of this one, the rock wall of the Acropolis stood in afternoon shadow. At first, she feared she was trapped in a dead end, but then spotted some steps leading up from the end of the road. She dropped the statuette to rest her aching jaw and ease the stiffness, but jumped at a shout from behind, and the scrabble of paws. She looked over her shoulder and her spirits sank.

Kratos had somehow reunited with three of his thugs and was barrelling towards her with renewed intent. Terror lent her new reserves of energy. She picked up her treasure and bounded forwards. The street rose towards the flight of steps, and the climb made her lungs ache. Daphne was at the limit of her endurance, and the chasers were closing fast.

At the top of the steps, following an instinct, she turned sharp right, relieved that this new road was flat. She accelerated once more, but the chasers were reining her in, and the object in her mouth made breathing difficult.

Past the last house she flew, and darted through a set of railings, barely breaking stride. Daphne had travelled in a circle, behind and above the Agora, and safety lay tantalisingly close. Panic was the only thing driving her forward now, but at least she was heading downhill between the trees, towards safety. Behind her, Kratos slid to a halt, frustrated. He was near the heart of his enemy's territory, but he didn't yet dare to venture further with so few followers accompanying him. He would be back sooner rather than later, but for now only one thing occupied his thoughts; his prize had been stolen, and he wanted it back. Badly.

CHAPTER 51
A NEW BEGINNING

drenaline and thoughts of revenge coursed through Apollo. Athena had failed to come up with any kind of solution, and there was no other help available. It was time to act. He chastised himself for failing to realise it from the outset: if you want something done, best do it yourself. A vision of the prison compound fixed in his mind's eye, and he set off on a determined run.

The bus driver saw him late; a ginger streak running out in front of his vehicle. Far too late to stop. In the end, he didn't have to do anything; his bus stopped anyway, with a loud bang, even before he could stamp on the brake pedal. He was lucky he had the wheel to stop his momentum, although it jabbed him in the stomach. Fortunately, he hadn't been going so fast.

Behind him, the passengers weren't so lucky. Some crashed into the back of the seat in front. Those standing stumbled over buggies and shopping bags or went sprawling on the floor, groceries and other belongings spilling down the aisle.

There were angry shouts and wailing babies, but the driver ignored them. He was struggling to take it in; the road had been clear. What had he hit to cause such damage? It couldn't be just a cat. The smashed windscreen and deep vertical indentation up the entire front of the vehicle was the sort of damage you would get if you'd hit a lamppost at speed. But he had come to a shuddering halt in the middle of the carriageway, not on the verge. The V-shaped dent buckled the floor and warped the passenger entrance. He was lucky his feet hadn't been trapped in the wreckage. Mangled plastic and metal had bent his steering wheel out of alignment; the dashboard had smashed, and the pedals twisted. Somehow, he'd escaped injury, but the door of his cab into the bus wouldn't open; he had to exit via the side door.

He stood back and observed the damage, scratching his head. The front of the bus looked even worse from outside. There was no sign of a body; no tangible obstacle anywhere. What could have caused such destruction?

Blackness, alternating with light, and strange visions. Sounds, amplified and distorted, drifted across his consciousness. Snatches of a conversation far away. Traffic, the song of birds, the backdrop of everyday life.

Apollo stood on a promontory looking across a turbulent sea. The day was bright, but the wind and the currents were always strong here. Waves broke in blue and green, and white spindrift spun from their crests. Behind him lay a small city of temples and squares interspersed with fine houses. Boats bobbed up and down by the quayside as citizens went about their business. This was a prosperous place; a place of commerce and pilgrimage. His island. But no one acknowledged him as he walked among them. No one seemed to see him or hear his friendly greeting. It was puzzling. Was this death, finally? The idea was almost thrilling. He'd never realised he *could* die, but…

Maybe it was some form of purgatory. He'd heard people

talk about that in solemn tones, but never paid too much attention. It was somebody else's religion; not his. If he was dead, why wasn't he in the halls of his uncle? An honoured guest in his dread realm?

Nothing made sense.

And now his vision shifted.

He was floating above an unremarkable patch of scrubby, yellowing grass in the middle of a city. It was criss-crossed by paths and dotted with the occasional struggling bush or stunted tree. Beneath a park bench was a body; one of the innumerable feral cats that infested this place. Thin, wasted, misshapen, with its limbs at odd angles. Dried blood caked the mouth. Mucus dripped below an eye. Flies had gathered. But there was still the faintest of breath, so they dared not feast or lay their eggs yet. No passers-by paid the cat any attention. It was just one of many. The park keepers would clear it away before long.

The realisation grew: what he was looking at, on the ground below, was his own body. His travel cloak. The shroud he wore in this version of reality. The vehicle in which they'd trapped him all these centuries ago, when he had foolishly agreed to their hasty transformation.

He had to admit, he had seen better days; but the dead all look like lifeless clay once the vital spark has gone. He didn't know what came next; perhaps a long, dreamless sleep? It wouldn't be so bad; he felt tired enough to sleep forever. Perhaps fresh adventures awaited in some far distant realm.

He was still musing on the possibilities when the pain returned, exquisite and agonising. Its intensity appalled him, but with a pang of regret, it forced him to acknowledge he was still alive. With this awareness came the all too familiar concerns and emotions: guilt, worry, anxiety, anger.

He already missed being dead, if that's what it had been. He'd had no worries. The experience had been soothing; peaceful, even. Now, he lay beneath the bench in the middle of a small park; more dead than alive, but wracked with pain and consumed by anguish at this additional delay in his race to rescue Olympia.

He was losing time; time she couldn't afford. And nobody – not even himself, with his full powers – could pause Chronos in his count.

The floating sensation ceased. His eyes flickered open and he licked his lips, tasting the congealed blood. It was far too soon to move any limbs; he had too much healing to do. Fortunately, it was one of his innate skills. He concentrated on knitting bones back together and weaving snapped sinews; healing punctured organs and closing wounds. He would ache for a long time. His mistreated body would just have to cope while its pilot rediscovered his form. For now, a brief sleep would help; he was still too weak to stand.

But far from sinking into deep and blissful slumber, vivid dreams took him once more, shaking off the torpor, steering him towards a distant, instantly familiar scene. He flew, invisible, towards the tableau, recognising all those present; his fury every bit as raw and impotent as before, as once again he saw replayed events he'd hoped would remain forgotten.

The sick were being healed, their lives extended and their health improved. Jealous Hades demanded resolution; insisted that Asclepius, favourite among all Apollo's children, be brought before him and faint-hearted Zeus agreed. His crime? Healing the sick and prolonging their lives kept them from Hades' jealous clutches longer than the lord of the dead deemed reasonable. The king of heaven killed his beloved Asclepius with a thunderbolt and sent him to live among Hades' folk.

Asclepius didn't deserve to die; he was the noblest of them all. He'd brought humanity such riches: knowledge of healing, an understanding of disease, the foundation of medicine, gifts beyond price. The injustice lent him reckless fury as with deadly purpose, he tracked down Zeus' armourers, the

Cyclops: the one-eyed giants whose weapons lent Zeus his invincibility. In revenge, he slew the forgers of those thunderbolts, one by one, his jaw clamped tight as, in his vision as in life, he relived every stroke, the memory of his anger still coursing through his sleeping mind.

This time, he'd gone too far. This time, his father was beside himself. This time, Apollo felt the heat of his wrath.

Glaring at each other, each god overflowing with righteous fury, neither was prepared to back down. But Zeus was still the stronger, and the others stood by his side.

For his temerity he faced an eternity in deepest, shady Tartarus. Hades grinned and held the gates open himself. To Apollo's lasting shame, his mother Leto, on her knees, pleaded his case, and the sentence was reduced: a year's hard labour at the Court of King Admetus.

In truth the sentence was lenient, and over days and months, as he undertook his daily toil, he reflected on his sins and the constant turmoil in his soul. God of light they'd called him, but light can burn and scald as much as guide. A ferocious temper sat uncomfortably alongside more peaceful intent – the aspect of himself he valued most. How to rein in the destructive side of his nature? Could he step outside himself? Or was his doom to forever cycle between those poles.

He'd always struggled to master the constant war between the two forces in his heart, but control them, he must. Apollo made a solemn vow to change his ways. As he contemplated the two sides of his nature, a phrase sprang into his mind. It would look good, carved into the lintel of his temple at Delphi, above the entrance. A lesson to his followers down the years: *know thyself*.

In this way, he rediscovered the beginnings of wisdom.

.   .   .

Night had long been swallowed by the dawn of a new day before he opened his eyes again and tried to move. To his surprise, his limbs obeyed their orders. He rolled onto his stomach, and with the trembling unsteadiness of the newborn, slowly stood. Bones cracked and sinews creaked, but they held firm. He walked around, tentative at first, then stretching and experimenting until he was confident of his movement once more. Then he sat and had a thorough wash.

Today would be a red day; a day of heroism and dread, haunted by the spectre of death, leavened by the chance to save lives.

He was ready. Apollo was still a stranger in this modern city, but he knew his destination with absolute certainty, and nothing now would stop him. The wind of his passing stirred the leaves on the trees.

CHAPTER 52
SECOND LIEUTENANT SAMARAS

Daphne stood before Athena. She dropped the statuette on the ground between them.

"I believe you wanted this."

The grey cat looked at her. Against all expectations, this most unassuming creature had delivered her prize back to her. The object she'd craved for so long lay on its side in the dust between them, covered in saliva and bearing a couple of new scratches, but remarkably well preserved considering the journey it had just endured.

"Thank you."

Athena rarely had occasion to be grateful to mortals, but there was something unusual about this young animal; something she couldn't put a claw on.

"You have hidden depths."

Daphne bowed her head. "Now, if you'll forgive me, I have things to do." Athena looked askance at the grubby statuette, but picked it up in her mouth and made her way into the trees, up the hill.

Her destination was not a great distance away. She skirted Areopagus Hill and bypassed Pnyx, heading towards the streets to the south of the National Observatory, and making for an area of neat houses next to the woods. She turned into them, took a couple of turns, and approached a modest but well-maintained property. Treating her possession with care, she slipped through the fence and walked around to the rear where there was a cat flap built into a door. Without hesitating, she stepped through and into the room beyond: her secret sanctuary.

Athena shared this house with her human servant: a divorced, middle-aged man whose children had long since left home. His job as a police officer meant he kept irregular hours, and given the cat would sometimes disappear for days, the arrangement suited them both. He enjoyed her company when she was there, and as long as he kept a well-stocked cupboard, she was happy enough. From Athena's point of view, this was a place she could retreat to when she needed time to think, or when she became bored with the petty politics of Athenian feline society. She kept it hidden from even the closest of her acolytes.

She placed the statuette in the middle of the floor and stepped back to admire it once more. It was still muddy, but she could clean it up later. First, it was time to reacquaint herself with its ancient mechanisms. She settled down on a nearby cushion and stared at it. Then she closed her eyes and studied it in her mind's eye. Once fixed there, she projected her thoughts towards it.

At first, she couldn't remember what to do; the old pathways seemed overgrown. But with persistence and time, she would surely re-open them once more.

After several failed attempts at connection, she opened her eyes and glared at the artefact. The last time she'd used this thing, she was her old self; as a cat, reviving her affinity might take longer than she'd like. It was just as well the human wasn't at home; she couldn't afford any distractions.

As the evening drew on, she made some progress but found it tiring. After a while, she hid the statuette behind a bookcase and fell into a sleep so deep, she didn't hear the detective return.

Athena woke in the grey light before dawn and returned to her practice, finally making the breakthrough she sought, as the muscle memory of her mind renewed acquaintance with the device. Elated, she wandered through the house, irritated that the man was not yet awake. Should she force the matter? She pushed at the bedroom door but saw he was still asleep. She considered jumping on him, but with reluctance rejected the idea as potentially counterproductive, and returned downstairs to wait.

How convenient it would be if she could simply reveal her true self to him, as she once could. That was no longer possible, and she had no desire to revisit the source of that grievance; instead, she would project an image of herself through the artefact.

She considered its range. In olden times she had used it to communicate with humans right across the Aegean without having to leave her palatial home. Did she still have that ability? And anyway, right now there was no one she felt like contacting. Not yet, at any rate.

Waiting upon a human was intensely annoying for any deity, and her frustration mounted. She vented it by ploughing furrows in the carpet.

At last, she heard him stirring upstairs; but it still took him an interminable amount of time to descend for the strong black coffee which usually passed as his breakfast. Athena composed herself and watched him intently as he entered the room. He gave her an affectionate greeting, but as he approached to tickle her between the ears, something incredible happened.

He and the cat were no longer alone; to the man's left,

glowing brightly and filling the room, stood a tall warrior woman in a shining breastplate, her helmet and spear tip brushing the ceiling. His eyes widened in astonishment, and he fell back into an armchair.

Dazzling green eyes surveyed him, carrying more than a hint of disdain. He groped for words, but before he could react, she spoke, her voice melodious but powerful.

"Mortal, well met. I am Athena, daughter of Zeus, Patron of this city. I have a task for you."

Her host appeared thunderstruck. He just sat there, his jaw moving but no words coming. This was not the reaction she'd expected or desired. With a small sigh, she reflected that today's generation was a little out of practice in greeting deities. If he'd known better, of course, he would kneel or preferably lie flat on his belly, eyes to the ground, awaiting her gracious invitation to speak or stand. He would have brought a goat or lamb to sacrifice at her altar, killing it according to the appropriate ritual before sprinkling its blood and burning some meat as an offering. He would have chanted an appropriate incantation as the smoke rose heavenwards in her honour.

But times had changed. At least he had cleansed himself before approaching her, she supposed; it had certainly taken him long enough.

The man stared at the bright apparition before him, then at the cat, sitting on its cushion and also giving him a piercing stare, then back at the woman.

She waited, her patience growing thin. Were today's humans even more stupid than their ancestors? Trying to regain some sense of dignity, the man clambered to his feet, but even at his full height, she towered above him.

"Greetings, my lady," he finally offered. "Welcome to my home. I am Giorgos Samaras."

"I know." A look of confusion on his face. "You would do

well to honour me, but in these godless times, the least I demand is due respect. You will do well to remember that." She glared at him until he lowered his eyes towards the floor. A wise first step, good. His next question was impertinent, but, she reflected, almost inevitable after such a lengthy time out.

"Are you the real Athena? The goddess?"

"The same," she replied, a little icily. This seemed to be the closest she would get to supplication this morning, so she might as well get down to business. "I need you to do something for me."

Second Lieutenant Samaras stared at her.

"There has been some criminal activity. Concerning cats. In the western districts a band of brigands has captured many animals, both cats and dogs, and is using them for nefarious purposes. Puppies are being bred for sale. Some cats, as well. Others are disappearing, presumably killed for reasons I have yet to discern."

A look of confusion on his face. "Cats? But…"

Athena cut across him, an edge to her voice, "You will put a stop to this barbaric behaviour. You are with the Athens police. It falls upon you to carry out my will. I require you to apprehend, eliminate, or banish the culprits according to your preference, and free the animals." She softened her tone, leaning towards him. "Do this small thing for me, and I will look favourably on you. I will advance your career as a detective. You will go on to greatness." She stood back, imperious again. "Thwart me and you will forever languish in obscurity, filing traffic reports, forgotten." She glared at him, her eyes burning with intensity.

The lieutenant shrank back into his chair. "Well… I'll have a look, of course, but with all this suspected terrorist activity…" He wavered. For a moment, her aura intensified, but she brought it under control. Athena did not like being rebuffed.

She arched an eyebrow.

"I'll get onto it immediately," he added.

The goddess gave him an appraising look. "Don't disappoint me," she said, and promptly vanished.

CHAPTER 53
RESCUE

At his desk, Police Second Lieutenant Samaras hung the jacket of his uniform over the back of his chair and tried to put the morning's episode to the back of his mind. In the bright light of day, here at work, it seemed too incredible to have happened. His caseload was already too long; a wild goose chase somewhere in western Athens to search for some stray cats and dogs wouldn't win him any favours with his boss. And anyway, she hadn't even given him an address.

He sighed and tried to concentrate. Most of his colleagues were chasing leads, no matter how tenuous, on the terror attacks that had struck without warning across the city to devastating effect. Samaras felt overlooked. His bosses had assigned almost everyone to the new investigations except him. He was one of a small crew expected to take over and keep on top of existing investigations. What did it say about his promotion prospects?

A new report had landed on his desk, passed across from one of his recently reassigned neighbours. Samaras scanned the cover page and summary with little enthusiasm, unable to shake off a nagging resentment that the really interesting work was passing him by. He tried to concentrate. An informant had told his handler about an illegal fur farming operation up north where garments were passed off as exotic pelts, but analysis had shown they were made from lower quality materials. Samaras frowned at the report, weighing its importance. The farm was at the other end of the country; surely one to pass on to colleagues in Thessaloniki. He put it to one side and moved to the next item.

The duty officer from the front desk stopped next to him and handed Samaras a handwritten note. "One of the patrol cars was doing the rounds in Tavros first thing, and they've reported something strange. A warehouse is being mobbed by an unusual number of birds."

The detective glanced at the note. "What do you mean, 'unusual'?"

"A huge number, they said. Hundreds. Crows and ravens mainly. Not seabirds. They said they didn't know so many lived in the city. It's like they're staking it out. I wondered if you'd have time to take a closer look?"

"Why didn't they stop at the time?"

"They got a call to assist at the scene of the derailment at Lefka, and now their shift's ended, but they think someone ought to look." He gave the detective an apologetic look. "You never know, with all the strange stuff that's been happening…" He scowled at the note, before dropping it onto the desk. "Place belongs to the Olympus Trading Company."

Detective Samaras wasn't prepared to give in easily. "What are they doing? The birds."

The sergeant wrinkled his nose, thinking. "Well, they said they're perching on the roof, and they keep flying over it, making a hell of a racket. It's just as well it's not a residential neighbourhood, but the local businesses will probably send in complaints if this keeps up, and there could be public hygiene aspects. I've never heard of anything like it, and the thought crossed my mind that these are all carrion birds, if you take my meaning."

The detective gave him a long appraising look. "As if I've not got enough to do?" he sighed. "Alright, leave it with me. I'll head out there. I could do with some fresh air."

The birds were still flocking above the place when Apollo arrived. He paused on the road before the front entrance. A large four-by-four and a van were parked either side of the door. As if on cue, the van door opened, and a man stepped out carrying a plastic crate with a briefcase balanced on top. For an instant, their eyes met, prompting the man to drop the crate. Apollo leapt for him, clamping his jaws around his throat, his huge claws ripping at the man's shoulders and neck. He fell backwards with a truncated scream.

The sound brought his companions to the entrance, but the instant they stepped outside they were attacked by wave after wave of crows, jackdaws and ravens, swooping down from above. Any exposed flesh was a target, as they darted in, pecked viciously and retreated for another turn while their place was taken by another. With no chance of rescuing their fallen colleague, the men struggled to defend themselves and regain the building.

Tavros was such a short drive from the police station, Samaras felt guilty taking the car. His initial doubts faded as soon as he saw the birds; he'd seen nothing like it. The number of huge black carrion birds thronging the compound below and perched on adjacent rooftops was astonishing. If anything, the report had understated their numbers. There looked to be thousands of them. It was surprising that people hadn't complained, particularly the owners of nearby buildings. But since the recession, many of them in this district were closed or abandoned. But surely anyone within earshot would want this avian menace dealt with. Most pertinently, though, what was attracting them?

He stopped a hundred metres short and got out of his car to have a better look. The cawing was cacophonous, as if they were trying to bring as much attention to themselves as possible. But there was a scuffle by the entrance. Some kind of fight seemed to be underway, with figures scrambling on the ground. He couldn't make them out; they were just a blur. Behind, a group of men retreated into the doorway, under attack from above. Samaras climbed back into his car and got on the radio to call for support, then advanced to the property. He parked so as to block any possible escape route for the van, and warily got out, keeping an eye on the skies above. The cacophony of cawing eased, and the aerial bombardment stopped. Birds perched on any available ledge, branch or lamppost nearby. Samaras paused, giving them a suspicious look. Had his arrival been enough to cause their attack to cease? Would it begin again the moment he turned away? In the watchful silence, every bird he could see seemed to be scrutinising him in turn. From the corner of his eye, a ginger-and-white cat slunk by, seemingly ignorant of the stand-off.

Samaras put his doubts aside and turned his attention to the building. As he rounded his vehicle he realised he was too late. A body lay next to the van, blood pooling about the upper torso, sightless eyes staring to the sky.

He bent over the victim, careful not to disturb the scene ahead of the arrival of the forensic team. The dead man was middle aged, perhaps in his forties, and overweight. Several days' worth of stubble adorned his chin. The immediate cause of death seemed clear enough: his throat had been savagely ripped open, his head and upper body covered in deep gashes. It didn't look like the work of a few birds. Samaras cast an uneasy glance about him, and then at the door of the building. Was the perpetrator still inside?

In the distance he could already hear sirens. He stood and studied the front of the building, a shabby one-story business premises with grimy, barred windows that had never been cleaned, and a single door. The exterior was unremarkable: flaking paintwork exposing the underlying render which in places was crumbling to expose the brickwork beneath. As with most nearby yards, the walls were spattered with graffiti. The white transit van in front of it was elderly and battered, but bore no company logo. Samaras approached the door and hammered on it, as behind him, three police cars and a van arrived from both ends of the street and drew up to either side of his car.

There was movement within, then the door opened. In the shadow of the passage beyond, stood a middle-aged woman. Samaras entered; first to witness the horrors beyond.

An hour later the building was still a hive of activity, driven now by animal protection officers rather than the police. They swarmed the inner yard, treating animals and bringing wire-mesh cages to remove them to alternative accommodation. Several police officers were scouring the office, sifting documents and gathering evidence for the investigation to follow. Samaras was continually distracted between their activities and the animal protection people. In the street, an ambulance drew up to remove the body. As it was placed into the back of the vehicle, he was approached by a member of the veterinary team.

"I know it may not be my business: you'll have medical experts examining him, after all," she nodded towards the body on the stretcher, "but you may want to keep a lookout."

"For what?"

She looked at him as if deciding what to say. "I'm a veterinary expert, not a pathologist, but I got enough of a look at him to make me concerned." Samaras frowned. "Those wounds; they're not... I don't know of a weapon, a knife or blade of any sort, or a gun, that would leave such a mess, for want of a better word."

Samaras took her elbow to guide her out of the way of a woman carrying a cage containing an emaciated dog. He nodded towards a side room, giving them a degree of privacy. "What do you mean?" he asked.

The veterinary officer looked him in the eye. "Those wounds, the way the flesh was ripped and torn. It looks like bite marks, to me. I'd say this was the work of a large predator."

He could see she wasn't joking. He recalled his arrival, the sight of some kind of scuffle, as he'd thought it, behind the van. Blurred movement obscured by flapping wings and the harsh calls of angry ravens. The frenzy of activity had moved behind the van, and by the time he'd drawn up outside, all he could see was the body.

"The marks on his neck and head," she continued, "I've seen nothing like it. And the severity of the injuries. They look like the ripping of claws, to me. The incisions are ragged edged, not clean slices. Then the puncture wounds at the neck... I don't have a lot of experience with large predators, but they look like the wounds you might get from a big cat." She looked him in the eye. "I mean a really big cat. A lion or a tiger. Something like that."

"But I was here. I would have seen it."

She shrugged.

"In the distance, anyway. There was no lion."

She looked at him. "Well, I can't explain it. Perhaps the pathologist will come up with another answer. She brushed past him to get on with her work, leaving Samaras confused. Just what had he witnessed?

·   ·   ·

Sitting behind a lamppost across the road for the past hour, Apollo had observed the arrival of the police and the comings and goings of cars, vans and other vehicles with interest. He hadn't tried to hide, but no one paid him the slightest attention. He noted, with satisfaction, the arrest of the three remaining humans from the site, but began to pay closer attention when the first animals were brought out, most of them in a sorry state. It was time to conclude his search.

He padded across the road, weaving between legs and around obstacles, ignored by everyone. What he found shocked him. The interior of the compound was like a war zone. The number of captives was higher than he'd expected, and many were in a poor condition: physically malnourished, or suffering from severe mental stress and anxiety, or both. They howled or wailed in their anguish, some flinging themselves at the walls of their cages, others staring hopelessly into the distance. Many might never recover.

Apollo's outrage grew with every step. He weaved a path between the cages until he came to one at the back in the corner. There, looking thinner than he'd ever seen her, was Olympia.

He pushed against the wire mesh. On the other side, Olympia did likewise as they attempted to butt their heads together.

"I'm here. You're safe," was all he could think to say.

At first she couldn't even reply, but just searched his face, as if unable to believe it was true; rescue was here. "Thank god," was the most she could come up with, followed by a keening wail of pain at the slow release of tension. She fell silent for several minutes, a haunted look in her eyes. He could do nothing more than purr reassurance. Eventually she spoke.

"Is it really true? Is it over?"

"It is. You're safe."

Doubt was still etched on her face, but Apollo turned his

attention to getting her out. He needed her alert and in the moment. Escape would demand quick movement and good timing. Humans were everywhere: taking photographs, making notes, opening cages and stepping in to treat the worst affected. Olympia's pen was one of the last to be opened. A young woman with latex gloves stepped in to collect animals and place them into a rescue-branded carry case. Olympia waited until she had hold of her cell companion.

"Now!" Apollo yelled, and she ran for the door. The woman cursed, annoyed she hadn't closed it, but she couldn't drop her charge. Olympia shot past. Following Apollo, she swerved and dodged past human legs and other obstacles across the yard and down the corridor. Fortunately, the front entrance had been wedged open, so they easily broke through into the street. They took a right turn and headed up the road. No one paid any attention; there were too many serious cases to deal with.

A hundred metres away, they stopped. Olympia was struggling, breathing hard. Despite her pregnancy she had lost weight and looked weak, swaying slightly on her feet. Apollo studied her with concern and searched her face. He saw the haunted look of someone who has witnessed too much horror and still struggled to believe the ordeal was over.

Instinctively he pressed his forehead into hers, stood close to her, body to body, purring gently. He nuzzled an ear. It was a simple, instinctive gesture, but he put all of his healing power into it.

Guilt was his overriding emotion. Guilt about the time it had taken to rescue her, and the disloyalty that had guided his thoughts; he'd let his dreams of Daphne rule him all this time. She'd been the one driving his feelings, and Olympia had become merely an afterthought. Apollo didn't love Olympia. Not really, not deeply, and certainly not in the way she'd hoped; but he owed her a debt of gratitude for her companionship, if nothing else, and for the litter of kittens she was carrying.

His legacy.

He closed his eyes and concentrated his thoughts. She would need a lot more time to be anything like her usual self.

On a practical level, they had to take it steadily. As far as possible Apollo walked alongside, keeping a watchful eye on her every step. His initial elation at rescuing her soon evaporated. Now he just wanted to get her somewhere safe, while all the time knowing he was late for his appointment with a different destiny. One that couldn't wait. They walked down the road into a deepening gloom as storm clouds gathered over the city centre.

CHAPTER 54
THE SECOND BATTLE OF MONASTIRAKI

As the day wore on, the heat built, becoming more oppressive by the hour. Bright morning sunshine gave way to dull, flat light, and in the city centre a sense of foreboding was building. The two sides gathered on opposite sides of the square, warily studying their enemies, all of them weary but on edge. Kratos and Zelus were confident they had the numbers, but even so, it would be tough to motivate their followers for one last effort. Most had expected to be resting, enjoying the rich pickings promised by their victory. Many of them grumbled when safely out of earshot of the leaders or their kin. Kratos would need to use all his assertiveness to stir them up for one last push.

The brothers avoided each other as far as possible, each taking a different wing of their army. Kratos was still reeling from the theft of the artefact by the infuriating little spy. He should have crushed her when he had the chance. Thoughts of revenge filled his head, together with a steely determination to make Athena pay. Now he had experienced the power of the artefact, one thing was clear: it was the key to all his future ambitions.

· · ·

A short way across town, purposefully moving in file, was another gang with Bia at their head. As Hermes had foreseen, she had circled the Acropolis and Athena's unknown forces, to rendezvous with her kin via the narrow, winding streets of the Plaka itself. She was in no mood to let her brothers take all the spoils.

In the Agora, beneath the trees, Athena was restless. Her thoughts flicked from subject to subject, never resting for long. Once more she ran through the scenarios, weighing up the opposing forces; their experience, and motivation. Where was her damned brother? She could certainly use his uncouth brawn right now. What of Bia? Could she resist joining in, and if so, how many should be held back to prevent them surprising her forces from the rear? She paced up and down, her mind's eye far away from the nervous-looking cats assembled before her. Daphne and Jason sat beside one another. Neither spoke much; just the occasional reassuring nervous purr or nuzzle. Both knew the stakes were high.

"I wish Apollo was here," muttered Jason. Daphne looked at him, marvelling at his forgiving nature. He hadn't looked into those eyes.

In Syntagma Square, a few battered survivors of the Plaka gang assembled. They grumbled to one another about their misfortune. Most bore barely healed wounds. Few looked in any shape to fight, yet here they were, hoping against hope for some sort of miracle, although first they needed to see their erstwhile leader.

He arrived, flanked by his sons, striding across the square, apparently without a care in the world. Large in person, and larger-than-life in reputation, Ares approached them with a cavalier attitude. "Well met, my friends," he rumbled in his *basso profundo*. He scanned them, offering a simple greeting here, delivering a hearty message there. His mere presence lifted their spirits. Despite their situation, with Ares beside them, anything seemed possible.

Phobos and Deimos held back on the edge of the group. By nature, they were cooler and more reserved than their father; far less emotionally engaged and more calculating. They would play their part, but they would not lead the attack.

Ares addressed them all.

"Today is a great day. Today is the day we reclaim our home," he roared. "Are you with me?" He didn't wait for the answer, but turned and moved off smartly, heading towards Monastiraki Square.

The day darkened as cloud built upon cloud, towering above the city. With the sun obscured, night seemed to arrive prematurely. Oppressive air trapped beneath the clouds sapped energy and willpower. Cowed, and deprived of free will they might be, but the members of the Botrys and Gizi gangs were moody and resentful. Both Kratos and Zelus heard them answer back, whereas previously they would never have dared. It would take more willpower than ever to goad them to fight. Perhaps the survival instinct might suffice.

The two leaders watched from the Library of Hadrian; Zelus keen to take the initiative and attack, Kratos instinctively cautious. The lost artefact played on his mind. Recovering it was paramount, but there was more than one way to win a battle. Should he commit his forces not knowing what they were up against, or would it be better to wait and watch the enemy waste their energy on a futile attack?

· · ·

A few hundred metres away, Athena struggled with similar thoughts. Finally, she could bear it no more. She nodded to her lieutenants, and they assembled the cats. They were too few, it was clear to see. This was the kind of gamble she'd not attempted for many a year; she just had to trust in others to play their part as had been agreed.

Slowly but purposefully, they made their way down Ifestou Street towards the square.

"They're here!" shouted Rea.

Kratos looked up sharply to see Athena and her rag-tag army, and his spirits rose. "Is that all they've got?" Turning to his troops, he raised his voice. "They're no match for us. Let's sort this rabble out once and for all." He led them into the square. They formed pods on either side, still reluctant, but leashed by the power of his will once more, snarling and resentful. The same was true of Zelus' forces as they shuffled forth, sullen and embittered. For a moment, there was silence; then it began.

Through the gloom and humidity, there was an intense flash as lightning hit the summit of the Acropolis, accompanied by a hideous tearing sound, as if the sky were ripping in two. It reverberated and echoed from the walls. Almost immediately, hailstones the size of marbles rained down, bouncing from the pavement, ricocheting from the roofs. Tourists caught out by the sudden downpour dived for cover in shops and restaurants.

The two armies, driven by the willpower of their leaders, focused intently on the enemy and took no notice. It was as if someone had fired a starting gun.

They hurled themselves at one another in a mass of yelping and yowling that was drowned out by more thunder and flashes of lightning. Duels broke out all over the square as cats fought bitterly to the death. No quarter was given or demanded; the fighting was vicious. Flesh was torn and bones were crunched between powerful jaws. Victims screamed in pain and fear, their cries lost amid the mayhem.

The fighting was at its most intense around the leaders, with Athena on the one side, and Zelus and Kratos on the other. They were kept apart by frenzied foot soldiers, driven on, on the one side, by the spiteful mental grip of their overlords; on the other by a desperate desire for freedom and a peaceful life.

Into the mayhem, Bia and her gang arrived. They paused at the southern tip of the square while she took in the scene before her and picked out Athena, surrounded by the remains of the Plaka gang and her followers.

"So few," she scoffed. "We could have taken over years ago." Facing them in the middle of the square were her brothers. They had the numbers and the momentum. She turned to her followers. "This should be easy," she yelled. "Let's sort the old grey fool out once and for all." She led the charge.

Jason was in the thick of the fighting, with Daphne nearby. She pawed nervously at the ground, desperate to play her part.

Lightning danced around the old town, and the walls reverberated with the sound of thunder. The hailstones gave way to torrential rain, but the combatants ignored it. Skirmishes rose around the square and blood flowed into the gutters. It looked bad for Athena. Kratos and Zelus, now abetted by Bia and her gang, were just too strong, and her numbers were thinning. But then, with a yowling battle cry heard even above the din of the storm, Ares and his band of survivors emerged from Mitropoleos Street.

Kratos looked up, shocked to see the old warlord back. For a moment his hopes wavered, but then he saw their low numbers and how feeble they looked. This was still going to be his victory. He shrugged off his immediate attacker and tried to make his way towards Ares to see off the big oaf once and for all. But the new arrivals had more of an impact than their numbers suggested. Phobos and Deimos attacked on the flanks, spreading confusion, havoc and panic, and Ares in his fury was unstoppable, flinging the bodies of his enemies aside with a hideous relish. For a while, the outcome hung in the balance.

Within the wider melee, warriors duelled all over the square. Jason and Daphne were in the thick of it, close to Athena. They dodged, struck, bit, wove, disengaged, reen-gaged and grappled for all they were worth. Jason closed in on Kratos, but before he could get there, Daphne ducked beneath an assailant and found herself face to face with the gang leader.

"Oh, it's the pretty little thief," he sneered. "Time's up."

He leapt at her in a frenzy of teeth and claws; but she surprised him, dancing backwards and sideways, leaving him swiping at thin air. She kept her focus on him as he turned towards her once more. Again he charged, and, like a small matador, she ducked under his blow and wove past him again, this time getting in a swipe of her own in passing.

A red furrow appeared along his flank.

Enraged, he spun and flew at her once more; and again she danced away, taunting him. Darting forwards with a speed he could not match, she clawed his nose. Like an aggra-vated bull, he charged on, and she spun away again. But this time it went wrong. This time, it didn't work. This time there was a screech of brakes and a heavy thud. Absorbed in her fight, she had danced too far into the road.

This time, she didn't get up.

At first, Kratos was bewildered, then delighted. He raised his head and let out a victory yowl.

Jason artlessly launched himself at the big cat, who swatted him aside. He tried again, but savage bites and blows left him wounded and panting for breath. The gang leader stood over him. It was all over.

Most animals would have given up by now, but Jason's mind was numb with a different kind of pain: *if she's gone, I don't want to be here.* Head spinning, he struggled to his feet and mustered all his reserves for one last attack.

He never got the chance.

A dazzling light cut across his vision, momentarily blinding him. Kratos barely saw it coming and had only just begun to adjust his position before he was knocked sideways and bowled right over by a glowing ginger-and-white thunderbolt.

The two of them rolled over in a ferocious wrestling match. Jason crouched, trying to take it all in. Apollo had clamped his jaws around Kratos' throat and was shaking him like a rag doll, his claws raking the russet cat's neck and head. Despite his size and strength, Kratos had no response to the sheer power and venom of his attacker. He tried to break free but couldn't. This was a force beyond nature.

Apollo's teeth held him in a chokehold that punctured his throat and would have quickly killed any lesser being. Beaten, the big cat teetered on the brink, but somehow clung to life. Apollo threw him down in disgust one last time and stood over him.

Bruised, bloodied and battered, Kratos glared up at his attacker. Despite his wounds, he managed a croaking laugh, taunting him. "Here. At last. Too little. Too late." His breathing was ragged, and his words came in short bursts. Kratos cast a glance at the mayhem surrounding them. "It looks like you've miscalculated, Shining One. I thought you were supposed to be the master of logic. I've won. Your time is over. Go back. This is no longer your fight." He paused, panting for breath, then continued. "You're stronger than you look, I'll give you that, but still you are weak. The world respects strength today, not useless chit-chat. You are feeble. Your time has passed." He paused again, sucking in air, while the ginger cat glared at him, then resumed his taunts. "You might have surprised me, but you can't kill me." He gasped. "I'm one of you. I'm *immortal*." He laughed once again, wheezing and panting, but flaunting his defiance. Still, he had to avert his eyes from Apollo's scorching glare; it was like looking into the sun.

"Titan or no, I can send you back to Tartarus, where you belong," the ginger cat snarled. Kratos lay in front of him, struggling to breathe.

"You can't," he managed, eventually. "Zeus protects me."

Apollo's glare intensified, as if it would melt stone.

Kratos continued. "We fought with him all those years ago. We were allies. Maybe you've forgotten? It was me who pinned Prometheus to the rock with those iron chains. Zeus likes me. He always has. Then, eventually, he set the rest of my kin free. All of them. Even Atlas. He's made peace with us. You cannot undo it. The sacred treaty." He dared a spiteful glance at his enemy and couldn't resist a sneer. "Everyone knows that the mighty Apollo always bows before Zeus."

It was as if time had stopped. Apollo glared at his foe, his expression unreadable. Behind him, lightning flashed, but he took no heed. The moment stretched. Then a strange look came over his face, accompanying a memory: a picture of a rustic barn in the mountains, long ago. His mouth parted slightly into an almost wolfish grin.

"I'll argue with him later. It won't be the first time," he said and fell upon his foe, joyously embracing all the dark and righteous fury in his soul. Kratos howled in unearthly agony as ten razors slashed his pelt, helpless to stop his flesh being torn and stripped away. His screams echoed from the buildings, searing through the storm, and as his followers heard them, all their fight drained away, soaking into the rain around their feet. Some shook their heads as if waking from a dream; others gazed blankly at each other, wondering where they were, and why. The invisible hold Kratos had over them, brittle as glass, shattered, and they fled.

Zelus could only gawp in horror. Bia bowed her head to hide her face, the urge for conquest gone. Even Athena and Ares looked stunned. Apollo raised his head to look at them, his maw red from his bloody work, his eyes still blazing in fury. Red, too, were his paws and chest; at his feet lay an unrecognisable lump of flesh that held no life.

Kratos' death sent shockwaves through the aether, like ripples on a still pool; unnoticed by mortals, but as high and clear as the ringing of a bell on the still midnight air to those who could sense that realm.

In exile on the slopes of Parnassus, Zeus and Hera looked up sharply.

Deep in the woodland groves of Arcadia, a white cat paused her hunt, momentarily distracted.

In a shepherd's hut high in the mountains of Thessaly, a large copper-brown tabby, dozing on the hearth, raised his head, his eyes narrowing in thought.

At the back of a cavernous beach bar on Mykonos, beneath a banquet seat, lying amid the detritus of the previous night's party and trying to sleep off its excesses, a long-haired red tabby – the one they all tried to forget – opened a wine-dark eye to a snake-like slit, and absorbed the news.

A god was dead.

CHAPTER 55
STYX

The rain eased. The battle was over, but there was little joy in victory. Athena, Ares and Hermes were slack-jawed. Zelus cowered at Ares' feet, both horrified and indignant. Bia slunk away with her supporters. All eyes fixed on the ginger cat in his ferocious, bloody glory. He flung back his head, and a roar filled the square; a noise no ordinary cat could make. It was over. He looked around at them, defying any challenge, his eyes still burning with righteous fire.

Athena moved to his shoulder. Even her warrior spirit seemed unnerved by his savagery; still, her proximity had a calming effect and his monumental wrath subsided. Across the square, an eerie silence fell.

"You'd better leave," she said. "Take the others and head to the Agora. I've got this."

As she spoke, vans drew up at the roadside, and humans clambered out, unloading wire-mesh crates. Wounded stragglers from the defeated gangs tried to escape the men, who deployed nets to catch them. Others advanced across the square, tending to the wounded, collecting the dead. They gave the Olympians a wide berth, as if they didn't see them.

Apollo turned to the victors, most of whom seemed to be unsteady on their feet and in a state of shock. His insane rage ebbed away, and the returning tide brought a strange ennui. The monster was defeated, but could he endure his victory?

He locked eyes on Jason, his voice suddenly flat but gentle. "Come on, old friend. Let's go."

Jason didn't reply. He looked lost. Instead, he walked towards the road, past the human animal welfare officers. He approached Daphne's lifeless body and sniffed at it, then prodded it with a paw. But there was no sign of life.

Olympia appeared at his side. She tenderly butted against him with her forehead.

"We ought to go," she said, gently.

"But where?" he asked. "I've got nowhere to go to anymore."

She had no answer. Again, she nuzzled him, offering comfort where there was none. "Look at me," she said, more firmly. "We can't stay here. There's nothing you can do." He stared at her with hollow eyes.

Olympia turned and strolled away, looking over her shoulder to check he was coming. Blindly, he followed. Together, they made their way through the easing rain towards the sanctuary of the Agora.

The victors assembled, but there was a hushed silence. They had won. The short but evil reign of the gangs was over, but with the losses they had suffered in two bitter conflicts and the wounds many endured, there was little celebration. Just relief. It would take a while before a merry band of misfits populated the Plaka streets again, teasing the tourists.

Daphne stood at the side of the road. What had happened? She'd been jousting with the horrible oaf, making him look like a fool, and then... nothing, for a moment. Then she was here. But what was that lying at her feet? It looked familiar.

Tentatively, she sniffed at the body, but it seemed to have no scent. She tried patting it, but her paw seemed to go right through it. Her fear verged on panic. She looked around wildly. Everything was in monotone; sounds were suppressed. What was happening? It all seemed strangely distant, as if she were watching through a fog. A large silver-white cat approached and turned his piercingly bright blue eyes towards her.

"Come with me," he said kindly. "Don't be afraid."

They passed down paths she could not describe, to a strange land.

After a long or short time – she could not tell – they appeared at a river where a boat drew up. The white cat stopped.

"I must go no further," he told her. She jumped onto the boat, hesitating, and looked up at the hooded figure of the ferryman.

"Don't be afraid," the white cat told her one more time. He turned to the ferryman. "She is bound for Elysium."

"It is not for you to say," the other replied, in a rumbling voice, deep as the river. "It is for the judges."

"I know."

He stood on the bank for a while and watched the boat cross. Onboard, Daphne gazed at the shadowy bank ahead, now more nervous than ever. As she approached the shore, she heard music; faint at first, but building. It was a beautiful melody; unlike anything she'd ever heard. Soothing and strangely uplifting. Behind her, the white cat gave her one last look, then left.

CHAPTER 56
DECISION TIME

F aint light crept in, apologetically, through the doorway to his mighty throne room. To the figure enthroned on the enormous obsidian chair the entrance was little bigger than a mouse hole and the dim illumination made little impression on this enormous liminal space, deep within the bedrock beneath the lake. How far it extended into the darkness, even he did not know, but it was not far enough.

Not far enough to reach to his ancient lands: the kingdom from which he was banished.

The god sat, brooding in the dark. He was one of the mighty ones. Among the oldest. The Lord of Chaos. Reduced to a shadow of his former self. An exile in foreign lands. This was his punishment for wanting nothing more than to reclaim his rightful throne. And for murdering his brother.

About his feet, drifting in from the further darkness: sand. The grains slipped between his sandal and his foot, sticking between his toes. It was the familiar touch of home, but no sun would ever reach this place to warm the sand or lend it a hot glow.

The enormous figure leaned back, deep in contemplation,

staring unseeing into the dark. He rested his left elbow on the polished black stone arm of his throne, the hand supporting his chin, while his right hand tapped out a rhythm on the other arm. He scarcely noticed he was doing it, so deep was he in thought.

It is time.

He could feel it. Like any immortal, he'd heard the knell of one cast out from the realm above to the next. It was as clear a sign of change as any. A signal. The time had come to wake up. To plan. To act. To return.

He came to a decision and stood. Then walked across the sand-strewn stone flags towards the doorway in the corner. As he did so, he shrank to normal human scale, his head transforming into that of a dark, curly-haired and bearded man.

Through chamber and antechamber he strode, then veered between the exhibits to a door in a side wall. It led to a fully equipped modern laboratory with work benches, microscopes, racks of colourful bottled liquids, petri dishes, scientific instruments.

He sat on a bench before a computer and tapped in the parameters of his search.

A search that would consume all his energies. A search for a weapon, different from those he'd accumulated to date. A weapon that would kill a god.

A weapon that would bring them all down.

CHAPTER 57
EAGLE

I n the hours following the battle, the survivors could do
little more than recover. There was no celebration. Feeling
deflated and weary, Apollo sought Jason. His friend was
struggling, but he scarcely knew what to say.

"I'm sorry I couldn't get there in time."

Jason gave him a sharp look. "What was that all about? So
many lives destroyed or screwed up, and for what? For the
pickings of a few streets, here in Athens? Why?"

"I can't say."

"Why did we come here?"

"You know the reason."

Jason stared into the distance, struggling to connect his
thoughts. "I'm glad she's safe. But I wish we'd never come."
He bowed his yead onto his paws again, staring at the
ground.

"I'm sorry."

Jason looked at him once more. "I suppose you're just
sorry he didn't kill me instead? Then you could do your
heroic rescue bit, and swept her off somewhere"

"You knew her better than that."

Jason glared at him.

"No," Apollo told him, "I was ..." he couldn't bring himself to say the word. "It wasn't meant to be. I understand that now."

Jason didn't look satisfied by his explanation. "I thought your kind never said sorry."

"Well, I'm saying it now."

"And that's enough, is it? Just a quick apology and move on to your next big adventure?" He raised his head, anger replacing bitterness in his voice. "She was special. Special to me, at any rate. You'll just forget her and move on. Pretend none of this ever happened."

Apollo struggled to put the words together. Explaining himself to a mortal was as novel as it was unsettling. "I won't. Ever." An uncomfortable silence fell between them. He tried again. "No one escapes their life unscathed. Not even us. We're all damaged one way or another; we all carry scars, even if you can't see them. We all make mistakes."

Jason still simmered. "But your mistakes are bigger. More deadly. And you don't die. It's just everyone around you." His eyes bored into the ginger cat. "I thought you were one of us. A friend. Someone I could trust. Do you really care about us, or are we just another one of your games?"

Apollo had no answer. He looked into the eyes of his friend and saw pain etched deeper than he thought possible; a desolation that would last a lifetime. There were so many deadly mistakes throughout his long existence and he was tired of hiding from them. The weight of the years was heavy today, and he had no escape. He envied his companion's brief existence. What time would he have to dwell on his own errors of judgement? Virtually none.

Behind it all was the knowledge he'd lost Daphne; she who'd lit up his life once more without realising it. He longed to see her again, if only to apologise for that last encounter. To try and explain, to make her understand, though he doubted he could. Perhaps there were some things that could never be unsaid. He thought back to Delphi, a matter of days ago, and playful times beneath the olive trees. Daphne had taught him that life could be worth living again. And she had made her choice.

"I'm still me," he said, finally. "The same animal you've known. I've always been around, and I always will be. Some have even been thankful to know me." He faltered and averted his eyes for a moment. When he resumed, it was as if he were talking almost to himself. "I hope you will, too. One day. Perhaps you just have to wait and look for me when you're ready?"

Jason gave him a searching look, then bowed his head, lost in thought. Apollo turned to leave, but immediately he heard a small voice behind him.

"She's really gone. What can I do when all I've got is a few memories?"

He turned back to the animal, so lost in misery, and understood his pain.

"Treasure them," he whispered, and walked away.

The golden eagle appeared soon after, as he knew it would. It circled overhead once, then swooped down to land on the Pnyx rock. Apollo stood before it.

"You have broken a treaty that has endured ten thousand years, and as a result, they threaten war. You must accompany me and explain yourself before Zeus."

"No."

The eagle fell silent. It had not expected rejection. It tried again.

"The Titans seek retribution. They must be appeased, or war is likely. Who are you to defy the Sky Father?" The eagle stared with unblinking eyes, awaiting his response.

Apollo's chin rose almost imperceptibly. Through flared nostrils, he could detect the faintest aroma of the trees and foliage of Delphi on its feathers; the scent of home. His eyes narrowed. The bird waited, still as a statue.

"This audience is over," said Apollo. "You may leave." He turned away.

The eagle gave the retreating cat a long look. "Is this your final answer?"

Apollo continued on his way, the eagle's eyes boring into his back. After a long pause, it departed.

Athena emerged from behind a tree. "Wasn't that rather hasty? You know he won't let it go."

"Maybe. But I don't care." Apollo walked past her and into the trees. She caught up with him a few paces on, walking alongside.

"We should talk, the four of us. I've got some ideas. Follow me."

CHAPTER 58
THE CAT INTELLIGENCE TEAM

In a shady clearing on the upper slopes of Filopappou Hill, four cats lounged, passing the time of day. They communicated much in the flick of a tail, the scratch of an ear or the occasional glance, whether furtive or bold. The rest they vocalised. Ares, Hermes, Apollo and Athena were debating recent events.

"I can't believe you did that," said Hermes.

"He deserved it. I couldn't let him go," Apollo shot back. It had taken him some time to make his peace with the messenger god again, but slowly fences were mending.

"Yes, and I will back you, even if they return in war." Ares' support was one thing, but all could remember the terrible ten-year war between the Titans and Olympians, and none of them wanted a return to those days. Apollo looked into the distance, deep in thought.

"What do you think he'll do?" said Hermes.

"I suppose he's going to get you to turn me in." Apollo looked at each of them; none could bear the weight of that golden stare for long.

"He might try," Athena admitted. There was an air of defiance in her response, which Apollo acknowledged gratefully,

ANDREW RYLANDS

even though it surprised him. If Zeus had a favourite among his children, it was surely her.

"You know as well as I that I will find it difficult to resist his call," said Hermes, returning a level stare. "Fortunately, he has not sought me for many a year, but were he to summon me once more, it does not mean he owns my mind. I will not act against you."

Apollo looked at him again. "You'll keep my whereabouts secret? You won't betray me?"

"I give you my word." Hermes locked eyes with him and held his gaze for a long moment. It seemed to satisfy the ginger cat.

"I'll have to go into exile, I guess."

"So soon? But where will you go?" Athena asked.

"I don't know, but it's best if you don't, either. I'll just follow my nose. I'm sure I'll end up somewhere interesting." He hesitated. "There is one thing you could do for me, though. Olympia's carrying a litter. She'll be having them soon. After all this, she can't go back to Delphi." He left it hanging.

"I'll look after her," said Athena.

"She can stay with us," Ares suggested. "Better for the little ones." He glanced across at Athena. "You wouldn't want them growing up among the sisterhood. They'd turn out odd." Athena glared at him but said nothing.

"You will keep their identity secret?" Apollo added.

Silence fell. They basked in the sun. After a while Athena spoke again, changing the subject. "Are you ready to resume your duties as head of your so-called Plaka gang?" she asked Ares.

He mulled it over. "I suppose so."

"That's not what I'd call an enthusiastic response," piped Hermes.

Ares flicked his tail. "I don't enjoy feeling trapped."

"None of us do," Athena replied. "I don't think it's a

problem to take the odd break. It's not supposed to be a prison sentence."

"I'll think about it," he grumbled and lay down flat on his side.

"Tabitha's an able deputy," Apollo suggested. "Jason speaks highly of her."

"How about Jason as deputy?" suggested Hermes.

"I don't know," said Apollo. "Maybe. I'm not sure if he wants to go home or not, after all that's happened. He's taken it hard." He lay his head on his paws and fell silent.

In the distance, the rumble of city life continued, but closer to home, the sounds of birds and insects prevailed; particularly the incessant buzz of crickets.

"Something has been troubling me," said Apollo. "I remember we all agreed to the transition into this form, but why? Try though I might, I just can't remember."

Meaningful looks passed between the other three.

"It's her fault," Hermes said.

Ares turned towards Athena; Apollo followed his gaze. She looked a little uncomfortable.

"Come on. You were all there at the meeting. It was a collective decision. We all bought into it. Even the Titans."

"Hades didn't. Neither did Poseidon nor Oceanus at first," Ares reminded her.

"I wasn't there. I'm sure of it," said Apollo.

Hermes looked at him. "No, you were too busy chasing that nymph," he said. "Your consent was just assumed. But you ate the same fruit as everyone else."

"Fruit?"

"From the tree," said Hermes, exasperated. "The Tree of Demeter. The one she and Athena grew specially. I can't believe we all fell for it." He looked away in disgust.

Athena shuffled her position. "Yes. There were one or two dissenters," she admitted, continuing as if she hadn't heard him. "And it probably makes little sense for them. But everyone else was up for it. We used to change shape all the time for our own various purposes. Just not all together as a group. It took a lot more effort and coordination. It was difficult. But after a lot of research and planning, Demeter and I put together a complex set of spells and enchantments, and we combined them into a new species of tree."

"We?" asked Apollo. Athena shuffled position. For the first time since he'd seen her again, she looked uncomfortable.

"It was a joint effort," she said, staring into the distance.

"But why cats?" he added. "And why little ones? Why not something bigger, like tigers? It's hard to think in something this small, let alone act. I feel almost powerless."

Athena smiled. "It's like hiding in plain sight. We can live among them, eavesdrop on all their secrets, keep on top of things and influence them when we can. It could be fun. We just get on with things right under their noses." She seemed pleased with herself, despite more than fifteen hundred years of "hiding". "Keeps me busy, anyway. After they stopped worshipping us, I needed something else to do to keep me interested. Something that would spice things up. What else can we do? Stay involved or just fade away into the background like old wallpaper? I'd rather do this than drive a taxi." She gave them a defiant look. "Anyway, it seemed like a good idea at the time. And they're bound to screw up sometime, and then we'll be ready to get more involved again."

"Except we can't," said Hermes.

"Oh, all right, then," said Athena. "I know it's my fault. You don't have to keep going on about it."

Apollo scowled. "About what?"

"About the fact we can't change back," said Hermes.

Apollo sat back in shock. He looked in horror at Athena. "We're stuck like this? Forever?"

She gave him a long look. "Eating more of the fruit should allow us to change back," she said. "But I think the tree died."

She looked down, but Apollo's eyes bored into the top of her head. "Or it might have been moved. I don't know if there are any others." She glanced up at him, a slightly desperate look in her eye. "I don't know if Demeter took the seeds or any saplings. I can't remember."

He stared at her, uncomprehending, and echoed her words. "You can't remember?"

"It may have been poisoned." Ares was serious now. "There were rumours. But whatever the truth, we don't know where it is."

"Why don't we ask Demeter?"

"No one knows where she is, either."

Apollo looked from one to another. "There's got to be another way. Surely one of you must be able to do something? Get us back into our old bodies?" Blank stares confronted him.

There was another long silence.

"What have you done with that precious artefact of yours?" asked Ares. He rolled onto his stomach and tucked his paws underneath, his ruby eyes on Athena.

She took her time to reply. "I've decided. I don't want it to go missing again, so it needs to be stored securely. I've decided to donate it to the museum."

"Won't that stop you using it?" asked Hermes.

"No. I've experimented with range. I think I'll still be able to use it from a distance, as long as I know precisely where it is. It should be okay. And you can all relax." She glanced at each of them. "I will not use it against you. You can do what you like provided you don't undermine the safety and security of the city." She gave the large russet-coloured cat a meaningful look and changed the subject. "I've been thinking about the future," she announced. "I think we need a new mission."

The others looked at each other.

"You mean a collective mission?" Hermes asked.

Athena gave an imperceptible nod. "Yes. It worked out well, what with the rescue and everything. I think we should capitalise on it."

Apollo gave a derisive snort. "Are you sure your policeman friend was up to it? He arrived late, and he didn't seem all there, if you ask me."

Athena defended her protégé. "He took a little time to adjust. But he gets it now. The briefcase dropped by the man you attacked contained some crucial documents that tied this bunch to an illegal fur farming operation up north. They were passing off cat fur as mink, selling it on to foreign gangs to distribute abroad."

"Cat fur!" Hermes spat.

"I'm afraid so. Those animals were held until they were needed up north at the garment factory. Then they were killed and sent on. That's why they hardly bothered to feed them. They were just waiting for slaughter."

There was silence while they absorbed the information.

"We rescued Olympia just in time then," Apollo said to no one in particular.

Athena moved the conversation on. "Anyway, as a result of cracking this investigation, Second Lieutenant Samaras is going to be promoted to lieutenant with greater investigative responsibilities. It's just the first step. He could go far. We have recovered the artefact formerly known as the Luck of Athens, and I've recruited a useful human who can be directly manipulated. They're the first two building blocks of a network. A network that can help us."

Silence. Suspicious looks.

"Explain," Ares demanded.

Athena continued. "I think you all agree that we are weaker when we act individually. And it is a sad truth that so many of our number have simply disappeared these past few centuries. Gone we know not where. I propose we track them down. And in doing so, we also search for the tree. The Tree of Transformation." She gave them another look. "What do you say?" She sat upright, tail curved around, warming to her theme. The others continued to look suspiciously at her. "We have agents everywhere. All of our followers and extended contacts represent a set of eyes out on the streets, in homes, in shops and businesses up and down the country, even in what passes for the corridors of power. As we grow, we can expand it into a vast network. A massive resource. We need to connect everyone, of course, but if we work together, it's achievable. Then we use our new network of eyes on the ground to look out for oddly behaving felines, or mysterious trees with unusual fruit."

"I'm not sure it's quite so simple," said Hermes, mulling it over.

"It might work," Apollo ventured, "but how do we get messages to you?"

Athena adopted full planning mode. "Well, you've got your crows and ravens. Hermes—"

"—has tortoises," interjected Ares.

"Hermes is our messenger," Athena continued, "and you can just send one of your Plaka tribe over here to talk to me. I have my own followers, and I can send my owls out to check in with people periodically. It should all work." She gave them a triumphant look.

The others shuffled their positions. It would certainly be different. They'd hardly ever acted together before unless they were under a collective threat, such as in the war against the Titans, and since that might be on the brink of breaking out again, this could be a useful move.

Athena took their silence as acquiescence. "That's settled, then."

"What are we going to call this new operation?" queried Ares.

"How about the Cat Intelligence Agency?" suggested Apollo.

Hermes yawned. "CIA. Been done."

"Feline Bureau of Investigation?" Ares prompted.

"United Cat Detectives?" offered Athena.

"Sounds like a parcel delivery service," said Ares. "You might as well go for United Pussy Spies." Athena shot him a venomous look.

"Let's keep it simple," Apollo said. "How about Cat Intelligence Team? Just tell it like it is. It's about teamwork, after all."

The others mulled it over. There were no objections.

"So, Cat Intelligence Team, it is." Athena tried to regain her poise. "Oh, and I've got a new computer." The other three stared at her in astonishment. "Yes. I spoke to the police officer and instructed him to get me one. I also told him I want a state-of-the-art voice synthesiser with Artificial Intelligence software to go with it. It adapts to higher-pitched sounds in our voice range, so it works with my speech patterns. And it learns." Another glance at the others. "A keyboard would never work with paws. So now I can do a website for us and boost our profile."

Silence.

"And just how many cats do you expect to Google us?" asked Hermes.

"Oh, I know it's not likely, but it's just a bit of fun. We've got to move with the times."

"Athena, the first digital goddess," scoffed Ares. "Whatever next? Cats in space?"

Athena turned to more earthly matters. "Anyway, as I was saying, the first building blocks are in place."

"And we've stopped another Titan insurgency," said Hermes.

Ares nodded. "And probably started a war."

"What's happening to Zelus and Bia?" asked Apollo.

"Well, I arranged for the city's animal protection service to collect the wounded after the battle, as you saw. Including

Zelus. Bia escaped. I believe Zelus is currently in quarantine. I've asked them to re-home him as far away from Athens as possible. On an island, preferably. Or up in the mountains."

"And Bia?" Ares enquired.

"I think she'll be easier to manage without her brothers around," said Athena.

"And what about Herse's boy, Erichthonius?" Hermes asked.

Athena looked uncomfortable. "I'll have a chat with him," she offered.

"See that you do," Ares said. He rose to his feet and stretched. "Well, I'd better check on the troops." He headed off.

Hermes made his apologies and left soon after, but Apollo made no move.

Athena lay beside him; for a long time neither spoke.

"It is good to see you after all this time," she said at last. He hadn't expected her to care. "Too many of our kin have disappeared, cut themselves off, or fallen into senility. But you've escaped that fate. How?"

He stared into the darkness beneath the trees recalling fragments of his conversation in the mansion beyond the maze, long, long ago. He had no desire to share any of it.

"For a long time, it's what I wanted, too. To sleep, to forget," he said. "The past is a heavy burden. Do you not feel it?" She gave no response, but her study of him intensified. He looked aside. "Anyway, it weighed me down. Became unbearable. I sought a different path."

"So, what changed?"

It was a while before Apollo answered. He sounded puzzled, as if trying to work it out himself. "Along came this lively young creature, a small force of nature, I suppose, and she woke me up. I thought I was in love again, but…"

He could hardly bear to go on; the emptiness in his heart was too great; the pain of her death too sharp. He looked

Athena in the eye. "You know, I only ever felt that way about one other. A long, long time ago. But this time it was different. Deeper. More profound, maybe. But I was cautious, not wanting to be hurt. I played the slow game, took my time, let her make the first move. It didn't work."

It would do as an excuse. That last look into Daphne's eyes, and what he found there, he would keep to himself. And the pronouncement of the Oracle would remain secret.

"At least the pain is different, this time around." He gave her a rueful look. "Anyway. I am here. For now." He wandered down the hill.

Athena stayed put, in no hurry to move. Modern life could wait. After a while, there was a rustle in the undergrowth, and a small black-and-white cat emerged. He ambled towards her and stood watching the spot Apollo had vacated.

Athena glanced up at him. "Well?"

"He still doesn't realise, does he?" said the newcomer. "Probably just as well. But it makes me wonder if he's all there."

"You shouldn't eavesdrop. Anyway, what did you expect? It's been a long time."

The black-and-white cat looked down at her. "It worked, though, didn't it? Woke him up. Got him engaged again. Dragged him out of his rural hideaway, whether he wanted to or not."

"Maybe. But at what cost? I'm still not sure it was the right thing to do. He doesn't seem at ease with himself. We may be playing with fire." She looked at the other cat for the first time, a note of caution in her eyes. "All of this has to remain secret, you understand."

"Oh, I don't know. All's fair in love and war," he said.

"I mean it." Athena studied Eros. In some ways, he was the most dangerous of them all.

"And speaking of dragging him here," she added. "The policeman revealed something interesting. The outfit that kidnapped Olympia. It went by the name of the Olympus Trading Company."

"A coincidence?"

"There's no such thing."

"How unoriginal, then. So... who?"

She had no answer. He gave a barely perceptible flick of his tail and walked away.

CHAPTER 59
A PROPHESY

Departing from his meeting with Athena, Apollo descended the hill then paused. He would spend one last evening here, on the wooded slopes above the agora, and then set off in the quiet hours before dawn.

He looked around. Small groups of cats were close by, resting or sleeping. Some prepared for an evening in town. He was, in his own way, at home among them. At the same time, he was in no mood for company. There was too much going on in his head. He needed calm. And soothing, mind-emptying sleep.

He lay down, but his hopes proved false. Instead of healing slumber he gained only a sense of creeping unease. He was back in Delphi, on the slopes of Parnassus, in the sacred grove across the hillside: a part of the mountain he'd almost forgotten. It was the hour before sunset, when the mountainside was bathed in golden light, but between the silver-leaved trees of the grove lay a permanent twilight. The dark trunks contrasted with their leaves; the air was warm. The sky above glowed, but never with stars.

He stepped into a clearing and stopped short. Before him, a darkness grew, coalescing from the shadows cast by the trees and from the dark underside of their leaves. They fused into one amorphous shape, then in its midst formed a U-shaped stringed instrument with a wooden frame.

A lyre.

Transfixed, Apollo stepped closer and reached out, but the instrument receded in equal measure to his approach.

A tune began to play. Discordant at first, as if the player was just learning his trade, then more confident. Soon, a tune emerged of beautiful intricacy, and through its notes, and between and behind the melody, strange symbols appeared, then morphed into words in his mind. Troubling words that made him frown and retreat.

"I am the Oracle of the Shadows. Guardian of the Evernight. The void between the stars."

Apollo tripped and fell backwards. The shadow lyre loomed closer.

"Heed me well, Apollo. Listen to my tune."

Half sitting, propped up on his elbows, Apollo hardly dared to move. Above him, the unearthly lyre continued playing its tune, and in the sky above, the heavens seemed to move in response. In his mind's eye, visions formed, and an inner ear heard words in place of notes and chords.

"Like a creeping vine, shadows have long pursued you, god of light. They wrap around your soul and drag it towards me and the everlasting dark. Come, Apollo, leave the world behind. Join me in the eternal dark."

"No!" He shuffled backwards in an effort to get away from the creeping lyre, its tune so sweet, so inviting, so hypnotic. Should he give in and let go?

"I give you a choice," sang the mellifluous voice in his thoughts. "To die and join with me, or..." A chorus swelled behind the music, with voices so numerous as to belong to a mighty host. Apollo held his breath. Above, beyond the shadowy lyre, he saw the moon and sun moving, their paths destined soon to cross. He swallowed. At who's command did they move so?

"Or you can see your sister's fortune, god of light. Would you abandon her to this fate?"

A vision forced its way into his mind: a dungeon, dank and cold, moss adorning the rough stone wall. His sister hung in shackles, her flaxen hair lank across her face and neck, her tunic soaked.

The vision pulled back and Apollo saw that this was no dungeon; she was chained to the exterior wall of a mighty fortress, dangling above the sea. Waves smashed into the rocks below her feet and surged over her, then receded, only to crash about her again. She was conscious, but clearly in discomfort. His viewpoint moved out further still, until finally he saw it: Typhon, looming offshore, the monstrous spawn of Gaia, mightier even than his brother, Python, free, somehow, from captivity, thirsting for fresh new prey. Eager to consume the daughter of his eternal foe, Zeus.

His heart pounded. This could not be. He had to stop it.

"A choice, god of light. Forsake her, faint heart, then go on your merry way as if nothing has happened, fearing no consequence, casting no shadow, continuing your frivolous life. Or die, and in so doing, save her and join me in the Evernight. It's your choice."

One last chord from the lyre. Behind it, faint but audible, came peals of distant laughter.

The lyre disappeared.

And now, in the sky above, an eclipse gathered.

This should not be happening, but Apollo couldn't drag his eyes away. As the moon slid across the sun's disc, he beheld a sight so strange it brought a frown. There was a symbol in the midst, and in the centre, a letter: Omega. Surrounding it: the Ouroboros, the serpent that encircles the world, forever eating its own tail. Between these two extremes, five trees were drawn, positioned at the points of a pentagram. He strained to see them in greater detail but could not make out anything more. A burst of fire gripped the edge of the darkened disc, like a celestial diamond in a signet ring, and the sun began to emerge. The symbol on the moon's disc faded into black. Apollo shielded his eyes.

He woke with a start but did not move.

In this way he began to understand fear.

For many long minutes he stared without seeing into the dark beneath the trees, the dream replaying in his head. What did it mean? After an hour he was no closer to knowing. Anxiety knotted his stomach: not the fear he'd experienced when he was searching for Olympia. This was deeper, visceral.

He'd been given a choice: sacrifice himself to save his sister or let her die in his stead. It was no choice, really, but where once, not long ago, he'd have welcomed death, his appetite had begun to wane. He had no desire to die at the command of some unknown entity.

Resentment grew. He was the god of prophecy. Oracles were his to command. But this was an oracle he'd never heard of, and had no idea existed.

Who or what was the Oracle of Shadows?

Apollo stood and shook the stiffness from his legs. It was just a dream.

A dream. Not real.

He should find Artemis. She would laugh it off. How long had it been since he'd seen her? Eight hundred years? A mere blink of the eye to the god of light.

Along silent city streets he plodded in search of open ground. The desire to leave Athens had never been so strong. In his mind, Apollo built a wall to hide the disconcerting visions of the night.

That's what she'd taught him to do when he wanted to forget.

CHAPTER 60
GOAT

She found him on a narrow street beneath the towering cliffs of the Acropolis, curled up next to a large plant pot and a wall with his head on his paws. She approached slowly, but he didn't acknowledge her. He was not asleep, but staring blankly into the middle distance. He looked utterly dejected. Athena respected his privacy and didn't sit too close. She hesitated, suddenly unsure what to say. Above them was the point Erichthonius' mother had jumped from. She chose not to look, fearing it might appear insensitive. How they had changed. Once, the death of a mortal meant little to them, unless they were a hero, or a favourite.

The young cat raised his head and gave her an accusatory look. She suspected he must know the story of his mother's suicide.

"You drove her to do it."

Startled at his accusation, the grey cat looked away. At least he was direct, which was a good thing; Athena hated animals who avoided difficult subjects. She regained her poise.

"I wouldn't quite say that."

"Then what would you say?"

Athena looked at him. "Your mother was..." She groped for words. "Mistaken."

The hostility in Erichthonius' stare was unsettling, even for her. She went on. "Look, I didn't mean it to happen. Of course I didn't. She just..." Now she was the one being evasive. She collected her thoughts and started again. "I'm sorry. Really sorry for what happened."

Times were indeed changing. At the back of her mind, she tried, and failed, to recall when she'd last apologised to anyone. "It was a misunderstanding. I was angry with her, and maybe I said too much. But she took it too deeply to heart. I didn't know how she would react." Even as she was speaking, Athena's discomfort grew. This was a feeble excuse. She shuffled her position. She didn't care two hoots what Herse thought of her dressing down. She had been rightly furious with the traitorous behaviour of her servant, and dismissal was absolutely the right thing to do in the circumstances.

Her thoughts circled round again. That was how she justified her actions to herself. But could she have done anything different? Could she have shown just a little empathy? The concept was alien to her. Perhaps she could have tried to be more understanding; see things from the other cat's point of view. Offer Herse a way to regain her trust.

Maybe.

Erichthonius was still looking at her, as if reading her thoughts. Pretty sharp for a mortal. "In fact, I didn't bother how she would react," Athena admitted. "I just wanted to vent my feelings. I was furious. I had been waiting for that artefact to be rediscovered for a long time."

For several long seconds, Erichthonius said nothing.

"She was worried about you," he said. "About all of us. And she was right. Just look what happened."

Athena considered the war and the many unnecessary

deaths. The murder of the kittens lay heavy on her conscience. "I know," she admitted. "I know..." She said it mainly to herself and sighed. "They're with Hades now; I can't bring them back."

"I thought guilt would be an alien emotion for someone like you." Erichthonius' anger turned to sarcasm. In an earlier era, she would have turned him to stone for his impudence. But not today. She realised that he was past caring and determined to vent his anger. "You can't go around playing with lives, like everyone is a piece on a board."

His denunciation was claw sharp. Deep down, Athena knew he was right. The gods' remit was to make things better, not mess them around playing games. She would repay her guilt as far as possible.

"You're right," she said. "Do you know, I think I might need some help? Someone who can keep me straight. Stop me from being unreasonable. Tell me when I'm going overboard." She looked at him again. She was going to break the habit of a lifetime and admit a male into her service. More than that, she was going to make him one of her right-paw animals. "Things are changing around here, and I've been sleeping too long. There are things to do, matters to put right. Like stopping the theft of antiquities. What do you say? Would you join me? Help me run this city?"

The other cat's eyes widened as he absorbed her suggestion.

"I will," he said, finally.

Athena purred in delight. This seemed right. This would be a new start. It would allow her to repay the debt to his mother in the way she knew best.

"Come on. Let's get something to eat," she said.

A few minutes later, they were sauntering through the Plaka. Pleased with herself, Athena mused on her recruit. He would become one of her most trusted followers, she was sure. He had a sharp brain, and he wasn't afraid to speak his mind. An old quote came to her.

I cannot teach anybody anything. I can only make them think.

"Socrates would be proud." Accidentally, she said it out loud.

Erichthonius started. "I saw him play once." Athena looked at him in amazement. He went on. "It was at the bar down on Prytaneiou Street, just before the last World Cup. They showed some films about famous old players." He stared into the distance, remembering. "He used to play for Brazil, didn't he? He was good, but Messi is better."

"Messi's quite good, isn't he?" Athena ventured, hoping not to appear stupid.

"Oh, yes. I think he's the greatest of all time."

They continued for a while in companionable silence, while she collected her thoughts.

"Personally," said Athena, "I don't think you can do better than Pelé."

They walked on down the street into the sunset glow.

CHAPTER 61
SIX MONTHS EARLIER

The Queen found him wandering along the black sands bordering the starless sea. She paused for a moment, watching him. The man was startlingly alive for one so long dead. He still retained his muscular physique, his proud bearing. It was partly strength of will, and partly the result of his steadfast refusal to bathe in the Waters of Lethe.

No forgetting for him. He still hankered for his old life.

Perhaps that was why he wandered forever along these shores, hoping against hope that a sail would appear on the invisible horizon, and take him away.

Persephone approached, her aura illuminating the black sand about her sandalled feet. Her glowing presence was like the fall of a faint yet distant star onto this baleful, lonely shore. He barely registered her arrival.

"My Lord," she said, paying due reverence to his legend.

The man stooped and picked up a pebble, then threw it far out into the inky water. He avoided looking at her. "What do you want?"

The queen took a few steps closer until he could no longer ignore her presence. Reluctantly he turned to face her. He gave no bow. This long-dead man clearly thought that death made them equal.

"You should at least do me the honour of pretending to acknowledge my status."

In response she received a sigh. The man gave the briefest, shallowest nod of appreciation.

Her eyes drifted off to the distant cliffs as if she had better things to look at. "I suppose that will have to do," she admonished, still hoping for more. Persephone walked past the man. Perhaps curiosity would bring him to heel. "I have a task for you." She ventured a sideways glance. "If you're interested."

He caught up with her and walked in step. "What sort of task?"

"Something I think you'll enjoy. A return to the overworld."

He said nothing.

The queen waited. She knew him well enough to realise he would be searching for a trap behind her bland words.

He bit. "To do what?"

For a while she continued walking, making him wait. Finally, she stopped and looked out across the dark sea. "I want you to keep track of someone for me. Well, two some-ones, actually. Just that. Befriend them. Accompany them. Make sure they follow the path that was prophesied."

"What prophesy?"

She looked him in the eye. "You'll find out in due course."

"Sounds straightforward. What then?"

"I haven't yet decided. It depends on how events unfold. But for the time being, just hang around until I send further instructions."

"What if I don't want to just hang around? What if I go travelling?"

For the first time a faint smile touched the corners of the

Queen's mouth. "Do you presume you will be able to outrun me? Have no fear. I will find you." Their eyes locked for a while, then he gave another subtle nod. "Good. Now to the practicalities. You will have to travel in disguise, but you can't change the way we immortals can. I have, however, found an alternative. Come with me."

With that, she grasped him by the wrist like a parent with a recalcitrant child. Her grip made him wince, and she smirked at the brief flash of anger in his eyes: a recognition of a goddess's strength.

We are not equal, you and I.

Persephone ascended into the sky, dragging the dead man with her, and flew across the land.

Onwards through dark skies they soared, over plains and hills, until he spied mountains approaching. Soon, they alighted on a patch of rough ground before a wall of rock. At its base was a portal; a doorway into the mountain. Or so he thought.

It was huge, tapered towards the top. About it, on each side and across the lintel far above were symbols carved deeply into the rock; the sharp, angular letters of a language he didn't know.

There was no door or gate across this doorway. Instead, it was filled, as far as he could tell, by coils of swirling mist.

"An entrance to another realm and the start of a new adventure," Persephone told him, still keeping a tight grip on his arm. "Come, Jason."

Persephone shouted a command in a harsh, discordant language, and the symbols around the portal's frame flared silver and white. Still holding him by the wrist, she stepped into the swirling, seething vapours.

EPILOGUE

I n the museum, they had opened a new gallery to house the finds from the recent excavations. There, in the centre of the room, in pride of place, was the small bronze statuette, on its own plinth, beautifully illuminated and surmounted by a glass box. A note below, written in Greek and English, described it thus.

Figurine. Believed to be of the goddess Athena.
Early Classical period, circa 480 BCE

It was early evening; the museum had just closed. A large grey cat with bright emerald eyes wandered in. The entire gallery was suddenly filled with the vibration of purring, far louder than any animal her size could reasonably produce. The deep hum seemed loud and deep enough to spread across the city; it was felt rather than heard. The cat walked around the statuette, continuing to purr. Finally, a guard arrived.

"Ah, it's you again," he said. He was fond of cats, and this one in particular. There was something special about her. "I don't know how you get in. You'll land me in trouble one day!" Athena raised her tail, pleased to see her favourite human again; one with proper reverence for the past. She wandered up to him and rubbed around his legs, then followed him to a small alcove near the staff entrance, where he placed a special bowl down, just for her. "Don't tell anyone," he said to her, smiling.

Later on, after he'd let her out, she padded back to the Agora. She enjoyed visiting the museum and renewing acquaintance with the old marbles, echoes of a past long gone. For a long time now, the fortune of Athens had lain in its stones; memories of a glorious past. Perhaps one day she should tell them some of the real stories. But for a while she preferred to be alone here, under the trees of Pnyx Hill, over-looking the city from the splendour of the Acropolis to the memories of the Agora, the ancient market square and heart of the old city, and beyond to the present. She needed to feel the open air and the starlight at night beneath the trees. It spoke to the wildness in her soul, echoing down the centuries. It had all worked out well in the end, thanks to those new arrivals from Delphi. Perhaps she should visit sometime.

But first things first; it was time to update her contacts in Geneva.

She passed the hill, went down through the Agora and arrived at Lieutenant Samaras's house. He wasn't at home, but she went in through the cat flap and to the room he had set aside as instructed. There, on a low table, was a computer with a screen and keyboard adapted to suit her paws plus the all-important voice synthesiser. A large crimson cushion was set before it.

She sat down and, using the voice interface, opened a video link to CIT HQ, the command centre of the international Cat Intelligence Team network.

A moment passed before the connection.

A view of a distant room appeared on her screen, with a cat at its centre.

"Geneva here," said the now-familiar voice of the Swiss tortoiseshell who normally answered.

"It's Athena. Trudie, how are you?"

"I'm fine, thank you. Good to speak to you. I'm glad you called." She wavered, looking aside. "Er, I'll just hand you over. There's someone who'd like to speak to you."

She jumped down and off-screen, and a magnificently battle-scarred black cat took her place. He was huge, with a heart-shaped white patch on his chest and a white blaze down his forehead. His ears were ragged, and he appeared to have only one functioning eye; the other was multicoloured glass. But his good eye had just the kind of penetrating stare she recognised.

"Who are you?" asked Athena, a little taken aback.

"Greetings, dear lady," the black cat said in perhaps the deepest voice she'd ever heard in one of their kind. "I have long desired to meet you. I have many names, in many languages, but you can call me Odin."

THE END

ACKNOWLEDGMENTS

Many people have been involved in some way or other in helping me to produce this book. I am hugely grateful to all of them.

In the early stages Fiona McLaren delivered pin sharp objective scrutiny and helped steer my direction. Debi Alper provided invaluable advice and encouragement, and among other things introduced me to the intricacies of psychic distance and much, much more. The editorial skills of Andrew Lowe have had a profound impact on the final shape of the book, but I have also benefitted from his extensive guidance. His input has been instrumental in getting me this far. Stuart Bache has produced a brilliant cover, and I am grateful to Lottie Clemens for proofreading. All have been invaluable and they have made this book a far better read than it would otherwise have been.

Thanks are also due to Lucy Evans, Paul Harrald, Rosemary Scott, Kai Hopcraft, Alex Copeman, Nicola Dahlin, Lianne Dillsworth, Cyntia Ocampo, Anne Mortensen and Nick Franck for reading complete or partial early drafts and providing detailed feedback, and most importantly, the encouragement to keep going.

Any native of Greece will realise that there is no police presence in modern Delphi, but with that exception all other locations depicted are real and many of them can be visited. If you find yourself walking the Sacred Way, keep a lookout for the local four-legged inhabitants who scratch a living on the margins of our world, and please treat them with due respect. After all, you don't want to get on the wrong side of Zeus.

ABOUT THE AUTHOR

Andrew lives near Edinburgh with a cat who insists on auditioning for a part in a future story. When he's not writing, or thinking about writing, he enjoys exploring both the UK, and the rest of the world, and planning his next trip. Greece, the inspiration for these tales, is always a favourite destination. There is nothing quite like standing among the ancient stones and listening for an echo of the stories they once witnessed. That was what started him down this road in the first place.

www.andrewrylands.com

ALSO BY ANDREW RYLANDS

Made in the USA
Monee, IL
02 May 2024

57841603R00239